Praise for *In a Book Club Far Away*

"We might not be able to choose our family, but we can choose our friends—and the books we read. *In a Book Club Far Away* celebrates both these blessings through a trio of army wives who, across the span of eleven years, learn hard lessons about true friendship and forgiveness. Adelaide, Sophie, and Regina are unequivocally real, full of foibles, compassion, moxie, and humor; I wanted to shake them, then invite them over for drinks. If you're like me, you'll turn the last page, then rush to call your friends and maybe start your own book club. Make this openhearted charmer your first selection; your friends will thank you."

—Sonja Yoerg, *Washington Post* bestselling author of *True Places*

"Tif Marcelo has a way of writing characters that invite you into their lives from the first page. *In a Book Club Far Away* finds us traveling through a tumultuous decade with three army wives navigating love and loss and grief and hope and life, against the backdrop of books from various genres and authors. Marcelo takes a deep dive into the crux of female friendship, and the result is a story that is equal parts surprising, raw, funny, and delicious. A perfect next choice for your own book club whether it's composed of twenty members or one."

—Amy Impellizzeri, award-winning author of *I Know How This Ends*

Praise for *Once Upon a Sunset*

"*Once Upon a Sunset* will sweep readers up in a heartfelt story of long-lost family secrets and bright new beginnings that spans from World War II to today. I always look forward to a new book from Tif Marcelo!"

—Julia Kelly, bestselling author of *The Light over London*

"Tif Marcelo does it again. *Once Upon a Sunset* balances a tragic family secret with a hopeful future, wrapped in an authentic mother-daughter relationship. Grab some sunscreen, dip your toes in the sand, and dive into this sublime beach read."

—Amy E. Reichert, author of *The Coincidence of Coconut Cake*

"A richly drawn and poignant tale of finding yourself in unexpected places and connecting with the unlikeliest of allies."

—Amy Impellizzeri, award-winning author of *Secrets of Worry Dolls*

"The lush backdrop of the Philippines brings new chances at love for both Diana and Margo as the old love letters connect them to a new family."

—*Booklist*

Praise for *The Key to Happily Ever After*

"A charming, fun read. I love these sisters! Clear your calendar—once you start, you won't be able to put down this wonderful story."

—Susan Mallery, #1 *New York Times* bestselling author of *California Girls*

"The de la Rosa sisters are much like the flower in their name: delicate and poised but also fiercely strong. As the trio takes over the family wedding planning business, they will need all those traits and more to transform their careers for a new generation. As they forge their paths both together and separately, these three sisters discover that love—like a wedding—is all about timing. Full of wisdom, wit, and, of course, wedding gowns, Tif Marcelo's latest charmer proves that, sometimes, the key to happily ever after comes along when you least expect it. This endearing, deeply poignant trip down the aisle(s) is full of romance, unexpected twists, and the perfect helping of family drama."

—Kristy Woodson Harvey, author of *The Southern Side of Paradise*

It Takes Heart

OTHER TITLES BY TIF MARCELO

Contemporary Fiction

The Key to Happily Ever After
Once Upon a Sunset
In a Book Club Far Away

Journey to the Heart Series

North to You
East in Paradise
West Coast Love

Anthology

Christmas Actually

It Takes Heart

Heart Resort Book 1

TIF MARCELO

Text copyright © 2021 by Tiffany Johnson
All rights reserved.

Published by Montlake, Seattle

www.apub.com

Amazon, the Amazon logo, and Montlake are trademarks of Amazon.com, Inc., or its affiliates.

ISBN-13: 9781542029650
ISBN-10: 1542029651

Cover design by Hang Le

Printed in the United States of America

For my mom, Lita, who named our homes
and who encouraged me to fly with my to-do lists

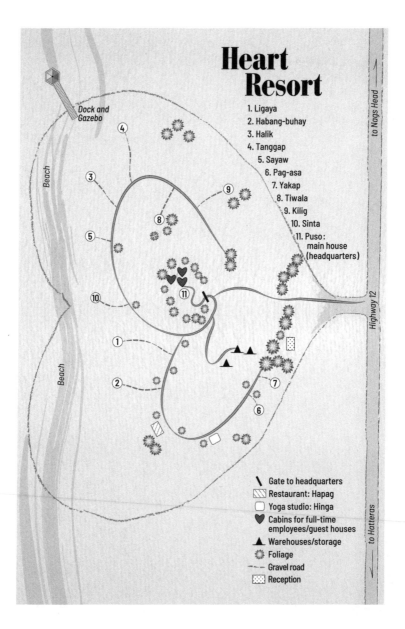

Heart Resort

1. Ligaya
2. Habang-buhay
3. Halik
4. Tanggap
5. Sayaw
6. Pag-asa
7. Yakap
8. Tiwala
9. Kilig
10. Sinta
11. Puso: main house (headquarters)

Dock and Gazebo

Beach

Beach

to Nags Head

Highway 12

to Hatteras

\ Gate to headquarters
Restaurant: Hapag
Yoga studio: Hinga
Cabins for full-time employees/guest houses
Warehouses/storage
Foliage
Gravel road
Reception

CHAPTER ONE

Four years ago
Las Vegas, Nevada
Weather: scattered clouds, 97°F

One didn't need to go to business school to understand that scarcity of goods increased demand, and in the case of the garter toss at a wedding it could escalate to a brawl. But Brandon Puso, a graduate of a bona fide business school, also understood that despite his objections against the garter-toss contest, the groom, his eldest brother, Christopher, had the final say. In everything. So he'd embedded himself with the three other single men at Chris and Eden's nuptial reception and given the contest his all.

And this was how Brandon found himself sitting in the dark corner of the reception venue, sans garter, and stripped out of his barong Tagalog. Now wearing a white V-neck shirt, he sipped a sinful dalgona coffee with a ziplock bag of ice pressed against his left knee (the bartender apparently felt really sorry for him) and watched the rest of the family dance the Cha Cha Slide. He had to nurse not only his ego from losing the garter to the wedding officiant, who'd decided to stay and party, but also the bruise blooming from a strategic tackle by said officiant.

The chair beside him screeched back, pulled by a hand with perfectly manicured nails.

"Well, well, well, this is where you've run off to," a familiar voice said. Brandon tore his gaze from the dance floor to the ever-elusive and gorgeous Geneva Harris, his big sister's best friend and the plus-one to all their family dinners growing up in Annapolis, Maryland.

He sat up, all but forgetting his knee.

Brandon had spent so many nights with Geneva across the hall during sleepovers with Beatrice that he'd had a natural simultaneous inclination to think of her like family and as his forever crush. And here she was, no longer in overalls but in a short, loose-fitting, and delicate peach dress that tied behind her neck, a few inches away from him. She had a smattering of freckles over her shoulders, her skin a golden brown from her Filipino and White American mixed-race heritage, though now, two years since he'd last seen her, she resembled her Filipino mother more than ever.

Then he remembered that she'd witnessed the wannabe WWE Royal Rumble he'd embarrassingly lost. He winced. "Did you see the reverend come down with the crane like he was the Karate Kid?" He lifted the bag of ice from his knee and shook it. "Direct hit."

She burst out a laugh, head tilting back. Her highlighted light-brown hair brushed against her shoulders.

"Yeah, yeah, yeah. Just because you caught that dang bouquet. It helps that it had a more reliable trajectory and that Eden has an arm of a pitcher."

"Whatever you need to say to make yourself feel better, Bran." She snickered. "You should know. I go for what I want, just like the reverend. Now *that* guy was intense. Talk about shameless."

"Like he's been practicing for it." With his head, he motioned to the guy not quite in step with everyone doing the slide.

"I'm going to have to take a picture with him later. That's going to be weird. I would rather be taking it with you." She bit her lip as she smiled. "Seriously, though, what are you doing back here? You could be up there partying it up. I mean, this is your song."

"Ha. You're never going to let me live that down." His face heated now; leave it to Geneva to bring up his brother Gil's wedding to Jessie about four years ago, where he'd break-danced to this song. It had been a dare, and at the time, his parents were still alive, and Brandon had not a care in the world.

It was different now.

"It was impressive, your dance." She stiffened into a straight posture with her arms at ninety degrees. She popped and locked like a robot.

"Please!" Brandon laughed. "You were lucky to see that in action." Still, embarrassment rushed through him. The one thing about childhood friends was that there was no way to be cool or act cool. He was sure she'd seen him at his dorkiest. He reached out and gently pushed down her bare arms, which made her cackle. Soon, they were both cracking up.

And were sitting much closer together.

Imaginary red flags waved in front of his eyes while his senses sharpened. What was it with weddings that all the single people became vastly aware of one another? He had been flirted with twice during this event, and if this wasn't his own brother's wedding, he might have considered.

And this was Geneva, which meant flirting was double off limits. Not only was he not going to touch that unsaid rule of never dating your sibling's best friends, but the woman was intimidating and clearly out of his league.

Still, those catlike brown eyes were channeling a different message. They were mischievous, and seeking. Was she—

"Hey, you two." Eden, the bride and Brandon's new sister-in-law, skipped up, pulling Chris by the hand. Her dark hair was swooped up in an intricate bun. Her cheeks were pink, and she exuded joy. All at once, Brandon was filled up with this feeling of he didn't know what.

Gratitude? Relief? Their family had lost so much, but here was Eden, a hopeful reminder that life would go on. He hadn't felt like this since his youngest niece, Kitty, had been born.

Brandon stood, wincing briefly, and so did Geneva in anticipation of Eden's hug. As if there weren't hugs being passed around all day. He'd arrived that morning from Annapolis, and it had been a nonstop hug and food fest, blunting all his initial suspicions that it was a shotgun wedding—because the two hadn't been dating that long.

All that didn't matter now. It was clear they were both in love—it was in the way Chris was looking at Eden at this moment, in awe.

"The photographer wants to take a pic of the Puso siblings with me before the party dies down," Eden said. "So c'mon, Brandon. Sorry, Geneva."

"No, don't be sorry. I'll head back with the rest of the party animals." She gestured to the front, where a *Soul Train* line was in full swing. "Make sure to send Brandon back. He promised me some B-boy action."

Chris laughed and hooked an arm around Brandon's shoulder. "It's a promise."

Brandon pressed his lips together to contain his laughter. He eyed Geneva, shaking his head. "Not cool."

She returned a wink, sending another thrill through him. Was that friendly? Naughty?

Maybe it was he who was lonely.

As Chris began tugging him away, he grabbed his barong and donned it, and they walked side by side as Eden rushed ahead to chat with another guest. Chris's similarity to their father was uncanny. His skin was the same dark brown, his black hair was full and slightly curly up top, and his languid swagger was so reminiscent of Joseph Puso it was like standing next to a ghost. It didn't help that Chris also didn't do small talk, and their interactions always felt a little stilted. "How's it feel being a married man, Mr. Christopher 'My Work Is My Priority' Puso?"

"Feels all right, I have to say." His voice was gruff. "But it was time, you know? You figure out some things are important."

It was a funny way to describe his marriage on his own wedding day, with no talk of love or commitment. Then again, his brother had never been the touchy-feely type. "Well, Eden's great . . . you know how I feel about her."

It was Brandon who'd introduced Eden to Chris.

"She's amazing," Chris said. "Respiratory therapist by day and a published author by night? I couldn't have asked for a better partner to build a home and business with."

Brandon frowned at yet another detached statement.

"Speaking of, Bran." Chris stopped and faced him, expression serious. "Your email about putting the Annapolis town house for sale. I'm sorry I haven't gotten back to you about that."

"Aw, that's no problem. You've had so much going on with the wedding and Heart Resort." The family business, a couples resort that had recently opened in the Outer Banks, had consumed all of them. It had not only drawn from each of their inheritances but relocated all his siblings to North Carolina, leaving him on his own in Annapolis. "But as I wrote, the market's really good—the comps are favorable. I want to go into business, and that share of the equity could go to start-up capital. Besides, I'm ready." He swallowed the rest of the explanation. A wedding was not the time to go into the fact that living in a town house with all his parents' things was *no longer serving him*—his therapist's words. In Brandon's words, it was more like suffocating, dismal, and sometimes crushing.

"That's the thing, Brandon. The market is *going* to get better, and the equity will continue to rise. I think staying in it a few more years will be to our advantage. You still have a large portion of your inheritance to use for your start-up. Besides, living rent-free is about the best deal you can get in the DC area."

Unease swirled in Brandon's chest; he knew it as anger. And if he wasn't careful, if he didn't express it, it could whip around and become something else entirely and put him back in bed as it had when their parents had died. It might not happen that day, or the next week, but he'd learned the more he repressed, the greater the chance anger would turn into self-isolation. Wedding be damned, he was going to put this issue on the table. He'd tried to communicate with Chris time and again. "Kuya, I've got plans. There's a condo in DC that's perfect and in walking distance to work. And the town house is too big—"

"You guys!" Eden called from afar. The rest of the family was already outside the hall's double doors. She was smiling, though it didn't quite meet her eyes. Her expression struck a chord of guilt.

He didn't want to ruin this day—her day—with one more disagreement with Chris. While it was their dynamic to fight, he couldn't make a scene. "We're coming," he yelled back. Then to Chris he said, "Can we talk about this later?"

"Sure, sure."

But as they approached their boisterous family, Brandon had a feeling that he'd lost the battle already.

♡

For Geneva Harris, weddings were the battleground between the angel on her shoulder swooning over the new couple and wishing for her own happily ever after and the devil cheering that it wasn't her walking down the aisle. The Chan-Puso nuptial was the sixth wedding in her schedule for the year, and Geneva had learned to appease these two parts of her psyche by engaging in some mild flirtation or a temporary fling. At this wedding, however, Geneva was facing a different challenge, and his name was Brandon Puso. At this moment, he was outside the glass double doors waiting his turn with the rest of the Puso siblings to take a solo photo with the bride.

Brandon had grown up. Or perhaps the last three years had matured him. Gone was the boy who used to try to spy on her and Beatrice's conversations. Gone was the college kid who'd needed help packing his suitcases for school—because she'd been there for that too. His face now bore his struggles, and it endeared him to Geneva all over again, except this time in a very sinful way.

This was bad, right? Very, very bad.

Geneva sipped the sparkling water just handed to her by the bartender to ease her parched throat.

"Neva?"

The mention of her nickname, only used by one person—her mother—doused Geneva in ice water. She righted her posture (yes, Lisa Harris noticed everything) as well as her brain because Brandon Puso was supposed to be like a brother to her. He called her parents Tito and Tita, gosh darn it. She should not think of him in any other manner but family. *Get your mind to G-rated thoughts, Geneva.* "Hi, Mom."

"Dad and I are headed to the hotel, iha. The Macarena wore us out." She gestured to Geneva's father, who was slowly making his way to the doors. He was a year poststroke and recovering slowly but surely, and he hated asking for help. As if his ears were burning, he turned their way and raised a hand.

Geneva blew him a kiss. "Do you want me to leave with you and hang out?" She hadn't been to her parents' retirement community home in Tennessee in about a month while she managed Harris Interiors, her start-up design and organization business. "We can have some quality time."

"No, anak, we're fine. You stay here and spend time with Beatrice and the rest of them. This was such a wonderful day. It's the first time you all have been together for a while—you have to celebrate."

The double doors opened, and the Pusos entered from their photography session outside, disrupting her train of thought. She watched them crowd her father like puppies to a papa dog vying for attention. "Tita Marilyn and Tito Joe would have been so happy."

"I like to think they're around still." Lisa smiled. "Okay, I'd better save your father. Unlike me, he is an introvert. Have you read about the Myers-Briggs—"

"Yes, Mother. I have." She kissed her mom on the cheek and turned Lisa by the shoulders before the woman dug into her E trait. "I'll be by your hotel room for breakfast tomorrow."

Geneva had turned to the bartender for another bottle of sparkling water when a body sidled up next to her, back against the bar. A little too close for comfort, she'd say, but when she turned, she was faced with Brandon, hands stuffed in his pockets. "Hey, that was fast. Need a refresher?"

"In more ways than one." His voice was gruff and low, and her skin tingled. Earlier, when they were sitting together, she'd detected the beginning of flirtation, and at first she'd thought it was just in her head.

Perhaps not?

And nothing thrilled her more than trying something different, discovering something new. It was what she loved most about design. It was the shiny, the fix. With Brandon, it was more. She knew his core, which made this both exciting and safe.

"Is there a way," she heard herself say with a shaky voice, for with doing something new, there was always a risk, "I can help with that?"

Brandon stilled. His face tilted ever so slightly toward her, his profile undeniably handsome, full lips with a hint of a smile.

Yes, Brandon, you heard correctly.

She sipped her water. While she wasn't much of a drinker, she kind of wished it was something stronger. She wasn't sure what she was asking, specifically, but she wanted to get to know this adult version of the boy she'd grown up with.

"I was thinking of calling for a cab, actually." He turned around and rested his elbows on the bar. "Everyone's headed out to an after-party after this, but my knee's killing me." He winced and shook his leg out.

"I've got a rental and am more than happy to give you a ride to your hotel. An easy favor, from a bridesmaid to a groomsman."

"I'm not at the hotel with everyone else. I'm at an Airbnb. It's super private—I've got the whole house to myself." His voice dipped almost to a whisper.

"Oh. How convenient." It was as if Geneva had looked down after climbing up one more rung in the steep ladder of their banter. She was breathless. "I can . . . tell everyone I'm hanging out with my parents."

Now this . . . she was entering recklessness. They both knew what "everyone" meant: his siblings, and most of all Beatrice. This was lying. A small lie, because Geneva was planning to hang out with her parents tomorrow, but a lie nonetheless.

But Brandon, so close, was temptation. He was a reminder of what had been the good times, of youth, and all the possibilities despite the struggles both their families had endured. She wanted to immerse herself in that comfort, especially now, thrust into the vast world of entrepreneurship.

She stepped in closer to test their connection. His shirt brushed her, and her entire body sparked. Then the formerly shy Brandon boldly turned so he faced her and, after a smooth examination of their surroundings, kissed her bare shoulder and raised the ante with a smoldering expression.

Inside she gasped, her decision made. "Let's get out of here, Bran."

CHAPTER TWO

Day 1
Heart Resort, North Carolina
Weather: clear skies, 97°F

Brandon Puso set down his duffel, took off his sunglasses, and hooked them onto his black shirt. He peered up at the large mahogany marker of his last name, nailed above the double doors of the Heart Resort headquarters office.

Wherever that marker, which had been handmade in the Philippines, had hung in the duration of Joe and Marilyn Puso's thirty-five-year marriage, that residence had been considered home. Apparently, it was now this elevated three-floor southern colonial beach home, rather than the Annapolis town house Brandon had driven from.

The marker had been restained, too, from its natural finish to a rich black cherry. A sign of the times.

He scanned the foyer and the reception area; its interior woodwork and design were at full blast with hand-notched hardwood floors and shiplap walls—this was all different too. The last time he'd been in this house, it had been a shell. It had been a box segmented into dreary basic rooms, and now . . . now the house—at least the first floor—was magnificent.

The only thing that kept his excitement from overflowing was that it wasn't he who'd helped build this place. His exile had prevented him from stamping a fingerprint on the final touches of this new Puso home, despite his expertise in building and design.

Voices from inside the office woke Brandon from his thoughts. Their pitches ranged from a mezzo-soprano to a tenor to an alto, and the cadence and flow of the conversation placed a smile on Brandon's face. For despite his frayed nerves, the familiarity was a relief. The last couple of years of his self-imposed solitude had placed too much time and space between him and the people on the other side of the door. Complicated relationships or otherwise, what they'd all endured, from Hurricane Dorian in '19 to, most recently, Tropical Storm Maximus two months ago, had left him with greater perspective.

With a breath, Brandon reached out to the bronze doorknob, squeezed it, and stepped inside. With what he'd imagined and practiced as a gleaming Crest-white smile, adrenaline rising with anticipation, he dialed up his voice. "You all started the meeting without me. What'd I miss?"

The conversation halted.

"Bran?" a voice said, coming from his right side. Chris stood from a chair behind an ornate wooden desk. His hands rested against the desktop, arms locked straight, and a curlicue of smoke trailed from a cigar in his right hand. His brother was smoking now? And something more—he had a trimmed beard and mustache.

"Surprise!" Brandon wiggled out a hopeful smile despite his slight shock and insecurity and Chris's incredulous expression. Arms spread apart, he said, "What, no hugs?"

Silence cloaked the room for an uncomfortable beat, long enough for Brandon to regret that he'd driven three hundred miles without telling anyone in this room of his plans. That he would be subjected to his family's raw reactions. That, perhaps, he wasn't welcome after all, despite their insistence that this was his home too.

Brandon's tummy dipped just as a woman's voice cried out, "Oh! My! God!" He turned to the clattering of footsteps on his left as Beatrice, two shades darker and a vision of color in a patterned dress, rushed at him at full speed. Relief invaded his body a second before she launched herself at him. He burst out a laugh while he steadied himself, rocked by her electric five-foot-two frame. "This must be how it feels to get tackled by the color wheel."

"I knew it, I knew it! I knew you would come. I told you, all of you!" Then, back on her feet, she promptly pinched Brandon on his left triceps.

"Yeouch!" Brandon grabbed his arm. "What was that for?" Beatrice and her pinches—he swore the pinch was an inherited weapon from their mother to forever torture him with.

"For the color wheel comment. And for not telling me you were coming." Then Beatrice wrapped her arms around his torso. "I haven't seen you in months."

"I came as soon as I could. The storm did a number on us up north too. The town house roof leaked, so I had to take care of that," Brandon said, avoiding Chris's eyes, the town house a sore spot. "And Mrs. Ling's garden flooded, and I didn't want to leave until that was taken care of."

"Then I guess you're excused. Anything for our old neighbors."

MY neighbors was what Brandon wanted to say, but he refrained.

"It's about time we're all together." Gilbert muscled his way through. He hooked Brandon around the neck and hugged him. "Hey, Bran."

"Hey, Kuya Gil." He fell into his second brother's hug, then stepped back, impressed at the change in him. The last time he'd seen Gil was after a quick meetup four months ago, and he had looked worse for wear after his divorce. Now, with a linen button-down and slim-fit shorts, hair combed back versus the disheveled mountain-man look he'd sported back then, he seemed more like himself, every inch the actor and model. Brandon whistled. "You look good."

Gil waved the comment away.

Chris entered their circle, followed by the smell of smoke. His brother wasn't a man of games, but it didn't mean he wasn't complicated to manage. Brandon's greatest worry had been this interaction.

His self-exile was from Chris and Heart Resort, not from the rest of his siblings.

Heart Resort had the reputation of fixing relationships; if clients only knew that the family who ran it had issues that ran deep.

"Hey, brother." Chris offered a hand.

That's it? Brandon stiffened at this formal greeting. Yes, a hug was rare on his brother's good days. Chris wasn't about PDA. But it had been two years since they'd stood in the same room. Wasn't Brandon's trip down to the Outer Banks meeting Chris more than halfway?

Still, Brandon took his hand. He'd imagined this interaction and practiced this first meeting in therapy. He wouldn't be thrown off course. He gripped Chris's solid handshake, refusing to let up first. Although they were the same height, Brandon felt the difference in power and stature. Chris was a force; he was intimidating, to say the least. He was eight years Brandon's senior, forty now, but was as wise and as cold as a vampire.

"How did you get through the gate?" Chris asked after letting go.

A wrought iron gate and a bank of trees encircled the main house and three tiny guesthouses, isolating the Puso family and the staff offices in the middle of the private peninsula. "I parked the Rubicon at the reception parking lot. Got a ride in on one of your handy resort golf carts. Sal, your head of security, remembered me from the last time I was here."

"Ah." He shook his head. "Still, he should have let us know. Better late than never, I suppose. You might as well get caught up."

Gee, thanks.

"C'mon. Sit by me." Beatrice pulled him to the couch, properly yanking him from his thoughts. Ten minutes he had been in this house, and already he was deflecting underhanded comments.

Once seated, she poured a glass of ice water and pressed it into his hand. "Welcome back to Heart Resort, dear brother. You've got a lot to catch up on."

♡

Brandon distracted himself by taking in all the details of the office, which, by the looks of it, had become central command. On one wall was a large projector screen; on another was a whiteboard with tasks scrawled in Chris's distinct left-leaning handwriting. Floor-to-ceiling shelves of books on the third, and on the fourth was a pair of large windows that led to views of a tree-shaded backyard. In the middle of the room was a diorama of the resort in all its glory, dotted by little figurines and houses, ridged with landforms and foliage.

The most prominent of details: the resort was built on a heart-shaped peninsula on the Roanoke Sound, connected to Highway 12 south of Nags Head by a narrow land bridge.

It had been this detail that had clinched his brother's attention when it had come time to purchase the property five years ago; Beatrice had called it serendipitous since the Outer Banks, and especially 12 South, had been their family vacation destination since childhood.

There were also small personal touches in the room: A Santo Niño statue sat atop a sofa table. Palm-size crucifixes hung over light switches. Chris's wide-brimmed gardening hat perched on top of his desk, which was littered with papers. All tiny sensibilities that were so reminiscent of their parents' vibe that, for a moment, Brandon's heart faltered. If their parents could have seen them, would they have been disappointed at how distant they'd become, or proud that they'd overcome their differences?

"Are you listening, Bran?"

Brandon spun his head to the front of the room and met Chris's eyes. "Um, yep. Tiny houses."

His brother sighed. After a beat, his gaze shot up to the whiteboard listing the ten tiny beach houses and two common-area houses and their statuses. "From the six out of the ten beach houses that need to be rebuilt from the storm, three have been completed. The last three modular homes are en route. The four that weren't affected by the storm are in process of getting an interior facelift so all of our clients will feel like they're being taken care of. As for the common areas: The yoga studio needs new flooring. The restaurant needs a rehab, according to our chef." He rolled his eyes. "But that restaurant is the last of our worries, since we have an extra commercial kitchen on the property. And I'm hearing of a storm brewing, on its way to Puerto Rico. Oscar." He meandered to the windowsill next to the whiteboard and gazed upon his precious pots of thriving orchids. "Bran, we're gearing up for a grand reopening at the end of the month, and we want to be efficient, no fuss. I'm assuming that you're home to help us out. Because if you are—"

It was a call to action. Brandon straightened with renewed purpose. He'd come down to the Outer Banks hoping he could lend a hand, among other things. This he was good at. "I'll just need to be equipped with all the contacts, contracts, and plans. I'm not licensed for North Carolina, but I can consult, and you know me, I can build, and an extra hand is an extra hand. Whatever you need. But—" He fixed the words in his head before saying them. "Is a grand opening deadline wise? Especially with Oscar?"

The thought of an upcoming storm shortly after Maximus triggered Brandon's anxiety, and his heart rate rose. It wasn't the rain that bothered him but the howling wind, the slap of leaves and branches against his window, and the dark, bleak night. He swallowed his thoughts and pushed through. "I imagine vendors are swamped bringing local business up to speed. Two weeks to get two common areas and three houses—that's pushing it on a good weather day."

"I said the same thing." Beatrice raised a finger. "But if we thought that way, Bran, then this entire region wouldn't get back up and running until the wintertime. We have to do our best to open back up."

"Exactly," Chris said. "We didn't have a summer season. Our cancellations go out to about two weeks, and after that, we only have half of last year's reservations. And what a great opportunity it will be for the resort to open before everyone else. Especially Willow Tree."

"Who's Willow Tree?" Brandon's gaze ping-ponged between his siblings.

Finally, Beatrice, with a flat expression—which only meant she was rolling her eyes on the inside—said, "Willow Tree Inc. is another family-owned business that currently operates an adults-only summer camp in Myrtle Beach."

"Though rumor has it that they're tapping into the couples resort space," Gil added. "Which in my opinion shouldn't be a big deal."

"I disagree." The tone in Chris's voice leaned toward bass. "We earned plaudits from the local community for bringing in more business to the Outer Banks than anyone else, and we've got to keep that up. We've got to show we belong. We can't let them down now. Gil, from the maintenance side of the house, do you think two weeks to get everything together is possible?"

Was Chris even listening? "Hello, I'm right here . . . I kind of know what I'm talking about. All the hard work you do from now until this storm arrives could be all wiped out in one fell swoop." Brandon half laughed and then realized that no one was laughing with him. He clamped his trap.

"Go on, Gil," Chris said.

Gil read his iPad. "We've done a lot of solid work the last couple of months. We can feasibly open once we have all the houses done. Yoga can be relocated, and restaurant services can be amended. But we definitely can't have damaged houses for clients to see. And we'll need a thorough cleanup of the beach, which should be done in about a week,

16

and then again after Oscar blows through. We can all hope it won't be anything but rain."

"How about client and employee relations, Bea?"

"Our teams are ready to come back." She turned to Brandon. "Admittedly it feels like we're pushing it, Bran, but now that you're here, I'm convinced everything is going to be fine."

Brandon's cheeks heated at the idea that he could be that valuable. Then he remembered that each Puso sibling acted based on their assigned birth order: Chris as the decision maker, Gil as the mediator, Beatrice as the optimist, and Brandon as . . .

He thought about it.

The muscle, the follower, the doer.

But to truly matter to them, to be with them, to be listened to . . .

The hope allowed him to rethink the situation. "Did you say that the newly constructed houses will be modular, Kuya Chris?"

"Yes, they're custom tiny homes in the last stages of build from a manufacturer in Georgia. They're quite strong and supposed to withstand the wind. They'll be transporting the already-built homes and, once they arrive, can install the houses within a day."

"In that case, it might be easier than expected."

"Ah, finally he agrees." Chris grinned and ran a palm against his beard. "This might actually work out, so long as we're on the same page and a certain someone doesn't go rogue."

Chris's intonation sent a spark through Brandon. No. His brother was *not* bringing this up now . . .

Beatrice shook her head in a marked frown. "Kuya—"

Chris held up a palm. "We need to talk about this."

At once, Brandon was brought back to their backyard games where he swore Chris had changed rules on the fly so that he always won.

Somehow, what had been a neutral family moment flipped onto its head, and the vibe was deluged with thick tension.

Chris continued, eyes solidly on Brandon. "We expect pure professionalism here. We have a mission to fulfill."

"Which I think unrealistic, by the way. Who are we to guarantee that we can fix a couple's problems and give them a happily ever after?" Brandon countered. While he'd invested his requisite part of his inheritance into the resort out of obligation, the business had yet to grow on him. Who were they to dispense relationship advice? Four out of four of them had issues.

Gil shot him a look—it said, *Shut up; you're on thin ice.*

Surprisingly, Chris seemed to perk, as if the challenge was just what he needed. "We're not the ones fixing their problems, Bran. But we become part of the solution. Every feature of our couples programs was studied and researched. We set the stage and provide every means so couples have no choice but to interact intimately. From the tiny houses to their private meals and activities and therapies. They're primed to address their issues, and they leave satisfied because they've achieved their version of happily ever after, together or not."

Chris was great at this, at this word scramble, probably from all the people he'd financially advised and the so-called important books he'd read. One would've thought that what also came of this was empathy. Instead he'd become more arrogant.

Brandon frowned. "What constitutes a happily ever after but togetherness?"

"Choice, Brandon. Choice. Choice sets the stage for a happily ever after. Because all of their misunderstandings, fights, and hard conversations will happen on this resort, and they will leave them here. From our data last year, about forty percent of our couples left the resort with the decision to divorce, but all with the true understanding that their divorce was for a reason. There are no years of wondering if they'd made the right decision. In short, their time here gives them closure. And most will agree that closure is the key to healing."

His brother broke out with a triumphant smile. And while Brandon wanted to rebut, since his role in this family was also the casual dissenter, it was all he could do to not reach across his back, to his tattoo. The remnant of his own lack of closure.

"All that to say, since the goal is to get couples to deal with themselves, while you're here, you're to keep yourself away from clients."

There it went, the unequivocal undercut. It socked Brandon below the belt, and his inner self folded over in pain. He should have known by now not to come in with his heart wide open, not around Chris. "Really? Are we going there? That was two years ago."

"Not long enough. That woman you messed around with is now one of the biggest self-help influencers in the online media space and could potentially affect our reputation."

Brandon snorted. "Self-help, all right. She didn't come to the resort to make up with her husband. She did it because of the prenup."

"And you threw yourself at her the moment she showed interest."

Brandon girded every part of himself so he wouldn't scream. "I thought she was a staff member."

"Argh, Bran. She was dressed to go golfing."

"It's not my fault the resort's uniforms look like golfing outfits."

"Look—it was your judgment. Just keep your nose clean." Chris advanced several steps toward Brandon.

"You always assume I'm trying to make trouble." Brandon stood, ready to defend himself for what he'd done and what he would need to do, even if he knew Chris was all bark and no bite.

Beatrice and Gil moved to position themselves in between Chris and Brandon. It was the familiar family standoff with the two middle kids dividing and placating the bookends of the family, who had a habit of getting into it.

"Bran?" A scream from the doorway cracked the veneer of Chris's face.

The room seemed to exhale. Brandon turned; Eden, Chris's wife of four years, took long strides toward him, with Gil's children—seven-year-old Izzy and five-year-old Kitty—at her heels, their squeals of laughter a fireproof blanket smothering the spark of conflict.

Eden wrapped Brandon into a tight hug, squeezing his frustration away. "I didn't know you were coming home."

"Not quite home," he said just loud enough for her.

Her eyes screamed in understanding. Eden was cut from the same cloth as Brandon. It was ingrained in their psyches to run toward the people they loved in their times of need. Eden was quite possibly his big brother's only soft side. With a low voice she said, "You okay?"

Brandon grunted a yes.

He knelt and opened his arms to Izzy and Kitty, who stepped in and wrapped their arms around his neck. They smelled like sunscreen. "Goodness. You both aren't so little anymore."

"Tito Bran, I missed you," Izzy stated. "It's been forever."

And just like that, the rest of his family faded away. Brandon's entire body slumped. "I miss you, too, and I'm sorry. But you and your sister have me all to yourself when I'm not helping your dad out. No matter what."

"Really?" A smile appeared on Izzy's lips. "We can go to the beach and skim the waves?"

"And hurt every bone in my body? Sure."

"Today?"

"Yes. Today. Well, after your Tito Chris gives me my bidding."

From above, Chris huffed.

"Okay. We forgive you," Izzy said.

"I'm glad you know what the word *forgiveness* means. Unlike some people in the world."

Chris grunted and crossed his arms.

Brandon sighed, audibly. "I won't let you down, girls. Starting with . . ." Brandon trailed his voice off on purpose, to build suspense.

Izzy was like him in every way. "There's a black duffel next to the front door." From his pocket, he fished out a key. "This is the key to the lock. There's something right on top for you and Kitty."

Her eyes widened into saucers. After grabbing the key from his hand, she turned to her father for permission. "Papa?"

Gil nodded. "Go ahead."

Izzy looped her fingers around Kitty's, and they ran off, feet slapping against the hardwood floors.

Brandon stood to Gil's wide smile.

"You're going to spoil her," Gil mused.

"I couldn't show up without getting her something. I can't remain her favorite tito without a pasalubong."

"I think it's so thoughtful," Eden said, an eyebrow raised to Chris. "See? Gifts. Not exactly my love language but still very much appreciated."

"We're still in our meeting," Chris grumbled.

Brandon pressed his lips together—how Eden had dealt with him the last four years, he had no idea.

"Thanks for taking the girls, Ate E.," Gil said.

"You kidding me? I'd rather be out there having fun." She rolled her eyes at her husband. To Brandon, she said, "We can take the golf cart across to the ocean side—be ready in an hour?"

Brandon nodded. "I promised."

Eden wiggled a wave goodbye without extra acknowledgment to Chris and sauntered out the door.

The room plunged back into ice. Brandon stuffed his hands in his pockets, mollified. If Eden couldn't smooth the rough spots of his brother's jagged personality, he didn't have a chance.

Then again, he wasn't there for Chris's approval, not technically. He was there for his other siblings and their consensus and would then head back on his way to Annapolis.

"Do you have any more marching orders, Kuya Chris?" Brandon asked. "I want to get unpacked, spend time with the girls. I can catch up later on tonight."

Chris shook his head. "No. That's it."

"Great." Brandon pointed at the door. "Then I'm out. I'll need a key to my apartment."

"You'll need to stay in the guest room. It's down the hall to the left."

Another stab in the gut. They'd built Puso with four separate living areas in the two floors above them. "Why?"

"We didn't know you were coming. Your apartment is still full of storage."

So they'd furnished all the living areas but his?

"I can help you unpack," Gil offered with a sheepish smile.

"Nah, I'm good," Brandon said, now raring to leave this unforgiving limelight. He spun on his heel and stepped out without fanfare, from what he knew would be a continued discussion about him. Part of being in a big family meant that opinions ran amok, that opinions about him and his actions were a given. When Brandon had been a kid, he'd been bothered by opinions—so concerned with pleasing his siblings.

These days, however, after all that had passed between them and the realization of the brevity of life, after he'd learned more about himself, it no longer bothered him. His siblings could talk about him all they wanted—the bottom line was that he was going to do what he thought was right. Nothing more and nothing less. He wasn't going to try to make up for a lifetime of misunderstandings—because no one should have to do that.

Not even Brandon.

Besides, he had a date with his nieces.

But as he walked out of the office, his phone rang in his pocket. He spied at the caller: Garrett Carter, his business partner up north.

He let the call go to voice mail. He could only deal with one problem at a time.

CHAPTER THREE

Day 2
Weather: partly cloudy, 88°F

It had been years since Geneva Harris had lived on the coast. And despite the ungodly time of 9:00 a.m., the Heart Resort's shore called to her.

"Nita to Geneva," the woman on her laptop said. "Yoo-hoo!"

Geneva tore her gaze away from the water view through the long and narrow window to the woman on her laptop screen. Nita Graves, her friend and remote freelance executive assistant from her side of the world in San Diego, California, leveled a no-nonsense expression at her. Though there was a barely pink sky through the open window behind her, at 6:00 a.m., Nita was effortlessly professional, in a pink blouse that complemented her dark skin, wearing makeup that added the right glow, and without a dark hair out of place.

Out of instinct, Geneva tugged on the collar of her shirt so she looked somewhat decent. She was, after all, the CEO of Harris Interiors. And yet, through her image on the chat window, it was clear her neckline was skewed permanently and the bun on her head was beyond fixing.

Perhaps she had been a little ambitious setting their meeting so early in the morning. Geneva had literally rolled out of the short platform bed hoisted up in the tiny beach house loft and was sitting cross-legged in front of her laptop, which was propped on a stool. Not quite professional. And though she'd slept like a rock the last twenty-four hours since her arrival on Heart Resort, in contrast to the months spent working late into the night, jet lag had nabbed her attention and energy. Geneva had pressed snooze one too many times, almost missing this meeting with Nita altogether.

Note to self: change morning meeting times.

"Can we perhaps discuss hiring a social media person?" Nita asked.

"This feels like a reprise of a request you made last week."

"Or, are you willing to take on this endeavor?" she said without missing a beat.

"Uh . . . no. Anyway, isn't this why I hired you?" Geneva peered at her friend playfully.

"I am your assistant for all of your administrative tasks between your clients and vendors. Social media is not my expertise, but even I can tell when it's not getting the right engagement. Besides, I can't take your pictures for you. You're the one on site. Like right now, you could take a random pic, upload, and voilà."

"Me, take pictures? Do phones even do that?" Denial. This was what Geneva was going for this morning. Just until she had her first cup of coffee. She reached above the laptop and tugged on the blinds pull so she could capture the full expanse of her view. With a soft nudge, she opened the window, and the warm air filtered through. Her lungs reveled in its comfort.

Luna, her rescue tabby, who had been asleep next to the stool, leapt onto the bed, away from the sunlight. Apparently she needed her first cup of coffee also. "Nita, I'm blissfully solo and beachside, and this is supposed to be vacation."

"A working vacation." Nita sighed. She linked her hands together in patient silence.

Geneva frowned. "Fine, you want serious Geneva."

She nodded. "I know she's in there."

That's the problem. Geneva, back to seated, scrolled through Harris Interiors' Instagram feed. "Everything looks fine."

"No, it's not. Very few likes, many with zero comments. It makes no sense that your business, which is based on design, aesthetic, and decor, doesn't have a gallery that's up to date."

Ugh. She was right. "Grr."

"Did you just growl?" Nita snickered. "I have never heard you growl in our two years together. First the pajamas and then the growling. Are you okay?"

"Yes. I just—" Geneva halted, because she didn't know what she wanted to say. She, technically, had nothing to complain about but a little jet lag, and possibly some social media remediation. "You're absolutely right. This feed is terrible. Can you canvass job boards to get some interviews lined up?"

"Happy to." Nita hummed as she scribbled on a notebook. "Next order of business. Helena's B and B."

She straightened and switched her phone for her iPad. "Now that— let me hear more of that. Are they ready to beautify?"

While Nita explained the details of the email, including some last-minute questions the proprietor had, Geneva pulled up her proposal. With a smile, she flipped through the designs she'd drawn up. Located in Charleston, South Carolina, Helena's B and B boasted a French colonial exterior, with a meticulously decorated interior that exuded cozy and shabby chic. Now under new management, they wanted a complete do-over with clean lines, color-blocked rooms, and absolutely no hint of lace or distressed wood. In the two-week break between Sedona, her previous job, and Heart Resort, Geneva had traveled to Charleston to meet the proprietor, tour the space, and make some initial plans.

"Oh, and they wanted to mention that you were referred by Beach Art."

Geneva's insides lit with pride. Beach Art was an art gallery in Austin, Texas, that had soon outgrown its space and had hired Geneva for a renovation consult and rebranding in 2019. The proprietor had been a tough client. She'd questioned every detail of Geneva's design as well as her minimalist philosophy that the less clutter, the more value placed by customers.

In the end, Geneva had prevailed.

There wasn't anything more valuable than word of mouth to a freelance mobile entrepreneur, and word of mouth, these days, transcended geographical boundaries. The design consulting projects she'd undertaken the last few years weren't splashy, but they were, in her opinion, quality work, and her clients raved about her in their professional circles. Their recommendations were what kept Geneva financially afloat, and she took every opportunity she could. It allowed her to make decisions like heading to Heart Resort as a favor for her dear friend Beatrice.

Geneva was exhausted, but she was accomplishing everything she sought to do.

"And they're all right with me starting in three weeks?" Geneva had moved on to her calendar on her iPad, spying at the seductively free hours of these next thirteen days. While being at the resort entailed work, she would have time for play. She'd done the lion's share of her list before arriving: ordering the furniture and decor, directing which homes needed their interior walls painted or wallpapered. Her job was to simply oversee that everything was installed and ready for its clients.

"Three weeks is perfect for them."

"Great. I—" The sound of something crashing interrupted Geneva midsentence.

On the screen, Nita frowned. "What was that? I heard it all the way from here."

A clanging noise followed. Luna jumped from the bed and hovered around the edge of the loft. Geneva's first instinct was to jump up and grab her cat—Luna had expended well more than her allocated nine lives—but she beat her to it, finding purchase on the empty floating shelves on the wall, and then moving down to a bookshelf.

"Whoa, what's going on?" Nita's eyes widened.

"I have no idea. Let me call you back."

"Oh, I'm not going to let you go until you confirm that you're safe."

Geneva smiled, and out of nowhere, her heart squeezed with emotion. She had been a nomad for several years, and what came with that, sometimes, was the lack of deep connections. Sure, she had her best friend, Beatrice, her parents, and Nita, but she buried herself with work, keeping many relationships at the superficial level.

Luna meowed as if reading her thoughts. Her tail whipped an objection.

"Human relationships," she said to the cat. "You're different."

"What?" Nita asked.

"Nothing! Anyway, you can't save me from all the way over there, Nita."

A thought occurred. Was there full-time security on the resort? When Beatrice had rung her up with a request for her to update the interior of the beach houses and a couple of the resort's commercial spaces in exchange for a two-week beach vacation, she hadn't bothered to ask about any logistics. Geneva had been due for a change of scenery; work was wearing her down.

The sound of something being walloped echoed through the tiny house, launching Geneva to her knees. The ceiling was inches from her head. She grabbed her phone. "I'm going to check it out."

"Okay. I'll be right here," Nita said.

She gingerly climbed down the loft ladder as the hammering continued.

There wasn't supposed to be anyone around her tiny beach house. The houses to the left and right of her, all west facing and located where the top of the heart met, were in bad shape from the tropical storm, with this one miraculously spared. Now, granted, it was indeed tiny and minuscule, and challenging even for a minimalist such as herself. At a total of three hundred square feet, the loft adding another hundred square feet, it was just small enough that a couple would have no choice but to work out their issues. And the current design—two wing chairs instead of a love seat, wooden kitchen chairs instead of padded ones, zero counter space in the kitchen, so only one could prep coffee at a time—wasn't conducive to couplehood.

In the lead-up to her arrival, she'd ordered initial pieces of furniture to be sent to the resort. But furniture was simply the foundation. The theme, her inspiration for Heart Resort, still remained elusive. This was why she'd asked to stay in one of the beach houses rather than at the Puso home; it was to understand the vibe. After all, the best design took into play how bodies moved in spaces. After fire and life requirements—nonnegotiables—it was then about flow, vibe, energy, and other intangibles.

As she pulled a sweatshirt over her head—she couldn't find her bra for the life of her—she was struck by a thought.

She spun around for her pen and notebook to write it down. Ideas like these flitted in and out of her head throughout the day, and she would soon forget it if she didn't record it somewhere prominent.

She spotted the corner of her brown leather journal cover under some papers that she had unloaded from her messenger bag when she'd arrived the other day. She fished it out, the leather smooth and cool against her fingers. It was worn, slightly wrinkled from years of travel, mostly with her dad, its original owner. She flipped it open, where two slim notebook inserts were nestled into the front and back flaps; one insert acted as her brainstorm notebook and sketchbook for this Heart Resort project, and the other insert was old, its pages delicate.

Out of instinct, she flipped the pages of the old insert first, three-quarters of the way through, to a list, each item preceded with a box. Some items had been checked off, others not.

Another clang sounded, shaking her from her thoughts. She flipped to the first page in the Heart Resort insert, above her small rough sketch of the resort, and wrote: *It takes two.*

Geneva stuck her feet into flip-flops and opened the wooden door to the screen door, grabbing the binoculars hanging on the wall. Stepping out onto the narrow front porch, just large enough that one round table and a chair fit next to the door, she raised the binoculars to her face and was bowled over by a sight.

It was a man. A shirtless man. He was wearing a baseball cap pulled down so it created a shadow, and his golden-brown skin shimmered with sweat.

Okay, Geneva hadn't been in a convent; she'd seen her share of shirtless men. But she'd been told this part of the resort would be empty. That there weren't guests around. Especially shirtless guests who'd have the thought to shake one of the wooden pilings of a tiny house on its last legs like they had a beef with it. Furthermore, the man was by himself and was not wearing the requisite hard hat. And when he turned his back . . .

Geneva gasped.

The right side of the man's back bore a tattoo. The way it wiggled on his scapula was familiar, and in that instant, Geneva's memory dragged her back, four years ago, to a tattoo parlor on U Street in Washington, DC, during a whirlwind three-week romance.

On instinct, Geneva touched the base of her neck, where a matching tattoo resided.

She lowered the binoculars.

It can't be.

She took another step so she was flush against the porch railing and lifted the binoculars once more. Her view magnified the tattoo of two black-eyed Susans entwined at the stem.

No way. No freaking way.

Geneva had known it was a risk that Brandon would be at the resort, but with Beatrice confirming that he had been keeping to himself—her assessment had been that the risk was low. Low to almost minuscule.

She also had this tool called social media, and Brandon's real estate business had just posted a photo of a home in Maryland that they'd purchased to flip.

From inside, Nita's voice was laced with panic. "Geneva! What's going on? Do I need to call for backup?"

At that moment, Brandon turned in her direction.

Geneva backpedaled and ducked into the house, stumbling over her feet. She pressed her hand against her heart. It pulsed like a hummingbird's.

Brandon's here.

Which meant that she couldn't be.

"Geneva! I'm going to call 911!"

"No! No need," Geneva whisper-yelled, making her way back up the ladder. Luna paced the loft like a guardian, eyes on the front door.

Could Brandon hear her in this tiny house?

Sweat had blossomed on her forehead from the humidity, the climb up to the loft, and the past that had landed squarely on her doorstep.

She didn't need a backup but an exit.

♡

Geneva wasn't good with the past. The past memorialized her mistakes and her worst, most impulsive decisions. Geneva wanted to be a woman who moved forward, onward to the next challenge, to the next experience.

But it didn't mean that the past didn't come back to poke her every once in a while.

Geneva sipped the cold iced tea and licked her lips, a reprieve from her thoughts and from a day that had gotten hotter and more humid. Though she was under a pop-up lunch tent temporarily erected and staffed by the resort's chef for those working on the resort, it was still torturous. Nothing could outrun the thick fog of humidity of the Outer Banks.

Though she couldn't beat the restaurant's location. From where she was sitting, she had a perfect view of the Roanoke Sound's waves as they rolled and crashed on the rocks. Earlier, after seeing Brandon, she'd stuck her feet in the water, and it had instantly eased her worries. After this conversation with Beatrice, she would need waist-high water therapy.

"Hey!" Beatrice came around the corner, black hair in a high ponytail. She wore a maxi dress with a geometric pattern, and large sunglasses concealed half her face. The other half was her bright smile, so much like Brandon's that it caught Geneva off guard.

She jumped off her seat and hugged Beatrice. "I love what you're wearing."

"Thank you. *Beachy*," she said in a singsong voice and struck a pose.

Beachy was Beatrice's subscription fashion-box side hustle. There was always a side hustle with Beatrice. She had been the girl who'd sold full-size candy bars in high school, all tucked into her JanSport backpack. She'd made a killing for herself and donated the rest to the school lunch fund.

"Impressed," Geneva mused. Beatrice's endeavors, at first glance, had always seemed out of reach but in the end materialized into something concrete and fulfilling. Her commitment and process were worth studying, especially as an entrepreneur.

"I should say this about you, calling for a meeting. I thought we agreed that you take at least a day off. And you even ordered me a drink.

Thank you." With both hands, she reached out to Geneva's arm as she sat in front of her iced tea. "But, before you begin. Guess what?"

"Spill it." She'd had enough of a shock this morning.

"Beachy hit our five-hundred-subscriber mark."

"Holy crap. Congrats! When are you not doing something amazing?" Geneva raised a hand for a high five. When they slapped their palms together, they kept their fingers intertwined, as was their way. She couldn't have been prouder if Beatrice had been her blood sister. A part of her wished that she could have been there to witness it all along, to be by her side as she grew Beachy from one customer to ten, to one hundred. They'd kept in touch as best they could, but this was the first time they would be together for more than a day or two.

Her tummy churned with guilt. Beatrice was the last person she wanted to disappoint.

Geneva took that back—the second to last.

"Thank you. But you're the one who's amazing, coming out here to help us," Beatrice said. "Anyway, what's up with *you*? Your text sounded very businesslike."

"I have something to tell you." Geneva bolstered herself.

"Oh?" Her eyebrows plummeted. "Is there something wrong? Oh goodness, I had a feeling last night that I couldn't shake. Then I had this weird dream that the resort hosted a wedding during a hurricane, and I was trying to get the officiator to speed it up. Ugh, I think the stress of everything is catching up to me." She shook her head.

Geneva scoured her mind on what to say. This was already proving to be harder than she'd thought.

When Brandon had finally left the neighboring house that morning after spending an hour examining, hammering, snapping pictures, and taking notes on his phone—she couldn't help looking because he'd made such a commotion out there!—her decision was solidified. She had to chat with Beatrice. She would tell her that she needed to leave; she would use another client as the reason and make up one if needed.

Geneva and Brandon hadn't had a playful, light affair. It had been hot and emotional, and hindsight was a devil in pointing out that they should've never thought that they could have walked away without some kind of consequence.

Splitting from Brandon, though a mutual decision, had changed her irrevocably.

Beatrice's worried expression, however, took Geneva off her game. Geneva wouldn't be able to give a legitimate excuse, and with a straight face, when she'd bragged about her flexibility—and then proved it by arriving well before she was expected.

And then where would she go to pass the time before her next job? *Tennessee?*

She pushed the idea away.

Bottom line, Beatrice was Geneva's ride-or-die, though they hadn't lived on the same coast for years. Their text messages had been the kind that ran like marathons. They knew everything about each other.

Correction: Beatrice knew everything about her *but* her relationship with Brandon, which was a pure miracle, with how Beatrice could sniff out trouble and lies.

Which meant Geneva had to be careful. She couldn't be rash. She couldn't upset her.

"Um, actually . . ." Geneva reconfigured her plan; she *couldn't* bail. If Brandon was just around for a couple of days, Geneva could technically hide out until then; she could find reasons to spend time in Nags Head, in Duck, perhaps to shop for decor. Worst-case scenario, she could find ways to sidestep his moves. So long as she didn't see him again or, worse, speak to him for any long periods of time, she could handle it.

That hour spying on—er, looking at—him through her windows had been enough to rile up too many NC-17 memories.

With a sliver of confidence, Geneva sat a little straighter. "Nothing's wrong. I just wanted to chat, about timelines."

After taking a long pull of her drink and pausing to swallow, Beatrice sighed. "Oh, okay. Whew. Yes, speaking of. We had a meeting yesterday about timelines . . . which didn't go so well because guess what?"

"What?" All Geneva's insides winced.

"Brandon's here! He's taking lead on all the construction project management, which we really needed. Gil had no idea what was up versus down, to be honest. We're now in the process of reallocating duties, and thank God. The stress dreams are probably because I've been dealing with both the HR and the customer side of the house." She took off her shades and set them on the table. Ruffling her bangs, she blew air up into them.

"Oh, wow," was all Geneva could say.

"Yeah, right? Anyway, Kuya Chris and Bran have to hash out the details still, but let's just say that the tension is thick. Those two are like oil and water. The dynamics of yesterday's meeting was exactly how it was when we were kids except we're taller, everyone's wearing more expensive clothes, and we all have much better haircuts."

Geneva threw her head back in laughter as the memories of the Puso family cycled through her head. She and Beatrice had spent equal amounts of time in each of their families' homes, but the Pusos had been infinitely more lively. They had been chaotic and loud, while hers was intimate, quiet, and calm. They'd both sought the opposites, and Geneva had found a little bit of solace in disappearing into the fabric of Beatrice's rambunctious family. Being the only child had had its perks, but having the sole attention of her parents had, at times, been overwhelming.

"How *is* Brandon?" Geneva slid into the question, curiosity gnawing at her. She brought her drink to her lips.

"Fine, fine, as usual. It's going to take time, but the mere fact that Bran came on his own—"

Geneva coughed. "So it was a surprise? You didn't call him?"

"I mean, I did. Of course I did. He and I spoke and texted almost every day. But no, he didn't let anyone know he was coming down, and especially to stay for a while."

"Chris must have been . . ."

"He was." Beatrice took another sip of her drink, then winced. "Personalities, am I right? Listen, I don't know how I would have survived my family without you to even things out. You always had your eye on some prize. You were always trailblazing and kept me on the narrow path and not down the wide road of my family drama."

Geneva tore her eyes away from her friend's face and bit her bottom lip. Trailblazing also meant day-to-day effort, and at the moment, all she felt was tired. But wasn't this exactly what she wanted? Work and acknowledgment for it? "You're selling yourself short, Bea. You kept me going too. You are so good at looking at the big picture, in everything. Except you're a lot more type B."

"That's why we make such a great team, especially at a time like this, when it's going to take a whole lot of different kinds of people to open up this place." Beatrice perked up. "Anyway, that's all to say that you'll be working directly with Bran. He's got a great head for design, too, but don't let him boss you around. You were here first."

Geneva pressed her lips together and willed a neutral expression. "How long is he staying?"

"For as long as we need him, through the grand opening at least."

Geneva stilled. Brandon was planning to be around the entire two weeks of her stay. There would be no way to hide. "That's . . . great!"

"Yep, and thinking now, he might have been on your side of the resort sometime this morning! God, with everything going on, I completely forgot to warn you. I know you're a night owl."

Geneva wiggled out a smile. "I . . . must have slept through it."

"Or maybe he was on the northern side? Anyway, you remember Bran. He's an early bird and can't sit still. He was up before the sun rose, knocking on my door, asking where the good coffee was."

A memory flashed of her waking to Brandon, a cup of coffee for her in his hand. Chipper, he had already completed most of his admin tasks of the day with his 5:00 a.m. wake-up, ready to take on work outdoors. Her cheeks warmed. "You Pusos are all alike."

"I guess we are." Her eyes rounded in concern. "Are you okay? I'm sorry. I've just been babbling. You asked *me* here. Oh, wait." Beatrice's hand shot up, her gaze now over Geneva's shoulder. "How long has it been since you were back in Maryland?"

"Years . . ." Geneva turned toward where Beatrice was looking—at a couple of Heart Resort employees in their uniforms.

Then they stepped off to the side like a curtain being parted, unveiling Brandon Puso, in a white T and long cargo shorts. His gorgeous face was split into a smile, eyes lit at the sight of his sister.

It was contagious, his smile. The tiredness she felt? It was swept away with it like a gust of wind.

But when Brandon registered Geneva's presence, his jaw seemed to drop in slow motion.

"It's my brother." Beatrice waved. "Brandon! Look who's here!"

CHAPTER FOUR

Brandon tripped over his own feet as his sister leapt from her chair.

"Now it's my turn to surprise you." Beatrice wrapped her hands around his bicep and pulled him toward the round table. She was laughing, enthused.

But Brandon, simultaneously exhausted from a fitful sleep and amped from laborious work that morning, could not grapple with what was before him. He was seeing a ghost. Or, rather, he was seeing the living, breathing apparition of the woman who had all but ghosted him.

He shut his eyes for a beat to clear his vision, but when he opened them and refocused, she was still there.

"Geneva," he breathed out.

The Geneva Harris he'd fallen for four years ago after a stunning three weeks together. The same Geneva Harris who, after an argument, had left him to wake alone the next morning with her side of the bed all tucked back into place as if she'd never been there. Like she had been a vivid dream.

The memory yanked Brandon's heart out of his chest, leaving a cavernous space. He'd had a myriad of feelings over the years after their breakup: loss, anger, sadness. Now, all he felt was nothing—was this shock? No, shock was the brick wall he couldn't get around when his parents died. This felt like . . . emptiness.

He was dumbfounded even as he got close enough to reacquaint himself with the details of her face: her high cheekbones, which even without makeup carried a muted shade of pink; the one tiny mole next to her nose; and what he now knew was a forced smile because it was this exact same smile she had placated him with the night before she had taken off.

"Hi," Geneva said.

Beatrice dragged him down to sit in the chair across from Geneva, then took the third seat at the table. "You remember Geneva, right?"

The cue threw him off his running thoughts. Time had passed. They were not in Las Vegas but in Heart Resort. His family didn't know about *them.* "Oh yeah. Hey. Sorry, I'm just a little . . ." He stuck a hand out.

What looked like relief played across Geneva's features. She shook his hand. "It's okay. It's the ocean air. Nice to see you again."

Was it nice to see him? Had she hoped to see him? Had she known he'd be here?

"How long has it been for the both of you? Since we left for school?" Beatrice asked.

Four years, actually.

"Four years." Geneva echoed his thoughts, eyes leaving his sister's face, then going down to her drink. "Chris and Eden's wedding."

"How could I forget." Beatrice bumped her forehead with a palm. "I take that back. Of course I forgot—I planned that event and was probably stressed to high heavens. Now *that* was a whirlwind." Then, to Brandon, in a change of subject only Beatrice could manage, she gestured to their surroundings. "Did you want me to order? I assume that you're here for lunch. Chef Castillo pivoted to feed us even if our restaurant's closed. Oh, just as an FYI, our new Friday dinners are now at Chef Castillo's and her sister's eatery, south on 12."

That took his attention for a beat. "A Filipino restaurant, down here?"

"Yep. So keep your Friday night free, both of you. It's required." She grinned. "So, what's your poison."

"Actually, I'm good." Whatever appetite he'd had disappeared. "I spotted your golf cart and thought I would stop to say hi before my first meeting with the team."

"Perfect timing! I was telling Geneva about your demo sesh this morning. You might have been exactly where Geneva was. She's in Ligaya."

Brandon had found it clever that the family had decided to assign a Tagalog word for each of the cabins, the yoga studio, and the restaurant. It had been Gil's idea, though taken right out of their parents' playbook of hammering their wooden sign at every residence.

"Ah . . . I was definitely next door, at Habang-buhay." Brandon snorted at the irony, that he'd demoed a beach house that was named *forever*, and all that morning, she had been just beyond his reach in a cabin whose name meant *joy*.

She had been his joy, once.

"What's so funny?" Beatrice grinned.

"Oh, nothing . . . nothing." He shook his head, then turned away from Geneva's unyielding stare to catch his breath. He faced his sister. "You didn't say she was going to be here."

"Yeah, well, I guess I didn't get a chance because you literally rolled in yesterday." Beatrice's words were slow and calculated, and she eyeballed him. "*You* surprised *us*, remember? I didn't have time to tell you who was on the entire team."

Right, right.

"And don't be rude," she added. "We're lucky to have Geneva working with us."

"No, it's okay," Geneva piped up.

Beatrice's words caught up to him, and the puzzle pieces clicked into place. Geneva was here to work, just like him. "You're doing the interiors."

"I am."

Beatrice's phone buzzed in her hand, cutting through the tension, and her lips pursed to the side. "Can you excuse me? It's my studio manager in Nags Head." She hopped up and placed a hand on Brandon's shoulder. "Don't be a weirdo, okay?" She glanced at Geneva. "If my brother's a weirdo, just ignore him."

Geneva smiled. "What are we, twelve? Go."

Beatrice meandered toward a quiet spot closer to the water and sat in a chair under the shade of a bright-red umbrella.

To his right, Geneva cleared her throat.

Every muscle in Brandon's body contracted, like he was in the gym attempting a heavy lift. His heart raced. Then he turned to her. It seemed the only thing he could convince his body to do. He opened his mouth, then shut it, clueless as to what to say, as to what to even feel. For this, he hadn't prepared.

"Look, Bran—" she said.

Hearing his name leaving her lips was like being pushed off a dock. Emotions crashed against Brandon like the shock of frigid water. It woke him up.

His instincts told him to go.

"It's . . . interesting to see you again, Geneva." He shoved a smile onto his face. His anger and disappointment should have been what leapt off his tongue, but the gentlemanhood his mother had instilled in him won out.

He'd witnessed his mother be disrespected because she had been quiet, petite, brown, and seemingly meek. And she'd turned the other cheek with a sort of gallantry. It had been her way to save face with her pride kept intact.

With Geneva, Brandon had so little pride left—she had taken it all from him when she'd walked out the door.

"Please tell my sister I had to go, and I'll text her later," he managed to say, standing.

"Bran." Panic laced the tone of her voice, and she reached out.

"No." Brandon jerked back before she could touch him. Despite his natural instincts to help, Geneva had a way of barreling through his impregnable boundaries. He couldn't allow her a moment of submission. "No, Geneva." Then a ribbon of guilt wrapped around him, because he didn't want to take this tone with her, or with anyone. "It's all right. I'll see you around, maybe."

His feet pedaled backward with a mind of their own, and he crashed into a resort employee. After sputtering a quick apology, he stepped out from under the tent. Sand dusted up around him in his long, fervent strides.

Work. What had saved him in the past was digging into work. So he marched to where his golf cart was parked and got the hell out of there.

$$\heartsuit$$

When it rained, it poured, and quite literally.

It began with a trickle as Brandon started back up the road that led to the yoga studio. In classic Outer Banks fashion, the partly cloudy sky transitioned to a dark-gray haze, and soon rain followed. By the time he pulled into the makeshift parking lot ten minutes later, the left side of his body was soaked.

Normally, storms triggered Brandon's anxiety, but his mixed-up emotions at seeing Geneva blunted it. Wanting to be clearheaded for the meeting, he took his sweet time parking next to the wooden sign that read HINGA. The building's name promised rest, a moment's breath, and while he knew what was waiting inside was not a yoga or massage session but his brother and his unrealistic expectations, he decided to enjoy the reprieve from the heat.

Sure enough, when the steam dissipated around him, the tension in his body lifted too.

What was left over was incredulity that he'd been docile to Geneva. Yes, it was probably the right thing to do at the moment—because he wasn't like Chris, who was always on the offense. But, for years, Brandon had waited for answers. In the first months after their breakup, he'd been hopeful for a reconciliation. Up to a certain point he'd been willing to forgive and to forget.

Yet when presented with the chance to tell her off, he'd skittered away.

Brandon shook off his embarrassment and wiped his face down with a hand, then climbed up the wooden steps. With the ascent he forced his personal thoughts away. Like Beatrice had said, they were now a team, and he would have to deal with Geneva's presence, somehow.

He squeezed water from his shorts and shirt and then, after fiddling for the correct key, found the door unlocked. He entered the studio and was hit with the smell of mold. The wooden floors were uneven and wavy—water damage. Its only saving grace was the view out the opposite side of the building through what looked like floor-to-ceiling accordion windows.

Voices echoed through the space. Brandon peeked over his shoulder; the resort's white van was parked just steps from his golf cart. He must have not noticed it with his occupied mind.

"Kuya Chris?" Brandon called in.

Chris walked out of a doorway that—from what Brandon remembered from sketches he'd received the night before—led to the private massage room. He wore the Heart Resort polo-style shirt and khaki pants. Chris had worn a version of this outfit throughout his life, whether working at the pizza parlor or as a merchandiser for a grocery store in college or at his internship at the Fed. Brandon would've bet that if he snuck into his brother's closet, there would be no fewer than five pairs of khaki pants alternating with khaki shorts.

Chris snorted, eyes widening. "Wow."

And already, Brandon knew he was in the doghouse. "Yeah, I'm sorry. I totally didn't read the weather."

"That'll happen, I guess." He checked his watch and visibly gasped. "You're early."

Brandon envisioned his brother's sarcastic comments rolling off his shoulders along with the raindrops. "You said that this was a meeting, right?" he said with more bite than he intended.

Chris's expression changed, and his lips quirked. "Jeez. Relax, man." Chris took two steps closer so Brandon could smell his cologne, could see the precise grooming of his beard and the iron marks on the sleeves of his polo shirt.

Warmth clambered up his neck. Against his brother, Brandon was going to come off to the team as a slob.

Still, he kept his head held high. Chris couldn't see him cower on day two.

"About yesterday," Chris started, "I know I wasn't quite as welcoming as I should have been. My reaction could have been better. God knows Eden and the rest of the girls are so happy to see you, and that alone—it's been rough around here, after the storm. Morale is low." He paused. "I *am* happy that you're here, and I appreciate that you came all the way, especially since you have your own business that you've taken a break from."

"I hear a *but* in there."

"There's always a *but*."

Brandon nodded. In his mind, he tried to flip the situation. If the tables were turned, would he be hesitant too? Wouldn't he assume that past behavior predicted present behavior?

His stomach gave way at this thought, relevant in more ways than one. He girded himself to stay in the moment.

Chris continued, "Just, please, run everything by me. I trust your skill. But what I'm asking for is communication. I'm asking that you treat me like your brother—you know, someone you actually like." His lips quirked.

Brandon bristled at Chris's attempt at a joke, when it had never been that easy between them. "I can do that. But will you treat me with respect?"

Chris's eyes flashed at his candor.

"You said choice was the key to a resolution, and I'm choosing to be here right now. Are you choosing for us to move on?" *That's right, big brother. I can stand up for myself.*

"I can do that." He nodded. "God forbid I chase away the only uncle the girls want around. And Eden would never forgive me," he said with a smirk. "My wife continues to remind me that you were her friend first."

With that, Brandon exhaled. *That's right.* He was there for the resort and family. For Beatrice, who'd all but begged him to come. For Gil, who needed a friend. Even for Eden, who he'd felt solidarity with from the moment they'd met. They were permanent.

And Geneva?

Discomfort pricked through him.

Geneva was temporary.

Brandon shoved his hand forward in agreement.

Chris took his hand. "Ready to meet the rest of the team?"

Brandon looked down at his half-soaked body. Not quite professional for a business meeting. "This okay?"

"No time like the present. Though we'll make sure Bea hooks you up with your own set of resort shirts."

Brandon followed Chris through the double doors, down a hallway, taking a left to what was the office, which hadn't sustained too much damage. Three Heart Resort employees in their matching polo-style shirts, with the resort's emblem of a heart superimposed over a sun stitched prominently over the upper-right breast pocket.

Chris provided introductions: a man of Asian descent, Chet Seiko, on the programming team; a pale-skinned, blonde-haired woman, Tammy Dirks, the resort's PR; and Mike Strauss, a blue-eyed and deeply tanned bald and bearded man, the resort's lead contractor.

Tammy trailed her light-brown eyes from Brandon's toes up to his face and grinned. "I'm so sorry for staring, but you look like you could be photogenic."

Chris burst out into a laugh. "Uh-oh."

Brandon looked from Chris to Tammy. "What's so funny?"

She tapped her chin. "Give me a sec to work it out in my head."

Strange.

"Let's jump into the meeting then, shall we?" Chris announced. As everyone pulled out their phone to take notes, he began dictating his expectations for Hinga's renovations. He walked through the massage room and opened the accordion doors, which spanned the entire rear of the studio. The rain had stopped, and the fresh, cool air unburdened the heavy stench of mold.

Brandon listened intently and scanned the blank space that he imagined couples had filled, surrounded by the sound of the water as they meditated.

"I have a good feeling about this. This team feels . . . solid," Chris added. "With Chet's innovative programming and Tammy's rebranding. Mike's teams. And then, well, Bran."

Brandon held his breath in anticipation of Chris's criticism.

"If there's one thing my brother loves, it's to build. It could be anything: Lincoln Logs, a pile of plywood, old electronics. Something about putting things together. He can oversee projects from a wide lens. I'm glad to have you on the team."

"Aw, shucks," Brandon said, though underneath the comment was a cautious optimism. He waited for the other half of that compliment sandwich to smack him in the noggin, but it didn't come. "I mean I . . . can't wait to get started."

Brandon shivered reflexively from the lie. Now that Geneva was here, he wasn't sure if he wanted to stay, if he *could* stay. Could he avoid her? If he couldn't, could he speak, much less work, with her?

And there was the other thing he had to bring up to his big brother that might change their entire relationship once more.

"A reminder to everyone that I need to be part of the process," Tammy said. "We want to be transparent with our progress, and we can use it to our advantage. The more we can inform future and prospective clients as we renovate, especially with the lead-up to the grand opening, the more excited they'll be."

"And we can finally lay claim to our position here in the Outer Banks." Chris's eyes gleamed.

"Exactly. So expect me everywhere with a camera in hand. For exterior and interior photographs." Her gaze darted between the two brothers. "But there's more. We're building the website and bulking up social media. To hop on my thoughts from earlier, I need people, models. Brandon, you would be perfect—"

Brandon took a step back. "Oh, no no no."

"We had a cancellation. A married couple was supposed to come and be additional faces to the site and . . ."

"But . . . I'm not a couple. And I'm not here to take pictures." He tugged at his neckline.

"Wait a sec. What kind of pictures are you talking about?" Chris asked.

"Candids mostly, and scenic."

"That doesn't sound so bad, Bran."

"Easy for you to say," Brandon said, with as little sarcasm as possible. Though perhaps he didn't succeed, his mind on how—and whether—he could juggle drama with work and all these little bits of information that kept dropping on his lap. All adding to a layer of guilt that he'd been ignoring his business partner blowing up his phone all the way from DC.

Chris's eyebrows lifted.

So Brandon tried again because he was going to be true to his word. He was going to try. "What I meant was . . . candids are okay."

"Great." Tammy brightened. "To confirm, who's on the interior design? I definitely want to be in on that action."

"That would be me," a voice said from behind.

Brandon turned, as did the rest in the group, to watch Geneva walk in. He held a breath, to slow the urge to either escape through the back or pull her into another room and demand a redo of those last three weeks.

What? The heat has definitely gotten to you. She destroyed you.

"Our secret weapon," Chris said, leaving their circle and wrapping an arm around her shoulder. "How did you know we were here, Gen?"

"Didn't Brandon tell you? We caught up briefly, with Bea. He said he was on his way here, and I thought that perhaps I should show my face too. After all, my time here's limited, and the faster I get started, the better."

Confronted with this new information, Brandon asked, "How long?"

"Two weeks, max. Then I've got to move on to a new project."

"As always," he whispered, just loud enough for her to hear.

Geneva shot him a look.

"You are truly a professional. Thank you," Chris said.

Brandon pressed a hand against the back of his neck to keep from rolling his eyes, because that statement sounded almost like another low blow.

Chris always did have a soft spot for Geneva. She'd been another little sister and a captive audience, and she had always looked up to his achievements.

As Chris introduced Geneva to the others, Brandon braved a total examination. Geneva, now thirty-four, was wearing a one-piece dress that hit just above the knees, and her arms were bare. But even though she was wearing a dress that was meant to erase a woman's curves, Brandon's eyes cut to her waist, at the spot where he'd rested his hand while lying by her side. How they'd fit—how he'd believed they fit.

He'd been a fool.

"Sounds like the both of you are going to make a great team." Mike grinned. "Since you all go way back."

"These two used to play house together," Chris added.

Brandon's stomach twisted at the flash of memory of him opening the town house's front door to Geneva, her duffel bag in hand, and stepping aside to let her in.

His brother had no idea how much house they'd played.

"Oh yeah?" Tammy's gaze darted from Brandon to Geneva and back in mischief.

"Oh, I don't remember that." Brandon shook his head, face heating.

"God, you should have seen it. Intricate blanket forts courtesy of Bran, and Geneva and Bea unloading the cupboards and stocking it up like it was a makeshift kitchen. Now, it's for real. Although"—Chris slapped a hand against Brandon's chest—"we have a budget. The goal is to be under. All right, I'm done here. I've got a date with my better half. What's your plan, kids?"

Chet and Tammy rattled off their to-do lists.

Brandon checked his watch. "I want to see what's under all this wood. Can you stay, Mike?"

"Can't. I've got to check on my crew. But I've got your digits. I'll text about tomorrow."

"I'll stay," Geneva said. "Bran, you and I have to get our schedule straight."

Brandon inwardly groaned.

"Sounds good. Go team." Chris raised a hand, and they each slapped him a high five. When it came to Bran's turn, Chris's smile widened. "C'mon, brother. This is how we do it here."

After a beat, Brandon slapped his brother's palm. Still, doubt remained; despite being 100 percent qualified for this job, he wasn't sure how he could actually do it with Geneva around.

CHAPTER FIVE

Geneva shut the door behind Mike, Chris, Chet, and Tammy and turned after a momentary but shallow breath to herself—the darn smell—only to find that Brandon wasn't in the room.

"Brandon?"

She walked out of the accordion doors onto the balcony. Her hair flew upward with a gust of wind, damp from the last bit of rain she had driven through in her golf cart.

Earlier, after Brandon had walked away from the lunch tent, Geneva had retreated back to her beach house. Seeing and speaking to him had affected her exactly as she'd thought it would—it had shaken her up. She'd never seen such blankness in his eyes. Shy Brandon, easygoing even in the most tense moments, had been angry at her.

Had she expected anger? Yes. Had she expected to care? No? Yes?

Turned out, Geneva cared a lot. In fact, it had lit a fire under her behind.

She'd taken out one of her two trusty black duffels; she'd thrown her clothes into it. She'd gathered her work items and stuffed them into her messenger bag.

Her focus had shifted to any place but Heart Resort and Brandon's judgment.

Because Brandon . . . he was today as he had been four years ago: a reflection. He mirrored back the past, when they were children and then lovers. Geneva didn't want to be held back.

But the Traveler's notebook, open on the kitchen table, had given her pause.

It takes two.

She'd thumbed the other old notebook open and come upon a box she'd checked when she'd arrived at Heart Resort: *Live next to the ocean.* Her thoughts had flown to Beatrice. And Chris, who'd advised her on her finances when she'd started Harris Interiors; Gil, who'd connected her with trustworthy people when she'd lived in Los Angeles for a short time.

And Brandon . . .

She couldn't leave Heart Resort, even with him there. She might be a rolling stone, but she knew what she was made of. The Pusos were part of her chosen family.

Geneva found Brandon around the corner, on the deck's east side. He was facing out, leaning forward onto the railing on his elbows. And though on the drive to Hinga she'd bolstered herself for this talk— because they would need to get this out of the way—she wasn't adequately prepared.

Because seeing his outline against the sky took her breath away.

It had been a long four years.

She halted at the building's corner and braced herself against the wood. After a beat she called out, "Hey."

"Hey," he said, out to the empty space in front of him.

"Can I come closer?"

"You're asking now?"

Ouch. She let out a breath. She wasn't sure if she deserved that, but she would let it go. She approached him and mimicked his stance, feeling the cool wood against her arms. When she looked over, straight on to his profile, what rushed back was familiarity and nostalgia, the memory of the bar at Chris and Eden's wedding.

What also surged back was need, a geyser unearthed.

She flipped around so her back was to the railing. She let out a slow, deep breath and imagined that need transforming itself into a force field to protect her heart. Because she was staying, and she couldn't let herself fall into this.

"I *did* see you this morning, next to Ligaya," she said.

"You didn't want to show yourself then?"

She half laughed, more to herself, remembering her kerfuffle with the universe, the bargaining with her heart, her apologia in staying. If only it were as easy as it sounded. "I was hoping I could get out of here without you seeing me."

His face sported a grimace. "That's funny and not funny, especially since you were the one who left without saying goodbye."

Shame rode up her spine, but if there was one thing she hated, it was revisionist history. She hated it more than reliving the past; with the real truth, no matter how painful, one could simply look forward and move on. "That fight was our goodbye. And before that fight you knew the plan. You and I *made* the plan."

"There were a lot of changes and nuances to the initial plan we made."

"And you can't expect for me to read your mind. You said you didn't want anything serious. You said I needed to go." Inwardly, she winced. *You need to go* had been his words, verbatim, and had been an unequivocal directive. He hadn't minced his words, and it had ground her heart to bits.

"I called you after you left, Geneva."

"Why would I have wanted to take your call when you made it clear that I didn't belong there?" Snippets of their last night ran through her mind. The final fight, the harsh words they'd said to one another. Geneva had heard once that fights were a protective measure to push away the people one cared about to keep from getting hurt. That fight? It was a shove toward the other side of an impenetrable boundary.

"Can we not rehash?"

"That's absolutely fine with me," she spat out. It *was* fine enough. Whether or not they talked about it—or whether or not she wanted to make sure he remembered what the real story was—it wouldn't change what they were facing now. She eased her tone. "But, we need to talk about us . . . and our current situation. Yes, earlier, when I saw you, I thought the first thing I should do was leave, but in thinking twice, I couldn't. I would do anything for Beatrice, and really for your entire family. I'm only here for a couple of weeks. Surely there's a way that we can make this work, maybe stay out of each other's way?"

Brandon laughed, face rising to meet the sun. "Oh man—stay out of each other's way? There is no staying out of each other's way with Pusos. You heard Ate Bea—there are Friday dinners. Heck, all of our dinners are planned, I bet. And frankly, our work overlaps. Someone's going to pick up on what's going on—"

"No one's going to pick up on what happened, *in the past*, especially if we don't talk about it," she emphasized. "I propose . . ." If she didn't say the words right then, she might change her mind. If Brandon was still the same man, he would think about her next words. "That we work together because it's in the best interest of your family. I don't need to be in your space. We can work our schedules so if I need to be on site, I'll send you a text to let you know. Heck, we can even share a calendar. We'll need to meet and coordinate, and yes, Friday dinners, of course, but we can be deliberate."

Finally, Brandon looked at her.

Score. She moved on. "I also propose that *yes*, we lie low while we're here. Two weeks is two weeks. Thirteen days, actually, before I'm back on the plane and minding my own business. I won't even be here for the grand opening—if I have the days mapped out, I'm leaving the day before. I'll be watching it from my phone when your sister decides to livestream it, because you know she will." The thought of the grand opening, of her friend's joy, brought a smile to her face. All this effort would be worth it.

Finally, he faced her. "You would do that?"

"I would. Look around, Brandon. All of this belongs to your family. The private waterline, this resort. What did my mom say? 'Buying a home means owning the land, the ground below it, and the spirit above it.' It took my parents so long to buy that town house in Annapolis. I knew their pride. And you four? This is your parents' dreams, incarnate. I remember how they wanted the best for you all, and they worked so hard." She conjured a vision of Tita Marilyn and Tito Joe, wise and gentle. Tears pricked her eyelids at the memory of them with her parents; they'd had a bond that Geneva had thought was indestructible. "A lot happened between you and me, but that was four years ago. The faster we can get this all done, the faster we get back to where we need to be."

Finally, he nodded. "Okay, I'm in." He met her eyes. In them, she saw her own conflicted emotions.

Because this tension between them? It was something. And it could grow to more, if they both weren't careful. Already, being this close to Brandon, she had the itch to wave the white flag, to get down on her knees, to apologize.

But, as much as Brandon didn't want to admit it, their breakup had been a two-person decision. He'd had a hand in it, too; now, hindsight was as clear as their current view. They weren't meant to last.

Geneva and Brandon were, at the core, seeking the opposite. Geneva chased adventure, the future; Brandon had his feet planted firmly in the past, and in Annapolis. In order to work on Heart Resort together, they would need to remember this difference.

A flash of light in her periphery took Geneva's attention, and she turned toward it. A camera was directed at them from below, on the surf. "What the h—"

"Hey! It's just me!" Tammy waved. "It's picture perfect with the sun shining on you both against the clapboard!" She gave them a thumbs-up and an exaggerated wink. "How about one more?"

Geneva spun so her back was to Tammy, her heavy thoughts about Brandon pushed aside. "I didn't know there were going to be pictures."

"It's no big deal, just candids for the website and socials," he said. "Anyway, she's gone now."

Geneva turned. "Yeah . . . I'm not a fan. Do you know how much we're exposed on the net? Our personal lives, our locations. Stalking is already a normal, accepted act. The very least I can do is keep my face—"

"Okay," he interrupted. "Enough with the soliloquy."

"It's not a soliloquy. I don't even post pictures of myself on social media." Privacy was precious, and social media never did serve its purpose in the end. Yes, it was a mode of communication, for networking, but it was also a tool that kept people in the past, stuck on their devices, full of regret.

"All right, Geneva. I get it."

His tone pulled her back to the present. She was unraveling, which was exactly what she'd done four years ago. Which also meant their time was up. She stuck out a hand. "Give me your phone, Brandon."

"Why?"

"You'll need my new number." Once he handed his phone over, she entered her contact information. "There you go. You have my digits. You know where I live." She took a step back, now wanting space between them. With this offer laid out, her angst was replaced by eagerness. Her to-do list materialized in her head.

She turned to walk away, then hesitated. She couldn't let one last thing go. "Brandon?"

He looked up from his phone. "Yeah?"

"We agreed to keep our relationship a secret from your family those years ago because we didn't want to cause any drama. We lied to them, and thank God, because we ended up breaking up. But I want to make it clear: I never once lied to you."

And before she allowed herself to fall into another conversation with him, she marched into the studio, the front door her destination.

♡

Geneva's phone buzzed in her pocket as her golf cart rumbled out of Hinga's parking lot. Nita.

"I swear you have a sixth sense," Geneva said, driving onto the main road. Her destination was Halik, a house on the northwest side of the island. Like its name suggested, it needed a kiss of pizzazz. Its initial pictures had depicted a dreary interior with dark-wood everything and without touches of color. Her plan was to paint a bright accent color against the back wall before its furniture arrived the next day.

"You might end up cursing me for it," Nita said.

"Give it to me."

"The truck carrying the furniture? You won't believe it, but it caught on fire."

Geneva veered onto the side of the road. "Say that again?"

"It was part of a multivehicle accident just out of Tallahassee."

Geneva leaned back in the seat and shut her eyes. *This can't be happening.* "No."

"Yes. I'm sorry. And, I called the warehouse, and unfortunately, they only have about half the items we need, and they won't be able to get them on a truck until the end of the week. The rest will take at least two weeks to get to Heart Resort."

"No, that won't do." That would run into her deadline for the grand opening; it might prevent her from heading to Helena's B and B on time. It was out of the question, especially with Brandon here. Geneva had planned to utilize the heck out of their shared calendar to keep distance between them; in truth, seeing one another would be unavoidable.

Their first conversation had been bad enough.

After putting Nita on speaker, she clicked onto her files on her phone and ran through the house names. Their images flashed in her head. "Have them send what they have. If you can email me a list of what those are, I can try to supplement with what I can find locally."

"Already done. It's on our shared drive."

"Thank you. You're fantastic. Are you sure you don't want to work for me full time? Do I really need to share you?" What had been the to-do list in her head scrambled as priorities realigned.

"All of this talent cannot be contained." Nita laughed. "In truth, I just channel your motto. 'Nothing stands in the way of Harris Interiors.'"

"You are absolutely right." Buoyed now by her assistant's reminder that she was capable and determined, and that every minute counted, Geneva said, "All right. I need to get off this resort and find some furniture. Talk soon." After she hung up, she looked back at Hinga, where Brandon was probably brooding.

And this was why she'd always stayed in constant motion—in her business, where she was the sole proprietor, it was all up to her.

Geneva pressed the gas on her golf cart and turned right toward the entrance of the resort. She passed a resort employee; he raised a hand. "Slow down! Ten miles an hour!"

She eased her foot's pressure on the gas. Geneva sipped her breaths to allow for her heart to slow.

This is going to be hard.

And it wasn't just about finding furnishings. Could she and Brandon work together?

Geneva arrived at the front reception building at the entrance of the resort, where five white resort vans were parked side by side, along with three personal vehicles; one she recognized was Gil's minivan for the girls. One of those white vans would be her best bet to get her to Nags Head, so she checked into the building, where she was greeted by the wonderfully frigid AC.

Geneva recognized Sal Medina, head of security, who'd picked her up from the airport the other day. She exhaled with relief. In that short ride, they'd bonded; she'd found out he was of Brazilian descent and one of the resort's first employees—he'd known the original owners of the peninsula. He was tanned brown from the sun and had more salt than pepper in his hair. He was sitting next to a sandy-haired, pink-cheeked younger woman also in a Heart Resort shirt, with a name tag that read *Rhiannon G.*

Surely one of them could help her. "Afternoon. I was wondering if I could borrow one of the vans?"

Sal's eyebrow plunged. "I'm not able to give you the keys, but we can definitely assist. Where would you like to go?"

"Nags Head."

"Where in Nags Head?"

"Actually, hold on." Feeling sheepish—she had been in a rush—she pulled up her phone. Nita had already texted her two furniture stores that might have stock. "I'm looking for boutiques and home stores. And I have these two places I need to go to." She zoomed in on her phone and turned it around so Sal could read it.

Sal tilted his head back and peered through his glasses. "Hmm." He passed the phone to Rhiannon.

"Yes, ma'am. I know exactly where that is," Rhiannon said in a southern accent. "I live in Nags Head, and shopping's my jam. I can even take you someplace better than those two stores." She did a double take with Sal. "That is, if that's okay with you, Mr. Medina. It's only ten miles away."

"Yes, of course." He moved to hand her the keys, but a strange look passed over his face. Geneva watched the interaction but forgot about it as Rhiannon stood. "But remember . . ."

"Yes sir, I know." Rhiannon opened the door for Geneva. "I'll drive safely."

"What's going on?" Geneva asked as she followed Rhiannon to the van. The doors popped open, and Geneva climbed in.

Rhiannon buckled her seat belt. "Oh, Mr. Medina thinks I have a lead foot. Which I don't. He's got a skewed sense of speed because he drives mostly on the resort."

Geneva snorted. "God, if he saw the way I was speeding in the cart earlier."

"I know, right?" She placed the gear in reverse and glanced at Geneva. "Ready?"

♡

Geneva hadn't been ready. Nags Head was only ten miles away, but in those short eight minutes—yes, eight—she lost ten years of her life. Rhiannon was not only a speed demon but also a swerver; she tailgated and wove, as if to instigate the car in front of her, all on the two-lane road.

Geneva all but kissed the ground when she disembarked from the van.

"Here we are," Rhiannon said, arms out. "Everything you ever need is in that magical place."

Geneva gazed upon the ramshackle barnlike building in front of them. There wasn't a store sign to be seen, nor was the parking lot marked by lines. She'd expected a bona fide building of a large furniture chain. She wouldn't even have minded an outlet mall where there was, at the very least, a Pottery Barn where she could order multiples of everything. "Um, *where* are we?"

"You said you wanted furniture and stuff for the beach houses."

"No, this won't work." Geneva shook her head. Beatrice had told her that they were looking for modern design, for a simple, understated look. They'd wanted their clients to be focused on nothing else but their relationship, hence having the same modern furniture in each beach house.

Not junk.

What she saw as she followed Rhiannon up the walkway were old doors and windows littered in random places. At the corner was a group of old-fashioned sinks. Against one side of the building were rusted gas station signs. These were the kinds of pieces that her parents would've ogled and discussed and reminisced about. Milk glass and sleds. Vintage Singer sewing machines. Framed stained glass left over from an old church.

"Why won't they work?" Rhiannon asked.

"I mean, besides the fact that this isn't what Beatrice wants, it's too . . . personal."

"But don't the houses have names? Isn't that personal?"

Geneva slowed as Rhiannon's words seeped in. Then the drive to Nags Head fell away. The day thus far, of dealing with Brandon and the truck fire, dissipated. In its place, her vision for the home's designs—*it takes two*—came into full clarity.

"Something two people could talk about?" she said, more to herself.

Antiques and one-of-a-kind pieces *could* augment the entire mission of the resort. Perhaps the Pusos had assumed the wrong thing. Perhaps another way to set the resort apart was to provide a unique, custom experience, down to the house, because wasn't every couple unique too?

These pieces could jump-start conversations. They could facilitate bonding, and bonding led to connection.

"Um . . . yes?" Rhiannon answered hesitatingly.

"Rhiannon, I was scared as heck riding shotgun, but this . . . this was a good move. How did you know to take me here?"

She shrugged, taking the lead to the front door. "I just had a feeling. I also know the owner, and I've been walking through his junk all my life, and I've got ideas. There's a little bedside table in there that's made out of a large tree log. It's neat."

Geneva followed her indoors and was overtaken by the smell of wood and metal and must. The barn seemed to have no end; it was as far as her eyes could see. The sight was overwhelming, with nothing in its place.

But instead of tensing, Geneva's body loosened. She gravitated toward a grouping of watering cans.

"Hello, down there!" A voice echoed from above. A man waved from the loft. He was Black and dressed in brown overalls with a white shirt underneath.

"Mr. Barnes!" Next to her, Rhiannon waved. "I've got someone who might want a whole lot of stuff."

"Well, that's music to my ears," he bellowed. "I'll be right down."

"What time does this place close?" Geneva asked, eyes wandering, taking in all the possibilities.

"Seven, I think."

"Good. Do you mind working past your shift to help me out?"

Rhiannon's eyes widened. "I definitely do not mind."

"I hope you hydrated, sweet Rhiannon." She turned on FaceTime and called up Beatrice's number. Chris would have the final say, but having Bea on her side when she presented the change would yield a better outcome. "We've got beach houses to design."

CHAPTER SIX

Day 3
Weather: fair, 83°F

At Habang-buhay, Brandon tipped his reusable water bottle back and squeezed water into his mouth. He glugged until he no longer could, then twisted open the top and poured the water over his head.

"Sure you don't want to come with us?" Mike said in his North Carolinian twang. He exchanged his hard hat for a camo bucket hat. "Food truck's only here another half hour or so. Adobo shrimp's the special today. Paula's is the best."

"Paula?"

He hiked a hand over his shoulder. "Uh . . . Chef Castillo."

"Right . . ." Brandon pretended not to notice Mike's blush. Instead, he looked back to the waves behind him, softly crashing onto the man-made beach, and considered his options. "I appreciate it. But that water's calling to me."

"I guess I don't blame you. With Oscar coming and all, might as well enjoy it."

Brandon scanned the clear blue sky; the hair on his arms stood, so he pretended to wipe dust off them. "Any more news on the storm?"

"It made landfall at the Dominican Republic, though it's not too bad for them so far. They're saying four days to us if it doesn't veer off course? Though it doesn't look quite like it now, you just never know."

He swallowed down his nerves. It could miss them altogether—there was nothing to worry about, yet. "That could mess up our schedule."

"Yes sir, it could. But we've got plans in place. Chris was on it as soon as we had word that a storm was possible. We can touch base on that after lunch. But the gist of it is that we work as efficiently as we can while considering that we may have to stop." He swiped his forehead with a rag. "All right. Maybe I'll order you some shrimp to go. Unless I eat it first." He grinned.

"I won't blame you, I promise." It had only been half a day, but Brandon had fallen right into the crew's routine. It had been important for him to get to know Mike—he hadn't wanted to step on his toes. Trust was the only way to go.

Today's crew was reinforcing the pilings, all in prep for the arrival of Tiny House Specialists, who would swoop down with the prefab tiny houses to replace those that had sustained the most damage: Habang-buhay, Tanggap, and Sayaw. Tanggap and Sayaw were on the north and northwest sides of the island, respectively, and their prep was complete.

They would be done with Habang-buhay in no time.

"But see you all in about an hour," Brandon said.

He watched the crew go. As soon as the last one was off site, he headed toward the surf and took off his shoes and socks where the grass ended and the sand began. He pulled his shirt off, unloaded his pockets, and threw the contents with his things.

With the prospect of water, he exhaled, already feeling refreshed, much like how it was to smell coffee brewing—sometimes that, alone, was enough to perk up the morning.

And he needed the pick-me-up. He'd tossed and turned last night, and caffeine would not be enough to get him through the rest of the day. The culprit behind his insomnia? Geneva's statement that his memory was serving him wrong. She'd claimed that she'd simply acted on their agreement to keep it simple and light, and that in the end, it was he who told her to go.

Yes, he'd agreed to that arrangement. But in those three weeks, he'd assumed . . . he'd assumed that they'd risen above "simple" and "light." They hadn't just been sleeping together; he'd thought that despite that final fight, they were in a place where they could have fixed it.

He'd tried to recover their relationship; he'd left her messages, written her emails. The ball had been in her court, and she hadn't lobbed it back. There hadn't been a hint of a game left between them. Losing her had been a repeat of his parents' death: sudden and drastic. He was only lucky that at that time, he'd already been in therapy, and it was accessible.

Seeing Geneva here and rethinking their history and that one sad night . . . he couldn't categorically declare that he was right and she was wrong. That he was the good guy and she was the bad. Geneva had never been the enemy.

And she was right: it was he who had told her to leave.

Brandon was steps into the sand when he heard the vibration of his phone ringing in his shoe.

Crap. He walked back to his things and fished his phone out. It was Garrett again.

Double crap. He would need to take this. He'd ignored his business partner for more than a couple of days.

"Where are you?" Garrett asked without pleasantries, voice morose in his ears. In the background was knocking, and then the familiar sound of a low-pitched bell.

"Are you—" Brandon frowned. "Are you at my place?"

"Yeah, I am . . . I drove all the way to Annapolis from Arlington."

"Well . . . uh . . . I'm not there."

"Obviously. So where are you?"

Brandon paused. "North Carolina."

"As in, the state?"

"Yes."

A litany of curse words left Garrett's mouth.

"I told you I was heading down here." Brandon bit his cheek. Despite his great show to stand up to Chris, Brandon was a sucker. He was a sucker for everyone who said they needed him, and sometimes it was at the expense of making rash decisions.

He really needed to get himself together.

"Yeah, but we're in the middle of flipping Illinois Way."

"I told you I needed to see my family," he yelled, more to the surf than to the phone. From the shadows of the rolling waves came the figure of someone on a kayak, coming back to shore.

"Which is fine, if you're there to finally move on the town house sale."

"I . . . I don't know." He was still trying to settle in—he would have been, already, if Geneva's presence hadn't distracted him.

"Bran, you said we would be equal partners, and I need help with the capital to renovate," Garrett said.

"It's not as easy as you think." Brandon shook his head, knowing where Garrett's train of thought was leading. They had been at this endeavor, namely P&C Homes, for a few years now. With the booming real estate market in the DC area, they'd jumped on that opportunity and flipped homes. Garrett was a Realtor, and with Brandon's construction expertise, it had seemed like a perfect combination. They'd envisioned themselves born of the HGTV home-flipping shows, their brains and brawn clearly a straight path toward a positive cash flow status.

Not.

They'd made risky decisions, in design, in negotiations. Twice, they'd bought homes that had severely deeper issues than they'd planned for. Still, they'd survived, until the pandemic, when their business had all but stopped—and for good reason. No one wanted to move into a busy city in the middle of a public health care crisis.

It had taken them a good six months to find ground to pivot. They'd decided to turn their sights to vacation homes. Together, they'd concluded in the end, it would be all right. But in the interim?

Garrett had been footing the bill.

Currently, his business partner was convinced their most recent purchase, a historic and somewhat isolated riverfront home on Illinois Way about ten miles away from Annapolis, was their ticket to cash.

As Brandon paced across the sand, he noticed something white sticking out next to his toe. He fished it out; it was a scallop shell the size of a quarter, but unbroken. He ran his fingers against the grooves, and it brought him back to beachcombing with his mom.

"You have to step up," Garrett said, interrupting his thoughts. "And you and I know that you have the ability to do so. You have been ready to move on."

The lashing was at the tip of Brandon's tongue. He wanted to say that Garrett didn't have the right to tell him he was ready to move on. But the truth was hard to deny: They'd been friends for almost a decade, both with high entrepreneurial hopes. He'd invested more capital than Brandon, who'd used almost half of his share of the inheritance from his parents' will. Garrett was his brother from another mother—Garrett had been there to catch him when his parents had passed, when there were days he couldn't get out of bed to get to grad school classes, much less complete his work.

Brandon was tied to the guy in cash, in business, and also in friendship.

And Garrett was right; he did have more, but it wasn't exactly in cash.

"You have a solid offer on the table," Garrett reminded him. "And inside, you know it's the reason why you're there."

"I'm here to help my family."

"And to help yourself. We talked about this."

Brandon shook his head, even if Garrett was right.

Why couldn't things be simple, like when he was young and reckless, when the worst thing to happen on any given day was the warped wooden floor of a project or an incorrectly chosen paint color?

Stop it, he said to himself. He knew that kind of talk was neither helpful nor productive.

"Bran." Garrett's tone softened. "You know it's time. Just bring up that the investor wants to turn it into commercial property for a nonprofit. It's for a school. But above that . . ."

"Drop it . . . please." To discuss the family home required a straight mind, and *that* he didn't have at the moment.

Garrett sighed. "Fine. This still doesn't take away the fact that I'll need to start the reno of Illinois Way soon."

"I . . . I know . . . and I'm sorry for not telling you that I was headed down. I just couldn't be in that house for another minute. I'll figure it out . . ." Brandon relented, eager for the change in conversation, eager for the end of the conversation. "Anyway, that last house we flipped— we sank too much into it. We can't play in the custom game. That was our downfall. We tried too hard, took too long, and missed the ball in negotiations. We were greedy."

"I know, I know." Remorse laced Garrett's tone. "It won't happen this time. I walked through Illinois Way today. Good bones like I suspected— this flip is going to be way more straightforward."

"I wish I was there to manage it." Brandon pressed his hand against his forehead to still his running thoughts and worry. Maybe it had been a bad move for him to come to North Carolina after all. It had, ultimately, been a last-minute decision, after another night of attempting to pack up his parents' things and then going through their old photo albums. Six hours later, he'd been driving across the land bridge onto Heart Resort.

"Is that my fault?" His voice was shrill. "Sorry, man. That's just not cool, you know? You can't up and leave and not say a damn word." He heaved a breath. "We'll try to do some things from afar. We'll work with the same guys we always do. You'll be back soon, anyway. Right?"

Brandon ignored the question. "What's your estimated budget thus far?"

Garrett whispered the cost.

"No!" he yelled. Realizing that the kayak had made it up to shore, he lowered his head and voice. This was a private beach, which meant that the person was with the resort. Brandon turned, and did a double take.

It was Geneva, in a swimsuit. She raised her hand apologetically as she dragged the kayak out of the water, though unsuccessfully. From his vantage point, he noted that it was caught in the V of two rocks. She was struggling, and Brandon's focus lost itself in her plight.

"I'll call you back," he said.

"Promise, Puso!"

"Yes! I gotta go." Brandon hung up the phone and tossed it and the shell onto his clothes. He jogged in Geneva's direction. As he came closer, he lowered his eyes, so tempted to stare. She didn't deserve ogling, despite his curiosity.

After she'd left him at the yoga studio, her words had sunk in. And after he'd taken his thoughts out on lifting up some of the wooden floors, mainly to inspect the foundation, he'd landed at the point of momentary acceptance of the truce she'd offered.

Geneva was out of breath. "I'm sorry—I didn't mean to interrupt. I was trying to paddle further away, but the waves took me here. I guess I'm out of practice."

And gosh darn it, he looked up at her face. At the glistening droplets of water on her skin, at the strands of hair that escaped from her bun. She was wearing a two-piece suit, and it showed the toned muscles in her arms she'd been using in the waves, and the soft flesh of her thighs.

"It's all good," he said, though every part of him knew that none of his thoughts were reflecting good. It wasn't okay for him to want to get closer. "Here. Let me." He lifted the kayak from where it had dug itself into the dirt.

"Thank you." She gestured to Ligaya just up the small hill. "I can carry it the rest of the way."

"I know." He grinned. This woman had not changed. "And, got it."

"You don't waste time."

Confused, he frowned.

She nodded at the construction site behind him. "I was shocked to see from the house how many people had converged. With the binoculars—that's what I used. Not that I was snooping or anything."

He flushed at how she stumbled over her words, and that it wasn't only he who was trying to get all this sorted out in his head. "You wouldn't be alone . . . snooping, that is. We had Tammy taking pictures most of the morning. But anyway, yes, the crew works fast, that's for sure."

"Well, I'm impressed."

Her compliment sent a thrill through him. "I wish I could take credit. It's all Mike."

She looked away with a smirk. "Ah, well, that's probably good. No one needs to see you bragging around here." She laughed. "I remember the time . . ." She looked up and seemed to think twice.

He half laughed. "What time?"

"That time when we went to Kings Dominion, and you got into a competition with a twelve-year-old, in basketball?"

Brandon remembered instantly. She and Beatrice had wanted to go to the roller coaster park but were only allowed by their parents if they'd agree to take a sibling. Since Chris hated roller coasters and Gil had been busy, Brandon was the one they'd dragged along. "I won by one basket!"

"He missed a basket because his mother distracted him." She threw her head back and cackled. "And you were like five years older than him! You were always so competitive."

"It takes one to know one," Brandon said.

Her expression turned curious. "I'm not competitive."

"Maybe not with others, but with yourself you are." At her sudden silence, he jumped in, "Or what do I know. We haven't seen each other in years."

A gust of wind rocked the kayak, causing the both of them to steady it in Geneva's hands. It cut through the vibe, reminding Brandon that this wasn't just a girl from the past but a woman he'd thought he loved.

"I've got to go. I was just on a quick break, but I have furniture to pick up," she said. "You free tonight? To get together and talk about plans? I know I suggested we would only communicate via text or email, but things . . . changed."

"That sounds ominous."

Her face lit. "It was at first, but I have a solution. So does tonight sound okay? Twelve days and all." She gave him a pensive smile.

"Right. Twelve days." In true Geneva fashion, she'd refocused the conversation. There were only twelve days for them to finish up this project. Geneva was being a professional, and he . . . he needed to step up. If she could let the past go, for now, he could too. "Yeah, I'm free."

"I should be back from Nags Head about seven. But I'll text to keep you posted."

"All right. See you . . . later."

With a final smile, she turned and dragged the kayak behind her. She wrangled it like it was a body pillow, with what he knew was her stubbornness, her strength, and her ambition.

Brandon watched Geneva go, soft curves against horizon, until she became an outline. Her shadow climbed the stairs to her beach house, where he imagined she began undressing, piece by piece, before stepping into the shower.

A wave lapped onto his feet, waking his runaway thoughts.

Then, with one last look at her screen door as it slapped closed, he high-kneed into the water to cool himself down.

♡

Brandon stepped out of the bathroom, finally clean of sand and dirt from the day's work, and was greeted by the cool AC of his bedroom.

Correction—not his bedroom but the guest room, which was sparse but pleasing. From the white cotton sheets to the textured beige walls to the hand-painted dresser and the french doors that led outside to a porch with rattan furniture—their mother's favorite—the decor was thoughtfully arranged.

The room, however, was a reminder that he wasn't home. He had nothing to ground him. His clothing was still in his duffel bag next to a growing pile of dirty laundry he had yet to wash because that meant going into one of his siblings' apartments. And without a single framed photo—he didn't belong. Except for three shells he'd found that day, set in a line on the desk, it was a far cry from the family home, where every piece of furniture or clothing was a memory that he had a part in.

Another correction—Heart Resort was now the family home. So what did that make the town house?

His house? A home simply for storage?

In all cases, Brandon had no choice but to ride out this parole. Chris's icy barrier was melting, though Brandon wasn't sure if he was happy about this. Without that boundary, Brandon was more exposed. By letting in the person who was the biggest critic and cheerleader in his life, he would be encumbered by his expectations.

His phone sounded while he made his bed, and the screen lit with Geneva's text.

Geneva:

Doing a final load. Should be a little after 7.

His annoyance at his brother flipped to thrill, but he tamped it down. Talk about boundaries—whatever anger and shock he'd felt yesterday were nowhere to be found. It was as if, as he crossed into the Heart Resort property, he was overwhelmed by everything. It was an introvert's nightmare of meetings, forced family time, memory lane, and watching his back all at once.

Bottom line, tonight's meeting with Geneva was simply a step forward in their work relationship. Nothing more and nothing less. Even if he couldn't get her—in her swimsuit and standing so close that he could count the freckles on her face—out of his mind.

He texted back.

Brandon:

See you then.

Brandon opened the french doors and stepped out to the wooden deck and breathed in the warm air. The sun wasn't yet on the horizon despite it being almost 6:00 p.m. He took in the sounds of birds trilling and leaves rustling to push his lingering thoughts of Geneva away and focused on the rough weave of the outdoor rug beneath his feet.

He felt the fuzz of fur around his ankles, and he jumped back. "What the hell!"

A black dog circled his feet.

"Goodness, it's just Roxy," Beatrice said, joining him on the deck.

"You have a dog?" He bent down and offered the dog his hand; it had initially retreated but trotted around the corner of a chair leg, its fur shimmering. "Hey, Roxy, come here."

"*We* have a dog, yes." She sat on the cushioned chair and without fanfare picked up Roxy and set her on her lap. "A dog, a stray cat, and the same cardinal-and-blue-jay pair that seem to travel together. They like to hover around over there." She pointed to a bird feeder, so far away that Brandon had to squint. "You should have binoculars next to the french doors."

With the binoculars—that's what I used. Not that I was snooping or anything.

Brandon focused on the horizon. If he did, it would help him stop thinking of Geneva. "You and your binoculars, Ate Bea."

"You know I like to know what's up ahead," she said, running a hand down Roxy's back.

"Another word for that would be *nosy*." He grinned.

"It's to ease curiosity! And I don't know. I tend to think that messages are sometimes a little beyond what we can see. Binoculars help."

He nodded. To him, Beatrice was otherworldly. She always had a reason for her actions, and sometimes the reasons weren't so clear from the get-go. She acted on intuition that disguised itself in outbursts of fuzzy motivation. To others, his sister might be perceived as emotional and irrational, but Brandon had witnessed it himself—that frisson of excitement that would arise from nothing and then a jolt of action. In the end, they would realize that it was for some important reason.

Brandon moved to the railing and wrapped a bicep around one of the posts. His eyes caught on the heart carved into it. Sure enough, upon inspection of the other posts, there were hearts carved into every one.

"Did you just notice?" Beatrice asked with a wry smile.

"Yeah, I did. He spared no expense in the details."

"Kuya Chris wanted our name and brand everywhere. Not only is this our business, but this is also our home."

Brandon felt a pang in his heart. If Heart Resort was home and he wasn't here, then what, exactly, was he? He decided to test the waters—was his sister open to letting go? "Is our town house home too?"

"Of course it is. That's a silly question." She peered at him.

"There aren't any hearts carved on the porch."

"But it has Mom and Dad's things. It has all their stuff."

Brandon shook his head, wishing she'd said something else, something to realign his topsy-turvy thoughts on how to manage a home he both loved and needed to get away from.

He couldn't bring up the possible offer now.

His gaze lowered to the flagstone walkway that led from the house to the driveway. Located in the middle of the peninsula, Puso was its heart, amid foliage but built tall so the roof balcony had 365-degree views. The crape myrtle–lined driveway led to three other cottages, some for permanent residents and employees of the resort.

Under the bright sun, the walkway shimmered with red and gold.

"Good-luck colors, according to Mom." Beatrice answered his thoughts.

"I saw those colors and the logo everywhere on the way here. Billboards, road signs. On every one of those vans. It was on the mug on Kuya's desk the other day."

"I won't argue that the branding can get a little bit too much, but . . ." Her voice trailed off.

"But what?" Irritation seeped into his words, prompted by the thought of his brother's ambitions, his motivation to produce, and the pressure Brandon carried on his shoulders to please him—and ultimately, his inability to do so.

"Our last name is all we have. There's only us and the California Pusos that are in our family tree. What most people see as branding is us really making a mark here, and not just for us but for our parents. After all, it's why they immigrated, right? They'd wanted us to blaze our own trail. And what more than our name?"

Brandon never knew what to say to lectures such as this. What could compare to the dreams and sacrifices of his parents? It was true— he'd been raised with this idea that he should accomplish more than his parents ever had. That he would help take their family name and rise above, honorably.

But Chris assumed this effort single-handedly, and sometimes, his martyrdom was tiring. His attempt at parenting was also old hat—because Brandon, at thirty-two, didn't need a father. He needed support, advice, and friendship. He needed someone who didn't constantly remind him of the things he'd done wrong.

Brandon did this enough for himself.

You knew the plan. You and I made *the plan.*

The moment at the yoga studio had replayed itself over and over in his head, and each time, it reminded him of what had happened between him and Geneva, of the snippets of conversations he remembered in full clarity, of what they'd wanted in life. Geneva was like Chris—she was ambitious. Her goalposts moved, and she'd written down what she wanted in her life; she carried them in that leather Traveler's notebook. Four years ago, that list hadn't included him.

"You're right. And who am I to stand between our name and greatness," he said, with disdain.

"Don't be like this, Bran. We're already great, but don't tell me you don't want to make a mark for yourself. It's just that you have a different idea of what that is."

Beatrice's blunt accusation assuaged the argument brewing in his belly; his sister was used to dealing with his complaints.

"Why are you here? Was it to give me a hard time?"

She grinned. "It's my privilege to do so, yes. But right this second? It's to let you know that dinner's starting in, oh"—she twisted the watch on her right hand—"now, actually. At Kuya Chris and Ate Eden's. Which I think is right on time because by the sound of it, *someone's* hangry."

Brandon allowed the tension to pass; it wasn't his sister who he had a beef with. "Hangry and dark. Look at this." He lifted the sleeve of his shirt, showing the shameful mark of delineation between his DC-area light-brown skin and the dark brown of three days in the Outer Banks.

"Ew!" she said. "That's awful."

He snorted a laugh. "Anything else? Any other orders? You could have just texted me to come down."

"Yeah, actually." She thumbed her phone and handed it to him. "This is the Instagram account for the resort."

Brandon spied the picture of the yoga studio with the bright sky behind it and an outline of two figures, the shadows of their hands blending into one another.

The figures were him and Geneva.

"Tammy took it, obviously. If you look at the pictures before it, it's of the Hinga construction. Did you read the caption?" Brandon said. "'Soon, soon, lovebirds! Imagine yourself on our man-made beach, surrounded by the calm waters of the sound.'"

She raised an eyebrow.

The need to quell Beatrice's suspicions superseded the alarm that was blaring in his ears. Because the picture was . . . nice. He waved the photo away. "Kuya Chris wanted in-progress pictures."

"Okay, but—"

To veer the conversation to the logical, Brandon said, "We probably have to set some rules, though. Geneva's not huge on social media."

"How do you know that?" She peered at him.

"She told me." *While we were talking about our affair.*

"It's exactly what I thought when I saw this, honestly."

"Oh, that's all?" His chest sagged with relief.

"Yes. I don't want her to feel pressured to do more than she needs to. She's helping us pro bono. I'll bring it up with Kuya." Seemingly satisfied, Beatrice picked up Roxy and stepped into the guest room.

But before they crossed the threshold, she said, "Kuya Chris is very much like a cat. Unlike this cutie, who will throw herself at you." She rubbed the top of Roxy's head. "Our brother doesn't do well with surprises; you know that. And, he doesn't want to admit that he's not on top at the moment. Tropical Storm Maximus humbled him." Beatrice's lips quirked into a smile. "If only it wasn't a storm that took out part of the resort, I would actually laugh at that. He needed it, the humility. But the bottom line is that he's happy you're home. So hang in there. You'll be out of this room soon enough. I know that it's bothering you."

Brandon halted at the doorway. "How do you know that?"

"Oh, Bran, I've known you since you were born. And besides, whether or not you know it, or whether or not you say it, your emotions are so on your sleeve, even if it's marked with an embarrassing farmer's tan. It just takes the right person to pay attention."

CHAPTER SEVEN

Geneva hissed as she pulled her hand out from under the table leg. It had caught her pinkie finger in a moment's inattention, when her Apple Watch had buzzed with a text from Brandon.

"Ms. Geneva, are you okay?" Rhiannon's high voice echoed from the other side of the resort storage warehouse.

"Yes. Just . . . nothing . . . ," she said, face burning, though it was anything but nothing. She had been unfocused all day; she couldn't get the image of Brandon's shirtless torso and low-slung cargo shorts out of her head. And that despite her best efforts to paddle away from him, as she'd done four years ago, fate, this time in the form of waves and wind, had led her kayak straight to him.

Beyond that was her anticipation of seeing him tonight.

Rhiannon came around the dresser Geneva was standing next to, with Sal at her side. By means of sheer proximity the two had become Geneva's helpers. Yesterday and today, they'd assisted her in loading and unloading the smaller pieces of furnishings into the warehouse, with the larger pieces being delivered by Mr. Barnes.

"That's it. The van's empty," Rhiannon said. "I also called up to Mr. Barnes like you told me, to let him know that we'll be back up there in the morning. He said he put aside the pine tables so no one would take them." She crossed her arms and lowered her voice.

"Though don't say I said so, but I don't think anyone was really going to take them."

"Thanks, to both of you," Geneva said to the sweating individuals in front of her. The warehouse had high ceilings, and the space itself was expansive, but to say it was claustrophobic from the humidity was being nice. "You guys didn't bargain for this kind of work."

"It's a pleasure," Sal said, still very formal despite his dusty shirt. "I *am* very curious as to how all of this will work out."

"To be honest? Me too." She led the way out of the warehouse, and Sal locked up behind her. "I've got measurements but only have walked into a few of the homes, though I've got a good sense of what needs to be placed where. Not to mention, I still need approval from the big boss." She winked. "Beatrice gave me the okay, but Chris could very well not like it. We'll find out tonight—I might be able to catch him."

"That's why you asked about returns," Rhiannon said. "That was smart."

"This isn't my first time dealing with particular clients, though I'll feel bad if I have to send all this back. There's also the lost-time component. But I'm putting my bet on Chris seeing it my way." She turned and caught Rhiannon's eye. "Sometimes you have to make a decision on the fly knowing that you're taking a risk and possibly making a mistake. But that's okay, because most mistakes can be remedied."

Her own words pierced at her.

Was there a way to come back from mistakes? And if so, was there a statute of limitations?

The click of the van doors snapped Geneva out of her thoughts, thank goodness, and she climbed into the passenger seat. Rhiannon jumped into the back.

After Sal buckled in, he said, "Where to?"

Geneva pulled down the visor, and sure enough, dirt marred her right cheek and forehead. She rubbed it, thinking of her schedule tonight. She had her meeting with Brandon, but before then she had a list of admin tasks on her to-do list: Following up with Nita about Helena's B and B. Getting together the accounting for the items she'd purchased. Coordinating outreach to past clients for referrals.

But seeing Rhiannon in the mirror, who was staring out the window, looking just about as haggard as Geneva felt, with her wispy hair askew and cheeks red, her heart squeezed. Rhiannon reminded Geneva of herself at that age, eager to please, willing to get dirty to learn something new. At that age, Geneva also hadn't known of the ups and downs she would experience, and if she had a chance now to say something to her younger self, it would be to take the moment to chill out and enjoy the ride. "My place . . . for some dessert. Will the both of you join me?"

"Oh, I don't know, Ms. Harris," Sal said.

"C'mon, Sal. We've been working all afternoon, and you'll keep me company." She pressed her hands together in a prayer pose. "It's really yummy."

Rhiannon's face lit up. "Oh, Mr. Medina. It's *dessert*."

Geneva watched Sal's face change from hesitance to acceptance, his wrinkles accommodating a small smile.

"Great, it's settled." She clapped.

It took five minutes and a quarter of a mile to get to Ligaya, where they parked the van behind the house. They were greeted by a lively surf, and in an instant, Geneva's tiredness lifted. While kayaking earlier today, she'd been enamored of the expanse of the sound. She hadn't lied when she'd told Brandon that she was out of practice kayaking, but her drifting wasn't due to the waves but rather to her joy in allowing the water to take her where it wished.

To not have to steer, even for just a moment, was freedom.

As Geneva unlocked her door with the two behind her, she realized that unlike at her previous apartments, where she could fit a handful of friends comfortably, there wasn't ample seating inside.

"Why don't you guys wait out here? I'll come out with blankets."

She entered Ligaya, chilled from the AC. Luna greeted her with a meow, comfortable on top of the small refrigerator in the kitchen. It was as if she read her mind. "Hi, baby girl."

The cat returned the sentiment with the knowing stare of someone who felt ignored. "I'll make it up to you later," she called out to Luna. "I promise. There's just so much going on." The last couple of days had been jam packed with spending the resort's money and transporting furniture, with a few moments here and there for a break.

With the newly purchased furniture in mind, the current things in Ligaya paled in comparison. They screamed bland, with fabrics and textures that did not make an impression. They had function, true, but didn't impart the feeling of home and, most importantly, the feeling of togetherness.

Without comfort, there was no trust.

In her experience, it was trust, not love, that made the difference. It was trust, not love, that got her to stay somewhere. Love was just as it was, a by-product. The work was in the trust. And trust was work.

She grabbed two bowls and a mug and two spoons and a fork—there were only two of everything in the house, and that was something else she needed to change, because who wanted to be pressed with dishes—and scooped ice cream into each receptacle. It was lychee flavored and special and imparted a little bit of home. Her mother had a fierce sweet tooth—with her biggest temptation ice cream—and she'd generously passed it down to Geneva. She had been under her mother's tutelage in everything, from the way she looked at material possessions to her appreciation of the delicious Magnolia ice cream flavors like ube, mango, mais queso, and langka. Their freezer had been filled with pints hoarded from the Asian market.

Geneva's heart dipped, but she scooped herself up from the moment by piling the bowls, the utensils, and a blanket from the closet into her arms. She brought everything outside, where Sal and Rhiannon had taken off their shoes and were sitting in the sand. "Quick! The ice cream's already melting!" She laughed, passing Rhiannon the blanket. Sal crawled like a crab to lay it flat against the wind. They all fell into a fit of laughter, with the moment so pure that as Geneva ate, the ice cream had never tasted so delicious.

"Ms. Geneva, Ms. Beatrice said that you've been all over the place," Rhiannon said. She tipped the spoon so it rested lightly on her bottom lip.

"I have. I lived in Annapolis—that's where I met her and the rest of the family—and then went to college in Virginia. But after that, let's see: Los Angeles, Austin, Kansas City, Dallas, Saint Petersburg, and my last address was Sedona. But I've also traveled to so many other cities in the US and abroad. I even went to the Philippines to meet my family there."

"Where's home, then?" Sal asked.

Geneva took her time with the ice cream, mulling over her answer. "My permanent address is Gatlinburg, Tennessee."

She opened her mouth to say more, to possibly explain the loose threads of her life, but it would have been too complicated. Her parents' move from Maryland to Tennessee alone was a half-a-dozen-doughnut conversation.

"Wow. I've never lived anywhere else except for my same old house in Nags Head," Rhiannon said, saving the moment.

Geneva thought about it, the upheaval, then the Harris family bucket list she'd undertaken in spades. "That's not such a bad thing, to stay in one place, but I love to travel. I'm sure that you'll find a way to travel, too, someday, if that's what you want."

She shrugged. "Hopefully. But I can't right now. I help out, at home, besides school."

"Our Rhiannon wants to be a nurse," Sal said, like a proud dad.

"Yeah, it's hard, though. A lot of math." Her face screwed up into a frown.

Geneva laughed. "Math was hard for me too. But I have every confidence in you. My mother's a nurse. Retired now, but she loved it. She worked a lot of nights. Do you know what nursing you want to do?"

"No. I don't mind blood, though. I got into the nursing program at East Carolina University. I've been in the community college getting my prereqs done."

"That's great, Rhiannon. And as someone who's been at your side the last few days, might I say that you also have a good eye for design."

"You think?"

"I keep telling you how smart you are," Sal said over his glasses. "And hardworking. But you have to keep it up."

Rhiannon rolled her eyes, and to Geneva she said, "Mr. Medina doesn't want me to, quote, 'get distracted.'"

"All I want is to make sure you're on the straight and narrow."

Geneva watched as the two continued to banter, and her heart tangled up in twin slivers of memory and melancholy. In what she used to have.

"God, I completely forgot about napkins," she said, shooting to her feet, eager to put space between them. "I'll be right back."

She shuffled back in the house, deep breathing as she entered. She hated being rude, but it had gotten to be too much. She couldn't wallow in these feelings, in emotions that did nothing but pull her back to a space where she was unproductive. There was simply no time for that.

On the way out, she stubbed her toe against the kitchen table, and the laptop—which she had been working on earlier today—lit to life to her in-box.

"Dang it!" she said, hissing while pressing her toe into the floorboard to stifle the pain. Her eyes wandered distractedly to the computer screen and the bolded new message.

The email was from Nita, with the subject matter: Foster's Hotel Group.

The group that owned a string of midlevel hotels in the Midwest?

She stared at the napkins, knowing her ice cream was melting outside, and then at the email. A debate warred as it always did. Work or play? She bit her lip.

"Ugh." She clicked on the email. In it was a link to her Dropbox. She scanned Nita's message, bypassing all the details but coming upon highlighted words. Request interior decor consultation for a chain of hotels.

She reached out to the nearest chair and perched precariously on it. A chain. This would be another rung upward. It would mean prestige. It would mean exposure. It would mean learning.

It would also mean money. Great money.

Of course she would say yes.

She typed a quick email:

Nita,

Please schedule a time for either a video chat consult or an in-person consult possibly en route to Helena's B and B project.

Thank you, Geneva

She moved the mouse's arrow over to the send button, but something pulled from deep in her belly, taking her inward. For a beat she wanted to crawl back into bed, into the sleep that she'd gloriously had the last couple of days. Into the calm of the beach air against her face.

A clanging took her attention to the kitchen. To Luna, spying at her from on top of the kitchen counter. The bugger had knocked her keys onto the floor.

Geneva clicked to send the email and stood to retrieve her keys. Face up was her Annapolis key chain from the tourist shop on Main Street, discolored from its original silver color.

"*Now* what are you trying to say?"

Luna's stare was pointed.

Not for the first time, Geneva wished she could read Luna's mind. How many years had her cat been at her side? She'd seen Geneva's best and her worst. Most of all, she seemed to have a sense of when Geneva was facing a fork in a road.

In between what two destinations? She didn't know.

Unlike when she made quick decisions in design, in her own journey, Geneva never knew what was right. She simply moved to the next opportunity, a lesson straight out of her father's playbook.

At times the opportunities brought something fantastic, and other times, like these days, with Brandon complicating the two weeks she was supposed to be on the resort, her decisions were yet to be judged as wise.

"I didn't know he was going to be here," Geneva said.

Luna's tail whipped in objection.

"I swear," she giggled, and scratched the cat behind her ears. Luna leaned into her hold, purring in bliss.

Then, as if summoned by the stars, her phone buzzed in her pocket with the calendar notification that her meeting with Brandon was in a half hour.

♥

The nine-foot wrought iron gate that shielded Puso and the staff residences from the rest of the peninsula was open by the time Geneva drove up in her golf cart, with Brandon standing in the middle of the winding driveway.

She cursed herself at the surprise—she'd expected to have the drive up to pump herself up for their meeting—and her stomach gave way for the second time at his appearance. He was in shorts and a white T, with an Outer Banks baseball cap shielding his face and what she knew was a pensive smile of mixed emotions.

Me too, buddy. Me too.

She swallowed her nervousness. "Hey. How long have you been waiting?"

"Not long. When you texted, I thought that I might as well open the gate and then realized I didn't know how from the house. After dinner, the rest of the family kind of went their separate ways, and I didn't want to have them help me out with one more thing. Anyway. I thought this was the easiest way." He held up his gate remote control.

"Did you walk all the way down here?"

"I . . ." His face registered the decision he'd made. "It's not that far."

She hid a smile, noting the speed of his speech and the high tone of his voice. At least it wasn't only she who was nervous. "Thanks. Um, where should we go?"

"Just up to the house. I've got everything set up in the HQ dining room. It has the largest table."

They paused, just looking at one another.

Awkwardness bloomed between them. From yesterday to today could have been weeks in emotion for Geneva.

"Do you want a ride?" she asked finally, scooting a smidge to the left.

"Yeah, sure. You, um . . . you look nice."

"Thanks. I've worn this thing a million times," she said of her sheath dress. It was made of a knit cotton, and though the fabric was light and airy, heat inched up Geneva's neck as Brandon climbed into the golf cart. When he brushed up against her, it sent her heart into running speed.

She glanced at him at the same moment he raised his eyes to hers.

This was silly—what was this, high school? Not even that, but middle school? In high school she'd come into her body and confidence and even as a freshman didn't fear facing her crushes.

Then she realized. This was reminiscent of them four years ago at Chris and Eden's reception: both shy, testing each other out, despite their obvious connection.

"So . . . did you need for me to give you lessons or—" Brandon woke her from her thoughts and gestured ahead to the road in front of them. "The pedal on the right side is the gas."

She swallowed to ease the memory that had filled her chest. "Har har."

"Now go easy on the—"

She pressed the pedal to go, and the jolt of the golf cart jostled them forward. Brandon yelped, and thank goodness for that and the loud whir of the engine to divert her thoughts. Up ahead, the house's outline grew and became a beacon of white amid the green of the trees.

Geneva heard Brandon whimper, and she risked a glance in his direction.

He was gripping the oh-crap handle with his right hand and bracing himself with his left. "Holy hell. Who gave you the license to drive?"

She slowed, laughing. "Are you really going to be a backseat driver?"

"Look. It doesn't help that I still have visions of you driving over our garbage cans."

"Oh my God!" she said over the engine. "I was just learning."

"Illegally, mind you."

"Legally. Chris was old enough to be my guardian at the time. And I had my permit!"

They quieted as she parked the golf cart among the others under the home. To the left was a space occupied by a Harley with a sidecar, glossy black gleaming in the setting sun.

Geneva jumped out and appraised it. "Wow."

"It's Gil's newest toy."

"Does he actually take the girls in the sidecar?"

"If Ate Bea has anything to say about it? No."

She followed him up the stairs into the house and veered right. They passed doors to a balcony and stairs that led up to the apartments above.

They arrived in a four-season room with floor-to-ceiling windows on three sides. A white hand-scratched wooden table with what looked like a three-inch board and pedestal legs took center stage. Curvy metal chairs surrounded it, giving it a modern touch. Above the table hung a capiz-shell chandelier, and the rhapsody it emitted as it swayed against the warm wind that blew through open windows caused Geneva to exhale a long breath.

"My mom loves capiz shells," she said. "My dad, on the other hand . . . we had one of those shell hangings in the living room, just above his chair, but he always hit his head against it." Her father was tall, over six feet, of Scotch Irish descent, but it was all in his torso.

"They never moved it?" He offered her a bottle of water from the bucket sitting on the buffet.

"C'mon, this is my mom."

He laughed after he took a swig. "True, true. I have actually witnessed her steadfastness. And I bet to this day—she's still the same way?"

Brandon's honesty, but without judgment, put her at ease.

"Still."

She loved that with the Pusos, in general, she didn't have to explain herself—they knew enough about her and about her parents to commiserate. As an only child, Geneva had no one she could turn to with the same shared experience. And knowing in full capacity the length of life . . .

"Anyway." Geneva pushed herself through the thought. "I really love this room. I'm almost jealous I didn't design it." She ran a finger down the edge of the sideboard against the wall, also in an off white. Above it was a mirror framed in mother-of-pearl.

"I said the same thing when I walked into the house. I was kind of insulted that they did so well without me. When was the last time you were here?" Brandon gestured to the table, where a map was held open by four tulip shells, while others were rolled on one side of the tabletop.

She dropped her messenger bag into one of the chairs and perched on its seat, cool against the backs of her bare legs. "A little over a year ago. I was within driving distance, so Beatrice and I met up for lunch, and she gave me a tour."

His eyebrow rose. "Even more recent than me."

"I guess." She kept her face neutral, though curiosity pulled at her. The Pusos were tight knit, even in their differences. Beatrice hadn't mentioned why Brandon was never there, and Geneva hadn't inquired.

"They've done a lot since then. I can take you on a tour after this, if you'd like. There's even a pond they'd filled up with koi, though they were relocated after the storm." He winced. "I mean, the koi are fine. Anyway . . . the plans."

"Right," she said, refocusing on the matters at hand, on the large sketch of the resort. It was best not to skip down memory lane—it would be a slippery slope.

"The x-ed-out squares are the prefab tiny houses that we're waiting on." He unrolled two tubes. "We have two houses in one floor plan, and one with this second floor plan. The facade for these new homes is also modern, unlike the cottage style we currently have. They're on track to be delivered and installed tomorrow and the next day."

She eyed the renderings and the dimensions. Geneva bit her lip.

"Is . . . this a problem? Do your designs not fit into your plans?"

"That's not it." She went on to explain her conundrum of the truck fire. "I've got quite a bit of furniture in our warehouse here on the resort, but I'll need more."

Worry was etched in the lines of his face. "Will you have enough in time? And budgetwise, where are we?"

"I'm totaling that up now, and honestly, it is what it is. We have to bend in order not to break. I haven't updated Chris, though."

"I'll tell him; don't worry."

She smiled at the sentiment. "I'm not worried, Brandon. I'll tell him myself."

"Excuse me . . . ," he said wryly. "I was just thinking I could give you some backup."

"I'll let you know when I need it. But here's what I have." Geneva pulled her iPad from her messenger bag and turned it on. The screen saver turned on to Luna.

"You have a cat?"

"Yeah, why?"

"I dunno. My sister has a dog, and you have a cat—"

"I adopted her when I'd returned to Tennessee after . . ." She cleared her throat. In truth, Luna had been her mother's idea after she'd left Brandon. "Anyway, isn't she pretty?"

"She is. I just thought . . . that you traveled solo. It's what you always said."

"Well, people change." A shadow passed across his eyes, and the truth of her words caught up to her. "And Luna's not human, so it's . . . entirely different."

She pressed the screen swiftly, to her photos. "Take a look at this." She swiped right, to the collection of furniture she had built up the last couple of days.

He leaned into the iPad. "That's kitschy."

She leaned back. "Kitschy?"

"Yeah, definitely not the modern or universal that was initially the concept."

"I mean, no, it's not." A sliver of doubt nagged at her, from the decision to pivot in design. "But this isn't about flipping or selling a house. This is trying to get people to stay. I admit I was hesitant at first, but I got to thinking—"

"Flip and sell a house?"

"Yeah, what you do. Your mission is to take potential buyers and make them feel like they could live there, whereas—"

A hint of a grin wiggled from his lips. "How did you know I flipped homes?"

"Well, because . . . I don't know. Beatrice must have told me." Her neck warmed at the lie. He didn't need to know that she'd once scoured his website last year to gaze at the "About Us" photo of Brandon and his business partner.

She had to fix this quickly before a guilty-as-charged giggle burst from her lips. "As I was saying. I got to thinking that this might set our accommodations apart. I've got most everything I need, but there'll sure be some last-minute shuffling around."

She rummaged through her bag for her Apple Pencil, pulling out a swatch of fabrics from her bag as well as sample wood. "Now that I've lived in Ligaya a couple of days, I'm really feeling the vibe of—"

"Whoa. What more do you have in there, Mary Poppins?"

Confused for a beat, she realized she was holding three fabric swatches in her hand. "Oh, ha!"

"Do you have power tools too?"

"Actually . . ." Amused, and slightly proud of this fact—because preparedness was her best trait—she produced, with a flourish, a Gerber tool.

"All right, all right, I'm impressed, probably because . . ." He fished something out of his pocket. "I have one too."

"Yeah, but is yours engraved?" She flipped her tool over and pointed at the deep grooves of her initials in calligraphy on the handle.

When he didn't answer right away, she looked across to see his shoulders shaking. His hands were on his hips, lips pressed together, eyes alight.

"What?"

He shook his head.

"Are you . . . are you laughing at me?" Except she, too, felt a giggle coming on. "Okay, I got a little carried away. I wanted to make sure no one took mine."

He wiped his eyes and coughed out a laugh. "I mean, I'm not even surprised."

"Only-child problems."

"Well, well, well, what is this, a bonding session?"

The voice came not from either Geneva or Brandon but undeniably from Beatrice at the dining room entrance. And while absolutely nothing shady was going on, Geneva froze, her gaze momentarily meeting Brandon's eyes, who reflected the same guilt.

Guilt from years ago, rushing up. Guilt that now reminded her of her proximity to Brandon, that somehow in their conversation they'd moved so they were inches from one another.

She spun swiftly toward the doorway and found that not only was Beatrice there, but Chris was too. "Hey! How long have you both been standing there?"

"Enough to see that you two are hard at work." Beatrice's eyes flashed, a grin on her lips.

"Was that work?" Chris asked in his usual wry tone.

Next to her, Brandon grumbled.

"You have perfect timing, Chris. I'd love to share what I have." Geneva waved him over to decrease the tension rising in the room between the brothers. Chris was very much like her mother, whom she had always called a Nurse Ratched: all mean on the outside, soft and gooey on the inside. Chris just needed a little softening up.

She swiped through the furniture choices. All the while, she discussed the truck fire and reinforced that they were still on track in the timeline.

Geneva loved this part of her work; she loved painting the picture and watching her client's reactions to it. The magic was in the transformation, and with sometimes little intervention. A tweak here and there, a coat of paint, a switch in perspective, and voilà: a brand-new room, a new identity, a fresh start. Her favorite reaction above all: surprise, at falling for the unexpected. And that was what Geneva was reading on Chris's face.

That she'd surprised him.

"I like it. I like all of it," Chris finally said. "I won't love it until I actually see it come together. But you had a quick solution, and you acted on it." He tapped the table with two fingers. "I want the budget in my office in the next couple of days. If we have to, we can take it out of the restaurant budget."

She nodded. "You'll have it."

"Since we're talking about the restaurant," Brandon chimed in. "Kuya, I was going to bring it up tomorrow, but since you're here . . . I'd like to bring in a restaurant consultant."

"No." Chris's answer was swift.

"You're not going to hear me out?"

"There's nothing to hear out. Everything is down to the dime." Chris's eyes flashed, and in them, Geneva read his unsaid words. That it was postdinner, that his shirt was already untucked for the day. And while he tolerated Geneva's presentation because she was a guest, this wasn't time for a brother's request. Timing was everything.

"A good consultant is worth their salt," Brandon asserted.

Geneva cleared her throat. "I . . . I can see if I can help. I've got some experience in restaurant design."

Next to her, Brandon grunted.

Chris nodded. "See, you have a resource right here."

"It's not the same," Brandon said.

"Well," Beatrice chimed in like the bell at the end of a round. "I'm headed up. My show's about to start. *Paradise Island*. I love watching who's about to hook up with whom."

"God, I haven't watched TV in forever," Geneva said to lessen the tension.

"It's all garbage." She wiggled her eyebrows. "Yummy garbage, and quite informative of the human condition. Drama, am I right? C'mon, Kuya, leave them alone already." She turned her brother by the shoulders, and as they walked away, Beatrice shot them a glance and mouthed, *Sorry.*

Once alone, Geneva looked down at her iPad, opened to a panoramic photo of the furniture in the warehouse. Furniture that might have taken up Brandon's budget.

The entire encounter between the two brothers replayed itself in her head. It was obvious that the exchange stemmed from something deeper.

She lifted her gaze to Brandon's clenched jaw, and the truth settled around them along with the heavy weight of his silence.

Geneva had messed up.

She'd interfered in his life. Which she didn't want to do; she wasn't on the resort to do more than her job. "I'm sorry. I shouldn't have done that—"

"No, you shouldn't have." He shook his head. "Wanna go for a walk?"

"What?"

"A walk. I need some air. I mean, you don't have to, just—"

"I . . ." Her first instinct was to say no. Because walking led to more talking, and it would lead to sharing of feelings—and this was Brandon. But then again, *this* was Brandon. He was a man who didn't bare his emotions to just anyone at any time.

And admittedly, she didn't want to return to her beach house, where nothing waited for her but Luna, who would have reflected her conscience. That she should be right here. "Yeah, a walk sounds good."

CHAPTER EIGHT

Brandon had been having a great day—an excellent day. A fantastic few days, actually. He was getting things done. Tonight was supposed to be an easy meeting, and he'd had every intention to remain rational and cool around Geneva.

But he'd been filled with embarrassment that he, at his age, still struggled to get ahead of his brother.

Once they were outside, the warmth was a relief. The soft wind was a bit of consolation, soothing what was white hot inside him. And as he continued up the hill, the chatter in his head dissipated so he could properly hear the rustle of the trees and the sound of crickets, and he could smell Geneva's perfumed lotion.

"It's so pretty out here," she said, looking up at the sky, lit bright by stars. "You have to get pretty far from the city to see this sky."

The way she knew how to steer the subject was something he always appreciated, so Brandon went with it, leaning into the ease instead of the defensiveness that he carried around like a brick. He strolled up the main driveway toward the back of the house, deep into the weeping willow trees, where it darkened save for the solar driveway lantern lights that were gentle reminders of the path. He slapped at the random mosquito on his arm trying to make a meal out of him. "Kind of reminds me of those art classes we took, when we poked holes on a black sheet of construction paper and shone the light from behind to make the solar system."

"Ha! The great Mr. O'Rourke," she said.

"You had him too?"

"Yep. He taught at the middle school for forever. I got him in seventh grade." She smiled. And though it was dark, Brandon could make out the shine in her dark eyes.

"Are you okay?" she said after an extended pause.

He rested a hand behind his head. "It's the same ol' same-o with my brother."

"I know. And you fall right into it."

"Me?" He peered at her.

"Yeah, you. It takes two to get into a fight."

"Not always."

"Most often," she said. "Especially with the both of you. You didn't have to bring up the restaurant consultant. You could have done research, had names to throw out, and yet . . ."

She wasn't lying. He couldn't help but say something. He'd wanted to see if his brother would have extended the same allowance to him as he'd done to Geneva just then. Yes, he was a masochist. "It was a business meeting."

"You were testing him and used me to do so, but I'm going to give you the pass. Look, I'm sorry about coming in between that. I won't do it again. But you were just raring to get into a fight. You're not thinking of what it's even about or what you could lose."

She was right. Of course she was right.

He shook his head, finally.

"It's also massively awkward. When one of you digs, another one punches the other below the belt, and it's painful to watch. It hurts right in the puso." She pointed to her heart.

"Oh, you're getting deep now, Geneva." He snorted, deflecting, and purposely doing so. As usual, she was seeing right through him.

"Kuya Chris is just him, and I'm just me. It's just that now we don't have to pretend. There are no forebears to please, and especially none to keep him in check. But I knew that coming here. I'm here to do a job and get out."

"Wow," she whispered.

"Isn't that what you do?" Except when he said it, it came out harsher than he intended, and he regretted it. "I mean—"

"It's okay," she said. "I know what you meant."

They'd come upon a fork in the road, where a hammered wooden sign read SECURITY CABIN. A few meters up, a light shone through the windows of a tiny house, and the scent of something sweet reached Brandon's nose. It was a reprieve; he didn't want to talk about his and Chris's roller-coaster relationship, nor did he want to delve into their drama. "Someone's cooking."

"Sal?" Geneva asked.

"Yep." He took another step forward on the path, when he was suddenly blinded by white lights.

"Whoa!" Brandon turned toward Geneva. He held a palm up to block the light.

"Who's out here?" a voice said. "Mr. Puso?"

"Sal, it's Brandon."

"Ah, Brandon." Sal waved them his way, toward the shadows. "I'm sorry about that. We have motion sensors all up and down this main driveway. It's rare that this one goes off. Oh, and Ms. Geneva. I apologize."

"It's okay, Sal. We were just on a walk." Geneva had gotten ahead of Brandon and was already by Sal's side. "We're sorry to bother you."

A shadow of a person was at Sal's door.

"Not a bother at all. Are you in the mood for food?"

"Well, n—" Brandon began.

"We're having s'mores."

"That's what I smell," Geneva said.

With a quick glance at Geneva, Brandon relented. He'd been taught to never say no to an elder. Though he'd only encountered Sal briefly throughout the resort, he was enough of a mainstay. "Sure, okay."

After a quick stroll up the pathway, they reached another man at the door. They made quick introductions. Jonathan Chang appeared to be Sal's age, dressed in a tropical shirt and board shorts. He had a deep tan from the sun; his thinning hair was white. They went around to the backyard, to a metal ring aglow with a small fire.

Sal grabbed folding chairs and opened them side by side, then set Brandon and Geneva up with sticks with marshmallows at the tips.

"I haven't done s'mores in forever," Brandon said to Geneva as he sank into the camp chair.

"Perhaps the sugar can pep you up a little," she said just loud enough so he could hear.

"Ha."

"Jon and I were just arguing on the best type of burn on a marsh-mallow. I like it barely dark but melty. He, on the other hand . . . ," Sal said, handing Jon a stick.

"We weren't arguing. It was a discussion." Jonathan loaded up marshmallows with a crooked grin. "I like my marshmallows burnt to a crisp. Why not go for it? Life's too short to wait for perfection."

"It's not about perfection but function. You can't make a s'more from something you can't smoosh," Sal countered.

"I beg to differ." Jonathan eyed Brandon, who had just retrieved his stick from the fire, the marshmallow sizzled and charring. "See, Brandon has the same theory."

"Don't waste your theories on that guy. He doesn't even like choco-late. He just eats the marshmallow from the stick," Geneva jumped in.

The two men gasped.

"That's blasphemous. No chocolate or graham cracker?" Sal asked.

"Nope," Brandon said. "Purely marshmallow. Listen, when you're the youngest in the family, it's all about grabbing what I could. Beatrice ate the chocolate separately, and my dad loved eating the cracker on its own. But we always had marshmallows. Whenever they took out the s'more stuff, I grabbed those in a hurry. It's the fight I knew I could win."

"That, too, says a lot about you," Jon said.

"You're not kidding," Geneva said. She carefully pressed her s'more together. The marshmallow oozed from the middle. "I, on the other hand, want every bite to have every single ingredient. It always drove me crazy, how the chocolate squares are smaller than the graham cracker squares, and the marshmallow is only half its size. So, I always do two marshmallows and six Hershey rectangles."

"Basically you want it all. Interesting," Jonathan said. "I like you."

Brandon thought about this as Geneva bit into her s'more, and as they chatted with Sal and Jonathan. While he participated—because he was always polite—her words, "You're not kidding," nagged at him. They were innocuous words, if cynical, and they were about marshmallows, for God's sake. But for some reason, the meaning landed a certain way he couldn't explain, except that he didn't like it.

♡

By the time Brandon walked Geneva back to her golf cart, the moon was high in the sky.

"I didn't mean for us to overstay our welcome," Geneva said, climbing in. The main house's front porch lights were illuminated over his shoulder. She set her messenger bag on the empty seat next to her. "I can't believe it's midnight."

"I don't think they minded at all," he said, then laid a hand on his belly; it ached. "They kept going back to the kitchen for more, and you know I can't ever say no to food. My mother would've killed me."

Sal and Jon had been masters of the outdoor kitchen. After their s'mores, they'd worked backward in the dinner party routine, grilling corn and brats. The last course was mango salsa with chips. All the while, each one of them told stories that seemed to have no start or end.

As if reading his mind, Geneva said, "God, it's been so long since I just sat there and shot the breeze."

"Same. I'm caught up most days."

"Same." She returned his smile. "But I had fun. Thanks for a business meeting turned food fest. It's definitely time for bed. You must be exhausted, Mr. Early Bird."

"Not really. I think I've got a little bit of a sugar high."

"Me too. Chocolate is truly my weakness." She giggled. It was so sweet; Brandon wondered how he could fit in another s'mores activity. "When I get back, I think I'm going to make myself a cup of tea and work on some of the designs, sketch a little. I leave in eleven days."

"Eleven?"

She looked at her watch. "Yep, it's now day four."

Day four. Was it already day four?

Then Brandon admonished himself for caring about this fact.

Then again, of course he would care, seeing that he needed to get his work lined up with hers.

As he mediated between the angel and the devil on his shoulders, she started the golf cart. She pressed a button, and the headlights turned on, dim against the shrub in front of her. The right-side headlight flickered.

Brandon peered down the pitch-dark driveway and then at Geneva in the rinky-dink golf cart that didn't even have a seat belt. What was it, a ten-, fifteen-minute ride to Ligaya?

"I should drive you home. Gil has the minivan parked in the back."

"I didn't think anything but resort vehicles were allowed on property?"

"If you saw how much effort it took to wrangle two kids into a car seat, you'd make a special exception. He brought the girls to art, and I guess they have something in the morning. But anyway, I can grab the keys from Gil real quick. He's probably up."

"I'm fine, really."

"Of course you are. You always are. But this place is a whole different animal at night. Most of our street and building lights are off with the lack of clients. I would just feel better if—"

"Bran, I can maneuver myself through this resort with one light bulb. I—"

Then, as if the world, for once, had decided to side with Brandon, both headlights went out.

From below, Geneva heaved a breath. "Ugh." She was biting her bottom lip.

Now this, this expression, he hadn't seen before. This biting-the-lip thing was new, and it riled up something inside of him. It lit him up like the fireflies that inhabited the Outer Banks at night.

It was adorable.

Stop it.

"I guess I can get a ride from you." Her tone seemed remorseful. "But I don't want to wake Gil and the girls."

"I'll take you in my golf cart, then."

"Fine."

He snorted. "Jeez. You're welcome." He gestured her to his golf cart. Also known as the only one in the row, he had realized earlier that day, that wasn't personalized. His was the standard white with gray seats, whereas each of his siblings' was personalized. Beatrice's looked like a mini-jeepney, Filipino style, with bling and lights and flags.

"I didn't mean it that way." She climbed into the passenger seat. "Thank you for taking me home."

"My pleasure. I know you don't like help." He turned on the cart.

"It's not that. I don't want to put anyone out." She fiddled with the rolled-up sketches on her lap.

"You've never put me out, Gen." He turned around out of habit and slung his arm behind Geneva, for when he didn't have a vehicle with a backup camera. As he did so, his skin brushed the back of her clothing.

His own words caught up to him, and the intimacy within their meaning caused him to pause. They were shrouded in darkness now, and he couldn't tell what her expression was. He could, however, hear her breaths, and detected the slow rise and fall of her chest.

An owl hooted in the distance, and it broke the spell. Brandon shifted gears, made a U-turn, and began the descent down the middle of the driveway, where the moonlight hit. Still, it was so dark that he couldn't see past ten feet in front of him, and he focused on keeping the outline of the road in his mind, especially as the driveway began to curve.

As they got closer to the end of the driveway, the full night sky came into view.

It was this big sky that his father had loved. On their vacations, he used to lie out at night, looking straight up into the night sky. He'd said it put life in perspective, to feel so small and to believe that their troubles were actually tiny in comparison to the rest of the world's.

Sometimes, his mother used to join him, and under their murmured breaths they would discuss the Philippines and what they'd left behind. They'd giggled and reminisced, and Brandon, despite his want to be out there with them—because being the youngest always seemed to put him on the outs on everything—had kept out of their way. Those moments seemed sacred.

"So romantic," Geneva said.

"What?" He did a double take.

"Sal and Jonathan. They're so romantic."

"Yeah, they are." He pressed the brake slowly as they got to the gate, which opened at their arrival after a quick press of his key fob.

"They seem happy."

"They do, like they've known each other forever."

"How old do you think they are?"

He glanced briefly at Geneva and mulled the odd question. He was no good at gauging age. If he didn't have his nieces, he'd think that a five-year-old was ten and vice versa. "I dunno. Midfifties? Sixties maybe?"

"Do you think they're your parents' ages, or mine?"

"I don't know." He tried to picture his mom and dad. They'd been dead seven years.

Seven years.

Brandon waited for the sucker punch of pain. But instead of the dread that used to descend upon him when he thought of his parents' accident, it was awe. Awe at how fast time had flown by and what had happened since. Brandon had been immature and naive at twenty-five. He was just starting to . . . if he was being perfectly honest . . . just figure out how to live on his own.

He had his parents and then his siblings, who had taken care of him, attended to all his needs. His hand-me-downs consisted of clothing, cars, and lessons passed along through three sets of sibling hands.

He had been so young. His parents had been so young.

"Know what's so funny?" he said, a memory flying in. "Whenever I asked how old my dad was, he'd always say, 'Thirty, iho. Thirty forever.'" He snorted.

"Tito Joe's dad jokes were always on point," she said.

"His hair, too, and maybe that's why I always forgot how old he was. I think he dyed it."

"Well, Sal's and Jonathan's were undeniably gray. Maybe they're in their sixties. They're both physically well, though. They're lucky about that." After a pause in which they went over a bumpy part of road, she said, "I miss my parents. They're in their seventies now. Can you imagine? I mean," she followed up in a rush, "I'm sorry."

Brandon shook his head, used to this kind of conversation with folks. Except he knew that in Geneva's case, she meant her apology. It didn't come off as pitying or apologetic because she wasn't sorry for him. She *was sorry*, because she had her own loss. "Do you think our parents ever thought we would be riding around in a golf cart in the middle of the night on a private resort?"

She laughed. "I think both of our parents just hoped we'd dream big and make something of ourselves."

"Speak for yourself. That was what everyone thought of me, but not you. Not perfect Geneva. You were the star."

"I was the star because I was the only star. And Tito Joe and Tita Marilyn thought so highly of you, Brandon. You brought sunshine into the room. You still do."

The last part of the sentence dipped into a whisper that made Brandon swallow a breath. He girded himself against falling into her spell. She was being nice; that was all. So he decided to call her bluff. "My mother always made it seem like each one of us was a favorite. She even used to say, 'You are my favorite bunso. The last and the greatest.'"

She laughed. "No, I mean it! You always lit up a room. Everyone felt your presence. *I* was under a lot of pressure to succeed, because I was the only. Then, of course, after my dad had his stroke . . ." She paused just as Brandon turned onto the little gravel path that would lead to Ligaya. The sound of the wheels over gravel was loud, and Brandon sped up. He wanted them to continue this conversation because Geneva didn't talk much about Thomas Harris specifically. She always referred to her parents, and most times only to her mom, Lisa.

The motion sensor light turned on, flooding the area around the cart, when he finally parked.

She grabbed her things. "Thanks for inviting me over. I'll call—"

"Wait a sec." He reached out and lightly touched her forearm. "You weren't done."

Her lips were pressed into a line. "Yeah, I am."

"Geneva, you are never done talking. In fact the moment that you clam up is when I know there's more to it."

She settled back into her seat. "It's just that when my dad had his stroke, I felt more pressure to be better than what they expected. To be better than I had expected for myself."

"The total s'more," he mused.

"I guess? I didn't think of it that way. But on top of all that, seeing them get older . . . it's a reminder that there's more to do." She looked down at her things.

"I think you're doing just fine."

"Eh." She returned a weak smile. "Anyway . . . thank you for meeting with me. I'll send you a linked calendar request, and let's keep each other abreast via text, especially about design issues."

And in a classic Geneva maneuver, she didn't leave Brandon any room for response. He could only watch her gather her things. She jumped out of the cart without pleasantries.

He said the first thing that came to his mind. "Hey!"

She spun around. "Yeah?"

"I'll make sure to get your ride fixed!"

Finally, finally, a sincere smile appeared on her face. A thankful smile. "Okay. Have a good night, Bran."

"I will." Now, especially, because for that one moment, he knew that that smile was because of him.

CHAPTER NINE

Twelve years ago, December 16
Paris, France
Weather: cloudy, 45°F

Geneva clutched a baguette wrapped in a napkin, and flecks of its crispy crust dotted her black knit gloves. From over the top stuck out a long sausage nestled in the bread.

"This is the most refined hot dog I have ever seen," she said, admiring it.

"Oh, before you take a bite, I want to take a picture," her dad said, while holding his own baguette. "Here, take mine for the shot."

Geneva cocked a hip, holding the two baguettes, while Thomas Harris backed up to encompass the Eiffel Tower behind her and lifted the camera hanging from his neck. It was a massive thing, with a long lens, so that his neck always bore the markings of the camera strap. Sometimes he carried two cameras for work as a freelance photojournalist.

"Ready?" He counted off, then took a series of shots. His specialty was portraits, which meant Geneva had learned from being his subject in every holiday and family event in her twenty-two years that taking a photo didn't mean one snap but several from varying angles.

So she stood still for a beat, then switched positions at his cue. Smiled at his encouragement, then pouted when he instructed. She imagined herself blending into the background of tourists, who were all doing the same thing.

From behind her dad, her mom arrived, coming from a shop. This was how they traveled: Geneva sketched, Thomas photographed, and Lisa Harris shopped. It was no surprise that she was holding a couple of bags.

Thomas lowered the camera. "All done!"

"Thank God." Geneva bit into her baguette and hustled to her parents' side, and the three slumped onto an open bench.

They'd been on their feet all day. Yesterday was Munich, today Paris, tomorrow Calais, and then across the English Channel. A whirlwind, but she couldn't get enough of it. Each new place filled her up. It didn't matter where they went—fancy or otherwise—she gobbled up sights and sounds and smells like a vacuum.

Her parents shared a baguette, and as Lisa ate, Thomas took out his leather Traveler's notebook from his camera backpack. He'd purchased it a couple of years ago while on a trip to Japan. Three notebooks were nestled inside. Two were for work; he flipped the third open to a list.

It was their family bucket list.

With a flourish, he produced a pen and handed it to Geneva. The list was a mixed bag of items they all had come up with. From *buy a convertible* to *walk across the Golden Gate Bridge*.

Geneva ran a finger down one page to *visit the Eiffel Tower* and checked off the box next to it with a satisfying stroke. She looked up at her parents, their cheeks bearing the chill of the cold wind as they grinned at her.

Checking that box and seeing the looks on their faces took a close second to actually seeing these places.

"We have something for you," her mother said. With a brief glance at her husband, she retrieved a meticulously wrapped package from the bag.

A sigh escaped Geneva's lips. The wrapper was a deep, metallic ocean blue dotted with the occasional gold, topped by a sheer gold ribbon. Only her parents knew how hard she geeked over wrapping paper, wallpaper, scrapbook paper, and fabric. Anything that brought a sudden pop of color, an emotion.

She almost didn't want to open it, but with prompting she did.

It was a set of notebook inserts similar to what was inside Thomas's Traveler's notebook.

Her father then did the unthinkable. He removed his two work notebooks from the leather cover's flaps and handed the leather cover to her. With the bucket list notebook inside.

Geneva's jaw dropped. "I don't get it."

Her dad urged her to take the leather-bound cover. "Because it's time for you to fly."

"But this is *our* list."

He smiled. "Sure it is. And we'll keep adding things and keep checking things off as we do them together, but you don't have to wait for us to get started. You can write down all of your dreams, to your heart's content."

"This feels . . ." Geneva wasn't sure what she felt, but it was familiar. It had started when she was filling out college applications and visiting colleges. Feeling a rush of independence at going away to college. Tagging along whenever her dad traveled. Knowing that it was only the three of them in their family. Good for the most part, though sometimes overwhelming. "Exciting."

"To mark today, let's write something down. Something silly," Lisa said. "Something wild."

Geneva bit the side of her cheek as she wrote: *Live next to the ocean.*

CHAPTER TEN

Day 4
Weather: partly cloudy, 92°F
Hurricane Oscar: Category 1, approaching Dominican Republic

It was as if Geneva had intuited her mother's phone call. She awoke the next morning to the shrill of her mother's ringtone, Elton John's "Tiny Dancer."

"Good morning, Neva," said Lisa Harris in her singsong voice. Geneva still had only managed to open one eye. From her bright screen, she read that it was a good two hours before her wake-up time.

"Hi, Mom." Her voice croaked.

"Iha, it's eight a.m. your time, and why aren't you up? I can hear it in your voice. You're still under your covers."

"I worked late last night." She raised the covers off her face and brushed the wisps of hair that had flattened themselves across her cheeks. "Okay, I'm over the covers now." Sort of.

"Good, good. How are the Puso kids?"

"Good. Same."

"Uh-huh. Helloooo! Good morning! Nice to see you!" Her mother was yelling, which only meant . . .

"Are you on a walk?"

"But of course, at Springtown Mall, my usual. But if I call you later, you'll be too busy to take my call." Her tone was like the sound's waves, undulating, with a whole lot more meaning than what was seen or, in this case, heard.

Geneva didn't bite. Distraction would be her ally. "Guess who's here?"

"Mm?"

"Brandon."

Silence ensued on the other end of the line except for the swish of her mother's workout pants. Geneva's mother was a woman of many words. In person, she could talk one's ear off, and if placed in front of a phone camera or on the phone, she rose to the occasion of the technology, using it as her personal karaoke machine.

The silence meant that her mother was thinking.

"How is our dearest Brandon?" she said finally.

After she and Brandon had broken up, Geneva had had to tell Lisa. She'd had no choice—she'd fallen into a sadness that even she couldn't outrun. Geneva had retreated to Tennessee for a few weeks, and her mother had nursed her back to emotional health.

Geneva felt her body relax into her bed. Her eyes were open now, and she stared up at the low ceiling.

Like most ceilings, Ligaya's was white, with nothing to visually grasp onto, so instead of muddling with words, she scrapped the roundabout and crashed into the truth head on. "He's beautiful, and sweet. And just everything."

Last night had sealed the deal. Their time together at Sal's . . . it wasn't the two men who made the time romantic and nostalgic; it was Brandon. In the way he was so open to it all, from tasting a little bit of each food to the conversations that flowed. Brandon had this soft confidence that she'd missed.

"And?" Lisa asked.

"We decided on a truce."

"Why do you need a truce if the both of you weren't at odds?"

She slung her arm across her face. "Are you getting technical now?"

"I mean, yes. You're not his nemesis. You're not two worlds fighting for resources in order to save your people."

"Oh dear. You're reading sci-fi again."

"Yes, but that's not the point." She sighed. "Maybe it's not a truce but a peace. And I think that's very good, Geneva. Being at peace is important. This makes me so happy."

"Okay, fine, a peace. And I'm glad you're happy, Mom."

"Why do you sound irritated? What did I say?"

"Nothing." Because in fact, Geneva didn't know why she was upset and irritated, except that sometimes when she spoke to her mother, the whole weight of the world fell on her shoulders. And while logic told Geneva that her parents had never put pressure on her, not in a way that was tangible, she was, in fact, not at peace. "I'm sorry. It's . . . I got home late from this planning meeting with Brandon, and then there was this little backyard food extravaganza, and then he drove me home. And it was friendly, and it was also a little weird. It felt like it should have never ended. But then I remember why it did."

"And what's that?"

"Because of time. His time, my time. It all didn't add up to our time."

"But right now? Is this the right time?"

"Mom! Where is this conversation even going? I'm not saying at all that either one of us wanted it to be a time."

"It's serendipitous that the both of you are there at the same time. Anyway." Her mother's voice dropped, and from there, Geneva picked up a hint that something wasn't right.

"Mom? What's wrong."

"I . . . I miss you."

Geneva turned to her side, and through the loft window, she caught sight of the beach. She imagined her feet dug into the sand, grains in between her toes, and the warm sun against her shoulders. She breathed out the tension that had built up in her chest. "I miss you too, Mom. How are the both of you?"

"We're doing fine, iha. We're doing so well. But it doesn't take away that I worry about you."

"You don't have to worry about me."

"I wouldn't be a mother who loved their child if I didn't worry. I just wish . . ."

"Don't say you wish you didn't make the decision."

It had been years since her parents had moved to Tennessee, but every few months, Geneva would hear the regretful tone in her mother's voice. "Mom, it was the best decision to sell the house in Annapolis. It got you a better house in Gatlinburg and more reliable care for Dad. More financial flexibility for the both of you. You don't have to deal with the cold in the wintertime, and you're with your sisters."

It was so logical, what was coming out of her mouth, but she felt the same grief, from a daughter's point of view. The loss of what had been their normal when her dad had had his stroke and then they'd left their family home. The growing anticipation of watching her parents get older, now in a retirement community. The fear Geneva carried that life was too short, and she had so many things to do, not only for herself but for them, so that they could be proud.

"But moving here has kept you from coming home."

"No, Ma. I haven't been home because I have work, like the rest of the world. And I've been to all these great places!" She infused light into her voice. Because herein was the confusion of her feelings—her life wasn't all bad either. Not having the tie to home encouraged her to go out into the world. Because of it, she had visited forty out of the fifty states. So many of her boxes were crossed out. "I have my career, I have my friends, and for the next week and a half, I have the Pusos."

"And Brandon."

And here we are again. And yet, despite her eyeballs rolling upward, she couldn't help but smile. "Yes, Mom, and Brandon. Because he *is* part of the family."

"You'll have to tell them that we miss them. That they can come here anytime."

"Okay, Mom, I will." And with that, Geneva detected her mother gearing up for her list of instructions. It usually began with an innocuous request and then tipped headlong into asking when the last time was she'd gone to Mass.

And Geneva hadn't yet had her first cup of coffee. "Mom, I have to go."

"No, wait." Lisa's voice skewed to panic.

"Yeah?"

"That was a good picture of you."

She slowly sat up in bed, wishing that she could stand and stretch. "What picture?"

"The one on the Heart Resort Instagram?"

She stilled. "The Heart Resort Instagram."

"Yes. You're on it. I wasn't sure who the man was since it was just an outline, though I know now it's Brandon. I could tell it was you immediately. Geneva, your posture. You really need to work on it. When you were little—"

Geneva put her mother on speaker and thumbed to Instagram. She wasn't even following the resort's socials. Sure enough, the last photo was the faraway view of her and Brandon at the beach, and they looked . . . close. Intimate. The photo was tasteful. Artistic.

She shook her head. "I'm not sure how I feel about this."

"It's no big deal, right? It doesn't even show your face."

Logically, Geneva knew this. None of her features were distinct. "I guess."

"But the chemistry." She clucked.

"All right already. I'm going. This is awkward."

A laugh filtered through the speaker. "I'll call you soon."

At that moment, Luna's tail tapped her on the cheek. Geneva turned to encounter her stare. "Luna says hi."

"My grandcat! Tell her I love her. I miss her too."

"I will. Love you, Mom." Geneva pressed the button on her phone to hang up, her spirit in a flurry. There used to be a time when all her conversations with her parents, even in college, when she was so busy sowing her oats and making her life, had ended on high notes. Their conversations had brought her to the next level of confidence.

These days, though . . . she was left with a film of regret all over her.

And now with these photos . . .

It wasn't necessarily photos but social media. At its inception, she'd gathered in online social circles, where she'd relished the camaraderie, the friendships, and the business relationships.

And then it had gotten to be too much. Her dad's sickness had kept her from checking in with the same fervor. Soon, she'd slowly opted for cat and dog feeds instead of those posts about milestones in families. Because not every family ascended in stature in the same manner. Then every post had felt like an announcement, an update via a bullhorn into a cavernous space.

She'd stepped back to recharge. Then, when she'd tried to jump into the fray once more, a truth had emerged. Everyone had moved on. It was like going to a ten-year reunion but with no context, jumping in midlife, into engagement and childbirth announcements without knowing anything about these newest family members.

With that, her life had narrowed to a tiny group of individuals. Even as her business had grown, which meant playing by online marketing strategies, she'd only taken it as far as posting curated photos and ads. She had enough obligations, enough pressure, to be checked up on and judged upon.

The phone rang again, but this time instead of her mother's face, Brandon's name appeared on the screen. Excitement ran up her spine, and she picked up. "Hi, I was just talking about you."

"Yeah?" Brandon was chipper, like he'd drunk three cups of coffee. Behind him was the whir of an engine.

"My mom says hi."

"Aw, tell her I say hi, too, next time. What are you doing right now? Still in bed?"

"Technically, I'm sitting up in bed. Why?"

"Sal fixed your ride. I'm headed your way to drop it off."

"Oh." Urgency sped up her heart. She looked down at her bare legs. She was wearing shorts and a T-shirt. Last night she had barely crawled into bed after staying up another couple of hours to look through the Foster's Group inquiry, research their flagship hotel, sketch out some ideas, and add to her and Brandon's shared calendar. Game planning wasn't necessarily doing new work, but it always set her up for a more successful day after. "Do you mean right now?"

"Yes. But no need to get up. I can drop it off and walk over to Pagasa. We're partway done with the renovation."

Pag-asa was one of two beach houses on the southeastern part of the resort. Its roof and windows needed repair.

"Oh, really? I'll go with you."

"Yeah?"

"I wanted to get a feel for the place again, for its personality." She put him on speaker as she dug through her duffel. Finding a simple summer dress, she climbed down the ladder, the phone in her hand.

"You sound like my sister."

"It's why we get along." She smiled as she gathered her iPad and stuffed it into her messenger bag. "But I've got to talk to you about something else too."

"Okayyyy." He lengthened the word.

"I'll be outside in ten minutes, fifteen max."

Geneva took a quick shower, brushed her teeth, and slathered on sunscreen. She coiled her hair up into a bun. She needed coffee, still; Brandon would have to be all right with a detour.

With Converse on her feet and a messenger bag across her body, Geneva opened the front door. The sight of the water took her aback and added to the rush of anticipation of getting in the water after work.

Of seeing Brandon again.

She must have been standing there for a while, because the next thing she heard was Brandon's voice. He was holding two to-go cups of coffee in his hand. "Geneva. You ready?"

She nodded, heart bursting at his thoughtfulness.

They were going to Pag-asa. Hope.

♡

Three minutes in the golf cart took them to the house's turnoff. A flatbed truck had taken up most of the road, and a group of workers wearing Day-Glo-yellow vests assisted in unloading replacement windows and shingles for the roof. A construction site was always worse before it got better, and right then, Pag-asa's status, if it had one, would be *in chaos*.

It was exactly the kind of chaos Geneva loved—it meant that soon, new would replace old.

"I love construction," she said as she disembarked from the golf cart. Someone passed her a hard hat, though most of the workers weren't wearing one.

She would protect her noggin, thank you very much.

"Same." Brandon popped the hard hat on his head. "So this is the same company who's bringing up our new homes—Tiny House Specialists. Chris managed a deal with them that they would reinforce some of the homes to withstand another storm. Since we're dealing with roof and windows for Pag-asa, they were better prepared versus Mike and the crew. But did you know what I just found out?"

Brandon was vibrating with giddiness. Geneva laughed. "What did you just find out?"

"The project manager working with us was previously a restaurant consultant."

"Brandon? Are you . . ."

He shrugged. "I'm going to ask a few questions. Research, right?"

She tugged back on his shirt, and he turned. "Just . . . try not to be pushy." Geneva knew that it was an imposition to lob a new request on a job already negotiated.

"I promise," he said with his boyish grin. "C'mon."

A woman emerged from the swarm of people. She was taller than Geneva by a few inches, fair skinned, with a light touch of pink gloss on her lips. Wisps of brown hair peeked out from under her hat.

"Morning, Brandon." The woman offered a hand.

Brandon shook it. "Morning. Lainey Mills, this is Geneva Harris. She's with interiors."

"Nice to meet you." Geneva nodded.

"Great to meet you. I know it's a great big mess right now, but give it a few hours and you'll see a new structure emerge." She gestured them closer to the site and pointed out a few features in the new windows. They veered down the path toward the water. Then she turned around to face the front of the home. "You'll notice we're nixing the gabled roof. Instead, we're popping it up a little higher to get more headspace in that loft. The roof itself will be made of metal that will withstand the wind."

"So impressive. So while you're not adding square footage, you're adding area."

"Yes, and in these tiny homes, it makes such a difference. Comfort is paramount, even to those who choose small spaces."

"On that topic"—Brandon crossed his arms in a casual stance—"customizations—can you do them?"

Lainey barked a laugh. "Customization is our business. There's nothing too specific we can't do. People might have their misconceptions about folks who live the tiny house lifestyle, but one thing is true: they are very particular about space management."

"Hmm . . ." Geneva avoided Brandon's eyes. "So how easy is it to plan a kitchen?"

Lainey looked from Geneva to Brandon, a grin appearing on her face. "Um . . . easy."

"How about a restaurant kitchen?" Brandon asked.

"This sounds like a question not pertaining to the current job."

"Research," Geneva said at the same time as Brandon. She stifled a giggle. "For our resort restaurant."

"I see. Very, very curious. We'll have to sit down and chat specifics—"

"Great!" Brandon's answer was swift, though he backtracked. "At your convenience, of course."

"My priority is to install the new homes coming in today and tomorrow."

"Oh yeah, of course," Geneva said. She tugged Brandon's elbow out of instinct, feeling the teamwork between them, and to hold him back. He looked like he was about to give Lainey a hug. "Priority always goes to the current build."

"But I'm sure I can arrange a little side consult." Lainey dug a buzzing phone out of her back pocket. "Sorry, I have to take this. How about I text you when we're about done here. Is that good?"

When she was out of earshot, Geneva raised a hand for a high five. "Oh my God, did you just do that?"

"*We* did that." Brandon slapped her hand. "And *we* are going to be in deep crap with my brother, you understand. But it's research, right?"

"We?"

"Was that only me who heard you jump in with questions? You can't back out on me now, Harris."

Geneva spun around to face the water, taken in by the moment. "Wow, this house is going to have an amazing sunrise *and* sunset view." "That's right." "It makes sense that it's named Pag-asa." Already, her thoughts moved to what colors should be in the space, what could be accentuated in the evening as the sun's rays beamed through the windows. Her mind wandered to the current set of furnishings in the warehouse. "I'm going to have to head out and find different things for this home. Everything I have thus far is rustic, and too cozy. We need something a little more modern. With this house, the view is going to be everything."

"And how about that one? That's Yakap." He pointed to a tiny house so exactly like its name, peeking out from behind a barrier of sea oats that seemed to be hugging it. "It's on the docket for Mike's crew today."

"I haven't gotten a chance to visit Yakap, since it's the least damaged on my list—just some cosmetic changes, right? I didn't realize that it was going to be done so quickly."

He nodded. "Staining the floors and replacing cabinet-front doors. A new toilet and sink. Otherwise, it will be ready to go soon. Hurricane Oscar's off the coast of southeast Florida, so there's a bit of a rush to get things done."

Geneva didn't like the sound of that. "Then there's no time to lose. Let's go."

She trekked through the sand, unsuccessfully at first, and then bent down to take off her shoes. Sand crabs peeked out and scuttled across her path. The sand was warm against the pads of her feet, a tickle at first, before she steadied her legs and stomped through.

It was a massage from the toes on up. Had it always felt this good to walk on the beach, with the smell of the ocean in the air? Of course she'd partaken and enjoyed since she'd arrived, but at times it felt like a renewal.

In her excitement, her legs tangled. But just as she thought she was going to get a face full of sand, she was held up by the waist. Cackling, she gained her bearings and turned to a grinning Brandon. His smile was beautiful, contagious, and, if even possible, made Geneva's smile bigger. Sweat bloomed on her forehead, and she wiped strands of hair away from her face. "Oh my God, thank you."

"What is this, a race?" He was still holding her, their bottom halves pressed together, and she felt every bit of support in his arms.

Brandon would never let her go—it was something she never had a question over. But it was exactly the thing that made her stiffen. Because Geneva had to be let go.

She had things to do.

Brandon eased his hold around her. After a beat, he took a step back and let his arms fall. His eyes darted to the left, and he bent down. "Oh, look."

"What is it?"

"Coquinas." With his thumb and pointer finger, he held up a shell, cute and sparkly with hints of pink.

"It looks like a butterfly."

"And it's not broken. Usually the ones here aren't intact." He held it out to her. "Want it? I have a couple that are close enough to perfect, but this one's definitely a keeper."

"Thank you." She held out a palm, and Brandon set it in her grasp. "You've been beachcombing?"

"When I can. It helps me think." His gaze strayed. "I used to beachcomb while my mom took a quick beach run, though at some point she roped me into it."

"You don't run anymore?" she said, forcing the moment forward.

"That's history. I'm a gym rat these days, or before these days. But if I'm running around here, that means someone's chasing me."

She cackled, marching on by his side, and this time, with focus to keep herself from falling.

Yakap was well set behind the sea oats on a cement foundation. The house was right out of a travel magazine, bright though unassuming with large windows. Instantly, this house became Geneva's favorite of them all. She squealed at the potential; it evoked innocence and a simple joy. "This is so adorable. I can't believe it made it through the storm without too much damage. This is it. I love this the best."

Brandon beamed.

"What?" Now her cheeks were burning, though it could have been from the sun and especially their walk over.

"I love your enthusiasm. You lit up talking about it. You were saying?"

She turned away from him, steadying herself from his unflinching, amused gaze. They were there to do a job, and she couldn't forget that. Last night had been comfortable, but it didn't mean they should take it to flirtation. She cleared her throat and started again. "This house is just a pleasant surprise."

He peeked into its windows. "I don't have the keys with me, but you can get a good view of the living area from here." He gestured to his side.

She sidled up next to him and propped her hand on the glass. Leaning closer, she squinted into the darkness, into the empty shell. "Hold the phone. This is a one-floor home?"

"Ah, that's my bad. I forgot to mention it. The resort needed an accessible home, and since this house is built on a foundation, it was the chosen one." He pressed a finger against the windowpane. "So if you can make it out . . . the loft was removed, and instead, a skylight added. The bedroom is toward the back."

"Excellent . . ." She backed up from the window and stepped into the space between the front door and the sea oats. "It's so private. This can be super romantic." A vision emerged, of hanging lights that set the mood, the sound of the water as the backdrop. The couple lying back on lounge chairs. Instead of Netflix and chill, it would be waves and chill. Solitude and chill. Serenity and chill, like Brandon's town house backyard in Annapolis, its periphery bordered by rosebushes, courtesy of Tito Joe and Chris. There, they'd lain back in Adirondack chairs, hands clasped in between, and they'd chatted about everything. At times they'd forget they were in public, ensconced in the backyard's seeming protection, and she'd climb on his lap, and . . .

Brandon stepped up next to her, halting her running thoughts. She willed her body to cool down, hoping he couldn't see her goose pimples and how her mind veered toward the proverbial gutter.

He gestured to the empty area behind the sea oats. "We shouldn't waste this space."

"I was thinking the same thing. Is there room in the budget for a wooden deck, with posts on four sides?"

"And some lights, maybe?"

"Yes!" she said a little too loudly. "And a love seat deck chair."

"Agreed. I see it."

"I feel it," she whispered, looking out onto the water.

"I do too." He stuck his hands in his pockets. "Great minds."

She nodded. They always had thought alike. In design, at work, that was perfect. But in love and relationships?

The air between them became heavy. She cleared her throat and infused levity. "We're geniuses."

"Tiny house geniuses." He laughed. "Anyway, I don't think it will bust the budget adding the deck. I'll need to run it by Kuya Chris."

"Great."

He cleared his throat. "Well, we should get back. I've got a full day, then the afternoon with Izzy and Kitty."

"That's sweet you spend time with them, Bran." Geneva slipped her shoes back on.

"Sweet? It's not being sweet. It's a requirement. Izzy has a list of things for us to do."

Geneva tied her shoelaces. Was there a way to take her shoelaces and somehow secure her heart in its place? Because Brandon and his nieces and their list? It was all too much. She stood, avoiding his eyes. "Can I drop you off?"

"That'd be great." He offered his hand. She took it and stood, and instead of waterside, he followed the path up to the main road. "I'll keep you posted about when we can meet with Lainey. And oh, you mentioned that there was something you wanted to talk about?"

She shook her head and pushed the issue of the photographs away. It wasn't a big deal, not nearly as important as the excitement over their teamwork. It was a good morning. Geneva couldn't fuss over everything. "It's nothing."

CHAPTER ELEVEN

"This . . . this isn't right." Brandon hefted a backpack onto his shoulders, and it weighed at least ten pounds. "Geesh. What else do we need? We're just going for milkshakes."

"Listen, little brother, the moment you forget something is the absolute same time you're going to need it." Gil pulled a folded umbrella stroller from the hallway closet. It was pink and shiny.

"Why do we need a stroller? Kitty can walk." This was getting ridiculous. What had been a simple, short break was turning out to be more complicated than the actual construction he was supervising.

"Girls! We're leaving without you," Gil yelled above the television playing in the other room. The volume was up high, recently jacked up by one of the girls. He looked at Brandon pointedly. "Look, Kitty walks until she refuses. I personally don't want to carry a fifty-pound grumpy little girl. It was fine at thirty pounds, but fifty? I'm too weak for that."

Brandon's words of reasoning—that he was there to help, that they weren't planning to go for a walk but sit and have milkshakes, that perhaps Gil should put his foot down and make Kitty understand she would not be carried—came to a screeching halt when his nieces rushed into the living room. Kitty was in her swimsuit.

Izzy's hair was skewed sideways into a wannabe ponytail. She bore an exasperated expression. "I can't get my ponytail like Mommy does it. And Tita Beatrice isn't here."

Gil sighed. "Where are your clothes, Kitty?"

"I was hot."

"Go change."

"But they're too hot, Papa. I want to wear my swimsuit instead."

"My hair's messy," Izzy said once more, but this time she was looking at Brandon. Like she wanted Brandon to do something about it.

"Um . . . ," Brandon hedged. "Kuya Gil?"

Flustered, his brother waved him away. "I can't right now. Just . . . try your best, okay? I need to find Kitty's clothes."

Izzy was already dragging him by the hand to the couch. She pointed at the seat.

Brandon removed the backpack and sat at her request. Izzy pulled out her ponytail and pressed the rubber band into his hand. He stared at it and then at the back of Izzy's head, hair now a mane down her back.

"Tito Brandon, hurry! My milkshake is waiting for me."

"Okay." Except it wasn't okay. He'd never brushed, much less styled, a little girl's hair before. It couldn't be that hard, could it? He took a deep breath, then set the rubber band on the couch. Wait, that was too far away. Instead, he slipped it onto his wrist, where it dug into his skin, and proceeded to palm Izzy's hair into his hand, scooping hairs that had fallen out of his grasp.

"Ouch!" Izzy yelped, slapping the back of her neck.

Brandon leaned back, letting go, and raised his hands in the air. "What?"

"You pulled too hard," she admonished. "But why did you stop?"

"I . . . okay." So he started over, concentrating now, scooping strands into one hand, attempting not to pull when Izzy hissed, and somehow, in the process of the chaos, threaded her hair through the rubber band.

Sweat beaded at his hairline, but he absolutely refused to let go. Fingers cramping, he twisted the rubber band and threaded the ponytail through one last time. "Done!" he yelled.

He looked around to see if he had an audience. Surely someone was going to give him an award.

Meanwhile Izzy had taken off to the hallway mirror. She was short enough that only her eyes peered over the bottom edge. He followed her and lifted her off her feet. "Well?"

She twisted her head left, then right. "I guess it's good enough."

"What?" He set her down. "That is runway-walk worthy. It's"—he spied the bump he'd totally missed on the left side, where he could see her scalp all the way through—"artistic."

She sighed. "Thank you, Tito."

"You're welcome. Now go find your dad. I think he went down a rabbit hole."

Izzy ran down the hallway, and Brandon's phone rang in his pocket. Seeing that it was Garrett, he took the call. They had been checking in regularly, bouncing off ideas about the Illinois Way project. So far, so good. They seemed to be on the same page.

Garrett was in a jovial mood. "I've got Will on board to manage the project while you're gone—we're walking through tomorrow. How's everything there?"

"Good. Busy."

"Attaboy. Did you talk to your siblings about Mulberry Road?"

Brandon pressed his fingers to the bridge of his nose. He and Garrett only named the properties they were managing, and usually after the streets they were on. The fact that Garrett had now named his house—it was a shove toward speeding up a process he had yet to figure out how to even begin. "No," he said truthfully.

"Bran. You know you have to tell them."

His friend was right. "I'll bring it up to Gil. I'll start there. But Garrett." He checked to make sure the coast was clear.

"What?"

"She's here."

"Who's there?"

When Brandon didn't answer, Garrett said, "No. Wait. What? Her?"

"Her."

"Hold . . . hold up." Muffled noises ensued; a door slammed. "Geneva?"

"Yes."

"Geneva Harris?"

"Yes, but . . . ," Brandon started. There was too much to discuss. Garrett had been there to pick up the pieces of his affair with Geneva. After all, Brandon hadn't been able to go to his siblings. But, with the sound of his brother and his nieces headed his way, he said, "I can't talk about this right now."

"You can't do that, Puso. First you ghost me, and now you can't fess up with gossip?"

Gil walked into the room with an exasperated expression on his face. "We go now, or I give up."

"Kuya Gil just walked in, and I've gotta go."

"No no no no no no," Garrett said.

Brandon spoke above Garrett's objection. "No decisions until I get to see the numbers."

"Of course. Don't freaking change the subject, Bran."

"Promise me, Garrett."

"Dang it, are you really letting me go right now?"

"Yes."

"Fine—fine! Have I ever let you down?" He laughed. "Don't answer that. What I mean is, have I ever done you wrong purposely?"

"No. No, you haven't." Brandon's chin dropped to his chest. For what Garrett lacked in logical decisions, he made up for in his intuition about good properties to invest in. This flip could be the one that could turn the tide, *if* they were wise. Part of that decision was Brandon stepping up to be the partner Garrett needed too. "I'll call you."

"You better!"

Brandon hung up. He slung the backpack over his shoulder. "You look like you got worked over, Kuya."

"I'm in trouble with these girls, Bran." Gil ran a hand over his disheveled hair. "I can't keep up."

The girls brushed past them and got ahead, screaming, "Milkshakes, milkshakes," and they bounded down the stairs and into the minivan, its doors already open. Izzy helped Kitty buckle into her booster and climbed into hers.

Brandon beamed with pride at how responsible his oldest niece was, at the natural way she took care of her little sister. He had been doted on the same way. His pediatrician had been worried about him when he was three because he was uninterested in speaking; his siblings had advocated for him. They'd anticipated his every need. "They're good kids, though," he said to Gil, while climbing into the passenger seat. It was a captain's chair, and in it he felt at least a decade older.

Gil double-checked the girls' belts and then slid into his seat and buckled in. "Don't let them hear you say that. They are sneaky." He side-eyed his girls.

"Who's sneaky, Papa?" Izzy asked.

"See?" Gil grinned. He looked over his shoulder. "What did I say about Papa's conversations."

She rolled her eyes. "They're yours and yours alone."

"Right." He lowered his voice. "Just in case, let me turn on a movie. Watch this magic trick."

More screaming ensued as a movie was decided.

Gil fiddled with the onboard entertainment system. With the press of a few buttons, music piped through the speakers, and the girls quieted behind them.

Brandon marveled at the effect. "You're right. It is magic."

"And music to my ears." Gil lowered the visor and raked his hair with a hand, then examined a blemish on his cheek before pushing the visor back up. "They're great kids, but sometimes I don't know if I'm doing a good enough job." He reversed the van out of the parking space. "It's a crappy deal. I get them for the summer, and then I don't see them for a couple of months. So I give them everything they want, and then what? They forget me all over again, until Thanksgiving, when I have to woo them once more? Divorce sucks."

Brandon remained silent; he didn't know what to say. Gil, too, was a quiet guy. As a former model and actor, his looks usually spoke for him, and even then, his image was so well crafted by his agent, by his choice, that people assumed so much about him. That Gil held few opinions, that he was happy about everything. That life was effortless.

Brandon knew better, now. Image was simply that.

"How's Jessie, anyway?" Brandon asked, reminded of Gil's ex.

"She's good. Fine, actually. Better than fine. She's done so well for herself. She's in LA doing her thing."

Brandon detected a pain in his voice. "And . . . you? I meant what I said—you look good."

"I'm . . . taking it a day at a time. The resort has kept me busy; the girls too. Though it doesn't quite fill the niche of what I used to do." He grinned. "They don't tell you about this stage, man."

"Stage?" Brandon's mind drifted as they exited the headquarters gate. A right turn would take him to Geneva's place.

Since they'd parted this morning, he hadn't been able to get her—or how close in proximity they were to one another—out of his mind.

He had to be careful. When together, he forgot the fact that she'd left him; she was another person in his life he'd relied on who was there one day and gone the next.

"The stage when you realize that you've taken things for granted," Gil said. "I could have done more, could have been more ambitious. And now I'm old."

"You're not old. You're not even forty."

"It's old enough. See my wrinkles, the sun spots?"

"No." Brandon never really thought about those things. He just didn't care. In his mind, Gil had always been Gil.

"I do. And so does my agent, and so do photographers. And aging has no place in media, man. You're appreciated for your youth or wisdom, and at this age, you're considered neither. Not enough gray hair to say I'm a silver and wise fox, but just enough sagging skin that they wonder if I'm spending enough time in the gym. And being a single dad, the reminder that I all but gave up my relationship with my kids' mother for my career? It sucks."

"Wow." Brandon, stunned, mulled over his brother's words. How often had they had a heart-to-heart? Obviously not often enough.

"Wow, what? Wow good? Wow bad?"

"Wow . . . I had no idea you were thinking this at all." He ran a hand through his hair, ashamed now. "I knew that you were adjusting to your divorce, but not about how much you cared about your looks."

Gil gave him a double take. "It's not about my looks, Bran. It's about how it's attached to my worth." He peered out in front of him as they got to the intersection that led out of the resort. "And how all that messes you up so you don't see what's so good in front of you. Why do you think I'm here instead of trying to get another job out there?"

Under his breath, Brandon said, "I guess I just thought that you wanted to go into the family business with Kuya."

He snorted. "I wanted to invest in the business, not work in it. But I'm here . . . to get away and regroup. To spend time with the girls, to just figure things out. For all the brands I represented, the roles I acted, where I fit in is still a question.

"Bran, let me give you some advice. When you find the person you want to be with for the rest of your life, don't run. You stay. You work it out. You don't think that something out there is better, that something can replace it. It's harder to stay, but it's worth it."

As they turned left onto Highway 12, the girls, bored of their movie, took Gil's attention. Brandon was left to look out the window at the passing view to contemplate his words.

If only it had been that easy.

♡

Hindsight was twenty-twenty, and Brandon had long since come to the conclusion that if Geneva had decided to stay after those three weeks, they could have been something.

But she hadn't, and he wasn't sure if he could forgive that.

"Are you saying that you could have worked it out with Jessie?" Brandon asked, the conversation in the minivan just catching up to him. They were sitting at a picnic bench next to Goodness Gracious, a roadside dessert shop. Situated across from a strip mall outside Nags Head, it was a white home trimmed in green. A line snaked from the storefront window and wrapped down the sidewalk.

"If I wasn't being a stubborn jerk. Absolutely." Gil, with half of his face covered by his aviator glasses, passed out napkins to Izzy and to Brandon.

"But I thought it was her fault, that she . . ." Brandon pressed his lips together as Izzy climbed on the bench seat and plopped down, cheeks caved inward as she sucked on a straw. Gil had told the family that it was Jessie who'd walked away first by admitting she'd had an emotional affair with the host of a long-running matchmaking reality show where she worked as the director of photography.

"Yes, but I definitely didn't make life easy." Gil lowered his voice. "I gave her a hard time about her ambition. She surpassed me. I'm ashamed to say that I was jealous of that. I fought her tooth and nail about everything, from whose family we spend Christmas with to where we should live."

"Papa, what's ambition?" Izzy asked.

"Something you have and you're always going to be proud of, iha," Gil answered.

Brandon handed Izzy his phone, to distract her, and his niece, a whiz after a couple of rounds on it, clicked on one of the apps Brandon had preinstalled for her.

"Where did you want to live?" Brandon whispered, latching on to that small worm on the hook Gil had thrown his way.

"Where else but here?"

"Not the town house?"

"You know, as much as I loved that place for Mom and Dad, I couldn't wait to get away." His tone was matter of fact.

"Interesting." If only Brandon was as nonchalant about it. Irritation buzzed through him, at the idea that he seemed to be the only one attached to the house yet didn't have full responsibility for it. "What do you think about me moving out and selling the town house?"

Gil coughed. "What?"

"I've lived there seven years on my own."

"But it's paid for. And it's housing in an area where prices are sky high. That doesn't make any sense."

"Does it have to make sense?"

"I mean, yes." He half laughed. "I know that you're not thinking of the future now, but one day you will. That town house is ours, free and clear. We need to keep it ours."

Brandon's stomach soured.

"Tito Brandon." With perfect timing, Izzy handed him his phone.

"We'll talk more later," Gil said.

But Brandon had heard enough. He would need to reassess; he was outnumbered. Perhaps it wasn't time. Gil was right—the town house was their nest egg. He turned off the calendar notification that had popped up, reset the game for Izzy, and handed the phone back to her, then shrugged, to ease the moment. "Nah, it was just a thought. You know me, always thinking about the next flip."

"That's probably something you shouldn't bring up to Kuya. You'll give him a coronary."

Oh, believe me, I tried.

After taking a long sip of his vanilla shake, Gil said, "I don't know about you, but goodness gracious, Goodness Gracious is worth the drive and all the effort."

"And . . . I admit, I thought you were being extra with that stroller. I was wrong." Brandon gestured at Kitty, slouched in the stroller, both hands clutching her strawberry milkshake in a kid-size cup. Frowning, she sipped ferociously. In a hushed tone, he said, "That was the most epic meltdown."

"Told you. I think I lost another two years of my life. Under this body, I am literally sixty."

Brandon laughed as he sipped and forced himself to be in the moment. He dug into the fries in the greasy paper bag.

"You have to do it this way, Tito Brandon," Izzy said. "You have to dip. See?" With purposeful hands, she gave instructions on how to properly dip and eat a fry. "Now, your turn."

"All right. I'm gonna try to do it as good as you." Brandon opened his cup. Little did his niece know that one of his favorite things to do in high school had been to sneak off campus to Wendy's for Frostys and fries. The last time he'd had the treat—because it had been forever—was with Beatrice and Geneva.

As he dipped the fry into his milkshake, something caught his eye from across the street. It was a flash of color next to a white van with a familiar logo.

He lifted his shades. It was Geneva, as if conjured by his thoughts. It could've only been her: hair caught in the wind, that messenger bag wrapped around her body. And those Converse shoes. The storefront sign behind her was bold—CARVER'S BOUTIQUE—and she was next to someone in a yellow polo and jeans. He was loading a myriad of things into the back of a white van.

Unsuccessfully, judging from the way they couldn't close the van door.

Then the boutique employee removed some of the items as if to start over.

"Tito?" Izzy asked.

"Hold on, Iz," he said, fully distracted, and reached for his phone. The scene was humorous and spurred a memory of him helping to pack up Beatrice's car for college, Geneva with them, filling Beatrice's Honda sedan up to the top.

He clicked to send a text: Looks like you need a pack master.

After a moment, while mindlessly dipping his fry, finally, into his shake and eating it—because his niece was not backing down—he watched Geneva dig into her messenger bag to check her phone. She thumbed at it.

He grinned as his phone buzzed.

Geneva:

> We're going to be here a while. Can't figure out how to fit everything.

> Wait. Where are you?

She lifted her hand to shield her eyes and scanned her surroundings.

"What's going on?" Gil asked.

"I . . ." Compelled, Brandon stood and signaled with his arms. "Geneva's across the street."

Geneva waved back, and Brandon climbed on top of the picnic table bench. His body was doing this automatically; his brain had zero control.

"You're acting like Tom Cruise, Bran. Quit it."

Izzy jumped up on the bench and followed suit.

Brandon hopped down and hooked his glasses to secure them on his shirt. He popped the plastic cup cover back on.

"Where are you going?" Gil moved down his glasses and peered over the top.

"She needs help." He was moving out of instinct.

"Oh, really now." Gil's voice was coy.

"Yep. We're supposed to get together with the tiny house builder later on, but she mentioned trying to get ahead of everything before she leaves. I should help her, you know?"

"You're leaving me?"

"You can handle it, right?"

"Are you really asking me if I'm capable of taking care of my own children?" He put up a hand. "Don't answer that. We'll be fine. Go help her. We're all on the time clock, and Lord knows I can't design worth a damn."

"Izzy?" His niece, Brandon knew, was the real person he had to ask permission from.

Izzy leveled a serious gaze at him. "That's fine, Tito Brandon. I understand. You like helping people."

"You are the greatest." He bent down and blew a raspberry onto her cheek, prompting her to laugh.

"But aren't you going to bring Tita Geneva something?"

"You're so dang smart." He spun to spy the line. "Ah, but there's no time."

"Here." She folded down the top of the bag of fries. "Bring this as a present. My mommy says food is the best pasalubong."

Brandon spared his brother a glance.

Gil's face dipped. "She's right. I learned the hard way." He gestured at the bag. "Take the fries. This milkshake is a meal in itself."

Brandon did what he was told and, after looking both ways, jaywalked across the street with half his milkshake and a bag of fries, sidestepping a truck that careened around the corner.

And as he got closer and Geneva's smile brightened, he found that it wasn't just his milkshake melting. It was every part of him.

CHAPTER TWELVE

Geneva fumbled at the lock of the warehouse door, as if she hadn't fiddled with it more than a dozen times in the last four days. She was giddy, hyped from the moment Brandon's text had come through at Carver's Boutique.

How did it feel seeing such a gorgeous man come for you, on his own, without prodding? It was indescribable. He'd had a smile that spanned from ear to ear, a bag full of hot french fries clutched in one hand, and a milkshake in another . . . what more could a woman want?

And she hadn't been a damsel in distress; she hadn't needed his help. But somehow, he'd known what was going through her head at that moment. He'd been able to detect her rising impatience at the boutique employee's inability to pack up the van and them losing daylight. And the fact that, unbeknownst to him, she couldn't wait for the meeting with Lainey because it would be another opportunity to spend time together.

Hence the shaking fingers and the excessive pulling of the lock.

Finally, the lock popped open, and the door slid wide with a sigh. From inside came the smell of wood polish and metal, and she took it into her lungs as if she had been stuck underwater.

To the left was a switch, and she flipped it up. The overhead lights flickered on.

"Wow. You've got yourself a stash here," Brandon said, voice echoing.

The warehouse was marked with orange cones with the name of each tiny beach house. Ten areas of varying themes, inspired by either the name of the house or the house itself. Ten areas also with varying amounts of furnishings. "It's coming along, don't you think?"

"Um . . . yeah. It's only been four days, Geneva, and this is . . . a lot."

She beamed. "What can I say—I work fast."

"I don't think it's about working fast. You just know what you're doing." He left her side, and Geneva was thankful for the brief time alone, to take it in. To soak in the compliment along with the sight in front of her. The enormity of what she had accomplished thus far, and what she would be able to do the last ten days.

She *did* know what she was doing. She had put her heart and soul into this business, and it showed in satisfied customers. Their happiness became fuel for her engine to push the goalpost further along.

And yet, when she looked around, what she also saw was stuff. Just stuff. More than that, stuff for others, when she herself only had the things in her duffel bags. It was a disconnect she couldn't shake.

"Where do you want this?" Brandon clutched a lamp in one hand and a stool with the other.

Geneva woke and cleared her throat. "Over to Halik." But as Brandon took a step, she pulled him back by the elbow. It was a moment of weakness, to ground herself to someone, but also to explain herself out of her thoughts. "Do you see the little bits of red right here?" She pointed to the carvings at the base of the lamp, with its crevices delicately painted. "Reminds me of gloss. Perfect, right?"

His eyes rounded. "Oh, I get it. Gloss like lip gloss, to kiss with. It's subtle, but it works."

For a beat his eyes darted down to her lips and back up. Her mind flashed to a night when she'd caught him watching her swipe gloss on her lips before an evening out, and then promptly kissed it all off and decided to stay in instead.

A delicious flush crept up her neck. "Never underestimate the quiet details." She cleared her throat and gestured to the open area. "But yep. Right there."

"Got it." Brandon set down what he had in his hands, and the muscles in his arms flexed. His shirt accommodated and grew taut over his pecs.

Brandon didn't have a range of outfits: a different set of shorts, basic shirts. He picked just the right kind of shirt, though, a little snug around where it counted. She bet it was jersey and ultrasoft . . .

"Where do you want this?" Holding up two nightstands with legs that flared out, like skirts on a dancer, one in each hand—when had he gone back for those?—he grinned.

Busted.

Her cheeks heated. "Uh, yes, over there, next to the rug for Sayaw." She scoured her brain for the correct stream of thought, the kind that kept her imagination chaste. "I texted Sal on the way here to help out. We may need to rearrange some things around."

"Sounds good."

She willed herself to go, to be in the present. Perhaps a little physical exertion would keep her focused on work rather than play.

Slowly, it did. With every item she brought in, her emotions leveled with her neutral thoughts of floor plans and timelines. Of colors and textures and themes. She assessed what she had and cataloged and arranged images in different drawers in her mind. Work pressed all the buttons in her body that made it want to sing. The puzzling together of resources and the anticipation of the picture that would emerge brought a reliable zen.

After she'd made three trips back and forth from the van, her phone beeped. A text from Sal: Walking up from reception.

"He'll be a few more minutes," she relayed.

Brandon leaned another rug against the wall. "Okay."

"Actually, can you take that rug over to Tiwala and switch them out?"

"Sure." He wrapped his arms around the rolled-up eleven-by-fourteen-foot, handwoven blue-and-white rug.

But as he walked it to the other side of the warehouse, the rope around the rug undid itself.

"Oh, Brandon," she warned, marching in his direction.

The rug unfurled, and it tipped, right on Geneva.

She burst into laughter as it unrolled itself completely on the warehouse floor.

"Oh my God. Are you okay?" he asked.

"Yes." She patted back her unruly hair and was met by Brandon's concerned expression. "It's just another day moving furniture."

"Here, let's roll it back up."

The rug itself was heavy, so it took the both of them to bring it to an area large enough to roll the rug uniformly. She knelt next to him.

"I have to say, this is pretty rad," he said, running a palm against the fibers. "Super soft."

"It is. I love the wood floors, but it's always nice to have a rug to sink your feet into, don't you think?" She mimicked his actions, the softness enticing. "It makes you just want to lie on it."

"Have you lain on it?"

"No."

"Let's do it," he said. "I don't know about you, but all this lifting is exhausting."

As he crawled onto the rug, Geneva grinned. "But it's not our rug."

"I beg to differ. Am I not a Puso? And isn't the rug's bill going to a Puso?" He clasped his hands across his belly and shut his eyes. "Ahhhhh . . . this is comfortable."

"C'mon, Brandon, get up." She reached over and tugged at his shirt, the soft cotton lengthening.

He lifted his arm, and one eye opened. "Is there a bug on me?" He play pushed her arm away.

Giggling at his touch, she shoved him with a little more force.

"Bran." Under her hands, his biceps constricted, his muscles tensing at her fingertips. Her heart leapt at the contact, at the excitement of the innocent moment. "If you don't get off, I'm gonna . . ."

Both eyes opened now in a playful dare, and a smile split his face. "You're gonna what?"

"I'm gonna tickle you," she said, taking it right out of their playbook. She hovered above him, enticed by instinct and the echo of their voices.

"No you won't," he dared, eyes alight. "No, no you won't." He held her wrists, though gently. "You *know*, Gen. *You know.*"

Oh yes, yes, she knew. Brandon was strong, fast, lithe, but he hated to be tickled. "I know you become like a puppy that's scratched at just the right spot. A maniac." She placed pressure against his hands, as if she was going for his ribs, and he scooted an inch away, squealing in a high pitch.

She hooted. "How could you be thirty-two and still be wary of the tickle monster."

"Don't you dare—"

She went after his ribs again, and this time, she beat him to it. Not only did she make contact with his sides and belly, but she was able to overcome and straddle him.

Over him, she had absolute full advantage. As she tickled, his eyes shut. And though Brandon was cackling, she was imagining something entirely different.

And she was definitely *feeling* something different.

Her fingers slowed. Brandon opened his eyes, first in concern—yes, she was indeed on top of him—and a dark look passed across his eyes, and his gaze, which ran down her body, lit her on fire.

Geneva's breath hitched. His abdomen rose and lowered with deep, slow breaths, and his hands came to rest over hers, tentatively.

The air around them crackled like the sound of film being passed through a recorder. With a blink, Geneva remembered all the times they had been in this same position, her core activated by his simple touch.

Her fingers crawled up his abdomen to his chest. Through his shirt, she felt the grooves of his body, and she imagined her fingers on his warm skin.

The pressure on her fingers increased as his torso rose, his elbows now bearing both of their weights. His face neared, lips coming closer, eyes canvassing her face before ending at her lips.

"Geneva," he whispered, and the sound of her name this time sent her spirits soaring. It was a plea, a need, and it was primal.

Her instinct was to satiate it, especially knowing that she could. That she could take this spark between them and turn it into a bonfire that could be seen for miles away. Because it hadn't been extinguished. What she had for Brandon was, after all, like the heat of the sun. It withstood time and distance.

It drew her closer to him, and she shut her eyes in trust.

At first, their kiss was like a feather across her lips. It was sweet, a memento of their very first kiss, sugar filled and spurred by an afternoon flirting at Eden and Chris's wedding. But this one escalated quickly. This one, in this warehouse, alone, with its echoing acoustics, brought out the hunger she had pushed down and away so long ago in convincing herself that the two of them hadn't been right.

Right then, their bodies certainly objected to that notion. Their lips parted and moved and accommodated in a dance that they had perfected in their fling. There were no rusty moves to shed—they took turns to lead and follow; even their breaths fell into a rhythm meant solely for one another. And her mind . . . Geneva's imagination strolled down a road that would take her to the lustful gutter. And she wanted it. Her body wanted it.

She'd missed it.

Off in the distance, the sound of a car door slamming halted her stroll, and it reeled her back from fantasy to reality. She opened her eyes as Brandon disengaged, head turned toward the warehouse door, which was wide open. As shadows darkened the doorway, reality came into full picture.

"Oh my God," she said at the same time Brandon said, "Uh."

Both of their gazes drew down to her skirt draped over both of their laps.

Because she was straddling him.

Straddling.

Brandon.

And there was no denying they both liked it.

She crawled off him as a wave of shyness crashed over her. She had never been a prude, but it had been a while since her lust had taken over in such a way. Because this warehouse? On a job? With a man she used to love?

Oh dear.

"I'm sorry," he said, offering his hand for her to stand, which she took without hesitation. "We can—"

"Talk later." She finished his sentence and watched as not only Sal but Rhiannon walked in while having a lively conversation.

"I don't know if I want to look at blood and guts all day," the young woman said. "I thought blood wouldn't bother me, but dissecting toads today made me ill."

"You won't be dissecting as a nurse," Sal countered. "But at least you know now what you don't want to do."

Geneva cleared her throat and straightened her dress, heart pounding. "Hey, you guys, we're"—her voice cracked, and she tried again—"we're back here."

Shadows rounded the corner, and Sal and Rhiannon appeared, each already with a load.

"You guys can put that down there. We're, uh, we're just relocating some things," she said, not meeting their eyes.

"Did everything go exactly the way you intended, Ms. Geneva?" Sal asked, with what she could swear was a knowing grin.

"I . . . what do you mean?" Her heart skipped.

"The van. Your first time driving it."

"Oh yes, of course. Thank you for arranging for me to use it, by the way."

"What are y'all doing?" Rhiannon said, walking toward her. "Wow, that's a nice rug."

Geneva was glad for the change of subject, and she took that moment to tear herself away from Brandon's side, knowing full well that they'd both unscrewed and thrown away the lid to a whole can of worms. Now, they would have to decide if they had to cobble together a cover or simply allow their attraction to overflow.

$$\heartsuit$$

Four years ago, Brandon's bed had been the ultimate escape.

With him, Geneva was a kayak on the ocean, swept by Brandon's goodness, his care, and the instinctive way he touched her.

But unlike the ocean, Brandon was not the type to move with the weather; he didn't go with the flow. Brandon was to his family and their home in Annapolis like the ancient southern oak trees were to the ground, rooted and unmoving.

Geneva knew all this, and yet she'd allowed the kiss to happen.

Why why why?

She'd just compromised this precarious working relationship, perhaps the job itself, and even the Pusos themselves as a worst-case scenario. She wasn't a math whiz, but by sheer numbers alone—from the Pusos' four to her three, and even then, her parents were too far removed—Geneva had the most to lose.

Geneva couldn't even bear to think about it.

"All set," Sal said, as he climbed into the van.

Seconds later, Brandon followed. The front doors shut, rocking the van, and from the back seat and next to Rhiannon, Geneva spied Brandon's blank side-view expression.

"Where to, Ms. Geneva?" Sal asked.

"Home for me, please." Her voice croaked out an answer, and she cleared her throat. "We've got a meeting to plan for. Right, Bran?"

"Oh, um, yep," he said.

Silence ensued, and it was protracted and painful despite only being a few seconds, as they got to the main resort road.

"Mr. Brandon," Rhiannon said in sheer perfect timing, breaking the silence. "How did you know what you wanted to do?"

"What do you mean?" Brandon lowered the visor and looked back through the mirror. For a beat Geneva caught his eyes and promptly looked away. There was so much to unpack in his expression.

"I'm supposed to be coming up with a major, but there's too much to choose from."

"I thought you were doing nursing?" Geneva asked.

"I did some dissecting today, and it was . . . something. I don't know if I can do blood and all that after all."

"To be perfectly honest?" Brandon said. "I didn't know what I wanted at your age. A couple of my friends got accepted to this college in Texas, and I applied to it, and there I went. I picked a major that interested me, though didn't really know what I could do with it. History." He snorted. "You see where that got me? Not using history. I went to grad school to do what I realized I wanted to learn, which was business. The moral of the story, just go with what you think is right. Time will tell, and if it's meant to be, it's meant to be."

"That's so easy to say," Geneva commented.

Faces turned her way.

Oh goodness, did I say that aloud?

"You disagree?" Brandon asked.

She shook her head and gave Rhiannon a small smile. She recognized the look of uncertainty across her face, the pressure she was probably feeling. She didn't know enough about Rhiannon to make assumptions, but her own experience had taught her otherwise. "I don't disagree, but I just feel a little different about it. I didn't know what I wanted to major in, either, but with what I decided, I put myself into it a hundred percent. I made it my decision. My major was accounting, and I had all these jobs I was considering, but an internship changed my mind."

"Such great advice from two successful people," Sal said as he pulled onto the gravel pad behind Ligaya—Geneva's stop. He spun around. "I went to trade school, but I took a chance there too. Just got lucky that I liked it."

Rhiannon nodded, eyes roaming the van and then meeting Geneva's. "It's so hard, being an adult."

"And in all honesty, even as adults we don't have all the answers. We still make a lot of mistakes," Geneva said.

The van was claustrophobic with all of them looking at her. Correction, with Brandon not looking at her.

"Well." Geneva slapped her hands on her lap. "I'd better go. Lots to do. Thanks for everything, Sal and Rhi; I'll keep in touch. See you soon, Bran."

Geneva didn't wait for answers and instead excused herself as she climbed over Rhiannon and popped the door open to the relief of the open air and the gravel underneath her feet. With a final wave, she put distance between her and the van and Brandon, and that scorching kiss.

In high school, Geneva had felt nothing for Brandon other than that he was Beatrice's baby brother. Growing up, she'd treated him like any older sister would. If anything, she had been more doting, aware of their family dynamic. Chris and Gil had each other, she and Beatrice were inseparable, and Brandon was left to whoever decided to share their time with him. Brandon had been the one always left behind.

When she and Brandon had reunited at Chris's wedding after years of seeing each other on social media, right away she'd been able to tell that he was the same Brandon but more.

Had *he* been primed for a fling?

Perhaps. He was still mourning his parents, and she was mourning them too. She had been lonely and had been searching for . . . she didn't know what.

Back then, it had started with a kiss, as it just had again.

Could she let this continue? He was still her best friend's younger brother. Their careers still took them in the opposite directions.

Geneva now entered Ligaya, mind swirling with thoughts. Of everything, really, in her life. Thoughts of the sparse furniture and of how none of the things were hers.

Yes, she had done this by design. She'd kept it bare and minimalist, and she'd been loud and proud about it. She'd touted it after reading books about the theory of minimalism, after mulling over the significance of the movement. Proud of being able to let go and simply move toward the goals she hashed out for herself year after year.

But at what cost?

Luna sauntered in from the kitchen, a queen awoken from her nap. She crooned at Geneva, then turned right around and made her way up to the loft, as if not wanting anything to do with her.

Geneva didn't blame her, because she was a mess.

She threw her keys on the table and dropped her messenger bag on the ground. She ran her fingers through her hair. Her body flushed with need of the unresolved, with the leftover heat of Brandon's hands all over her, along with all the subsequent consequences of their togetherness. This was also another reason why she left things, places, and people. She could not deal with drama. Brandon was, in every possible way, drama.

She was filled with tension, with irritation, with energy misspent. She didn't need to exercise, though she knew exactly where she wanted work done, and by whom.

A knock sounded at the door and she whirled at the noise.

"Geneva." The voice was low, a growl through the wood, and her tummy flipped.

She laid a hand on the doorknob. "Brandon?"

"Can we . . . talk?"

"I don't know," said her mouth, straight from her brain without a filter. She wasn't sure if she could do it, just talk. Not after the warehouse, and in her current state, bothered and hot.

"Are you okay?"

"Yes, I am." She nodded, instantly comforted. He cared for her—he did. And then she laughed, because while he was worried about her, she was trying to get over this . . . need for him. She turned the knob and popped the door open a sliver.

Brandon's hands were braced on each side of the screen door. Seeing her, he stepped back and stuffed his hands in his back pockets.

He was still wearing the same clothes, yet she was seeing him with a different filter. The kind where he was naked.

Her breath hitched at the thought.

"Hey," he said, after the silence between them. "I'm sorry . . ."

The statement made her frown. "You're sorry?"

"Not that it happened, but that . . . that we didn't talk about it first. We had decided . . ." Then he straightened. "But no, I'm not sorry that we kissed. That was . . . I had been wanting to do that ever since forever."

"Forever?"

"Yeah, Geneva. Forever, yesterday, four years ago. Being with you was never the problem. It's everything else. My family, our circumstances, is what always gets in the way. Are you . . . sorry?"

146

"That we kissed?" If he could feel the heat steaming off her now, the need that was growing inside her, it would make him blush. But admitting it would be a catalyst for her to open the door all the way, for him to come in and possibly create a bigger mess than this was. Because it was a mess. "Brandon, we're both visitors in essentially your family's home."

"So you're sorry."

Yes? No? She pried the truth from her teeth. "I don't know."

"What do we do?"

"We . . ." *Continue to kiss all day and night.* "We can't do this again. We have work to do, and I'm only here—"

"I know, I know, eleven days. You're right. You're absolutely right. Okay." He took one step back. Then he turned, then spun to her. Lifted his hand to say something. Geneva stilled at the doorway. Her own defenses were down; a slight bit of temptation would be enough for her to give in. "I'll . . . I'll keep in touch for when we can meet with Lainey?"

"Yes. In public."

He breathed out a laugh. "Yes, in public, and purely platonic." He took one step back and heaved a breath.

He was going. She was going to let him go.

Again.

She shut her eyes tight as the word wormed its way out of her mouth. "Brandon."

He looked over his shoulder, then turned, slowly this time. He looked up at her through impossibly long eyelashes. "Yes."

Geneva's body was going rogue. It pushed the screen door with a squeak. Heat rose up her chest. Because she and Brandon had belonged to one another once upon a time, and she knew that in his kiss was pure bliss. "Maybe just one more kiss?"

He scooped her into his arms. They didn't have far to go, just steps to the kitchen, with their lips interlocked, breaths as one. Brandon was strong, solid, and he propped her up on the kitchen counter, perched precariously, as his lips trailed across her cheek, earlobe, and neck.

"Longest kiss ever. Time it," he said against her skin. The vibration made her giggle, and he followed suit, until his lips met hers again, and they found a groove.

She dug her hands in his hair and found purchase with her legs wrapped around his waist. "*Guinness Book of World Records*," she said in between kisses. "You win."

This part was so easy with Brandon. It was simple and comforting and safe and wonderful that she could just put everything aside.

Why *couldn't* they do this? They could meet off resort. They could make things work.

Something vibrated against her ankle, but she ignored it, relishing Brandon's hands as they made their way up the sides of her bare legs.

But the vibrating didn't stop. It kept on and on and . . .

Brandon pulled away, snapping the moment in half. He growled as if in pain. "I'm sorry. I have to get that."

She dipped her chin into her chest, nodding.

He plucked the phone from his back pocket and answered. "Yep." After a beat, he frowned; then he shook his head. He stepped back, away from her, and as the distance between her body and his increased, the moment rushed headlong into reality. She hopped off her kitchen counter and grabbed a bottled water from the refrigerator, taking a second to breathe in the cold air.

What had just happened? What was she about to allow to happen? Where was her logic?

"See you soon," Brandon said.

She turned, taking a swig of water, and with it swallowed the nerves that had built up inside her. "What's going on?"

"Two things. It seems that Chris and Lainey ran into one another, and she mentioned us meeting with her and why."

Her shoulders sagged. "Oh crap."

"Yep." He linked his hands behind his head. "So he wants a meeting with all of us tomorrow. He's got some overnight thing with Eden, but eight a.m. sharp."

She righted her thoughts and took one deep breath. Back to work. "I mean, it wasn't ideal for him to find out, but if he's not insisting on a meeting tonight, it's probably not so bad?" She shrugged to inject levity. "What's the second thing?"

"Beatrice has a proposal for us. It's about our pictures."

CHAPTER THIRTEEN

Day 5
Weather: mostly cloudy, 87°F
Hurricane Oscar: Category 1, over The Bahamas

It wasn't as much a dining room as it was a boardroom, with Brandon and Geneva on one side of the table and Gil and Beatrice facing them, with Chris at the head.

Chris was always at the head. And, of course, he was in full lecture mode, which put Brandon on the defensive.

"Honestly, I wasn't too surprised that Brandon went against my suggestions, but I didn't expect it from you, Geneva."

Brandon opened his mouth to object.

"Aw, Kuya, you don't have to go there." Gil beat Brandon to the punch, leaning back in his chair with his arms crossed. "She was looking out for us, weren't you, Geneva?" His tone was relaxed, too relaxed, and almost placating.

Geneva was looking down at her clasped hands.

This was getting ridiculous. Chris was treating them like they were children. "Wait a sec—" Brandon started.

From under the table, a searing pain jolted his shins. Gil eyed him pointedly as if to say *shut up*. "And I think Brandon has a point.

Restaurants aren't his expertise, and since the contractor is here, why not?"

"It's about the budget. We're down to every line item, and we *all* know this. Everyone except these two apparently. They seem to think that they have carte blanche over decisions."

"I'm sure some of our decisions were made in a vacuum." Gil raised his hands in defense. "That's my opinion."

Silence descended over their group; Brandon calmed. He nodded at Gil in thanks. Sometimes his own temper got to him. Much like grabbing the marshmallows while making s'mores, Brandon really needed to ease up and let things play out instead of grabbing for the first opportunity.

Around his family, sometimes, he regressed back to acting like the youngest, the smallest, the most immature, even if he had already made a life for himself. Even if he was a grown person.

Brandon tipped his coffee cup toward himself; it was empty. They'd had eggs, bacon, and garlic fried rice for breakfast first as a family, because nothing could get between Pusos and food, especially when Chris cooked, but as soon as the last of the plates had been cleared, the small talk had disappeared along with it.

Yesterday had started with a bang and ended as a dud. This morning, the tide changed as drastically as the ocean's undertow.

He and Geneva had kissed. They'd touched. They'd laughed. They'd somehow foolishly put away history. Foolishly, because history never did end in the past—*that* was at least something he'd learned from college. He'd also learned that history dampened the naivete of the present day, just as Chris's call yesterday had virtually snuffed out the smoldering fire between him and Geneva. After hanging up, without fanfare, he'd left Geneva's house as if their kiss had simply been a passing thought.

Maybe it was better that way. That kiss was too close to falling into what history had deemed a mistake.

The *m* word—he hated that word. He hated it with a passion, for what it connoted. Because he was the expert on this, on making mistakes. In his family he was always atoning for something, being the last to learn.

Chris wiggled a finger. "I'd wondered, you know? When you mentioned the consultant the other night, I wondered if something else would come down the pipeline."

Brandon was tired of this. "I was doing research. Why is this so bad?"

"You're not getting it. You didn't keep me in the loop, and it's me who looked like a fool. Lainey asked me about it as if I already knew, and I didn't."

"Aw, Kuya, you didn't look like a fool—" Beatrice interrupted.

"Yes, I did." He crossed his arms as he meandered to the window. "I played it off, though. Because you might be right."

Geneva met Brandon's eyes, mirroring how he felt. Was this concession?

"I asked her about her rates." He rubbed his beard impatiently. "They're acceptable, but she can only help us while she's here to install the houses. We're cutting it close, in everything, and I don't like it. Oscar is a day away from Florida, which means it'll be on us in a couple of days."

"We can get quite a bit done in two days," Brandon piped up. Optimism ran through him despite a ball of nervousness threatening to form in his throat. There was no storm yet. He was okay. They were okay. "Mike and I have come up with a plan to prioritize securing the homes and wrapping up some tasks. I can send that to you."

Chris nodded. "Good. I just hate to lose ground or change the date of the grand opening, because the marketing and publicity is working. And speaking of publicity. There's another proposal on the table, which I wholly am against."

"But," Beatrice piped up, "I insisted that I at least share it. But it's totally up to you both." She rose from her chair.

Once again, Geneva met Brandon's eyes.

"It's about the pictures Tammy took for social media. They're very good."

Chris raised a hand. "And weird."

"Not weird," Beatrice said. "Obviously they're not weird, because they're doing well. Engagement is up."

"Okay. So, great." Brandon peered at his siblings.

"No, you don't get it, Bran," Chris said. "The pictures she's talking about? They're of you and Geneva. Show him, Gil."

Gil sat up in his seat and woke the screen of his phone. After a couple of presses of a thumb, he slid the phone across to Brandon. Geneva scooted her chair closer, and with bent heads, they spied at the resort's Instagram.

Admittedly Bran had been caught up. Being on the resort had been a whirlwind. As if by crossing the land bridge, he'd been taken away from the real world. He hadn't been looking at anyone's Instagram or Facebook, not since Beatrice had shown him the first picture of him and Geneva on social media.

He also wasn't the expert on what made a good feed and what didn't. Except that this one looked uniform and pleasing, with outlines of couples against the horizon or running on the beach. Of standing next to the baby-blue house, a guy holding a woman's hand, spikes of sea oats in the background.

Wait a sec.

It was he and Geneva, at Yakap.

"That's us," Geneva whispered. "You were helping me up after I tied my shoes."

Three emotions warred inside him. Shock, that someone had been watching them. Vindication, that they should have been together, that they should have remained together. Anger, that Geneva had left him.

"Oh my gosh, it's of the two of us. All of these photos are of the two of us," Geneva said, reaching across him to zoom into the photos. "This is when I almost fell while running in the sand."

"Aren't they great?" Beatrice said. "She captured you both so well."

"Too well," Chris grumbled. "It looks so real."

"It's not real. Not at all." Geneva's face contorted into a frown.

Brandon sat back in his chair, dismayed by her words. They took the air out of his chest, despite the logical part of his brain saying *I told you so.*

Had he expected a different answer?

Brandon felt the eyes of everyone staring at him, waiting for his take. "This is . . . a lot."

"It's not enough," Beatrice said.

"What do you mean?" Geneva asked.

"You are *the couple*, and Tammy agrees. We needed one couple, *the* couple on our website, on our pamphlets. We hired other models, and we've seen their photos, and you are just . . . it."

Brandon shook his head. How could one breakfast conversation have taken so many turns? Then, like a curtain rising on a stage, Brandon realized what his sister was asking. "Wait a hot second. You want me and Geneva to look like we're a couple?"

"See, it's a bad idea," Chris declared. "That is incestuous."

"I mean, by definition? It's really not," Gil said. "And from my point of view, if it even matters at all—"

Beatrice leveled him with a look. "You *know* it matters."

"Logistically, you're already here on the resort, so the background is true to the environment. In general, photographs of people bring engagement. And optics? You're both Filipino American, which is representative of us. That's something we've always discussed as important—we wanted people to know exactly who we represent and that we're inclusive."

Brandon pinched the bridge of his nose. "Wait a sec. Neither one of us are models. You, Kuya Gil, are. This is totally up your alley. In fact, why aren't you doing any of this image and outreach stuff? This is supposed to be your career."

"The voice of reason!" Chris said. "I have been saying this all along. Why are we even messing with models when we have you, Gil—you're a freaking celebrity."

Gil leveled all of them with a glare. "You *know* I'm on a break. A self-enforced break. Do I have to be blunt about it? I'm burnt out, and I refuse to compromise the few weeks I have with the kids. My focus is them. And honestly, Bran and Geneva, you have an undeniable chemistry. I don't know what to tell you."

"Ugh," Chris spat out.

Brandon could feel Geneva stiffen beside him. She was sitting on her hands, posture straight, and utterly quiet.

His answer was swift. "No."

His siblings countered with their stances, either in support or against.

"No," Geneva said next to him.

Chris's smile of triumph lit up the whole room. "That's my girl."

Irritation gripped Brandon, and against his better judgment not to act protective, he said, "She's not your girl."

His eyebrow went up. "Goodness, I apologize. Thank you, Geneva, for seeing it my way."

"What I meant was," Geneva continued in a steady voice, in contrast to his and his siblings' bickering, "it's not incestuous, and I'll do it."

The room quieted. Brandon faced her. "You're okay with this?"

"Yes."

"But you said, about social media—"

"That was different. This is posed, planned. And I want to do it, for you all."

Beatrice beamed. "So I'll tell Tammy that it's an all clear?"

"It's no big deal. Right, Bran?" Geneva looked to him with pleading eyes. "Ten days. We're together all the time anyway. We take them and then move on."

Her words called up a familiar theme from years ago: *Three weeks, and we move on.*

In truth, everything between them was a big deal, and moving on was no simple matter. Already, being in close proximity to Geneva had broken down the first layers of the wall he'd worked hard to build for himself since their breakup.

But, in the end, Brandon couldn't say no to his siblings, with Geneva already on board. "All right, then."

The question was, How would he protect himself to come out of this unscathed?

♡

The beep of the drip coffee maker snapped Brandon out of his thoughts and he approached the machine with his to-go carafe in hand, glancing out the kitchen window.

One by one, golf carts backed out from under the house and motored down the driveway. An hour after their morning meeting, life and work resumed, and each of his siblings jetted off to their assigned projects. Geneva was up the hill, making arrangements with Sal.

Brandon had needed a moment for a refill, and for a breath.

Pouring the coffee into his carafe, all but draining the pot, he caught a nice big whiff of java, and he reveled in it for just a moment.

He would need all its strength to deal with this jumble of a situation. As if it wasn't complicated enough with the logistics of rebuilding Heart Resort, and this messy limbo in his and Geneva's relationship, now they would be under a camera lens.

"Still here?" a gruff voice said behind him, and he turned to Chris, who, despite looking more polished than he had been at breakfast, had an unreadable expression.

"Last top off." Brandon lifted the carafe. "You look like you need this coffee more than I do."

Chris pressed his fingers against his eyes. "I need a double."

"Oh, wow. Okay." This was a rare moment of vulnerability. Chris was a man who kept an image even with his own family.

So Brandon pulled a coffee cup from the cupboard, noticing once again how his siblings had seemed to move on. Their apartments, their golf carts, and now this cupboard of perfectly matching cups, saucers stacked perfectly next to them. That the dinnerware had been bought all together as a set, the opposite of how they'd grown up. The Annapolis town house still stored their parents' mismatched dining sets, a result of having four children at home who dropped dishes, who accidentally tossed utensils in the garbage, and parents who never threw anything away.

Brandon poured the last of the coffee into the cup, splashed 2 percent milk from the fridge on top, and handed it to him.

Chris perched himself on the stool on the other side of the counter. "Thank you. And for remembering."

"You're the only one I know who likes milk in their coffee."

He shrugged. "Anything to cut the tar a little. Especially with how you make it."

"Pardon me. I make it to the standard, actually. Two tablespoons for every six ounces of water, just like Dad taught me," Brandon said, eyeing his brother—he didn't look right at all. "What's up?"

He sipped, swallowed, and shook his head. "Just stuff."

"Is that why you were extra bossy this morning?" To his attempt at a joke, Brandon didn't get an answer, and he frowned. This was serious. "Can I help?"

"That's the thing, Bran, if only someone could."

"I don't like the sound of that." He leaned against the counter wholly to steady himself, and his heart rate rocketed. Sweat bloomed behind his neck.

It was his anxiety.

Since his parents' sudden deaths, Brandon's reactions to certain stimuli had changed. Storms rattled him; his body reacted viscerally to bad news. Just the idea of someone he loved hurting—he simultaneously wanted to jump in to help them and get the hell out of there, like the push and pull of emotions run amok. He'd learned a lot of things along the way. Seven years of grief, most of those years addressing it in therapy, and slowly reaching out to people had been helpful. Lifesaving. But it didn't mean the anxiety was gone forever. He just got better at sensing it, coping with it, and asking for help when it got to be too much.

"Hey, Bran," Chris said, an eyebrow up. "You okay?"

Brandon exhaled. He had been holding his breath. "Yes, I'm . . . can you say what's up?"

Chris rubbed the top of his head. "It's me and Eden."

"Eden? Something's wrong with Eden?"

"No. No!" He shook his head. "Well, I mean, if you want to talk literally, something *is* wrong with Eden, but it's because of me."

Oh. He inhaled slowly, and his body began to unclench itself. "You're Eden's problem."

"Yeah . . ." He half laughed. "We are having problems, in our . . . marriage. We've . . . been. And it's been weighing on me, a lot. We fought again last night, on a date night no less. Notice she wasn't at breakfast?"

"I thought it's because she and the kids—"

"All excuses. Eden doesn't want any of you all to know that we're not great right now."

Brandon listened for any noise, for the sound of footsteps. For a child coming from upstairs, or even a crack in the veneer of reality. Chris was opening up, to him? "I . . . I'm sorry."

"Don't be sorry. This is all my—our—doing."

"Is it for a specific reason? Are there . . . other people?"

"No. Is that what you think of me?" He frowned.

"That's not . . . never mind."

"No, I want to know what you mean."

Brandon pulled the threads of his thoughts together, the reasons why things had never really worked out with others, and with Geneva. "It doesn't have to be another lover, or an affair. It could be other people in the way of responsibilities, or loyalties."

Chris's shoulders dropped. "No, there aren't any other people. There are other issues, in the name of Heart Resort and Everly Heart."

Eden was also known as Everly Heart, a romance author of fifteen books. For as long as Brandon had known her, Eden had clacked away on her computer or dictated into her phone. From Eden, Brandon had also learned to respect novel writing and romance as a genre. He was proud to say he'd hand sold his share of Everly Heart's romance novels.

Brandon also knew of Eden's drive and ambition, and it rivaled Chris's. She had goals, and no one, not even Chris, could keep her back from them.

"Is it serious? The fighting, I mean? I can't imagine you both fighting. I don't think I've ever seen her raise her voice," Brandon asked.

"She doesn't have to. She carries a big stick. And she's the expert at the silent treatment. My back's screaming from the tossing and turning I've been doing. I've been on the couch." He winced. "Anyway . . ."

Brandon locked into his brother's change in subject, but there had been more. "You said Heart Resort. The resort's coming in between you both?"

"Yeah. She thinks . . ." He looked down into his cup. "She thinks that I'm obsessed."

"Obsessed. Clinically?"

"No. Those were my words, I'm sorry. That was ableist." He heaved a breath. "Eden thinks I'm too competitive with Willow Tree."

Brandon relaxed and rolled his eyes. "This—this isn't a big deal. This isn't even competition. Different states, and we have a freaking island practically."

"Peninsula."

"Whatever. There can be more than one couples resort in the US. There's one on Martha's Vineyard, another in Vermont—"

"They tried to poach Mike from us."

"Our contractor?" Brandon frowned.

"They called and asked him to join their team for some chief of some division—his sister is married to a McCauley—Dillon McCauley the third is the CEO. Anyway, when Mike said no, they tried to mine him for information."

"That's shady."

"No doubt. None of what we do is proprietary, but I certainly don't want to make it easy for Dillon. He's third in a line of business guys, cutthroat, old money. Bran, I just can't let up. I want them to think that Tropical Storm Maximus strengthened us rather than hindered. I want them to know that we belong here too."

Brandon nodded. He understood his brother's pride. He also understood Eden's issue with it.

"Anyway, I'm headed into town to meet up with the bigwigs to talk up the resort. What are you doing today?"

"Floors for the yoga studio, meeting with Lainey, hopefully. Speaking of, can I make a couple of PB and Js? I don't think I'll be able to stop for lunch."

"Go ahead. This is your house too." Chris waved a hand across the kitchen.

Brandon stilled for a beat. He begged to differ, seeing that he hadn't yet been invited to move into his own apartment upstairs. But that was another conversation for another day. This had been the most his brother had shared with him. And he . . . he was in turmoil.

"Bran, this is also why I'm not down with this idea of you and Geneva being a couple for the resort. I don't need you or her to, first of all, be exposed to Willow Tree—I know they're watching us closely. And secondly, the idea of fraternization is unconscionable." He harrumphed. "But, I have to trust your professionalism. And Beatrice is insisting, and I do trust her judgment."

Chris took the first sip of his coffee.

Though Brandon commenced making his sandwich, food was now the furthest thing from his mind. He, too, was as torn as Chris was. Pretending to be a couple was not a good move, but it was too late to worry about fraternization. He and Geneva had already crossed that line.

When she'd left him those years ago, Brandon had gone day after day of being distracted. Of forgetting tasks, of worrying for a human who didn't want to be contacted. Of trying to jump-start his body and brain so he could be the productive, competent person he was raised to be.

He hated how he had been. And he hated this state of limbo that they were in now.

It's not real. Not at all.

Goodness, they'd shared a kiss. A freaking kiss. A hot freaking kiss, but still. He had been intimate with others in a quicker time frame. Why wasn't he surprised that she was willing to downplay it? "Can I ask you some advice?"

Chris looked up from his cup. "Of course. Is this about your business? It did make me wonder how you can take so much time off."

Brandon winced, because yes, he had the town house to discuss, but he could only do one thing at a time. "No. It's personal."

A grin broke out on Chris's face. "Personal."

"Yes."

"A woman?"

Brandon nodded.

Chris peered at him. "Is this going to be like one of our ten-questions games?"

Brandon laughed at that, though admittedly he likened sharing his emotions to yanking his own baby teeth. It was like his first time in therapy—it had taken the full fifty minutes to pull more than two-word sentences from him. "No."

Chris raised his eyebrows. "Good golly, man, just say it."

"Since we were talking about Eden . . ." He heaved a breath. *Just say it.* "How do you know when it's right for a relationship to continue?"

"Ah, you're involved with someone."

Involved was probably pushing it. Tangled? Hooked on what-if? Utterly confused? "Maybe?"

"And the way you're being so open means you're probably not going to give me a hint as to who this is."

"I'd rather keep that private." Brandon dropped his gaze for a beat, tempted to tell Chris—he wanted to talk this over with someone. Though it was one kiss, the situation felt urgent.

Chris ran a finger over the rim of his cup. "I'm going to allow that, just because I know at some point Beatrice will weasel it out of you. It will be more satisfying to watch it happen."

"*Kuya.*"

"Okay, I'm listening. Give it to me."

"How do you let go? How are you the way you are?"

"And what's that?"

"Stone cold, man."

Chris shot him a bewildered look. "I'm not sure how to take that."

"Oh, c'mon. As if you don't know." Brandon grinned, leveling a look at him. "You're not exactly warm, or touchy feely."

He shrugged, a hurt look on his face.

"Aw, you're not being serious right now." Brandon did a double take. Sure enough, Chris's shoulders had dropped, and he didn't have a hint of a smile. "You're serious."

"Look, intense doesn't mean cold." Chris held a hand up. "And just to prove it to you, I'm not going to let this conversation derail. You're asking me how I let go, and I'll tell you something. I don't. I wish I could crack the code, Bran, because I can't seem to let anything go. What I do isn't the most healthy or probably helpful, but I push it down, deep on the inside. Anyone like me? Type A? Repression is our superpower."

Brandon took in his words and ruminated on them. "Wow, Kuya, that is incredibly self-aware."

"I have a romance author for a wife. Empathy is her business, and she has schooled me more than once about my"—he made quotation marks with his fingers—"*wound, or that which motivates us in all of our actions.*"

"That's super interesting. And your wound is . . ." Brandon leaned in, curious about this new side of Chris.

"None of your business. But my advice would be that you should do what's right for you. Bottom line, I have no advice."

"That might be a first."

"Keep in mind that it's only for this question. Because the rest of it? I have ideas and advice. Like perhaps when you speak to Lainey about the kitchen, I want you to keep the plans as simple as possible."

Brandon glanced up at the ceiling and laughed. "Ah. And he's back."

"Oh, and just an FYI, Friday dinner tonight. I'll grab and take you to the restaurant, and apparently per Beatrice, you and Geneva are doing a little photo shoot tomorrow morning, as the sun rises, with Tammy. I'll text you the details later on."

"Even better," he said softly, except without sarcasm. With his brother's lesson on self-awareness, Brandon now wondered if Geneva running, avoiding him, and leaving were due to a wound too? And what was his?

Brandon swiped the bread with peanut butter, and he grabbed a couple of clear ziplock bags from the drawer. His phone beeped with a calendar notification for tomorrow afternoon. He gave it a glance: *Walk-through of Illinois Way.*

Garrett with his perfect and awful timing.

When he looked up, Chris was drinking his coffee and checking his phone.

If there was a time to bring up Mulberry Road, it was now, while they were alone. Then again, Brandon had done that four years ago, and he'd been shot down two sentences into the discussion.

You have been ready to move on.

"Kuya."

"Yep." Chris placed his phone facedown.

"You know, real estate prices have skyrocketed in Annapolis."

"Yeah, I heard. Thank God—after the dip during COVID, I was a little worried."

"Currently homes are selling about ten to fifty thousand more than prepandemic."

"Wow. Our parents bought our place for a little more than a hundred and fifty thousand. Can't imagine."

"Yeah, it's easily four times that."

Brandon would say it. He would say it today.

"And it's all ours." Chris grinned. "It's really our nest egg. If everything goes up in flames here, I'm just glad to have that house to come home to."

"Would you, though? You haven't lived there for a decade."

"Yeah, of course. That's home. It belongs to us." His phone buzzed, and he glanced down at the notification. "Are we having this conversation again? You know how I feel about this. It's our home, Brandon. We can't sell it."

A slew of emotions overcame Brandon, from anger and irritation to guilt. And the overwhelming feeling of being trapped.

"Um . . ." Chris pointed at the sandwich. "You forget something?"

Brandon looked down at two sandwiches, smashed under his palm, with the closed bottle of jelly next to them.

He'd forgotten the jelly.

"I hope you're not as forgetful at work." Chris laughed, though underneath it was sarcasm, bordering on cynicism.

"Nah . . ." He stuffed a sandwich in the ziplock bag. "I meant to do that," he said, pretending.

Which seemed to be the story of his life.

CHAPTER FOURTEEN

Brandon:

Tried to catch you today

Geneva:

Met up with Beatrice after work

She needed help

Brandon:

Can we talk?

Geneva:

Later?

As dots appeared on the screen, Geneva stuffed her phone in her back pocket.

If she didn't see it, she wouldn't have to answer it.

"What are you complaining about over there?" Beatrice walked into the sparse white room, carrying a box. "I hear those impatient deep breaths."

"Work, what else," Geneva lied, and looked up from the box she had temporarily set on the floor. She was on her knees, on a quick break to finally answer Brandon's text. She'd kept him on read—she really needed to switch out her settings—most of the day, still unsure how to deal with him and their situation. In the span of a day, they'd changed the trajectory of their work and personal relationship. Not only did they have to contend with their kiss, but now they had to play a couple on the internet. It didn't help that Beatrice didn't hold back in laying on the guilt trip that Geneva was spending more time with Brandon than she had with her.

It had been an easy decision to escape Heart Resort to help with Beatrice at Beachy's Nags Head office for a couple of hours before the Pusos' Friday dinner.

"Can I help?" Beatrice asked.

Definitely not. "Nah. I'm avoiding a conversation because I'm not sure how to approach it."

Beatrice winced. "Eeps, sounds sticky."

"Like molasses." She waved the topic away. "Honestly, I don't want to think about it right now."

"I've got a good solution to that." Beatrice slung her arm across her chest to stretch it and gestured at the boxes littering her office floor. "You can put your energy toward all this."

"I'd better be getting a bonus." Geneva flipped the blade of her box cutter up and sliced one of the boxes open.

"The bonus of my ever-loyal friendship, duh."

"Mm-hmm." She rolled her eyes, but her faux sarcasm dissipated when she gazed at the contents of the box. "Ooooh, oranges and yellows. So pretty!" She took each plastic-wrapped item out of the bag and stacked them on the worktable. Then, after a quick look through the rest of the box, she popped the tops of the other boxes too. It was a feast for the eyes, of stripes and polka dots and paisleys in a rainbow of colors. "Are these all caftans?"

"Caftans and sarongs, and muumuus and maxi dresses," Beatrice said in a most flirtatious voice. "Go ahead, open one in your size. You can change behind the wooden partition."

"Are you sure?" Geneva felt like a kid in a candy store, sorting through the bright colors.

"Of course I'm sure. How else to sell clothing but word of mouth, especially from a comfort-dress aficionado like yourself?"

After finding a pin-striped orange-on-white linen caftan, Geneva popped behind the wooden partition. It was a temporary fitting-room setup, with a small bench and an umbrella tree, from which hung padded hangers, and a stand-alone full-length mirror.

Geneva took off her shorts and tank, slightly dusty from the day's activity of hanging wallpaper and painting accent walls. The projects in tiny homes were such a pleasure because they only took a fraction of the time. Which was what she needed after the doozy of a meeting this morning.

Slipping on the V-neck dress felt like a luxury, the fabric sliding on her skin with ease. It draped over her like a good friend's hug—fun, loose, and reliable—and came down to just below her knees. The sleeves were flowy and comfortable.

This dress could be rolled up and stuffed into her already-full duffel bag.

She halted at this added requirement; portability was a criterion she had held dear for years. All her belongings had to have a function. But more: they had to fit in the scheme of her life, which meant they had to fit in her bags.

It had been a badge of honor to be so nomadic, so unattached. How would it feel to have a big closet and a collection of things just because?

"You're quiet over there," Beatrice said.

"I just love it, is why." She stepped out from behind the partition, and Beatrice turned around, arms crossed.

Her face lit up. "I love that on you. The orange is perfect for your skin tone. Hmmm." She tapped a finger against her lip, then rummaged through the pile next to her, retrieving three packages.

"What are you doing?"

"I want you to take these."

"I can't. It's too much."

"Have them. Wear them. They'll also be perfect for your photos on the resort. They're complimentary."

It wasn't about cost. But she plastered on a wry smile—Beatrice's face was too sincere, and she didn't want to disappoint her. "Ah, so I get it: I'm going to be your *brand ambassador.*"

"Ha ha. No. But, if we're talking about quid pro quo . . . how many dresses would it take for you to stay and design this office?"

She inspected the fabric closely—the weave of the cloth was divine. "That's easy. I can design this place remotely. I can even take measurements before I go."

"It wouldn't be the same." Beatrice stomped, and her voice took on a more frantic quality. "Did something happen the last day? I feel like something happened. You seem different. Was it because of our meeting this morning? If you don't want to play a couple with my brother, you don't have to. I shouldn't have brought it up—"

"No—nothing happened." As she answered, Geneva willed her gaze to focus on the very tip of Beatrice's nose. This was not the time to bare the truth, for where would she start? Four years ago when she'd slept with Beatrice's brother, or last night when they'd almost done it again? Or her concern that playing a couple wasn't even the issue so much as the fact that it would purposely bring them closer, and she would be tempted to kiss him again.

Brandon's kisses were glorious. They were perfect. Making out had been the wrong move on both of their parts, but damn, did she want to do it again.

Geneva only wished that his kisses could remain simply kisses. With them, Brandon had dug up all the deep feelings she'd pushed down and away from her sight.

"Uh-uh. No. We're going to talk about this. You're not looking at me straight on."

The front door of the shop slammed open, the bell ringing the arrival of two other women: Giselle, Beatrice's office manager, and Eden. Each was carrying a box. With them, a gust of sticky air floated in.

"Later," Beatrice told Geneva pointedly as she rushed to hold the door open for them. "Thanks, you two, you are heaven sent, I swear."

"These are the last of them." Giselle set the box down and swiftly twisted her curly reddish-blonde hair into a bun. "I think the Fed Post guy was super happy we were there to help him bring all these boxes in. He's new and didn't quite realize what he was getting himself into."

"No, I think the Fed Post guy was just happy because *you* were there," Eden countered, taking off her sunglasses and sticking them on the top of her head. She had a hint of a glasses tan: half of her face was a lighter brown than the rest. "He was drooling all over himself when you were standing next to him. He could barely figure out how to work his scanner."

"You and your meet-cutes." Giselle rolled her eyes.

At that statement, Geneva straightened, attention now fully on the two women, and shot Eden a look. Across from her, Beatrice did the same.

"What?" Giselle asked. "What did I say?"

"Oh!" Eden said. "Don't worry, you guys; I told her. I couldn't not. She was fangirling me too much."

The store seemed to exhale. Eden's identity, as communicated to Geneva, was an utmost secret.

"Oh yeah. Your secret's safe with me." Giselle nodded enthusiastically. To Geneva, she said, "I was going on and on about one of her books. Which I didn't realize was written by her! I about almost peed on myself. Anyway." She eyed the boxes, suddenly laser focused. "I'm going to start creating areas so we can sort through the inventory."

Along with the rest of the women, Geneva hopped to it.

"All righty. Let's go with sarongs at this table. Caftans in this area, boho dresses here, and muumuus here. Empty boxes can go back here." Giselle pointed to the corner of the room. "Does that sound good, Beatrice?"

Beatrice nodded. "Yep, and can we make sure the shipping area is clear? We've still got to deal with returns."

Giselle nodded, thought about it, and redirected the rest of the group. It was soon followed by the dragging of boxes, the crinkling of paper, and the low murmuring of voices. The room warmed, and Geneva, after unpacking and breaking down her boxes, surveyed the space in all its inventory grandeur, as well as the women working in their corners with such dedication. All the day's chaos fell to the back of her mind as she envisioned built-in hanging racks and long, flowing curtains on the windows that were currently covered with basic window blinds. She imagined hardwood to replace the laminate floors and, behind the partition, a proper fitting room.

"I can see your evil mind working." Beatrice wiped her forehead with her arm.

"I was just thinking."

"Uh-oh," Eden said. "I detect that something has to do with wallpaper."

"Am I that transparent?"

Eden and Beatrice both sounded off with a resounding "yes," while Giselle simply shrugged. "I'm going to agree with my boss."

"My question, Bea . . . does this space need only to be a storage area?"

"Um, yeah, because my business plan is for a subscription box business."

"And not a retail front?"

"No, that is a whole other can of worms. It's perfect right now. Giselle and I are able to handle it along with a couple of paid hourly workers. Once you add a retail front . . ."

"Once you have a retail front, then you have a showroom," Geneva mused. "You can serve your community and tourists who also want these dresses."

"I don't know. I have the resort to deal with. *That's* my job." And yet, the smile on Beatrice's face said something more. It said that she was thinking about it. "Although . . ."

"Although what?"

"It's nothing."

Geneva peered at her friend. There was no such thing as nothing with Beatrice. She had a light touch on everything, but it was most certainly a purposeful touch.

♡

"I thought we were going to meet everyone at dinner," Geneva said, riding shotgun in Beatrice's pristine white Tesla sedan. They'd left Beachy and were headed east instead of south toward the restaurant for the Pusos' Friday night dinner.

"It's not for another twenty minutes. And they know I'm always late. Patience," she said, looking askance.

"I have patience, just as long as I know what's coming," she declared.

Truthfully, Geneva was simply restless. Despite the couple of hours of inventory, after which they'd split ways with Giselle and Eden, who'd wanted to sneak in a few minutes of writing before dinner, she was still antsy. It was everything, the culmination of the entire day, that made her want to scream or run.

"I thought you should get a tour of Nags Head. You hadn't mentioned going to the beach."

"Uh . . . there's a private beach at my front stoop."

"Yeah, but it's so empty, right? Sometimes when I'm on the resort I forget an entire world exists out here. Because we work and live there,

there's no separation. The place is all-encompassing, and I can get cabin fever. After all, I see the same people every day."

"Ah, but you're also an extrovert, and that, I am not." Geneva pushed down her visor to block out the last of the sun, still at least a couple of hours from setting. The streets were packed with pedestrians. The way to the beach entrance was clear from the path people were traveling. Like watching a trail of ants, one only needed to follow those with portable beach chairs and large totes through the dunes and over wooden walkways to the ocean.

Beatrice swerved to the last alleyway in between the first two rows of beach houses, perched on tall and skinny pilings, sidings painted with all the colors of the rainbow. Every home they passed had a vehicle parked underneath it, except for one, which Beatrice turned into.

Her friend had done it with such ease that it took Geneva a moment to put the pieces together.

"Bea, why are we parked under a beach house?"

She turned off the car and unbuckled her seat belt and with a deadpan expression said, "Are we really parked under a beach house?"

"Yes, and a first-row house too."

Her friend's flat expression switched to a cheesy grin.

"No way."

The cheesy grin then turned to a joyful, unhinged smile, eyes wide, her eyebrows sky high on her forehead. "Way. It's mine."

"Oh. My. God." Geneva slipped out of the car and followed her friend up the steep white stairs, gripping the railing as the beach—the ocean—came into view. The strong waves, the crash of the tide. The squeals of people, and colorful dots of umbrellas and beach towels.

"Come on in!" Beatrice tugged her inside a white door, into an open-concept space.

The great room was sun filled, with light-gray walls, and with a white kitchen.

"There's more." Beatrice led the way into a hallway, pointing out a laundry room, and then up a flight of stairs. On the second floor were four bedrooms, two with en suites, and a separate hallway bathroom.

"This is spectacular," Geneva said, now in one of the en suite bedrooms, captivated by the sheer number of windows, at the feeling of being high up. "This room would be beautiful as a light peach."

"Light peach?"

"To bring in the light and the sunrise. It would be so pretty to wake up to that contrast." She shrugged. "That's just me. For others, I'd make it more neutral, maybe a soft light blue, almost gray."

Beatrice crossed her arms and leaned against the window. "For others?"

"Yeah. The guests. I especially like the fact that there are two en suites. Great for families that want to stay in one home."

"What guests? What families?" A smile pulled the corners of Beatrice's mouth.

"The ones you will be . . . renting . . . to . . ." With an eyebrow up, Geneva drew out her words. "Because you live on the resort. Didn't you buy this as an investment property?"

Beatrice hiked her hands on her hips and shook her head. "Uh-uh."

She mimicked her friend's stance. "What's up, Beatrice? First, you casually suggest that I help with your business, and then this place. Out with it—don't mess with me."

"Okay, but for this, I need to take you to the pièce de résistance. C'mon." She gestured with her head.

Geneva followed her out another door to the front deck and then up another set of stairs. With each step upward, her heart beat faster and louder.

Finally, she stepped onto the roof deck, surrounded by a wooden railing. It was easily the highest of the rest of the houses around them, and Geneva could see far and wide. From this vantage point, the sky seemed more attainable than the ground. She felt free but safe.

"This view, Beatrice."

She held her flyaway hair back with a hand. "It's pretty amazing. My mother would've loved this view, don't you think?"

"Undoubtedly. Poor Tito Joe would have had to drag her away. The only other thing that would have enticed her would have been . . ."

At the same time, they both said, "The kitchen."

A laugh bubbled through her along with a stab of pain. It was for herself, as well as for her friend. But when she looked at Beatrice's profile, what she saw was peace. "This view is why you bought it."

"Yep. It was this, and then feeling her up here." She turned to Geneva. "But I have a different reason for taking you here."

"Okay?"

"It's on the DL, Gen."

"Got it."

"You don't understand. You can't breathe a word, not until I figure out how to approach it. Because if done wrong, I could really mess things up. Then again, if I wait too long, then I could miss out on an opportunity."

"This sounds pretty serious." Geneva took a step closer.

"It is." Worry etched lines on Beatrice's face.

"Tell me."

"I want to do Beachy full time."

Geneva opened her mouth, then shut it. She tried once more and shut it again. Then she reorganized her thoughts. At how serious of a declaration this was.

Beatrice, above all, never strayed from family. That light touch was like superglue that kept all the Puso men together, and she knew it. Beneath her constant smile was a resilient woman placed under enormous pressure.

But trailing these thoughts was pure pride. It was pride and joy, and everything that one felt for a sister who had found her love.

Beatrice's love was her business.

Geneva reached out and clutched Beatrice's hand. Then she started to laugh. Beachy's rise was fast—driven by Beatrice's determination, by this love of entrepreneurship—and inside, Geneva again felt that yearning. She wanted to be like Beatrice—exactly like this, *in love* with her business. "Bea . . . Beatrice Cayuga Puso. Are you serious? That is fantastic, and bonkers, and oh my God."

Her eyes watered. "Oh God. What did I just say? Tell me I'm being completely irresponsible."

"What? No. Never. This is just going to be . . . oh shoot, your family!" Because there would be consequences. Scrape off the glue, and everything might fall apart.

Beatrice cupped her mouth with the other hand.

"Tell me. How did you get here? When did you decide?" Geneva asked.

"I don't know. I started Beachy as a side thing. You know how I am with that. But then the first customer came in, and then the next, and then came the business plan . . . and it just changed."

"Beatrice," she said pointedly, though inside was not surprised that the business plan had come *after* the actual business.

"I know. I love Beachy. Love it, and every part of it. The seasonal looks, the buying, the selling. The joy it gives people who wear clothes that fit well and comfortably. I have a feeling about this." She retrieved her hand from Geneva and ran both over her hair. "Earlier, when you mentioned me going retail in front of the girls, I pooh-poohed it, but it was only for show. I already thought about it. I have been thinking about it for a while. You reflecting it back to me was a sign. But I said the same thing about Heart Resort, remember?"

Geneva nodded. She'd gotten the phone call a few months after Tito Joe and Tita Marilyn had passed. Beatrice had been on a solo vacation, in Hatteras, and read in the local paper about a heart-shaped peninsula abandoned by a couple who'd passed before opening a resort.

With her parents' substantial legacy, Beatrice had been looking for an investment property.

It's heart shaped, Geneva. I have a feeling about this. It's a sign.

It had seemed so far fetched, but just as Geneva heeded Beatrice's advice, so did the rest of the family. Her idea was so good that Chris had taken it an extra step and decided to follow through with the couples resort concept. The negotiations for the property's sale had gone without a hitch.

"I believed in you then, and I believe in you now," Geneva said.

"Heh. I'm not so sure the rest of the family will feel the same way. Not with how much we've lost. The cost of rebuilding after Maximus—"

"Beatrice, no one blames you for a tropical storm's murderous wind speed."

She laughed. "I know, but if I hadn't brought up the resort at all, then we would—"

"You would what? Not have a business that has a mission of healing relationships? Not infuse the local economy with business and jobs, even during the pandemic? Not have gone into business with your family and who you now spend every day with? Heart Resort was one of the first businesses to open after the pandemic, if I remember, because it was already well suited for social distancing. Don't even go there."

"Well, I'm so glad you feel that way, that you feel strongly about this, and me. And this house. Because I have something to propose."

Geneva braced herself. Every proposal thus far since her arrival had involved a secret and a pivot. "What is it?"

"I propose that you move here to the Outer Banks to live and work with me."

Geneva was stunned. "I . . ." With so much to unpack, she grabbed onto the thing that jumped out the most. "You mean live in this house? Here, in North Carolina?"

"Yes, here." Beatrice's arm shot out toward the beach, and she sported a bright smile. "With all this. Ocean air, every day. Vitamin D just outside your bedroom door even when it's gray out. The water steps away, which I know you love."

The squeals of beachgoers took Geneva's attention, and she looked out. The beach was packed at the moment, but it wouldn't always be so. There would be nights and early mornings when the crowd would be sparse, and from fall till spring it became a ghost town. And oh, did she love putting her feet in sand and in water every day.

A gust of wind woke her from her trance, reminding her that there was one problem with this proposal. "But you sell dresses, and I'm—"

"The best designer I know. Your work on Heart Resort sealed it for me. It's not just about space for you but feeling, vibe, spirit. It transcends. It can transcend."

Geneva shook her head. "I don't know what you mean?"

"Besides coming to design our retail space, I want you to be my partner. To expand Beachy to house decor and housewares."

"Do you mean—"

"You get to design for yourself."

Myself. Designing for herself was never something Geneva had considered. Her whole mission was to please the customer, to exceed the client's expectations. Most of Geneva's hours weren't spent buying furniture or laying out rooms. They were spent getting to know the client, feeling them out, weighing what they said versus what they actually showed in their Pinterest boards or magazine cutouts. She believed in this mission through and through, never settling in wherever she laid her head to rest, and only living with the barest of things.

Yes, these were her choices, and she didn't regret them. But here she was, presented with another choice, a pivot.

"Geneva," Beatrice said, drawing her full attention. "I propose that you and I make Beachy a lifestyle brand."

CHAPTER FIFTEEN

Brandon pressed on the button, and the metal measuring tape slunk back like a slithering snake. "I think we can definitely fit a six-by-five-foot island here." He stood from a half-kneeling position, then took his place next to Lainey, who held an iPad and wore a serious expression on her face. Brandon pointed at the empty area in the digital drawing. "What do you think?"

Lainey nodded. "I think that will do. But let's do a trial run, shall we?" With the digital pen, she dragged the island icon to the empty area in the drawing, completing the full picture of the future kitchen of Hapag, Heart Resort's restaurant.

Seeing the plans on the screen, Brandon breathed a sigh of relief. He relied on experts, even with his residential flips. He employed kitchen consultants because he wasn't a cook, and the pressure to get the kitchen right was real. It had to be functional, practical, but attractive and inspiring. It was, at times, the one thing that either made or broke a sale. And a commercial kitchen? That was an entire animal unto itself.

Lainey stood at the kitchen entrance. "Watch the production." She took Brandon step by step from order retrieval, to the refrigerator and freezer, to where certain meals would be made, to the dishes and sink areas. Brandon followed along and nodded and took more notes on his iPad.

His phone buzzed in his pocket. He all but dropped the iPad on the ground as he fished his phone out.

Geneva:

We need to chat at dinner, somehow.

His body deflated, staring at the words. There were no emojis, nary an exclamation point. So much was lost in text messages. Was Geneva upset? Regretful?

"Ahem."

Brandon glanced up. Lainey was still holding the imaginary plate. "Sorry."

"It's all right." She heaved a breath. "Now, once plated and garnished, it goes up here to heating lamps, where the waitstaff grabs it and . . ." She backed against the swinging door, then stepped in as it opened inward. "Voilà! Happy customers."

Brandon annotated final notes into his iPad. His head started to spin with his to-do list of kitchen-equipment brand names, as well as a woman completely beguiling to him for reasons known and unknown. "Voilà," he repeated back. "Right."

"Knock knock?" Chris entered through the swinging door, accompanied by Tammy, and both had smiles on their faces.

"Perfect timing. More photo ops," Tammy said.

"Photos?" Lainey's eyebrows rose.

Tammy held up her camera. "I'm shooting in-progress photos. Do you mind?"

"Actually"—she winced—"I do. I just . . . like my privacy. I hope that's all right."

"Oh, of course."

Lainey turned the watch on her wrist. "And it's actually time for me to head out. I want to walk through the houses." She shook Chris's and Tammy's hands, and then to Brandon said, "Let me know if you have issues finding materials and appliances—I can hook you up with contacts. I also found out that I'll be in the area next week and can arrange to be here for installation, if needed."

"Sounds good. I'll walk you out."

"Thanks for your fantastic work, Lainey." Chris waved as Brandon shut the door behind her. With the click of the lock, he added, "What was that about appliances?"

Brandon grinned. Of course his brother couldn't help but micromanage. "She had some suggestions on reliable appliances and restaurant equipment that could serve us pretty quickly, because, you know . . . we have a deadline coming up."

"Just watch your cost. We don't need to have anything fancy."

"Fancy and reliable are completely separate criteria. And they both entail money."

"Hapag is going to serve ten couples at most at one time. The kitchen we had before the storm was good enough."

"Maybe that's something you'll need to ask your chef. At the very least, you'll want a commercial kitchen that can provide your chef the comfort to make high-quality special meals. If we're building from scratch, why not make it better? And . . ."

Chris hiked a hand on his hip. "And what?"

"The restaurant needs a paint job, inside and outside, and possibly new dinnerware."

"That's ridiculous, Bran."

"It's not when everything is a hodgepodge mess. Your house behind the gates has more modern-looking dishes. I was there this morning, remember?"

Tammy cleared her throat as she stepped up; Brandon had forgotten that she was there. "Shall I reschedule the pictures for another time?"

Between them, the tension was thick, but Brandon didn't budge. Chris might have had a say when it came to most everything in their lives, but with this, Brandon knew better.

Chris's face was rigid as he spoke. "No, this is fine, Tammy."

"Yeah, it's all good." Brandon heaved a breath, knowing full well this was the first round in the discussion. Chris was twelve times worse than Brandon's pickiest boss and client, holding the power of that intangible position called big brother.

"All righty then," Tammy said, voice lifting in faux enthusiasm. "Let's have you both stand in the middle of the room."

As she backed into the corner, Brandon took the moment to address his brother once more. "You have to let me do my job, Kuya. I've no issues working within the budget. But you have to trust me with *my* judgment. We want the same things."

"All right, you two, put an arm around each other," Tammy said, with half her face hidden behind the camera.

Chris wrapped an arm around Brandon's shoulder. It was a strong hold. It was unthreatening, but a reminder that Chris was formidable. That he was the CEO of Heart Resort and, ultimately, who was in charge. "Sometimes, I *don't* know if we want the same thing. And sometimes, I think it's simply because you're looking for a fight. And *that* is what renders your judgment faulty."

Tammy peeked from behind the lens. "Brandon, how about an arm around your brother?"

He slung an arm around Chris and smiled as instructed, but all he felt was the sting of the little razor cuts of his brother's words.

♡

"Are you giving me the silent treatment too?" Chris said from the driver's seat of his black Chevy Suburban.

From the passenger seat, Brandon gave his brother the side-eye, then quickly glanced to the back, where Eden was speaking into her phone, headphones over her ears.

"She can't hear us," Chris said. "She's in first-draft mode, in what she calls brain dumping, and she's dictating. Those noise-cancelling headphones are state of the art."

"Ah. That's interesting."

"It saves her wrists for editing. It's how she can write so much. But anyway. We need to continue our conversation."

"What conversation?"

Chris snorted a laugh. "Look, I didn't say anything in the restaurant that I wouldn't have said to anyone else on the team. Am I not allowed to give you feedback?"

"What do you want me to say?"

"That you understand where I'm coming from."

"I understand that you can't help but correct everything I do, despite the fact that this has also been my industry the last decade."

"Bran, I gave you my professional input. It's what I have to do. The problem here is that you don't want to move on from our fight. I'm trying, if you can't tell."

Brandon looked out onto the road. The scene flipped from sand dunes to glimpses of the Atlantic Ocean to lush greenery. Golden hour was probably a half hour away.

He tried to put his mind there, where all those colors were, away from their bleak conversation. Yes, his brother was trying. But it wasn't as simple as accepting his professional opinion. It was everything—the fact that Chris controlled every part of their family. No one should have that much power.

"You're always like this. You clam up. You bundle up all of your thoughts and keep it all inside."

"And you've got a way of spewing yours without the thought of others," he snapped.

Chris's face lit up. "There you go. I thought for a sec that I had a cardboard cutout of my brother next to me. Was it so hard to give me something? Try me again."

Brandon shut his eyes and let his anger take the words from his chest. "You chose that influencer over me."

Chris frowned and glanced at him for a beat, before whipping his gaze up front. "What do you mean?"

Brandon dug deep, to the source of his anger, and scooped it out with his voice. It took a breath, effort. "For all your talk about family and loyalty and our name. When all that went down, and it got out that the woman and I slept together, I was the one canned and shipped off."

"Bran." He shook his head, and remorse laced his voice. "It was a tough situation."

"Right. I get it. She was the customer, and nothing can be changed now and all the rest, yada yada. So I don't need a lecture about moving on, or how to act, or my crap judgment. You don't make it easy for me to be here. How can it be when I feel like you don't have my back."

"Damn, Bran. I do have your back." He repositioned his hands on the wheel. "And I didn't say your judgment was crap. I . . . look, I'm sorry. About what happened."

That isn't a true apology, was what Brandon wanted to say. He nodded instead, because what else was there to discuss? Though he did notice that the tension in his chest lessened; for all the trouble it was to express his emotions, he knew it was good for him.

They were a few miles south on 12, and the car crossed over Bonner Bridge.

"We're going pretty far," Brandon noted after a few minutes.

"The restaurant is in Rodanthe."

"Rodanthe." He snorted a laugh, with one image popping up in his memory. "God, that movie was depressing."

"I know. But Mom loved it because it was the only movie that mentioned our spot, so by default . . ." Chris shrugged. "Though I think she liked everything."

"It's because our father liked nothing at all."

Chris laughed. "Do you ever think about their relationship?"

Brandon nodded. His parents' relationship was what he gauged all others by. While he wasn't rushing to the altar, he eventually wanted what they'd had. "Thirty-five years was a heck of a long time."

"This year would have been forty-two years. They would have been close to retiring."

"Ma would have never retired," Brandon declared. "And she would have gotten sick of Dad at home."

"Truth. She can't sit still." Chris paused. "Couldn't."

The car slowed as they crossed the Rodanthe city limits. Chris flipped his blinkers on and drove into a parking lot. Gil's minivan and Beatrice's Tesla were already present.

Brandon was glad for their arrival, needing some food in his belly. There was never really enough time to eat during the day, not in a way that he wanted, and after his conversation with Chris, what he needed was comfort. Apparently, this restaurant was supposed to provide it.

He hopped out of the SUV and opened Eden's door for her. She took off her headphones. Her eyes were glassy as if in a daze. *In the zone*, was how she'd described it in the past.

"Got some words in?" he asked.

"Mmm? Yes. Sorry. I'm under deadline and just had a breakthrough and had to dictate it before I forgot."

He offered her his elbow. "No worries. Everything going okay?"

"It's going to hell in a handbasket." Her face scrunched. "My characters are going rogue. Why can't they do what I outlined for them to do? What's the point of me outlining ahead of time?"

"Um." Brandon never knew what to say when Eden asked theoretical writing questions. "Maybe . . . going rogue is a good thing?"

She shook her head, and she leaned into him, ducking as the wind whipped past. "I don't have time for them to go rogue. I wish I could take a lasso and tie them up and they can ride the arc like I told them to."

"You . . . yes, you're absolutely right." He snickered. He had no idea what she was talking about. Up ahead, Chris was on his phone, leaning back against the door of a nondescript building. Its walls were made of brick, the roof of metal. Behind it was the Pamlico Sound.

Eden groaned. "He's on that phone again. He can't even put it down for one dinner a week."

"He's a busy guy." Awkwardness clawed at his neck. He'd been Eden's friend first, but Chris, as prickly as he was, was his brother, and Brandon was supposed to have his back. Had he not known he and Eden were fighting, Brandon might have commiserated, but now?

"We're *all* busy," she said. "In fact, you've done so much since you've been here. You must be exhausted."

"It hasn't been too bad, actually. It's like a working vacation."

"Yes, but are you really resting? You were kind enough to come down, so you should take advantage of all the perks of Heart Resort. Put yourself first while you're here."

"Yes, Mom," he quipped and released a breath when she tugged him closer.

In contrast to the outside, the vibe inside the restaurant was colorful and festive, with music piping through the speakers. A sign above the front podium read SALT & SUGAR, and when the delicious smells from the kitchen reached his nose, his mouth watered.

Eden unfurled her arm from Brandon's. "We always sit in the back." She sidestepped through the half-full dining room, then out to the patio. Bulb lights hung from the pergola, and beyond the deck railing was the shimmering sound. There, they were greeted by Gil and the girls and Beatrice. Everyone stood and gave each other hugs and kisses as if they all didn't live on the same peninsula. Their voices rose above the sound of the wind and water. Brandon was sure they were causing a scene.

Honestly, this exuberance was the best thing about their family, and he attributed it to their Filipino-ness. Though their parents had been private in their own ways, in public spaces, they'd celebrated each and every small thing as if they'd won the lottery. They'd responded to news with excitement. They'd been overt in their hospitality, and none of it was fake. Perhaps it was a cultural trait, maybe generational, but despite all the threads that sometimes were pulled taut in the relationships within their family, it was all excused during these events.

Everything—all of it—centered around food.

It had been a grounding thing for Brandon that Chris and Gil had taken it upon themselves to make these Friday dinners mandatory even after their parents had died; he'd loved the weekly routine. It had become so important to him that even when three-fourths of the family had moved to North Carolina, Brandon had still taken himself out. Before his big confrontation with Chris, they'd met on video chat or sent pictures of their food. It was a tradition he couldn't kick even if he tried.

To be here with them, at this Friday dinner, was a boon despite his topsy-turvy day.

Beatrice gave him a high five, grasping his fingers. "What's up, Bunso?"

"Nothing much." He dipped his chin.

Then she stepped aside to reveal Geneva, already seated.

"Hey," he croaked.

"Brandon." Her face was unreadable, though it changed suddenly when Eden came from behind him to hug her. The stark difference of her greeting was a stab to the heart, but he pushed it down. They were in public. He couldn't expect her to jump him and stick her tongue down his throat.

"I ordered for everyone already. You guys took so long," Gil said. "You know the girls' timeline. If we can't be out in an hour, all hell breaks loose."

"Who, these angels?" Brandon took the seat next to Kitty, grateful that his attention would go toward someone who considered him pretty cool. Kitty had already broken half her crayons and was coloring her place mat with such fervor that the crayon was being ground into a nub.

"Angels, right!"

"No fear, Tito Brandon's here. The fun uncle." He picked up a crayon and joined his niece in her endeavor to color the entire place mat. "Unlike these old heads, huh, girls? Enunciate with me. Old. Heads."

"Old heads," Izzy announced.

"Dinosaurs," he whispered.

Kitty roared.

"Nice," Gil said. "They'll return to their mother growling their requests."

Brandon winked for effect. With a quick glance, he caught Geneva looking at him, though she swiftly shifted her gaze.

At some point four years ago, he'd begun to envision this very scene—the both of them with his family, with, perhaps, their own. Was it foolish to hope for it?

Had he always been foolish? He'd never once thought that he'd have to live life without his parents, that his brother would choose someone over him in a conflict. To expect a woman to stay after a fling . . .

Brandon colored with greater fervor.

"I beg to differ," Beatrice added, an eyebrow plunged downward. "Jessie will be getting back girls who are well adjusted after spending quality time with their family, unlike how they were being doted on by a nanny who fed them nothing but those fish crackers."

Chris tsked.

"All right, we don't have to go there," Gil said pointedly.

The table quieted.

"Awkward," Brandon whispered. This—this was new. The last Brandon had heard, there was an agreement drawn between the two families to keep the feud peaceful so the girls wouldn't be pressured to choose.

"Eden," Geneva asked with perfect timing. "How are things going with your book? I'm always so curious how you get your words. Three books a year. That's a lot of writing."

Thank goodness for the distraction, because Brandon was starting to sweat. Beatrice was like their mother, in that she kept life light until she didn't and every single person around her felt it.

"Oh, thank you for asking. Yes. Um." Eden, eyes wide, caught on to the charade to neutralize the environment. She discussed her research for her upcoming book and then her drafting plan, using an app to map out her word count in an oscillating pattern so she could have rest days.

Not only did her soliloquy drag Gil and Beatrice from whatever drama they were having, but 100 percent of the adults at the table were paying rapt attention, including Brandon.

"I can't imagine sitting there all those hours, Eden," he said. "I need to be outside, in the sun. And literally pushing things around instead of words."

"Yeah, we know about Bran and words," Chris said, eyes alight with humor.

"Did you even go to English class, Bunso?" Gil asked.

"Ha ha. So I admit I wasn't so great in English class," Brandon mumbled.

"Not . . ." Beatrice coughed in between the words. "In . . . any . . . class . . ."

The table roared, and Brandon's face warmed, not out of embarrassment but from the realization that this was a family joke.

That *he* was the butt of the family joke despite being away from it for a couple of years.

Which was something. And on this day, when he was reminded all his relationships were in precarious positions, he would take it.

CHAPTER SIXTEEN

Geneva's lips were sore from laughing. The nonstop banter, spiced with the combination of sarcasm, corny dad jokes, and old stories, lifted her spirits. By the end of the main course—a combination of inihaw na bangus, pinakbet, bistek, grilled vegetables, and steamed rice—her belly was full of homestyle Filipino cuisine, and her heart brimmed with a contentment she hadn't felt in a long time.

How had she gone so long without this? How had she dampened her need for this? Her days hadn't been idle. She'd filled them with what she loved—work.

But this—being with all these people—was different.

All through dinner, she tried to find the word for it. *Simple* didn't convey the deep ties she had with them. *Nostalgic* didn't give proper value to how much these people meant to her today. *Easy* was a complete lie, because her friendships with each of these family members were hard earned.

And then there was Brandon, who was sitting two seats over and across from her, who was entrenched in this joy. He reflected exactly what she was feeling, with his unyielding laughter and relaxed posture.

Geneva could feel her defenses dissolving. Goodness, just watching Brandon interact with his nieces brought down every single one of her barriers. His jovial nature was on full display in front of them. She wasn't a believer in a woman's biological clock. But were her ovaries aching? Yes.

It's incestuous.

Chris's words rushed back, and Geneva coughed. She choked on her own spit, and she brought her glass of water to her lips.

"Oh my God, are you okay?" Beatrice laughed as she patted her back.

She fanned her fingers against her chest. "Yep." She caught Brandon's inquisitive expression, and her face heated. Incest wasn't the problem between them, nor was the fact that he was her best friend's little brother—though that was problematic, obviously, for Chris. This was about where Brandon belonged in her life. He was in the past, and perhaps it had been easy to fall back into this . . . situation . . . because it was physically comfortable between them. But that didn't mean they belonged in the future.

They had to speak and figure out the way ahead, especially with Beatrice's proposal hanging in the balance. A lifestyle brand was a major effort, and it would be a challenge; Geneva loved a challenge. Just the thought of being in creative control made her giddy. But she was on her own current trajectory, her own journey, which was six years in the making with projects lined up at least for the next year. To walk away, even if it was toward a business that was located at the beach and with her most favorite people, would be setting aside everything she'd built that was already a success.

Geneva hadn't been able to give Beatrice an answer today, and her friend hadn't fussed. But she knew she would want an answer soon.

First things first: Brandon.

The next time Brandon's gaze darted her way, Geneva channeled a message of *follow me* with her eyes, then drank a long sip of water. "Restroom time," she announced, though everyone was deep into dessert plates of leche flan. She pushed her chair back, then headed toward the cavernous hallway that led to two restrooms.

Chef Paula Castillo had just stepped out from the restroom on the left side, tugging her chef's jacket straight. She looked up in surprise. Her lips were bare, cheeks with just the right amount of rouge. Her blue-black hair was pulled tight into a bun on the top of her head. "Oh, hello. Is everything going well?"

Geneva stepped out of her way; the woman's voice was loud. "Yes, it was all delicious. I'm just so impressed at everything. This place, it's so unassuming, but as soon as you enter—wow. And the view."

"I'll definitely let Chef Priscilla know."

Yep, her voice could be classified as *outdoor*.

"Oh, it's not your place?" Geneva asked.

"No, this is Pris's, my twin sister's. I only come to lend a hand on the weekends. Our parents do the cooking during the week. Though *Salty and Sweet* represents the two of us. Do you want to guess who I am?"

"Ah . . ." Geneva hesitated, and winced. This sounded like a trick question, sort of like *guess how old I am*. "Um, sweet?"

"Yep! Even if *she's* the pastry chef." She beamed. "Anyway. Back to work! Our bathrooms are gender neutral, and the right one is free."

That last sentence, if rated in volume, was an eight.

Geneva thanked her and slipped down the hallway but didn't go into the bathroom. Instead, she leaned against the wall, hoping that Brandon got the hint and wasn't scared off by Chef Castillo's strange declarations. And speaking of—hadn't she come from the left restroom door?

Maybe Geneva had misheard.

Across from her, on the wall, were black-and-white photos in a mishmash of frames hung in random fashion. The common things among the photos were pictures of Chef Castillo and of a woman who looked exactly like her in features, though had a different hairstyle. Or perhaps one was the other?

The connection was undeniable between them. Upon closer inspection, everyone else in the photos appeared to be related too. It dawned on her—these were family pictures, much like the ones her mother displayed proudly on the refrigerator door with magnets that she'd picked up from souvenir shops.

At the memory, an ache began in her heart. The fun she'd felt out there with the Pusos, and these pictures on the wall of the Castillo family? Geneva could have that. She could have all of this: Friday dinners, the Pusos, the Atlantic, Heart Resort, and Beachy. Hell, she could have and be with her parents anytime. A bedroom remained free for her to use, without notice.

Was that what she wanted? Or did she want to keep living the life she'd been living, which wasn't awful by any means? Her everyday affection was channeled toward design and Luna, and even then, the cat demanded her attention whenever she faltered. Life on the road, checking those boxes, treading lightly, was exciting—it was fulfilling in its own way.

If she'd hung on to people, if she'd stayed in one place, what could she have accomplished?

The hallway darkened, grabbing Geneva's attention; she turned toward the shadow.

Brandon.

Geneva sighed in relief.

As he approached her, she picked up a hint of his cologne. It was sweet, like him, through and through. She turned to face him fully. Every doubt and negative emotion she'd entertained slipped away. She felt herself light up at his presence, drawn to him immediately.

Brandon pulled her deeper into the hallway. Steps away was the entrance to the storage closet. "I've been wanting to get you alone all day. I missed you. And this dress."

"You like it?" The fact that Brandon noticed everything was also such a turn-on, and she basked in it. She looped her fingers in Brandon's jeans, bringing him close. With her back against the wall, he covered her with his body, hers fitting into his like a key into a lock.

It felt so right.

He nudged her nose with his; she detected a hint of citrus from the lemonade. They kissed, chaste at first, but one, five, ten seconds passed, and it flipped to a fervent need. Geneva wanted more.

She groaned. "You know exactly what to do to me." She pressed her torso against his.

He lifted her leg, making her gasp. Her flowing skirt draped backward. "Like this?"

"Yes. Yes." She moaned at the slide of his hand up her thigh, and she fisted his shirt, bringing him closer. Her lips crashed into his, and soon she was lost in his taste, in his arms, which held her steady.

The echo of dishes clattering from the kitchen broke their kiss. Brandon's face was hot, his breaths heavy, and knowing she did that to him revved her up. She wanted to revisit all the things she could elicit with her touch.

But a random voice from afar halted her running thoughts. She took the moment to breathe, to bring some oxygen into her brain. She'd called Brandon alone for a reason, and it wasn't to make out with him, even if her body was going rogue.

"We really shouldn't be doing this," she said with a swallow, as bits of her wit returned to her. Strands of hair had fallen out of her bun, and a few were stuck to her cheeks.

"I know. Chris and everyone are out there."

"No. I mean, this wasn't why I asked you to come meet me."

He ran his hand through his hair. "Damn."

"I mean, I loved . . . that . . ." She stood from the wall, and the excitement from their kiss flipped to dread. She hadn't actually planned it this far; she really should have thought about what she wanted to say. But his expression begged an explanation, so she heaved a breath and allowed her instincts to take over. "I love all of it. I can't get enough of you. I can't stop when I'm around you. But we can't keep doing this—you know that, right?"

"You said that before."

"Yes, but this time I mean it. I can't deny that I'm attracted to you. In fact the more time we spend together, the more I want to be alone with you, like this. But none of our situation has changed. You're still you with your goals, and I'm still me with mine."

Geneva had cut right to the heart of it, but after Beatrice's proposal, it was evident that she had choices to make: a new career with Beachy, or a solid, reliable life as Harris Interiors. Fall back to once again playing house with Brandon, or move forward in a professional relationship. Though she was still unsure about Beachy, in Brandon's case, forward was the only option.

Brandon took a step back, and with it, the temperature dropped. Seconds passed. "I don't know what to say."

"Say you're not mad," she pleaded. "Say you don't regret it. Agree with me that we got a little ahead of ourselves. But we can push through this. Because all those people out there are depending on us."

"So . . . no regrets, then?"

She looked back up at the pictures over Brandon's shoulder to focus her thoughts. "No, no regrets." Geneva reached out for his hand, heart dropping, the truth an anvil. "I'm s—"

He shook his head, though he took her hand. "Don't apologize. I had a feeling from your texts . . . though I'd hoped . . . I don't know what I hoped. But you're right. We tried once to keep it simple."

Relief pulsed through her. "There's no such thing as simple." Yet, even as she said it, she knew that they'd had a choice back then, and they had a choice now. They were that much older; they were more self-aware.

But at the heart they were still the same people.

"Especially not here on Heart Resort." He heaved a breath. "Are we okay?"

"Yes." Then she said with more conviction, "Yes, we are totally okay. I don't want to lose you, Brandon. That was the worst part about breaking up last time."

He nodded, understanding in his eyes. "I don't want to lose you either." He squeezed her hand, and it was like another hug. Geneva leaned into him, wrapping her arms around his torso. He kissed the top of her head, and she felt his entire body exhale.

The left-side bathroom door opened, and the squeak threw Geneva and Brandon apart. Geneva laced her hands together, still feeling the warmth of Brandon's skin.

A man walked out. He looked familiar, but she could not place him.

"Mike?" Brandon asked.

The contractor. Geneva's gaze dropped to the floor. She turned her face away. How much had he heard? Had he been in the bathroom all that time?

The right one is free.

"Hey, uh, nice to see you both. I'm actually just heading out." Mike gave a limp salute and stepped out of the hallway, then out the front door.

"That was weird," Brandon said.

The pieces of the puzzle locked in. Geneva covered her mouth with a hand, though it couldn't contain the giggle rising from her chest.

"What's so funny?" Brandon asked.

"I swear, Bran. Sometimes you can't make this stuff up."

♡

Geneva watched the sun set as they drove north on 12 to Heart Resort; the earth was bathed with the last bit of light. She ended up in the back seat of Chris's Suburban with Eden after their group had shuffled like a deck of cards. Chris and Brandon were both in the front seats and in some sort of heated discussion.

Next to her, Eden furiously thumbed on her notes app. "Sorry I'm being so rude. I have to get this out." The screen lit her face, showing her full concentration.

"It's okay. Been there, done that." Geneva grinned. It was admirable, her ambition.

With a final push on the screen, Eden raised her face with a smile. "Chapter twenty-five is done."

"Impressive."

"Thank you." She pressed her fingers back to stretch them. "This book is due in a month—which feels like far away, but it isn't, especially with all the resort stuff going on."

"What do you have to do for the reopening?"

"Just be a plus-one. Smile, be sweet. Act like the perfect couple."

Her sarcastic tone sent up warning signals. Curiosity nagged at Geneva, but while she was close with Beatrice, she and Eden were still surface-level friends.

Everyone knew what happened to the curious.

"Speaking of acting like the perfect couple." Eden's eyes slid right to the guys up front. "I hear you two have a photo shoot tomorrow."

"Yeah, I guess we do. It's supposed to be pretty PG. Just us looking at the sunrise. No biggie."

"It *could* be a biggie. It's a perfect setup for a rom-com."

"What setup?"

"A close-proximity, best-friend's-younger-brother romance? Oooh, that's good inspiration right there. Hold that thought." Eden woke her phone, and she typed feverishly. "Older woman, younger man. It can be funny but angsty. There will be deep-seated issues that won't make it easy for the couple to get together."

"Oh, wow." Geneva blinked back. Eden was sharp.

"Easy on who?" Chris peered at them through the rearview mirror.

Eden rolled her eyes. "No one."

"Oh, I thought you were talking about yourself being easy on me. I can't seem to do anything right." His eyes flickered to the front as the car rumbled over the resort's land bridge.

"Hmm, perhaps simply listening to the needs of others is a good first step in doing something right."

An uncomfortable heat rose in the van, and as silence permeated the vehicle, with Eden looking straight ahead with a deadpan expression, and now with Chris's eyes solely on the windshield, Geneva counted the seconds.

Something was up between the two lovebirds, and she didn't want to be around to see it.

It wasn't as if Geneva avoided these uncomfortable emotions. Scratch that—yes, she avoided them, but only because she couldn't help fix them. Geneva only wanted to spend her headspace on things she could change, on factual, tangible items that could be revised. That had been the story of Geneva's life.

With emotions—she only dealt with them to a degree, because at some point, problems recycled themselves and were hopeless to fix.

Much like with her and Brandon. Keeping it simple wouldn't have worked at all; history had taught them otherwise. Four years ago, what was supposed to be a weekend in Annapolis after the wedding had turned into seven days, then twenty-one. She and Brandon had gone from eating out to eating in, from getting takeout to cooking at home, then from shopping for clothes to doing laundry together.

Turned out, playing house brought out *feelings*. It increased expectations. Soon, making love had no longer masked the conversations that they weren't having. They couldn't *not* talk about family. They couldn't not talk about the future. Then what had been a fantasy had slowly peeled back like unsealed paint, into what was underneath: real life and responsibilities.

The SUV rocked as Chris parked it, and Geneva bade a quick goodbye and exited the vehicle. The humid air was a relief.

Only Brandon met her at the back of the truck.

"Are they coming?" she asked.

"I . . . don't think so." He ran a hand through his hair, then glanced behind him. "Let's get out of here. I think they need more privacy beyond the SUV."

"You don't have to tell me twice."

"Can I take you home? I don't see your golf cart here."

Temptation pulled at Geneva. She was exhausted after a long day, and the scant half mile on the pedestrian shortcut to her house would be hell on her sandal-clad feet. The humidity was punishing despite the sunset.

But, she had too much in her head. Tomorrow would begin bright and early, and the ocean air would do her good so she could sleep on time tonight.

"No, I'm good. I'm going to walk."

Brandon opened his mouth to say something, then, as if thinking twice, shut it. He nodded. He hooked an arm around her neck for a quick hug. "See you tomorrow, Harris."

Geneva squeezed his body tight, and in her hug she hoped that all her complicated feelings were communicated. Despite her monologue in that restaurant hallway, her biggest fear was that if she didn't watch it, that next trope and book Eden was typing out would be about them.

CHAPTER SEVENTEEN

Day 6
Weather: cloudy, 80°F
Hurricane Oscar: tropical storm, southeast Florida

Brandon:

Rise and shine!

Geneva blinked awake when her phone buzzed, and squinted at the sun shining through her window. She patted her bed for her phone, and a frisson of excitement rode up her spine, as she knew full well who the text was from.

She bit against her cheek as she texted back.

Geneva:

No.

We've still got 20 minutes.

Brandon:

Eighteen, actually.

Geneva:

I'm warm in my bed.

Brandon:

I have coffee.

Geneva sat up.

Geneva:

Good coffee?

Brandon:

Yep.

Geneva:

Fine.

Brandon:

And I've got good news.

Geneva:

What is it?

Brandon:

You're going to have to get here to find out.

Geneva kicked off her covers.

Geneva:

What are you wearing?

I want to match.

Brandon:

Jeans and a button down white shirt.

Bleary eyed, twelve minutes later, Geneva stumbled out of her beach house in one of her new caftans and climbed into her golf cart. Five minutes after that, she was on the northwest shore of Heart Resort and trudged toward Brandon, who clutched a cup of coffee in each hand, energy radiating off him. Tammy was farther down, toward the shore, and fiddled with her professional camera.

Upon seeing Geneva, Tammy raised her hand in an enthusiastic wave.

"How are you both so happy?" Geneva asked. She might be glad to be there, but her body rebelled at each step. She felt like she was moving in slow motion. God, she hoped she could smile for pictures.

"It's called sleep."

She grumbled. "I slept. Though not till about one in the morning."

"Ah. I hit the sack by ten." Brandon heaved a breath as if the air had additional life force. He handed her a cup.

Geneva didn't even have the energy for that. She wrapped her hands around the cup, grasping onto the first threads of cheer.

She did, however, notice that the first button of Brandon's shirt was unbuttoned, and she could see the upper part of his torso. Around his wrists were a couple of handmade beaded bracelets haphazardly tied with string, probably from his nieces. It was a combination that made her insides flutter.

"Why were you up?" he asked, startling her out of her imagination. "Did it take you that long to walk home?"

"No." Last night, the walk that she'd hoped would tire her out had energized her. She'd ended up knocking off a few things on her to-do list. She grinned. "Did some coordinating with a client who happened to be a night owl too. My client after Heart Resort."

"Right after?"

She nodded, her timeline materializing in her head. With it came the unending list of inherent tasks, along with a tinge of dread. She bit her lip, willing it away—she was just being grumpy, a side effect of being undercaffeinated. She sipped her coffee and sat with the heavenly, bitter taste on her tongue. With it, more words processed in her brain. "There's about a week in between this project and the next one, but many of the decisions need to be made ahead of time. Hopefully there won't be a truck fire like we had to deal with."

"God, I hope not." He gave her the side-eye. "Despite you still being in bed fifteen minutes ago, you clean up nice, Harris."

"You don't look half-bad yourself," she said, pretending not to care. Inside, she thanked Beatrice for intuiting that she'd need something fresh in her wardrobe rotation. "Though you're maybe a slight bit too chipper."

"I've got something that'll put a pep in your step."

"Yeah?" She stood straighter.

"How do you feel about modern dinnerware and fresh linens for the restaurant? New exterior paint job and, depending on what you had in mind for the interior, new paint and light fixtures."

"What?" Geneva woke, for real. Forget the coffee; this was like a jolt of IV caffeine. "How did you manage that? Chris barely agreed to Lainey coming."

He shrugged. "We had a talk last night."

"And he agreed, just like that?"

"I think he's trying, you know?"

Geneva nodded, impressed at Brandon's empathy. "Maybe it's good that we agreed to the pictures, then? All of us meeting in between."

"I'm still shocked you said yes to this. With the way you were with Tammy that first day—"

"Is it weird to say that this feels different?" Geneva squinted up at him. "This photo shoot is planned, and it doesn't feel quite as intimidating. My dad took a ton of pictures of me, but I had warning. He asked before he snapped. And, I got to pick the photo for him to use for our albums or to send to people. It's the candids, the unexpected, the posting, that I don't like."

"Ah, choice." Brandon nodded.

"Yeah, I guess." Geneva was reminded of the choice she would have to make soon, about Beachy. As she'd worked last night, she hadn't been able to come up with an answer. Pros and cons didn't seem to apply, because so much of this decision was about who she thought she would be a decade, two decades, three decades from today.

Tammy walked their way. "All right, you two. Ready? I already started to take photos. See?" She leaned her camera closer and flipped through images of them chatting as if they were sharing an intimate secret. "You both have such great chemistry—and so photogenic too." Her face twisted in a wince. "I hope that I didn't put you both in a spot by asking for couples photos. You just have an oomph. Those teaser pics on social media? They've been shared and liked because you look good together. Natural, you know?"

Hovering over the camera, Geneva raised her eyes to Brandon, who had a sad smile on his face.

Her heart twinged with remorse. Yes, Geneva definitely knew.

"You're good at this, Tammy," Brandon said, eyes flickering over to the other woman.

Tammy's shoulders drooped. "Thank you. I appreciate that. PR is my position, but photography is my specialty. I've loved it since high school." Tammy thumbed a few buttons on top of the camera. "Awesome . . . the sun is at the perfect spot. Let's get a little bit closer to the water."

They followed her toward where the grass turned to sand. "I'd like to take a few of you looking out into the water, with the pier in the background—you'll have to wrap your arms around each other. Is that okay?"

Brandon looked upon Geneva to answer.

"Yep, just fine," Geneva said.

Tammy's face lit up. "Great! And then . . . can I put my hands on you both?"

They both nodded.

Tammy guided them by the elbows. "Please look at one another . . . yep, that's it. Geneva, look up at him . . . raise a hand here. Yep, now lean your foreheads together. Great. So versions of this, and when I say to raise your heads, just step back, but still have your hands intertwined like this . . ."

If either the news about the restaurant or the coffee hadn't woken Geneva up, the posing would. Brandon's closeness, the touch of his skin against hers, his gaze, slightly shy. It all made her body hum.

Geneva was grateful for the warm wind, which she could blame for the uptick of her internal temperature.

"Got it?" Tammy asked. "You know what to do?"

"Mm-hmm," Brandon said, with a slight tilt of his lips. "Do *you* know what to do?"

Geneva's entire body lit on fire with his adorable expression, but she countered. *Deflection, Geneva, deflect!* "Look, *I* think that if there's anyone here who can handle a few directions, it's me."

Brandon laughed.

Tammy ran back to where they had been standing. "All right, make that magic happen, you two." She lifted the camera to her face.

Brandon's eyebrow went up. "Magic. What do you think she means by that?"

It was an innocent question, but their history put that sentence in a different context. "Not in the ways you're thinking, Puso."

His eyes flashed.

"Heads together, you guys!" Tammy said. "Like you like each other."

She and Brandon burst into a fit of giggles.

"If she only knew," Brandon whispered.

Geneva cleared her throat against this truth.

As the seconds passed, Geneva wondered how they appeared from afar. It was unnerving, because her best side was her left side, and Tammy was shooting from her right side. Did she look all right?

Her thoughts trailed to her father, and sadness tugged inside of her. She really missed him. He had this talent of bringing out the best in people, and it showed in the photographs he took.

Doubt seeped in. At her decision to not make more of an effort to visit her parents. And now, with Tammy, should Geneva have worn more makeup? Maybe this caftan didn't look good on her after all. "Tammy needs an assistant to give us encouragement or something. Is she even snapping pics? I don't hear the click of the camera."

"Hey." Brandon let go of her hands and rested them on her waist. "Let it go."

She settled, his words taking effect. She placed her hands on his hips, stepping into him so their torsos touched. "You're right."

He bent so their foreheads touched. "You okay?"

She nodded, heart returning to a steady beat. "I just want to do things right."

The sides of his cheeks crinkled upward. "I know. That's your thing."

"My thing."

"Yep. You see most things as opportunities, and you just go for it. It's why you have your lists, your calendars, your rules. You don't do anything halfway, and that is part of why you move on. But it's also what makes you great, because you don't falter, Geneva. You're what makes the world turn."

Geneva's heart splintered, because she read his mixed emotions on his face.

She pressed against his chest to squeeze a smile out of him. Their decision not to take things further was the correct one, and they both had to remember that. "You are the ultimate encourager—officially. I've decided."

He half laughed, and the sound was music to her ears. "That's good, right?"

She looked up at him, pleased to see him grinning at her. "Brandon. It's not people like me who make the world go; it's people like you, who are the foundation." Geneva tallied Brandon's qualities, often overlooked. Brandon made up for many of the things she lacked, and she wanted to make sure that even if they weren't going to be together, he knew how special he was. "You think of other people first. You make them laugh, make them stop and smell the roses. I think that sometimes I, and maybe other people, can take that for granted. You don't ask for enough, to be thought of first, but I see you. You are better than good."

Movement ensued on their left, and they both looked at Tammy, who was sidestepping and making motions with her arms.

"I think she wants us to step apart," Geneva said, clearing her throat. Still, her heart ached at her outpour. She hadn't expected to say all of that.

"Let's do it."

With fingers interlocked, they stepped back.

"I appreciate . . . you saying that, Gen."

"I meant every word." She looked into his eyes, at the vulnerability in them. "I don't want you to get a big head over it."

He laughed, glancing down for a beat.

It was endearing, sweet.

"Speaking of a big head, are you down to give Tammy a run for her money?" he asked.

She peered at him then. His voice had taken a mischievous tone. "I have no idea what you're getting at."

"How about a recreation of our first dance?"

It took a few seconds to piece together what he was implying. "No. *Noooo.*"

"Sure?" He took both of Geneva's hands into his. "You were pretty arrogant when we were paired up. God, we practiced it for forever. And at the party . . ."

"The party was magnificent. The decor, the music, the food. Your sister's debut was perfect. But me, arrogant?"

"You literally strutted when the instructor put us front and center of the group for the dance program."

"No, I did not!" Geneva gasped. *Had* she been that rude?

"Yes, you did."

"Can you guys face the horizon?" Tammy called from far away.

"We're running out of time, Gen. C'mon, you know you wanna."

She and Brandon turned toward the water, holding hands. He was daring her, and when she glanced at his mischievous profile, everything about that night came into full photographic memory.

It was Beatrice's debut, her Filipino, grand wedding-scale eighteenth birthday, and Geneva was one of eighteen of her girlfriends who'd each carried a candle to the center table, all dressed in various versions of a taffeta navy-blue dress. They'd each been partnered with someone—and she'd been partnered with Brandon. *Stuck with Brandon* was what she'd thought at the time, since he was that much younger.

But he'd become the best dancing partner, in the traditional waltz, the cha-cha, and the tango, and that was before the DJ had taken over the music. Brandon had rhythm.

"I haven't ballroom danced in forever," she said.

"Don't worry; I'll lead."

Brandon had led back then too. While all the other guys had noodle arms, Brandon, in his quiet way, had taken charge. He'd made her, for a moment, feel like she could rest.

Geneva looked up at the sky and envisioned the steps, the three-count move of the waltz. Then, as if he read her mind, Brandon spun her out, then tugged her back into position. And with a gesture of his head, he pushed off to the first step.

With his cheesy smile, she was unable to contain her own joy. Did she imagine she was in the movie *Step Up*? For a moment, yes she did.

Ballroom dancing was an art of cooperation. It was the combination of trusting your partner's strength and mirroring it. It had been a joke when they first were learning how to waltz; they had been a bunch of teenagers in a dance class, joking about succumbing and following and how the man *supposedly* led.

But she'd learned the nuances: a weak partner could cause the dance to fall apart. A stubborn partner's miscommunication could cause errors.

Geneva would not allow them to err in front of the camera. With a straight back she danced to the sound of the water, her internal metronome, and Brandon's lead.

Slowly, her embarrassment fell away. Her spotlight attention focused on their movements, on the push-and-pull relationship that had started when they were eighteen and sixteen. On a bond that continued to this day. A bond of teamwork, connection, friendship, and love.

Love, because that was what she felt for Brandon at the heart of it, and respect.

It was what led her back to him, despite her best efforts to stay away.

Someone clapped, bringing Geneva back to the present. She was tipped back into a dip, with Brandon's handsome face above hers. Except he was looking off to the side.

At Chris and Beatrice, Chet, and Sal.

Geneva swallowed down her lingering giddiness. With a swift pull she was back up straight; she fixed her clothing.

Next to her, Brandon bowed, proud of himself.

But all Geneva could see was Beatrice's curious expression.

♡

A video call from Nita took Geneva out of the group that formed after the photo shoot. It had been ten minutes since Tammy had passed her camera around to show off the dozens of photos and a long string of video.

It had been ten minutes of awkwardness and strange emotions.

"You have perfect timing," she said to Nita.

"I aim to please." Nita shuffled the papers in front of her. "I've got a couple of things to go over."

"Go ahead."

"First thing: For Helena's B and B, I received the list of furniture items confirmed for availability. They'll ship in the next few days."

"Great."

"Second, the CEO of Foster's Hotel Group prefers an in-person versus video-chat conversation and sent over their availability. They made it clear that they're very interested, and they're eager for you to be part of the team."

"Sounds good. I'll take a look at my calendar today." In front of her, Chris, Chet, and Sal climbed into their golf carts, Brandon into his. He turned and waved. She returned the greeting, and with a smile watched as he left the area.

A flood of warmth covered her from head to toe. That photo shoot had been comfortable and romantic and deep all at once. He'd calmed her down, encouraged her, made her laugh. With him, she had no problem giving up more of herself, or more of her control, even if it was for just a set of photos.

They had another shoot planned the next morning, this time with them frolicking in the waves. Would they need to be in swimsuits? Would she be able to keep herself from ogling him?

But all her thoughts promptly fell by the wayside when she noticed everyone had left except for Beatrice, who was sitting in her cart with the phone against her ear.

"Geneeeeva," Nita said.

"Yes, I'm still here. Sorry."

"Foster's Hotel Group has a stipulation regarding your arrival time."

"All right." She clicked onto her iPad calendar app.

"You'll need to leave four days from now."

Her Apple Pencil hovered over the screen. "Whoa. Why?"

"The CEO is heading overseas and won't be returning for about a month, around the time when they would want to begin work."

"This would rush me through Helena's B and B."

"Yep."

Geneva blew out a breath and leaned back against the seat of the golf cart. In her head, the days clashed along with her priorities, her wants and needs. If she took this interview with Foster's, that would mean she only had four days left on property. Four days to get everything done on these houses. Four days of being next to the salt water, and being with people she loved. Four days to be with Brandon, who, despite their back-and-forth, made her happy.

Leaving Heart Resort early was also a definitive decision . . . to not take Beatrice's offer. And not taking Beatrice's offer meant saying no to a new opportunity to design for herself.

Herself.

The more Geneva thought about the possibility to come up with original design, to perhaps be the provider of inspiration rather than the one executing it, the more it tempted her. But could she give her business up? There were also other repercussions, like letting go of Nita.

No, you can rehire Nita for Beachy.

"You don't look excited. I thought you'd be jumping at the chance." Nita interrupted her train of thought.

She shook her head to wake herself. What was she thinking? Foster's was *a chain*. She altered her expression. "Foster's Group is playing hardball with the timeline."

"You know the big dogs always do. In looking at the calendar, you can adjust your week break in between the resort and Helena's B and B, and that will give you enough time to transfer to Foster's Group."

Geneva nodded, but despite her best efforts to be motivated by this challenge, the thought of that alone made her bones weary. "One to another, and another."

"You've done it before."

Yes, she'd done it before. And successfully. But right then, looking at the water, and then at her best friend waiting for her, it felt less like an opportunity and more like she was being cornered.

"Geneva? This doesn't sound like you. By now you would have plugged everything in your calendar." Nita placed the papers down and brought the phone closer. "Hey. Tell me."

"It's nothing."

She crossed her arms. "I don't believe you, and I'm not going to schedule your flight until you tell me what's up."

"Hate to break it to you, but I can schedule my own flight."

"Ah, but if there's one thing I know about you, Ms. 'I Don't Know My Frequent Flyer Number,' it's that you hate administrative details. You wouldn't last ten minutes doing research for rates—it's why you hired me in the first place."

Geneva sighed. Audibly. Loudly.

On the other end, Nita imitated her.

Geneva lowered her voice. "All right, it's just that . . . I've been feeling . . . out of sorts."

Nita leaned into the screen and whispered in turn, "But I thought you were loving it there."

Was it love? Or was it just different? Being at the beach, her first time designing tiny homes, designing with antiques, a spark of something with Brandon, and a partnership offer. "Being out here is making me wonder if I'm simply on a hamster wheel."

"Not a wheel. It's called a career, a job, a business. Must I remind you that Foster's Group is the opportunity you've been waiting for? Must I repeat your words? Nothing stands in the way of Harris Interiors."

What Geneva could only describe as heartburn swirled in her chest. Because Nita was right. Foster's was the epitome of her next step. Working this project would open up more opportunities.

"Can I ask you a personal question?" Nita asked.

Geneva smiled at this. "You know most everything about me."

A pensive smile appeared on her face. "Okay then. Does this have anything to do with the guy in the photos?" Nita waved the words away. "Let's put a pin on that for a second and let me say on the record that you have appeared on our social media probably four times the last year; yet, in six days you appeared on Heart Resort's social media eight times. Does all of this—this entire change of heart—have anything to do with that guy?"

"Brandon Puso."

"Even more interesting. A Puso."

Geneva thought about it, remembering the first day she'd arrived at the resort. How she'd felt her entire body exhale, and that was before she'd known Brandon was around. "No, not in that way. It's just that I am, for lack of a better word, tired." She winced at her words. Saying it felt like she was admitting defeat, especially when she was surrounded by people—Nita, the Pusos, the Heart Resort staff, even the retailers and vendors she dealt with—who hustled. Who was she to be tired, when everyone was working? She avoided Nita's eyes.

Nita leaned back in her chair. "Hey, Geneva, look at me."

Geneva dragged her eyes to the screen.

"I know it took a lot to say that, and I commend you for it."

"I feel horrible."

"You shouldn't—"

"It's not like anyone is holding me to some standard. I work for myself."

"And yet, we are hardest on ourselves. You notice that I said 'we,' because you're not alone. You have to be a little type A to be an entrepreneur, a little bit of a hustler and a workaholic. It's huge to admit when you want to rest. What do you want to do?"

"I don't know."

She slapped the desk, lightly. "This is what *I'm* going to do, because I'm an amazing assistant. I'll set the flight in four days. Like you said, Foster's Group is negotiating. It's in your pocket to do what you want with it. But if I don't set the flight and you end up wanting to go, then it will be a bigger issue."

Geneva heaved a breath. "Thank you."

"Of course. And not to sound like I'm placating you or anything, but I'm proud of you."

"I don't feel proud."

"Then maybe a little rest is what you need. Because if you're not your best cheerleader . . . well . . . but I'm not going to lie, as someone who's worked with you for a couple years, I'm rooting for something to happen with this Brandon Puso. He's cute."

"Our families are too close."

"So you've thought of it. Interesting." Nita looked around as if being watched. "And can I tell you a secret? That families-too-close thing is an absolute weak excuse. You know that, right?"

This can only be temporary. I have a home to go to, to manage, and you . . .

The words she'd told Brandon four years ago rushed back. It had been a logical excuse. Was it relevant today?

"Look, I've no right to judge," Nita continued, "but I also know your travel patterns and . . . well . . ."

Geneva snorted. "Travel patterns? What am I, a bird?"

"Yes, for all intents and purposes. And your migratory patterns seem to veer away from commitment, except at this instance, when . . . maybe your subconscious knew that Brandon would be there."

"I don't want to talk about it anymore."

"See? A bird. Fly away."

"Nita, seriously."

"I am. As a heart attack. Sometimes you need to talk about it. Sit long enough to ruminate where it's uncomfortable." She thumbed her phone. She hummed a litany of opinions.

"What are you doing?"

"Going through the Heart Resort website. It looks like it's under construction."

"Yeah, about that." Geneva chose her words carefully and prepared herself for her friend's onslaught. "We're one of the models for the resort website."

"On the website!" Nita threw her hands up. "That's it, then. My expectation is for you to be involved from here on out. Not only for pictures, but videos"—she counted the list on her fingers—"and DIY tips, and day in the life. I can think of a million things we can do to amp this sleepy social media up. In fact, since it's taking a bit to scour through the applicants for your social media assistant, I'm going to start reposting these photos! Your clients need to know that you're working on such an exciting project. Anyway . . . you need to plug in."

"All right, all right, we'll talk about it. I won't promise anything, but yes," Geneva said.

"I don't even know what to say. Except that I'm hurt."

"Are you really?"

"No, I'm not—I'm irritated. But I'll table it since you're my boss, and I'm way more curious at what happens between you and Brandon."

Geneva spied at Beatrice, who was still chatting. There would be more to report to Nita once this was all said and done. She heaved a breath. "Thank you. For being, well, on it."

"It's what I do. Keep me posted on your decisions. I know it doesn't seem like it, but you have choices. We can move things around, and you can always say no."

But that was the problem. When it came to business, she rarely said no. Her father had taught her about the magic of yes; their family to-do list was the epitome of it. To say no to Foster's would be like stomping on the brakes, only to watch the world pass by. Then again, saying no to Beachy felt like bidding farewell to an entirely new career path.

After Geneva hung up with Nita, she stepped out of her golf cart. Beatrice was off the phone. "Hey, Bea." She kept her voice light as she climbed into her cart. "You didn't have to wait for me."

"My next meeting isn't until much later. Everything okay with work? That looked pretty serious."

"I just got a contract proposal for a job with a hotel chain." Geneva filled her in about all the details, and Beatrice listened with rapt attention.

"Wow."

Geneva avoided her eyes because Beatrice was surely putting all the pieces together. "I would have to leave earlier if I'm interested."

Her eyebrows plunged. "How much earlier?"

"In four days."

"That's . . . soon."

"I know."

"Have you decided?"

Geneva shook her head. She knew what Beatrice was alluding to—her offer for Geneva to stay. She shrugged. "It's a hard decision to make. There are so many loose threads."

Beatrice nodded, gravely, though she kept a smile on her face. "This is a huge deal."

"Huge. And . . . I feel like I'm in the same spot as you."

"You're debating what you ought to do versus what you want to do."

"Yes. I have built something. To leave it means . . . I don't know what that means in full. That alone is overwhelming. From the jump, it means having to figure out how to support myself." Geneva thought back to Rhiannon's question in the van the other day about college majors. Geneva's approach had been to put her body and soul into her studies, and even when she'd changed focus, she'd only done so when she could financially risk it. "Everything takes money. Others have the ability to take risks without consequences because there are backups in place, and I just don't have that. For me to pivot would mean that I have to be comfortable with someone's life raft nearby."

"I get it. I have three life rafts available, and I'm the life raft for others."

To be a person who everyone leaned upon was a responsibility that was both a privilege and a burden. "Our decisions are hard. In a perfect world—" Geneva started, and thought of her to-do list in that leather Traveler's notebook. She tried again. "In a perfect world, it would also be easy to achieve everything we set out to do."

Beatrice grinned. "We shouldn't even talk about the perfect world. It's not one. We have responsibilities."

"This is why I love you. We can dream and be real all in one conversation."

"And it's why I want you here all the time. But I understand, Gen. I know you'll make the right decision."

"Thank you."

"Since we're being real." Beatrice looked down for a beat. "I've been sitting here trying to figure out how I can talk to you about something. Not Beachy related."

"Just tell me."

"Promise not to take it the wrong way?"

"Promise."

"I think . . . I think my brother likes you." She shook her head. "I saw it today, at the photo shoot, and it makes sense, with the way he's been acting lately, so weird and giddy. Whenever he's around you, he simply lights up."

Geneva conjured up a blank expression, though panic ran through her. Beatrice continued to be the most important woman in her life aside from her mother, and she didn't want her to mistrust Geneva, or to be angry. "Are you sure?"

"Yes, I'm almost positive. I hate to even bring it up. I don't want for it to be awkward. The both of you are working together. I was all for this setup, for this fake-couple-for-pictures situation, but today it was apparent—this chemistry Tammy was talking about. No wonder your pictures are so good . . . in real life, you're a perfect fit. But now my brother's got a crush on you. And I . . . I can't tell if you like him back." She shook her head. "Do you? Like him?"

Geneva held her breath. She would not be able to lie around Beatrice, but what of it, at that moment, could she say? She formed her words carefully. "Of course I like Brandon. I love him, much like I love you. We have chemistry because we were dance partners at your debut. I lived in your house half of my high school life. He and I know each other for who we are." Saying it aloud was like a thunk against her chest. Because it was true, though it didn't mean they were meant to be. "That connection is what you see, Gen."

"You're right." Her face broke out into a relieved smile. "Okay, I just don't want you to feel any pressure. I know what happens when you do."

There was so much to unpack from the conversation, but her friend's last statement gave her pause. "What happens?"

"You get the hell out of here, and I don't want that to be the reason why you don't stay. For a time there, we lost touch."

"You mean after the wedding."

Beatrice nodded.

The lost months. With Geneva's breakup from Brandon, she'd naturally avoided Beatrice. She had been too much a reminder of him. The result was another breakup, though an unofficial one.

And there was one thing worse than a breakup with a love interest—it was a breakup with a best friend, even a temporary one.

"I'm sorry that happened. I was going through something," Geneva said.

"I don't mention it so you have to apologize. Nor do you even have to explain. Everyone needs their space sometimes. But here's the thing. If my suspicions are right, *and* my brother has a crush on you, it's only a matter of time before you like him back, because I just have a feeling, you know? Unless you end up married, you'll break up. And I don't want our family, which includes you, to break apart. We already went through it with Gil."

"Whoa, ease up on the gas," Geneva joked, though inside dread bloomed. Beatrice was verbalizing her own worry—she had laid out all the reasons why she and Brandon couldn't be together. There was too much at stake. The friendships, the connection, the future. Geneva couldn't believe that a second chance existed, because one couldn't go back and fix the past, could one? It was fruitless. What remained was learning from it and not making the same decisions. With a steady voice, she said, "The family won't break apart."

Beatrice heaved a breath and laid both hands on the steering wheel. "You're right. Okay. I'm sorry. I'm worried, and I don't know why. It all feels like we're on the verge of something. I'm picking up drama from everyone, and I'm not sure if I'm projecting my own indecision about Beachy."

"There's a lot going on, and it's emotional, and it's okay." Geneva leaned in to hug Beatrice and hoped it was enough to ease her worry.

But she knew that the hug wouldn't do a thing to assuage her own mixed feelings.

CHAPTER EIGHTEEN

"You're breaking up," Brandon said to his iPad, propped on the steering wheel of his golf cart. He was parked in the shade, steps from the yoga studio, from where the smell of wood stain mixed in with the cooking from Chef Castillo's food truck wafted in the air.

"Is this better?" Garrett came into focus on the screen. He was standing in one of the empty rooms of Illinois Way, wearing his usual, an oxford shirt with rolled-up sleeves and jeans. "My reception isn't great out here."

"My reception out here isn't that great either. You know, this probably would have been better if you properly scheduled the call with me. I wasn't expecting you to check in for another hour."

"I know, but I had a house to show in the neighborhood and thought, what the hell, right? Besides, I gotta catch you while I can."

"I suppose you're forgiven."

"So, how are things?"

"They are . . . complicated."

"With Ms. Harris? Do tell."

"That's the thing—there's almost nothing to tell, but it's not awful."

"That's vague."

"I know." Brandon reflected on it, on how good he felt with Geneva in his arms and yet completely understanding that nothing was to happen between them. "It feels hopeful even if there's nothing to shoot for."

"I can't say I understand. That, to me, means you're in limbo, but who am I to judge? I'm happy you're happy."

"*Happy* is an overused and probably an overrated word." Though the limbo comment wormed into his psyche. He tried to mentally pluck it out of his head.

"That is some fatalistic business." Garrett laughed. "Happiness just is. It doesn't need to be deep."

Brandon pressed his lips together and mulled. He and Garrett could wax theoretical all day long about happiness, about what was realistic and attainable. It made him a great business partner, because work was never just about numbers. "I don't know. Shouldn't the goal be happiness?"

"That's a high standard to keep, my friend. I agree to an extent that it's good to know what aids in achieving happiness, but the true goal, in my opinion, is joy."

Brandon snorted. "They are synonyms."

"Depends on the context. Anyway." He peered. "Do you know what can achieve both? Financial security."

Here it comes. "Garrett—"

"And that means unloading Mulberry Road."

Brandon dropped his chin into his chest.

"Have you talked to—"

"No, I haven't."

The rumble of a truck sounded, followed by Mike's dusty blue F-450. He stepped out and raised a hand, then pointed to the studio's open door, presumably to check on the crew's work.

He nodded and gave Mike a thumbs-up. Perfect timing. "Let's get started. My contractor's here."

"Yeah, I know when I've worn out my welcome." Garrett flipped his screen, and the camera tracked his exit to the outside. After a quick scan of the front circular driveway and the exterior of the home, he did a systematic walk-through of the indoors. On his iPhone, Brandon took notes.

The process took a quick twenty minutes, and Brandon foresaw a straightforward plan. He breathed a sigh of relief. "That's an incredible property."

Garrett was sitting on the front stoop, and behind him showed the breadth of the wraparound porch. "Right? And we got it below market value. The lot's small, probably half an acre, but coming up the drive, it feels isolated with the trees. Then the rear view of the river—that's what makes it special. We can go two ways, as with all our flips. We can go the easy way—fix the broken, slap paint on everything else—or we go custom."

Brandon winced at the truth bubbling inside of him. Because the house had all the markers of a success: big enough to accommodate a growing family, close enough to town, but far away for some seclusion, and most of all, it was cheap. "To be honest—"

"You love it, right?"

"I do, and—"

"I knew you would. Are you tempted, like I am, to go all the way?"

"I am, but—"

"But that's not smart." Garrett frowned and completed his thought, as was their way. "I agree. If this was a property any other time, we could do something magical with it. Right now with the economy, we need this flip to do well for us. But Bran."

"What's up."

"It's my turn to be honest. This could be my last flip. I've been thinking the last couple of days, man, and I can't do this alone. I know we touched on it a little when you left. Now that we're somewhat face to face, I need you to know that if this doesn't make money, or if you can't come to the table with more, I'm going to have to bail."

Brandon rubbed his forehead, the guilt sitting right there, up front and center. "I know I shouldn't have left without saying."

"Look, we're friends, Bran. I understand a lot of what's going on. But as a business partner? I have to tell you—man, you've got to get yourself together. I can't do this alone. If anything, I don't want to lose your friendship. Working with friends, with people you care about, creates a fuzzy line. And I'd rather be your friend than a business partner. So if you can't do something to come up with more investment, then I'm out after Illinois Way.

"I love you, man. But you've got to take what's yours sometime. If you want something, you've got to take it and move forward. If you wait too long, then there's a chance to lose all of it."

Brandon was left speechless. He knew that Garrett was talking about Mulberry Road, but it felt like a déjà vu, with Geneva. What settled was this indescribable sick feeling of people speeding past him, of leaving him behind. What was so wrong with double-checking and thinking twice? Why was it a disadvantage to hold on? Holding on meant building a foundation, and without a foundation, how would the rest of a house stand?

Brandon didn't understand. He didn't want to be pushed. But seeing his friend with this regretful and obvious disappointment on his face made him want to fix it.

At the end of the day, he didn't want to be left behind, especially by people he cared about.

"Garrett—"

"I know. You're going to try. But I need you to know where I stand."

There was nothing else to say, then. "I . . . I'll keep in touch, then?"

"Yeah, we will. Send me what your thoughts are on the project, and we'll go from there, okay?"

"Okay." When Brandon hung up, he typed up the beginning of what he knew would eventually become pages of an itemized list when he got back to the house later on that night. As he did so, he realized that that wouldn't be enough. He knew what he had to do, but the question was whether or not he could do it.

A gust of wind directed him toward the sky, where a flock of birds fought against the wind, a reminder that time was flying and there was more to do today. So he entered Hinga, where the industrial fans drying the wood floors became a relief from the punishing sun outside.

Mike was just getting off the phone when Brandon entered. "Boss! Thanks for meeting up. We're ready to start picking paint colors." He directed Brandon outside, where swatches of three different colors of blue were painted on the siding.

Brandon pointed to the middle swatch. Colors were his forte. "I like that one. But I'll have to run it by Geneva."

"I like the cobalt blue too."

"I'll get back to you by later on today. Though we may have to hold off from painting, right?"

Mike thumbed his phone. "The storm's in Charleston."

"Shoot." Brandon shivered reflexively, but he girded himself. "That's pretty close."

"We'll be ready. My team will board up windows tomorrow morning after our meeting. Maybe the weather will do us a solid and take a right turn."

"Well, thanks for working right up to the line."

"That's what I'm here for."

Brandon's phone buzzed with a calendar notification, a notice for him to head northeast, to Tiwala. Unlike the rest of the houses, Tiwala was shrouded by foliage. It had survived Maximus, only needing its front porch repaired. "I have to head out. Anything else?"

"Yep." He strode through the front entrance. "We'll need to decide on the outside paint colors for Yakap and . . . oh, wait." He looked up at the sky before digging at a box in his truck bed. "Scratch that. I'll text you the houses. But if we can get the samples up and chosen, we can keep moving forward."

"No worries; it's in my brain." Brandon lifted his iPad.

Mike handed Brandon paint swatches with a gritted smile. "Thank you. I'm losing my mind these days."

Brandon heard the shake in his voice. Keeping it light and flipping through the swatches, he said, "Everything okay?"

"Yeah." He waved it away. "Sort of. Woman problems. Actually not a problem . . . just, never mind."

"Do you mean Chef Castillo?"

"How did you—" His cheeks pinkened. "Oh, right, the restaurant. Yes, it is, but it's on the DL."

"You don't have to tell me twice. Or tell me at all. I didn't mean to pry. But if you need anything . . ."

"Thanks, I appreciate that. Let's just say I didn't expect for one meal to turn me to a one-woman kind of guy."

"Ah." Brandon offered him a smile of understanding, because his life forked much more often than he wished it did. "We can only do our best to adjust, right?"

"You're right." He pushed up the door to his truck's cab. "You've been a lifesaver, and I'm glad you're here, Brandon." In a lowered voice, he said, "I gotta admit that when I first met you, I wasn't sure how it was going to work out, with the two of us. I thought there would be too many cooks in the kitchen, know what I mean? But this has been good. You're a great team player, acting as the go-between to what needs to happen on the ground." He climbed into the driver's seat.

Brandon grinned. What Mike was saying was code. "You can say my brother's bossy."

Mike scrunched his face as he leaned an elbow out the window. "That's not it. I've seen bossy and worked for jerks. That's not your brother. He's exact, methodical. The kind of person you need up there. Don't know about you, but I'd rather be out here in the sun and getting my hands dirty, and not doing *his* job."

Brandon responded with a nod, but inside, a heavy feeling settled in. Brandon hadn't considered this. He'd assumed that if Chris could have his hands in everything, he would, but never questioned his own preferences. "I'll get back to you on paint swatches for the houses."

"See you in a bit."

Brandon gently pounded on the hood of the truck before Mike started it back to life.

Once alone, he texted Geneva, eager not only to discuss paint but to see her once more. Anything but to think of Garrett's ultimatum.

Brandon:

I've got paint swatches.

Where are you?

Geneva:

I'm at Halik.

Brandon:

I can come to you

Geneva:

I don't mind you picking them

Brandon's hand stilled on the phone. This was a turn of events.

Brandon:

You want me to pick them?

Geneva:

You're capable?

Brandon:

I know I am.

Geneva:

Great.

Super busy.

Halik was on his way to Tiwala, so Brandon decided to make a detour. The last text was unsettling. In the few days they'd worked together, he and Geneva had become a team. They'd discussed most decisions together.

The cart bumped down the uneven road. At Halik's turnoff, he parked behind a line of resort vans, doors open, with furniture ready to be hauled out. Music blared from the house's open windows, with voices interspersed. A quick peek through the shadows, and one was Geneva, wearing jean shorts and a tank and a headband, hair up in a ponytail. She was bent at the waist, wiping down the lamp with the red engravings with pure concentration.

Dang, she's cute.

He knocked on the window. Geneva looked up, head cocked to the side, then, after a painful few seconds, opened it. The cold blast of AC and Geneva's perfume were a wake-up to all his senses.

He lifted the paint swatches.

"I thought we agreed you'd pick them," she said without preamble. Her expression was unreadable.

"I also thought that you and I were good." he said.

"We *are* good."

He shook his head. "I don't think so. I know you, Geneva Harris, inside and out. Something's up. You have opinions on paint colors, on everything."

"Shh." She bent down lower, face closer to him. So close that the cupid's bow of her mouth was inches from him—so close he could have kissed her frown away.

Keep focus, Puso. "So what's this about, then?" Brandon asked.

"What do you mean, *this*."

"This . . . that you can't look at me in the eyes. Like you're planning to bolt."

Her expression changed. "You know?"

Brandon stiffened, and his internal monologue began: Was this about the dance? Had he been too forward? "Know what?"

"Shoot." She shook her head. Then a noise from inside the house caused her to turn, and a faux smile appeared on her face. To someone, she said, "I've got to step out and talk to Brandon, but I'll be right back. Just carry on. The iPad tells you where everything needs to go. Give me about ten minutes."

To Brandon, she gestured toward the front door.

Brandon came round and walked toward the water. The north side of the resort, which was the right curve of the heart of the peninsula, was the most scenic. A pier extended out into the sound, punctuated by a gazebo. It had been one of the first things reinforced after Maximus—besides the beachfront—since this pier was the most photographed view.

While Halik did not have a patio, about fifty meters away was an overlook with an overhead covering. From it hung two hammocks. Brandon moseyed to the spot and leaned against one of its posts. The view was spectacular, despite the fast-moving clouds in the sky, mirroring his running thoughts. He scoured through his morning—what had he done wrong?

"So, I'm here," Geneva said.

Her impatient tone smashed Brandon's initial worry and turned on his defensiveness. "As far as I know it's you who has something to tell me."

She stuffed her hands in her back pockets, though she barely looked at him. "My list . . . it's getting longer, and the days are passing quickly."

He swallowed the continued reminder that they would both be going their separate ways. "But this is why we have to work more closely, right?"

"Right. But it's also why perhaps we should make some decisions on our own. More a divide and conquer rather than a double defense on it, don't you think?"

The strategy was logical, but it was the complete opposite of their initial agreement to keep each other in the loop in all decisions. It also didn't explain her attitude. "And that's all?"

"That's all," she said.

Brandon thought back to the photo shoot earlier that day. To how good it had felt to have her in his arms. Was the dance cheesy? Yes. It was probably the corniest thing he'd ever done. Whenever he watched a scene like that in a movie or read it in a book, he couldn't bear it. In real life, with Geneva, it was natural and romantic.

But right then, it was as if the dance had never happened.

"Fine." It was the only thing he could say, even if everything inside him was screaming otherwise. There was more to her indifference, but Brandon also knew that the more he pushed, the more she'd clam up. "I'll send you my suggestions, then."

"Sounds good." She nodded. She hiked a thumb to the house. "I've got to go."

"Yeah, okay."

"See you at the meeting tomorrow?"

This meant she wasn't planning on touching base the rest of the day. Brandon clenched his jaw at the whiplash. What else could he do? "See you."

He watched her stride away, then turned toward the view, the ominous sky.

♡

Brandon scooped a sleeping Kitty, limp and sweaty, out of her car seat. He fluffed her pink ballet tutu down, though unsuccessfully, and it popped up and slapped him in the face.

"God bless dance class, am I right?" Across the van, Gil carried Izzy in a teal tutu. With great precision, he bent down and plucked the monogrammed dance bag as well as her ballet slippers from the floorboards.

"Yeah, and who knew dance was so serious. Was it just me, or did those mamas give me dirty looks?" Brandon rearranged Kitty after he shut the van doors. His niece breathed hard against his ear.

"You called out someone else's seven-year-old."

"That kid was causing havoc, spinning clockwise versus counter-clockwise. Izzy could have done better, and deserved the solo."

Brandon clutched Kitty closer to him as they climbed the stairs. It had been a good break, to get off the resort to help Gil with dad duties, even if dance class was a whole other world he wasn't ready for. While his intention had been to get his mind off Geneva for a couple of hours, he'd thought of Geneva the entire time—she would have had a field day sticking up for his nieces.

"Seems to me that *someone* was annoyed the whole class time," Gil said, popping the hallway lights on.

Brandon grunted as he followed Gil into a bedroom with two twin beds with matching teal sheets and mimicked his brother as he pulled the sheet and laid Izzy down. As Gil tucked her in, Brandon noticed that she had a grin bursting from her lips.

The stinker wasn't asleep at all.

Brandon half laughed to himself while pulling the sheets up to Kitty's chin. He caught his brother's eyes, and gestured toward his niece.

Gil caught the message straight away. "Bummer these two fell asleep in the van. Root beer floats sound so good right about now."

A frown appeared on Izzy's forehead. It took everything out of Brandon not to cackle.

"Maybe I can surprise them with floats tomorrow, so long as they have a good night's rest," Brandon added.

Izzy's wrinkles flattened out.

"You're such a sucker. All you do is spoil."

"Fun uncle. That's my name."

Gil kissed Izzy on the forehead, came around to Kitty's bed to do the same, then turned off the lamp, gesturing to the door. In the hallway, he said, "You *are* a fun uncle, and I wish you were with us all year long."

"You won't have them much longer, will you? Don't they go back to Jessie in a couple of weeks, when school starts?"

"Yeah . . . well . . . normally . . ." He shrugged innocently.

They'd reached Gil's kitchen, where all healthy foods lived. There was absolutely nothing on the kitchen counters, and Brandon bet that his cupboards didn't have a lick of junk food. It was 100 percent the opposite of the rest of the family's, with favorite savory snacks and crunchy bags of chips from the Asian market overflowing from their pantries.

But Gil's pristine white marble countertops and state-of-the-art appliances didn't distract Brandon from his shock. "Kuya?"

"We met up yesterday."

"Who?"

"Me and Jessie."

Brandon worked out the US map in his head. "But, um . . . she's in California."

He twisted the top of a bottle of kombucha and tipped it toward Brandon. "Want a sip?"

An acidic scent wafted toward him, and Brandon's mouth watered, but not in a good way. "Ah, no thank you. But go on."

His brother took a long pull. "She's here a week early. Filming wrapped up, and she didn't have much to do. She missed the girls—"

"And she missed you."

Gil nodded and leaned back against his countertop. His chin dipped into his chest. "Look, I know what you must be thinking."

"You'd better believe it. *Kuya Gil*—" Brandon said, exasperated. "The ink just dried. I meant what I said when I got here. You look really good now . . . because four months ago you were . . ."

He had been a mess. More than that: desolate.

"It's complicated, Bran. Do you know how hard it is for Jessie and me to live away from one another and juggle the kids? I feel guilty not having them all year long, and so does she. With you, the girls are exhausted and happy. You help keep their minds off their mother. But before you got here, they were crying every night."

Brandon's shoulders dropped along with his pending lecture. "I'm sorry, man. I didn't know it was that bad."

"Jessie says they're that way when they're away from me, so at least I know it's not personal." He took another sip. "Can you keep a secret?"

"Can I?" He laughed out loud. If the guy only knew. But at Gil's serious expression, he backtracked. "Yes, I can."

"She's here this week to look for a small condo in Nags Head."

Brandon opened his mouth to reply, but nothing came out but air. Because if his and Geneva's past relationship was a can of worms, Gil and Jessie's was a crypt—previously nailed shut and buried six feet underground more than once—being resurrected.

It wasn't just about the relationship between the two of them.

"The family—" Brandon started.

"I know . . ." Gil's voice trailed off. "And speaking of the family . . . we notice. Or at least, I notice."

Brandon's brain had been squarely on the Gil-and-Jessie situation, on the vociferous objections that would surely come from Beatrice. "Notice what?"

"You and Geneva. I heard about this morning's photo shoot, saw the looks across the table at Friday dinner. I can't believe you waltzed to no music. Can you be more cheesy?"

"I don't know what you're talking about." Brandon skirted his gaze. "You asked us to take pictures, and that's what we did, and she was *sitting* across from me at dinner—how could I avoid looking at her?"

"You almost got sideswiped running across a four-lane road to see her."

"She needed help."

"Help? Sure." He shook his head. "You're not fooling me, little brother. I see it in that face of yours. You always had a crush on Geneva. And while I was watching you almost die on that street, I remembered that you and Geneva spent quite a bit of time together at Chris's reception. In fact, if memory serves me right, while we all stayed in Vegas, the both of you left within a day of one another—you much earlier than expected."

"I don't even know what you're getting at." Brandon went to the fridge to escape his brother's interrogating gaze. Except nothing good was in there but kombucha and beet juice. "Damn, there isn't one can of Coke in here. Are you even my brother?" Brandon took his time selecting just the perfect bottle of water and twisted it open.

"Bran."

He turned.

Gil's eyebrow rose in a dare. "I think you're lying. Just come out and tell me."

"Tell you what? Geneva and I are friends. That's it." His brother's gaze didn't flinch, so he kept on. "Sure, I had a crush on her. Everyone had a crush on Geneva. The whole school wanted to be Beatrice and Geneva. But Geneva now? Yes, she's beautiful and smart and creative and all that, but she's a flight risk." He heard himself getting louder, but the message wasn't only for Gil but for himself. Because something was up with Geneva today, and he wished he could break through her barriers. And yet, who else could he blame but himself? He knew who she was. "I can't deal with games. I need a for-sure thing. I need someone who'll be around. That's not Geneva."

Gil pointed the tip of his bottle toward him. "The man doth protest too much." His eyes sparkled in mischief. "Looks like you put a lot of thought into it too. Runners. That's what the both of you are, and not even literally but figuratively. Because I don't remember the last time you put on real running shoes. Perhaps that's what you need. You and I should go for a run because the ocean air is so good for you. So . . . did she follow you back to Annapolis after Kuya Chris's wedding?"

Brandon peered back at him, at his attempt at trickery. "No idea what you're talking about."

Gil's front door creaked open.

"What are you two fools doing? I can hear you through the freaking walls."

Kuya Chris.

"I've been interrogating Bunso," Gil said.

"Oooh, this sounds fun. What about?"

"Nothing. Nothing at all." Brandon heaved a breath. The last thing he needed was Chris to be suspicious.

Gil shook his head. "It *is* something, but nothing he wants to admit." With a quieter voice, he added, loud enough just for Brandon, "But I'll get to the bottom of it. No worries. I have my secret, and you have yours."

"Is this about the woman?" Chris asked.

Gil beamed with righteousness. "Interesting."

"I'm out," Brandon said. Being in Heart Resort was like 2020 all over again. Every day brought something unexpected, and he'd had enough for today.

"Before you go, can we talk?" Chris asked.

"Yeah, sure." To Gil, Brandon said, "See you in the morning?"

"Yep."

Brandon followed Chris out the door, onto the lit deck. Chris gestured toward the outdoor chairs.

Chris stuffed his hands in his pockets and leaned back against the railing. "Listen, this is totally overdue, and you're likely settled in the guest room, but I had everything cleaned up for you to settle in upstairs."

"Really?"

"Yeah. There's furniture in there now. Just the basics, and you can add more as needed."

"I . . ." Brandon was flummoxed at this distinct honor of being asked to live in his own apartment, because it was also ridiculous that he'd needed Chris's permission.

"I know it took a while. I wasn't sure how long you were really staying . . . we still have our town house . . . but the last few days, you've worked really hard, Brandon."

"Thank you." Except for those two words, Brandon was unsure what to say through his web of emotions. Pride that he'd somehow earned his way in? Irritation at the expectation that he wasn't going to stick around to get the job done? Guilt because despite all this, he hadn't said anything about Mulberry Road? Vindication that Mulberry Road was where he truly belonged?

Above that was the question of how long he would truly stay. Was he welcome, finally?

"Your apartment is on the side without a deck, if you remember, but it has quick access to the roof deck." Chris looked side to side, then, as awkwardness began to settle, and said, "I'd better go. Eden and I . . . anyway, she wants me back right away. I've got duties."

Brandon winced. "Aw, man, I don't need to know that."

"No!" He barked out a laugh. "She wants me to read pages. You know, for my thoughts."

"You read her books?" The thought of it, of Chris reading romance, was far fetched.

"Yeah." He rubbed the back of his neck. "They're pretty good." He clapped his hands. "See you in the morning. And oh, I sent a text that the meeting is beachside tomorrow."

Brandon nodded. He watched Chris disappear into his apartment without fanfare, leaving him with the question as to whether or not that was a reconciliation. For once, Brandon wished for a hug or something physical and tangible. Chris was like a text message without an emoji: all-commanding, and sometimes in all caps.

Gil's front door opened an inch. An eye spied through. "All clear?"

"Were you listening all that time?"

"Of course I was. But I wasn't going to get into it. I've got my own issues."

Harkening back to dinner, Brandon's mind flipped to a new page, back in the sudden groove of the family, where if one didn't like the current situation, one only needed to wait a second before the next issue popped up. "Since you interrogated me earlier, it's my turn: Why is Ate Bea so mad at Jessie?"

The door widened, and light spilled onto the deck. "That will require a nightcap."

"Oh, you're drinking now?"

"Yeah. I meant it about the root beer float. Let me make one for you."

He followed his brother inside. "And all this time, I thought you'd gone cold turkey. You and your sweet tooth."

"Puso is what Puso does. I'm just warming you up so you can spill finally."

"Spill about what?"

Gil pulled out the ice cream from the back of the freezer. "You can keep at it, Bran. I'm patient."

CHAPTER NINETEEN

Seven years ago
Washington, DC
Weather: heavy rain, 57°F
Flood warning in the National Capital Region

Brandon entered his apartment on R and Sixteenth, soaked after running through the rain from his Metro stop. At the front door, he paused at the hallway table and unloaded his pockets, including his now-dripping phone and his Fisher Construction ID attached to a lanyard, and kicked off his steel-toed boots.

"Garrett?" He called out for his housemate.

The apartment was quiet, which meant Garrett was at work or at his girlfriend's place. Sweet. He had been craving rest and silence, two rare things for the youngest of four kids.

What a day. His spirits were flying high even if his wet clothing was weighing him down. With a grin, he peeled off his shirt and his pants and threw them into the laundry room and strutted through the house in triumph even if no one could see him.

It was then, and only then, that he hooted.

He'd completed his first residential renovation as a junior contractor.

In his boxers, he went to the kitchen first to stick a beer in the freezer. Then he padded over to the bathroom and turned on the shower. To celebrate, he was going to turn on HBO, drink a beer, and put his feet up. Not exactly sexy, but his body was bone tired from early-morning classes and work straight after. The real partying would have to wait.

He was a step into his shower when his phone rang from the hallway table. Brandon growled but got under the warm, soothing water and let the stream hit him in the face when the ringing stopped.

As he soaped up, the ringing began again. Then the landline trilled. Damn, when it rained, it poured. Literally.

So, he rinsed and toweled off haphazardly. The landline quit, and his cell rang once more. Water dripped as he made his way to the hallway, the towel wrapped around his waist.

"I'm coming," he yelled to the empty room. Brandon hated phone calls with a passion and avoided them at all costs, especially if it was off hours. Anybody he knew and loved left a text.

Reluctantly, he picked up his cell phone; it was Beatrice. Brandon pressed the button to answer, a sarcastic remark on his tongue.

He was met with his sister screaming. It was a guttural sound, where there were no beginnings or ends to words or sentences. No punctuation marks to be discerned. It was a series of sounds of high and low pitches.

Brandon, a solid 170 pounds on a five-foot-eleven-inch frame, dropped to his knees. His heart was tearing in half, though he wasn't sure what had happened. He had begun to cry, though he didn't know why. "What's wrong? What's wrong, Ate?" Brandon's voice shook.

"Mom . . . Dad . . . home . . . Brandon. Come home."

CHAPTER TWENTY

Day 7
Morning weather: cloudy, 20% chance of rain, 80°F
Afternoon weather: thunderstorm, 100% chance of rain, 70°F
Tropical Depression Oscar approaching the Outer Banks

"I've got to say, I have never had a bona fide meeting on the beach. You guys are spoiling me." Geneva dug her toes into the sand while leaning back on the reclining beach chair. Under a raised tent in front of Tiwala, the cold iced coffee in her hand counterbalanced the rest of her surroundings. "What a way to wake up."

"I thought it would be a good change." Chris passed out bottles of water and soda from the cooler. "To wash down the coffee." He then checked his phone. "We have to hold on for Tammy and Bran, and we can get started."

Geneva closed her eyes. She focused on the sounds of the active waves, the murmurs of the people around her, and the shuffle of bodies. Her thoughts meandered to the list of houses on Heart Resort needing her attention, then to the yellow house behind them, the perfect color to exude faith. All night and this morning she'd been besieged by her thoughts on what she should do about Foster's Group. Maybe, working in Tiwala—depending on how the weather held up, she would be installing a new ocean-blue-tile kitchen backsplash—she would find her answer. Or, perhaps, finishing up the wooden patio for Yakap would shine a light on her decision.

Could it be that it had only been a few days since she and Brandon had been looking through Yakap's window? Back then, she'd been naive enough to think that she wouldn't fall for him again, only to be swooped straight to the moon and back by that first kiss in the warehouse.

"Coffee's not helping, I see," a voice said next to her.

Geneva's eyes flew open, and her mind did the descent to reality with a quick flicker of images ending with her sitting atop her kitchen counter with Brandon between her legs. She gasped. "I wasn't sleeping."

Brandon tipped a glass bottle of soda onto his lips. He looked so handsome, but smug, in the chair. "Sure, just like how you don't have enough time to pick out paint colors."

Her gaze darted around the tent for prying ears; no one was paying them any mind, all engaged in their own conversations. "With the time I spent not mulling over paint colors yesterday, I finished up two whole houses."

"Congratulations," Brandon said. "Even if picking out paint colors would have only cost you a few minutes. But what do I know?"

Geneva bit her lip as guilt wiggled its way through her. In truth, she'd spent much of yesterday combing through her pros and cons while putting up wallpaper and creating accent walls. And still, she wasn't sure what she should do.

Her dilemma wasn't about leaving earlier than she'd anticipated. It wasn't even whether she would be able to complete her tasks at the resort. The entire crew at Heart Resort was now in the flow of work—she had been transparent with her design plans, and the Pusos had enough capable people to finish out the final to-dos on her list.

It felt as if her next decision was the domino to jump-start the next phase of her life. Foster's Group and Beachy were massive, rare opportunities that would require 100 percent of her effort and heart.

She knew she would be excellent at either job, and that made it more difficult to decide.

It was a relief when Chris called for the team's attention.

He directed everyone to their devices, to which he'd sent the grand opening rollout plan yesterday. Geneva clicked on the file; she had yet to scan through the topics.

Ten pages.

She took a sip of her coffee to bolster her.

"Damn," Brandon said, swiping left on his iPad.

"By the shock on some of your faces, I can tell this is the first time you're seeing the file. No worries—what I did was compile your updates so we all know what's up ahead for the grand opening. I wanted to make sure we were all on the same page. We don't want anything to fall in the cracks. First up: Tammy"—he gestured to her—"has been ramping up our social media as well as ads on Facebook and other related travel sites. Do you want to continue?"

Tammy stood and nodded at Geneva and Brandon. "Thanks to these two, and along with other models I've been able to hire, we are on our way to a brand-new website. I'm also amassing our own stock photos we can rotate out over the months. In fact, we have another session after this meeting, in front of Kilig. Perfect, right? Exhilaration."

Next to Tammy, Chris winced. "Not that there will be anything exhilarating going on."

Geneva gritted her teeth and avoided looking at Brandon.

"We've got a commercial queued at a local cable channel. We updated our billboards on northbound and southbound I-95," Tammy continued. "We've got a few media spots for Chris. Podcasts too. I've reached out to local brick-and-mortar Outer Banks businesses to develop partnerships, since they need to love us too. Right now, well, we're kind of like outsiders trying to mingle in with locals. In fact, there's a rumor that another competing resort is in the works, and its owners are local residents of the Outer Banks. They're called Willow Tree Inc.—"

Geneva's ears perked. As the owner of a mobile business, she was intrigued by the politics of small towns. In a large cosmopolitan area, what she'd run into was cutthroat pricing competition and invisibility. In a small town? It was all about acceptance.

"We don't have to involve everyone with that, Tammy," Chris said. "It's all politics, and I'm taking care of it."

"Oh, okay. Moving on then." She cleared her throat. "Finally, I'm working on cross-promotions with our vendors. That's it for me."

"Next? Gil?"

Gil cleared his throat. "Since Brandon and Mike are dealing with maintenance and building, I've been moved to employee management. Our retraining has begun. We've retained about ninety percent of our employees since Maximus, so we've got some recruitment to do. So far, for the expected amount of clients, we have enough in our teams to open."

"Brandon and Geneva?"

Geneva glanced at Brandon. He nodded back, to give her the floor.

An unexpected sliver of nervousness ran up her spine, which was silly. Nothing she was about to say would be new, but there was more at stake. From her relationship with the Pusos to how each home, albeit tiny, had come to be. And now that her work here was almost done, she was going to let all of them—the people and things—go soon.

Sadness washed through her; it was such an unexpected, visceral reaction that Geneva had to take a breath, and she blinked back tears.

"I started with a theme: it takes two. I wanted each space to feel comfortable and intimate, where a couple felt like they weren't on top of one another despite the home's square footage. From there, I really tried to give each home a personality," Geneva said, voice croaking. "One of our part-timers, Rhiannon Gold, reminded me that names mattered. Just as each house has a name, I thought, shouldn't each embody what that name means? If you swipe through the pages and zoom in, you'll see that Brandon and I worked to give each house a little something new."

All around her, the team swiped through the pictures she had taken along the way.

"These are gorgeous," Tammy said. "Can I grab a couple of these for our social media?"

"Yes, of course." She glanced briefly at Brandon. "My hope is that those couples who stay in these beach houses glean what they need from the house. The spirit, if you will."

She thought of Luna, who'd been immediately at ease in her own beach house, Ligaya. At the joy she felt opening her doors to the view of the water. And how, now, she didn't think twice about the climb down from the loft or how small the place was. She looked to Brandon and said, "Bran?"

"We still have to do the exterior painting on a couple of the homes," Brandon said. "The yoga studio's floors are done, mirrors and office installed the next day or two—fairly straightforward, and we don't anticipate any issues there. We're waiting on the delivery of new equipment for the restaurant, and we've still to update its interior decor."

"Just remember. It doesn't have to be complicated," Chris said.

Geneva detected a blip of a frown on Brandon's face, but it disappeared just as quickly.

"Thank you both. Beatrice?" Chris prompted.

She startled, looking up from her phone. "Sorry, I'm keeping an eye out on this storm. It looks like it's been downgraded to a tropical depression, which is a relief, but as the day passes, let's be flexible in stopping what we need to do in order to board up or shutter windows. We have materials at the ready from Maximus, and we have to keep on our phones for changes in plans. Anyway, if you take a look at the next slide, you'll see our client numbers." Beatrice outlined all the couples that were set to arrive for the first session back, and seven of the ten houses would be occupied. On a chart that only Beatrice could make whimsical despite all the moving parts, she showed occupancy depending on the current couples retreat plan.

Beatrice gestured to Chet, who stood and, without exposing their identities, discussed the myriad of relationship issues their upcoming clients were facing and what programs they were seeking. He directed everyone to his chart, which indicated which of the staff members would be involved, from the yoga instructor to the acupuncturist to the chef to the therapist on call, and the specific crews involved with the outdoor couples activities.

Geneva was swept up into the discussion and the team's sincere intention of making the couples' experience perfect. She thought of each house and which couple would be assigned which home. Of which home would give them the best luck for their couplehood.

Geneva wasn't at all superstitious; her spirituality, she admitted, needed some fine-tuning. Work was how Geneva expressed her intentions, her manifestations; work was her prayer. But her mother had called their house in Annapolis their good-luck home because it had witnessed so many of the Harrises' holiday celebrations and most of Geneva's birthdays. Geneva had felt safe in that house; she'd known every nook and cranny. That house had represented her childhood.

She yearned for that same comfort. When else had she felt that same safety?

Right here. With Brandon.

No.

She was simply emotional at the moment. This project was special, and the lines were blurred. She pushed her thoughts down and away as Chris took the stage.

"I'm just . . . I'm so impressed," he said. "In the beginning, I thought this was going to be a hard thing to accomplish, but here we are. I'm so proud of this team. I know I don't say it enough. You aren't just part of the executive team. You're part of this family. This Heart

Resort family, the Puso family. And, while some of you have to move on, you will always have a place here. These last few months . . ."

What had been a formidable force showed a crack in his veneer.

Were those tears in Chris's eyes?

Beatrice placed a hand on his shoulder, and the two shared a glance. Chris took another breath. "After Maximus, I wasn't sure how we were going to get it together. All I knew was that we had to try, for all of us, for our parents."

Geneva braved a glance at Brandon. He looked bereft; he was looking off into the distance, not quite at his brother.

Geneva had been on the road when Tita Marilyn and Tito Joe passed away. She'd been in the middle of a drive, leaving Kansas City, Missouri, en route to New Orleans. She had been looking forward to the new environment, another state to check off her family bucket list.

She had been driving a renovated van, which she'd gutted and furnished with a built-in mattress. The van itself didn't have bells and whistles, nor did it have Bluetooth capability, so when her phone had rung the first and the second times, she hadn't answered it. *It can wait,* she'd told herself.

By the third round, she'd dug her phone out of the center console. It was Beatrice.

"They're gone," she'd simply said with a stark one-toned voice. Beatrice "Inject All the Emotion" Puso, with a monotone one-liner? While Geneva hadn't known what it meant, she'd pulled over anyway. After she'd pieced together the horrible news, she'd turned her van around to be with friends.

Geneva knew how important this resort was to Brandon, to Beatrice, to Gil, and to Chris. The bittersweet joy Chris now expressed—she felt too. Geneva had been intent on making something out of herself before Tito Joe and Tita Marilyn had died, and their deaths had started her firing on all cylinders, wanting to accomplish all she had written down in the family bucket list.

Chris straightened, his stoic demeanor returning. "All that to say: I want to thank you for all of your hard work. And I would be remiss if I didn't thank Geneva especially for coming to Heart Resort on her own volition, since she's leaving us earlier than expected. But don't you worry, Geneva; we'll finish out what you started."

"Earlier?" Brandon echoed next to her.

Geneva kept her eyes on Chris, though her heart leapt in panic; he'd dropped a bomb of a half truth. "Actually"—she raised her hand to object—"I . . . I haven't decided yet." She smiled to ease the news for those around her, especially to Brandon.

"Right, right. Undecided yet, but important for me just to say, especially on the precipice of another storm. We don't know what we could have done without you. But enough of the sappy stuff. Let's keep things moving . . ."

With that, Chris continued on with the meeting. The man was right. There was, indeed, a storm coming, and she felt it from the chill next to her.

♡

"Hey, wait up!" Geneva chased after Brandon from under the tent. The meeting had concluded and the staff had dispersed, each with a laminated info sheet of storm and hurricane precautions. Once they were out of earshot, she raised her voice. "Bran!"

Brandon climbed into his golf cart, rocking it to the side. He took his time to put away his things but avoided her eyes. "Yep."

"Could I hitch a ride with you to Kilig?"

He turned the key. The cart beeped to life.

Geneva noted a flush across his cheeks, his tight grip on the steering wheel.

She rested her arms on the roof. While she didn't owe Brandon an explanation—technically, she hadn't made a decision—perhaps him finding out through Chris wasn't the best. "I'm sorry I didn't say anything. I'd mentioned the possibility to Beatrice, and she must have told Chris. There's a lot going on with my upcoming work, and this literally came up yesterday, after our photo shoot."

"Geneva." He looked up then; a small smile played on his lips. It made it to his eyes, but in this sad way. "I just want to be alone. I can meet you at Kilig, all right?"

She glanced at his foot, squarely on the gas pedal. Hands at ten and two. Brandon wanted to go—he wanted to get out of there, much like he had the first time they'd reunited. Internally, she grimaced at the backward slide, and at how everything was topsy turvy.

This was why she left before it got too deep. Because she couldn't manage this. Logically, her decisions about her business were her own, and yet, in the last day, what Brandon and his family thought, unbeknownst to them, mattered. It was why she couldn't spend but five minutes yesterday talking about paint colors. Ultimately, she wanted to make her own decisions, untouched by another person's opinion.

Still, she couldn't let Brandon go, because damn it, she *did* care about him. Despite her intention to stay away from him, he was under her skin; he was in her soul. She wanted to make things okay, though that would mean that he had to speak to her.

"Are you mad?"

He heaved a breath. "I'm not mad." Each word was measured and clear. He looked out of the windshield once more, and that was when Geneva caught it. His tell. A crinkle on the sides of his eyes, as if he was wincing, like he was resisting a hard truth.

Brandon was so good at small talk and easy talk. At banter. But not with his true feelings. Right then, it reminded her of them four years ago, with her chasing his thoughts and him holding back. Even at their last fight.

Right then felt like a breakthrough.

Geneva rounded the golf cart and hopped in.

It earned her an eye roll. "I guess we're riding together."

"Yes, because our conversation isn't over."

He sighed a heavy, impatient breath. "Geneva, I feel like talking's all we do."

When she didn't budge—did he know that she was as stubborn as he was?—he backed up from the space, and they set off.

There were more people milling on the resort these last couple of days. Golf carts whizzed down the main road. Chef Castillo now had two food trucks to accommodate those staying on during the day.

Geneva waved at the familiar people walking up the path: The crew that helped load and unload vans. Sal, with his walkie-talkie on his hip, directing traffic. The gardeners tending to the newly planted flowers she'd helped pick out. She'd had a bit of interaction with all these folks, and while with every job she'd learned to build a community, it wasn't quite like this.

"You're like the mayor around here," Brandon remarked above the noise of the engine.

"It's kind of hard to believe that it's only been a week, and I feel so . . ." The words rushed out of her, with the emotions of the morning.

"So . . . ?"

"Settled." She glanced briefly at him. Seeing the hurt on his face, Geneva's heart dropped at her mistake. She'd only been thinking of herself: her work, her adjustment, her schedule, her feelings. "Bran, I did get an offer I can't—I shouldn't—refuse. I was taking my time to think about it, to make the right kind of plans, and to make the announcement properly."

After a beat, his voice cut through the engine. "As someone who's working with you directly, it would have been nice to know. We're in a partnership."

She nodded. "What good is a notice if there's no decision?"

"Spoken by someone who doesn't run their decisions by anyone." He laughed. "Even a whiff of a decision could change the course of everything. Then again, even if you had feedback about your decision, it wouldn't matter. When you make up your mind, Geneva, there's no changing it. You up and go at a moment's notice."

Her insides burned at his accusation, feeling the words sear deep in her gut. There was a measure of truth in it, but defensiveness rose like a phoenix. No one had walked in her shoes. "I'm not stubborn for the heck of it." She dared him with a look, because two could play this game. "But you can't understand. You and I aren't the same person. We don't have the same kind of pressure."

"And what kind of pressure do you think I do and don't have?"

"I don't know, Brandon. But you're surrounded by these people. You will always be able to rely on them. You've even had the flexibility to stay in one place. And the consequences . . . you don't feel them like I do."

"Noted," he said.

Guilt overcame her; she'd overstepped. "I don't mean that you haven't had your struggles, Brandon. It's that I had mine too."

She halted there. Explaining more would have dug into their deepest issues, and none would be easy to discuss or solve in the next few minutes. There was too much between them, including everyone under this morning's tent who was relying on them. So she said nothing else for the rest of the ride to Kilig.

Minutes later, they drove onto Kilig's lot. Tammy was already there, setting up her camera, the tripod at her side. She waved.

As Brandon started to get out of the golf cart, Geneva reached out and pulled him back by the elbow. "I'm sorry that I didn't tell you about the offer, Bran."

"Just keep me posted, okay?" he said, sincerity in his voice. "We just want to make sure we can pick up where you leave off."

Stung, Geneva could only nod at his words.

CHAPTER
TWENTY-ONE

Brandon hammered the final nail into the final board on the last window at the restaurant. They had been at it since lunchtime, securing houses and equipment, and at 5:00 p.m., the sky was a dark gray, and wind had picked up.

"That's it," Mike said, after a swing against the plywood on the window he tended to. He looked at his watch. "It's time for me to get out of here."

Brandon spied his phone. It was a half hour before he was due back at Puso, as planned by Chris. The whole family and the on-site staff were expected to hunker down together.

He walked up to the parking lot with Mike. "Stay safe. And thanks for hanging back to help out. Hopefully we'll just be pelted by a mild storm."

"Wilmington isn't reporting a ton of damage, but you never know. We'll be good, though."

Brandon nodded, though inside him another kind of storm was brewing. It had started as an annoyance when he was sideswiped with the realization that Geneva had contemplated leaving without telling him, and then a sense of foolishness at his expectation that they were on the same level of intimacy. And as the day had progressed, the vibe on the resort had become ominous. It had become a ghost town. Employees had left to deal with their own homes, to stock up on last-minute necessities in case the storm worsened.

And God, he hated storms. He'd been able to cast his nerves aside most of the day, mentally occupied with Geneva's possible early departure and physical work. He'd taken his uncertainty and insecurity out on every nail he hammered. He was thankful that at least tonight he would be with his family when Oscar came through.

Mike climbed into his truck and, with one final honk of the horn, made a U-turn and headed down the hill.

Brandon did one last walk around the restaurant and inspected the plywood boarded up against the windows. He looked out over the sound. The water, normally mild even during high tide, had waves that broke forcefully over the surf. There were no ships on the horizon, no birds skimming the water. Far away was gray haze.

He'd better get going.

As he started his golf cart, his phone buzzed in his pocket. It was a text on their family group chat.

Beatrice:

Everyone should head this way.

A series of thumbs-ups against the text showed acknowledgment.

Brandon:

Done at the restaurant. Does anyone need help?

His brothers answered, each with a no.

Beatrice:

Can you check on Geneva? She's at the storage

warehouse. She hasn't texted me back.

Brandon:

I'm on it.

As he got going, it started to sprinkle, pelting gently against the top of the cart, but Brandon knew, as he watched the trees bend with the wind, that it would only be a few minutes before it became full-fledged rain.

When he got to the storage warehouse, he found the doors locked and the parking lot free of golf carts.

Brandon:

She might be driving to you. Not at the warehouse. I'll check her place in case.

Beatrice:

Not here yet.

Back on the treeless main drive, he pulled the hood of his sweatshirt up over his head. Normally he would have known where Geneva was—their proximity to one another via text and their shared schedule enabled that. And perhaps this was why he'd felt hurt that he'd had no idea that she'd been contemplating an early leave. He'd thought . . .

That was the problem. He shouldn't have assumed, even if it was about their working relationship. After their awkward photography session and that conversation where they'd both said some zingers, they'd parted ways without another text.

Brandon passed Geneva's turnoff and decided that he would check Ligaya, just in case. To both his worry and relief, her golf cart came into view. Through a sliver on one of the windows, he caught the shine of her lights.

He came around the front; the screen door slapped open and closed. He yelled into the screen. "Geneva?"

"Bran?"

"Yep, it's me."

"Oh my God, come in. Come in!" Panic laced her tone. "I'm in the loft."

"What's going on?"

"I can't find Luna." Her voice shook. "She hates storms, hates them with a passion, and I thought I would get back in time before she realized one was coming, but I can't find her."

Brandon systematically scoured the living room and bent down to look under her seats. "I don't want to add alarm, but how do you know that she didn't leave?"

"Because I kept the door closed and locked when I left. One thing she hates more than storms, it's the outside. She's in here, and I can't leave her. And anyway, I already searched. Even if she was outside, she wouldn't have gone far. She never does."

Thunder crashed down. Outside, the rain strengthened. Geneva's face appeared from the edge of the loft, and it was wrinkled in worry. "Brandon, you don't have to stay. You can go."

"Come with me. If she's in here, she'll be okay."

"Are you kidding? I'm not leaving without Luna. She's my ride-or-die. She's been with me every day for three and a half years." Her face disappeared once more, and a singsong tone followed. "Luna, sweet sneaky thing, where are you?"

Brandon weighed his options. He could insist they go. Cats were resourceful, and if Luna was in here, she would remain indoors. Only minutes remained before the start of this storm. But the shake of Geneva's voice, the way she was now searching every corner—Brandon knew that Geneva's attachment was true and unbreakable.

This realization was a chisel and pried his heart from his chest cavity. Geneva had claimed she was a rolling stone.

She wasn't, not really. Not with Luna.

So there was only one thing to do. He had to help her find this darn cat. If she loved this cat that much, if she loved this cat as much as he had once loved her, then she wasn't leaving without her.

Brandon started from the door and searched every hiding spot in the living room twice: under the seats, behind them, in the planter of the fake tree. Then he moved to the kitchen, spied under the tables and chairs; he searched in the kitchen cupboards, top and bottom. He peeked behind the refrigerator.

"She's not up here." Geneva's voice echoed. "She has this way of fitting herself into everything. And she'll do it if she's scared."

The only room left was the bathroom. Brandon peeked his head inside—which was a mistake, because the bathroom smelled of Geneva. Her perfume, her shampoo, her body wash. Her lotion. The thought of these things on her body turned up his temperature.

They might have only spent three weeks together, but in that time, he'd found out everything about her, down to the kind of lip balm she used at night before she went to bed, before he kissed it off her for another round of lovemaking. He knew that while she preferred to keep a small wardrobe, her skin care was complicated, with a mix of organic, Korean, and Japanese brands.

Once, he'd had the pleasure of being her apprentice, and she'd applied a serum to his face that didn't bring out the glow to his skin more than his ravenous need for her. Yes, that night had also ended up with them frolicking in bed.

"Where are you?" Geneva's voice woke him from his trance.

"Here!" His voice croaked. As he stepped out of the room, something caught his eye. He halted, then let out a long breath of relief. "Oh, you sneaky Luna."

The cat was hiding behind the toilet, crouched and hidden in the shadows.

He gave her the side-eye, careful not to make any sudden movements. Then again, the increasing sound of rainfall reminded him that they were losing time. As it was, it would be a heck of a time to drive up to the main house.

Brandon whistled the first tune he could think of: "Mary Had a Little Lamb." Then slowly, he bent down. Perhaps the tune worked, because Luna eyed him without much suspicion, tail curling. And by golly, she didn't resist as he plucked her from the ground.

"Oh thank goodness!" Geneva rushed the open doorway, relief playing across her features. Her hair and shirt were wet from her initial outside search.

Still, she was beautiful even in this worried state. Lips glossy and skin now shades darker than even days ago, Geneva glowed. She scooped the cat into her arms, and in feeling the brief contact of her skin against his, Brandon had the urge to take the extra step forward and bring both of them into him, their conversation earlier be damned.

Whether she left or stayed, he would always care for Geneva.

"Thank you, Bran. I was starting to get scared. You stubborn cat."

His first thought: How many more cats would he need to save to smooth what they had between them? His second: What *did* he want between them that was realistic? All he knew was that this proximity to her was a rush.

Perhaps that was why the idea of her leaving was like blunt force to the head. That she'd considered it without telling him meant she was willing to let this go without thought.

Thunder sounded, and it broke the moment. Brandon cleared his throat; they had to get back to Puso. "We'd better go."

"Okay." She nodded.

But as he followed her to the porch, it was clear that the drive up would be dangerous.

The rain had ratcheted up a notch. The wind whirred like white noise throughout the tiny house. The surf crashed on the beach. Sand swirled. There was just enough light in the sky that five-year-old

Brandon's imagination would have run amok on what monsters lurked out there.

"Crap," she said. "It's pretty strong now."

"I don't think we'll be able to make it with the golf cart." He took out his phone while a sliver of his anxiety inched up his spine. "I'll text everyone. It'll be okay."

♡

"Just breathe, Bran." Chris's voice was directive through the phone, which was pressed against Brandon's ear. "It's going to storm until dawn, so you'll have to hang in there with Geneva until then."

"Okay," Brandon said, though he knew he was still far from okay. After he'd texted the family group chat, Chris had immediately rung back. Right then, his kuya was not a big brother but a friend. His support system.

"This is not a repeat," Chris said.

"No, it's not," Brandon declared. In his head, he counted off where each of his family members were.

They're home, not even a half mile away.

Geneva is here with me.

Geneva and her darn cat. "Everyone is accounted for," he added, just as his therapist had instructed. *Say it aloud.*

"And you?"

Months after his parents had died, Brandon had blunted his feelings so he could express the swath of his emotions but couldn't get to the depths of them. Except for when he was angry. Or when he was worried. Or when it stormed. In these occasions, his body had crumbled like tissue placed in a cup of water. What had been a reliably jovial and relaxed Brandon became one who tensed over changes.

It wasn't just he who'd exhibited their grief. Beatrice had become an insomniac; Chris wouldn't leave his office; Gil drank to excess. They'd turned to one another, true, but the lost couldn't lead the lost.

Beatrice had dragged him with the rest of the siblings to family therapy, where all of them had sat in different chairs and muddled through their collective loss. Eventually, they'd attended therapy separately and found their own paths on the slow and arduous journey to healing. His siblings, as complicated as their relationships with one another were, had unified under their efforts to heal.

But the wound never really closed. It scabbed and protected for a bit; then something would tear through.

Brandon's task was to name his emotion and walk himself through the emotion. It had been hard and still was. The shock of an event became like a boulder that he could see neither over nor around. Putting what he was experiencing into words was as complicated as stringing together letters dumped out into a pile.

"I'm anxious. It's dark outside," Brandon said.

"Okay."

"The wind is really loud. I don't like how it's howling. But I'm safe."

"Good, Bran. You *are* safe. You're with Geneva. We are all okay."

"Yes. We are."

From behind Brandon came cursing, and he turned to see Geneva coming down from the ladder, with Luna scurrying away with a final screech. Luna was reflecting the chaos of the storm and vacillated between howling meows and hissing.

"What's that noise?"

"It's the cat."

"Darn animals. Tell you, Dad had a reason for not having them. Do you know how many times Beatrice's dog has nipped my heels?"

Brandon shed a couple of tears at Chris's comedic timing and sniffled. He pressed his fingers against his eyes. "Thank you for calling."

"Hey, it's what kuyas are for. And anyway, it makes *me* feel better to talk to you. I don't like not having you all around when stuff like this happens too. It's why, during Maximus, Beatrice called you a million times. I'm sorry I was too proud to call you myself. You needed me, and I wasn't there."

His mention of their fight reminded Brandon that he had Mulberry Road to bring up, but at the moment, he didn't have the bandwidth. What he wanted was the ability to breathe easy and not slip into his foggy thoughts. "I wasn't there for you either."

"But *you* came here. You're pretty brave." His brother's voice trailed off. "Call me straight away if you need anything tonight. I don't care what time. The phone will be right next to me."

"All right."

Brandon bade his goodbye and hung up. His heart had slowed; his conversation with Chris had eased his breathing. Through the screen door, he watched Geneva try to coax a frightened Luna from the top of the fridge. She was talking to her cat as if she was a human, with this absolute care.

His chest tightened, but now it was for an entirely different reason. Here was more proof of something he both cheered and dreaded. Geneva was capable of commitment.

The truth was right there, in plain sight. Geneva had to *choose* to stay, with anyone. Four years ago, he hadn't been her choice. And just because he'd allowed himself to fall into the same behaviors with her didn't mean he should expect her to reciprocate. She had to choose to stay in Heart Resort; he didn't have say over it.

Brandon repeated what his brother had reminded him of. This was not a repeat, and that applied to him and Geneva too.

He couldn't make it one, if he intended to survive it with his heart intact.

CHAPTER TWENTY-TWO

"Looks like we're staying put until dawn," Brandon said, thumbing through his phone. He'd just entered from taking a phone call on the porch.

Geneva was holding a shaking Luna. She ran a hand down the length of her body and glanced at her open doorway, through the screen door. The porch had provided some protection from the rain, but the whistling wind had swept droplets of water into the living room. They would have to close the door soon.

Which would render them together, and alone.

Geneva wasn't sensitive to small spaces, but right then, she could guess how many steps she was away from Brandon. It was too few.

She wasn't over their conversation from earlier today. Though their teamwork to find Luna had broken up the tension between them, since then, she had replayed this afternoon on loop.

I don't mean that you haven't had your struggles, Brandon. It's that I had mine too.

Could she have been more insensitive? Could she have been more selfish? She had deserved a snub after that.

And still, he'd chosen to stay to find Luna.

"We're going to be okay," Brandon said, finally plopping down on one of the seats. It was the second time he'd said it, as if she needed the reassurance.

Was she scared of the storm? A little. But Ligaya was on pilings; it had survived a tropical storm just two months ago. It had been inspected since then. And she'd been in storms in her tiny RV van.

She respected storms, but she wasn't scared of them.

Fear, real fear, was what happened to her when she couldn't steer the ship but could see the iceberg coming. Fear was about feeling helpless when she had the opportunity to affect something and failed. Right then, she and Brandon had done all they could with what Mother Nature was challenging them with.

No, it wasn't fear she was feeling right then but vulnerability. For the next several hours, she would not be able to avoid Brandon. Ligaya, after all, was only three hundred square feet, and her emotions were like live wires. Since she'd arrived at Heart Resort, it was as if she was undergoing her *own* renovation, except stuck at demo.

"Well, I'd better get to work." She spun and made to climb the ladder. The place had never seemed smaller.

He snorted, watching her. "Work? Now?"

"Weren't you just outside working?"

"That was a phone call."

"The rest of the world doesn't have Tropical Depression Oscar coming through, and I've got a business to run." She focused on the coordination of her hands and feet making contact with every rung. Brandon didn't push boundaries, and that loft would be her boundary. "We've got internet and power and water, which means we might as well take advantage. Don't you think?"

"Um. Sure."

Geneva made it to her bed and sat. She placed the computer on her lap and ran her fingers across her keyboard, though she didn't press on any of the buttons. She clicked on random emails, noting the myriad of incomplete boxes in her productivity app and glossing over the list, knowing Brandon was downstairs doing goodness knew what.

Luna hopped up next to her, without a care in the world.

She gave Luna the stink eye. "This is your fault, you know," she whispered. "If you had come exactly when I called, then we would be at the big house, and I wouldn't be sitting here hiding."

"What did you say?" Brandon yelled. The top of his head appeared as he stood near the front door.

"I was just talking to the cat."

"Did you tell her that this is her fault?"

"Actually, I did." She bumbled a laugh.

He ducked back deeper into the house, chuckling. Then his voice boomed from under her. "Is it okay that I raid your fridge? I didn't have anything to eat."

"Oh my God, yes, of course." Now she felt guilty. Here she was "working," and the guy was starving. "Help yourself."

She stared at her in-box in an attempt to jump-start her productivity.

A banner notification of a text from Nita popped out from the right side of her screen.

Nita:

I'm so glad you're online. I'm watching the storm on the news. Everything okay there?

Geneva:

Yes. Am in the house.

Nita:

In that tiny thing? Why aren't you in the main house?

Geneva:

Long story with the name of Luna.

260

Nita:

Are you alone?

Her fingers hovered on the keyboard.

Nita:

Geneva?

Geneva:

No

Nita:

?

The clanking of plates was a reminder that there was a certain someone downstairs who she couldn't ignore.

Geneva:

Brandon

Nita:

Oh my God. I'm getting off this text. What are you doing with me?

Geneva:

You're the one who's texting me.

Nita:

I'm cutting you off.

Then seconds later, another text appeared.

Nita:

Go, Geneva.

There was no way that Geneva was going to just *go*. To "go" would mean that she would have to either pretend that she had no emotions for Brandon or act on them. And neither was possible.

Nope, she would simply stay upstairs until her bladder demanded a bathroom break.

Another text appeared on her screen, this one from Brandon.

Brandon:

Hungry?

She was tempted, in all the ways. To have a meal with him. To just spend time with him.

But right then was too close.

Geneva:

I'm good. I'm in the middle of something right now.

Brandon:

Ok.

She focused on her emails and her to-do list. Only two more homes needed work: Ligaya and Sinta, the beach house to the right of Ligaya. Sinta was proving to be a challenge. What exactly represented love?

She moved on to the next emails. The delivery dates for Helena's B and B furnishings were confirmed. The contractor had finalized the dates for work.

Foster's Group needed an initial sketch of ideas, so Geneva tugged the leather-bound Traveler's notebook to her lap and grabbed her pouch of colored markers. In her sketch notebook, she started the beginnings of a color palette inspired by Foster's corporate website. Then, on the next page, she wrote down bullet points and questions to bring up to its owners.

The work was straightforward. It was almost old hat. She had a groove, a routine. Soon, she fell into thoughts of colors and fabrics, and her page was covered with doodles.

An email popped in from Nita. It was Geneva's flight confirmation to the Foster's Group meeting in three days. It was a straight shot to Chicago, to their headquarters, leaving at noon.

Above her, the light flickered, taking her out of her thoughts. She lifted her gaze to the window and noted the time. Only a half hour had passed, and the sky was pitch black, without a hint of light from the stars or the moon.

Then the house plunged into darkness, leaving the glow of her computer and iPad, luckily both still with power.

"Shoot." She crawled to the edge of the loft, where Brandon's curses trailed upward. "Brandon?"

"Aha!" From downstairs exuded a glow. "Ate Bea and her preparedness—yes!" The glow transitioned to a clear, bright light that he shined upward. "A flashlight, and a good one." Shadows played across his face. "You wanna come down? Or are you good up there?"

"I'll come down." Now that it was dark, admittedly the fear had begun to creep in, especially as the wind howled through the shuttered windows.

"I'll light your way."

"Thank you." Eyes on where he aimed the spotlight, she stepped down, keeping her hands solidly on the ladder rungs.

As both feet found purchase on the ground, the house groaned. The spotlight moved to the front windows, to where Brandon aimed and was turned. Geneva sucked in a breath.

Then their surroundings descended into another level of quiet.

"As soon as it all settles down, Chris said he would drive down in the van to grab us," he said.

"Okay." Unexpectedly, her voice shook. "Sorry. I thought that this wasn't going to be a big deal, but that was super loud."

"Yeah, I know what you mean. It's all much worse in the dark." He moved past her to the kitchen, avoiding her eyes. "But I saved you a sandwich."

"Thank you." She lowered herself into one of the kitchen chairs, where the plate, covered with plastic wrap, sat. When she peeled it back, her appetite returned in full force, and her stomach rumbled.

Brandon leaned against the kitchen counter and took a drink of tap water. Unease radiated off him; his left hand clutched the rim of the sink. She could have sworn that the glass shook as he tipped it back to drink.

"Wanna join me?" she offered, not liking the looks of him.

"I already ate," he growled.

"I mean, just to chat." At the rear of the house, the wood settled with a groan, but she tamped down her nervousness with a smile.

"I'm good right here."

Geneva pushed the chair with a foot. It squeaked against the floor. Brandon eyed the chair.

"What. Do I have the cooties? You weren't so scared about it the other day," she dared. This was the worst kind of low blow, and not Geneva's style at the very least. It wasn't that she didn't know how to flirt, but flirting with Brandon was like playing with wood laced with lighter fluid. One spark was all it took.

Luckily, her bluff worked, and Brandon walked over. He sat down in the chair, though he leaned back, legs out in front of him. He stuffed his hands in his pockets.

She split the sandwich in half and wrapped one piece with a napkin and offered it.

"It's yours," he said.

She smiled, warmed once again. "I only had three slices of bread left, which means that you left me this full sandwich and you ate a half one, and the heel of the loaf at that. I also know how much you eat." She shook it in front of him. "PB and J. You love it as much as I do."

"Sure?"

"Yep." She gestured toward the chips. "You can't have any of the salt-and-vinegar chips, though. That's all mine."

He brought the sandwich to his lips. "Oh, I know about you and your salt-and-vinegar chips. I have a permanent bruise on my shoulder from when you tackled me when I once grabbed a bag that you were keeping for your midnight snack."

Her cheeks burned, and a giggle escaped her lips. "Only-child problems."

They both ate in silence. Brandon gobbled up his sandwich in one and a half bites. He always did inhale his food.

"So, what's up? What's wrong?" she asked, examining her sandwich. It was very much Brandon's way, with the ratio of peanut butter to jelly at two to one.

He shook his head. "Do you mean besides the fact that we're in a tiny house during a tropical depression?"

The crack of thunder brought Geneva's gaze upward.

Next to her, Brandon jolted.

"Bran?"

His napkin was in a ball, and he fussed with it. Just as she was quick to express herself, Brandon was methodical and careful. He took his time. So, she waited, eating a chip.

"My parents." Brandon's words were almost a whisper. "It was a storm."

"Oh." Geneva exhaled. Of course. She felt foolish now, forgetting. "Their accident."

Tita Marilyn and Tito Joe's car accident had happened on the Beltway, on what had ended up being a six-car pileup during a rain-storm, triggered by a vehicle hydroplaning across three lanes. A thorough investigation had found that the driver of that hydroplaned vehicle had had a blood alcohol level over the legal limit to drive. These days, none of the Pusos drank—not even a glass of champagne during Chris's wedding—for this very reason.

He nodded. "It's stupid that I'm scared of storms when nothing happened to me."

She shook her head. "It's not stupid."

"Yeah, well, I wish I didn't feel this way sometimes." The muscle in his jaw worked; he was clenching. "Because it wasn't me who was out there. I had been so cocky that day. It had been a great day." He shook his head. "And then Beatrice called, and I got in my car to head to Annapolis, and the rain was bad, still. While driving I had visions of them and what they looked like, what the car looked like." He swallowed. "While I'd been thinking about how awesome I was, my parents were being sideswiped." He shut his eyes.

"Oh, Bran." She reached to his shaking hands and slipped hers in between his. He clutched onto them. "It's not your fault."

"It doesn't have to be my fault, does it, to feel like I could have done something?"

The question hit Geneva in the soft spot of her heart, in the place she kept shielded most days. It was a place she didn't visit often or allow anyone else in, where loss and regret resided. Even if she didn't know how it felt to lose her parents, loss was deeply ingrained in all the things she would never experience with her father.

Things changed in a split second. With one hydroplaning vehicle, or the rogue blood clot that had embedded itself into her father's brain, their lives changed. There were also secondary effects, like the acquisition of Heart Resort and her parents moving to Tennessee. Then the tertiary effects, like Brandon's regret and Geneva's indecision.

She was thankful for the tabletop, which grounded her. "You're right—it doesn't have to be. How can I help?"

"Thank you for asking. I'm . . . okay right now. Times like these . . . they're getting better, but I have a ways to go. I'm working on it, figuring out what is what."

She squeezed hard against Brandon's strong hands, hands that she had witnessed create something out of nothing. They were capable, a reflection of him and his spirit. He was so self-aware; he wasn't afraid of vulnerability. He smashed all her preconceived notions of bravery—this was probably why it had been hard for her to move on.

Then why do you?

Silence settled between them while Geneva searched for the answer to her own questions.

"Are there games in here?" he asked, the change of subject like cold water to the face.

It nudged Geneva from her thoughts. "Games?"

"Lemme go check." He let go of her hand and stood in a flurry, taking the flashlight from the table. Geneva breathed out as it darkened around her, releasing the pressure that had built up in her chest.

It didn't take long for Brandon to come to the conclusion that there wasn't anything to pass the time with. There was virtually no storage to scour through.

Then she remembered that they *did* have one source of entertainment. "Oh, duh. I have my iPad. I downloaded some shows from Netflix. I've got a full charge."

"You just said my most favorite word besides *pizza*."

"Except." Her gaze darted to the two uncomfortable chairs. "There's no real place to watch movies except for—"

Upstairs.

The mood flipped, and Geneva's thoughts gravitated back to the stark present of their solitude.

"That's all right," he said, as if reading her mind. "We can watch right down here at the kitchen table."

♡

Back up at the loft, Geneva grabbed her iPad from her bed. Luna was stretched out in the folds of the white sheets, paws extended, clearly communicating that the mattress would be way more comfortable than those kitchen chairs.

That's asking for trouble.

But this isn't the bad kind of trouble.

Yes, it is.

Luna meowed and slapped at the air, waking Geneva up from her argument with the devil on her shoulder.

This was all silly. What was wrong with her? She and Brandon were adults. Surely they could watch a show together on a bed. Brandon was more than a gentlemen, and she could keep her hands to herself.

"Everything okay up there?" Brandon yelled up.

You're going to be mature about this. Geneva nodded at her decision. "I have a better idea. Do you want to come up here?"

Silence ensued from the first floor.

"Um. You sure?" he asked.

"Yes." With the answer, she became more and more convinced. "Yes. Yes, of course. What was I thinking? Come up here." She waved him up. "I'll light your way this time." She turned on her flashlight phone.

Brandon climbed the ladder and entered the loft, making the space twice as small.

She backed into the loft, without much choice but to sit on the bed as he crawled in. He stuttered in his movement, unsure where to go, because it became clear that there was no other option but to get on the bed with her.

The awkwardness was so thick that it brought Geneva to giggles.

He stilled. "What?"

"Look at us, Brandon. We're acting like we're in high school. Come on this bed, jeez."

His facial expression eased, and he joined her. "Can I . . . lie down?"

She straightened and sat cross-legged. "Of course you can. But I appreciate that you asked."

Brandon stretched out on the bed, and his eyes just about rolled to the back of his head. He groaned. "Sweet relief."

"It's a comfy bed." She laughed, but her heart squeezed. It had been a long day for the both of them, and with what he'd revealed downstairs, he'd needed a moment to relax.

"Yes it is." His eyes shut for a beat, his voice a rumble, sending heat through her body. He turned so he faced her, sliding a hand under his cheek. There was a slight bit of fuzz on his chin, and she noted the few curls in his thick black hair. Like this, he was a mix of young and grown Brandon. More than once, when they were together four years ago, Geneva had watched him sleep. Alternately, she'd loved knowing that she would wake up with him already up and about. Then his dark eyes opened, and he looked at her through long, thick lashes. "So what's on the docket?"

She had been so entranced with this man in her bed that she'd accidentally pressed one of the app icons so that it prompted her to delete it. She snatched her finger back and reset the screen, then tapped on the Netflix app. She flipped the screen around, showing the list of all the movies she'd downloaded.

She braced herself with a grin because she knew exactly what he would say.

"Noooooo." He threw himself backward on the bed. "Not thooooose."

"Did you expect any less?"

"For a woman who doesn't like to stay in the same place, you sure have a reliable movie list."

"Some things really can't change."

He held out a hand. "Give me that thing." With the iPad in his hand, Brandon read out the choices. "*Titanic*—nope, no drowning ships and dying people please. *Top Gun*—nope, I grew up with my own version of Ice Man, and watching Val on the screen doesn't really excite me. *The Holiday*—dear God. And *Notting Hill*? Jeez."

As he continued to critique her list of nineties movies, Geneva watched the predictable expressions on Brandon's face and her heart swelled with the familiarity of his smile.

"You're really going to make me pick?" he asked.

"Surprise me," she said, though it wouldn't be a surprise. She foresaw his answer much like she knew Beatrice's favorite dessert, halo-halo, at any celebration dinner. As dependable as her mother's phone calls.

Her mother.

Geneva had been so fixated on Brandon's presence that she'd forgotten about her mother. She'd intended to call her as soon as she was at Puso; Lisa's worry over Geneva's safety rivaled any helicopter parent's, and it hadn't stopped after she'd become an adult. While her mother was sensitive to Geneva's need for independence and privacy, she expected a check-in when there was something big, such as a storm, coming through.

"How about I compromise and we watch *Twilight*. There's at least a plot in there, and a fight scene."

She giggled and hopped onto her messages on her phone. "Hold up a sec—I need to text my mom."

Geneva:

You're probably watching the weather, but don't worry I'm fine.

When she pressed the green button, the status bar inched but stopped just shy of completion.

He blinked up at her. "Connection down?"

"Looks like it."

He pulled his phone out of his back pocket. "Yep, I don't have signal either." He pressed to call one of his contacts and put the phone against his ear. "Looks like there's no cell reception."

"My mom's going to be worried sick. She's already on the verge of getting on the road herself to drag me back home."

"That would be a sight." Brandon snickered, then stopped as he caught her expression. "Something up between you and Tita Lisa?"

Inside, the two sides of Geneva's brain battled for how to respond. On one side was the part of her that trusted Brandon, especially after he'd admitted his own fears just a few minutes ago. Then there was the other side—the shame. "You're going to think I'm the worst."

"I doubt I'll feel that way."

"You thought that way a week ago."

"I was angry and a little bitter, but I never thought you were the worst." Brandon set down the iPad on the bed and sat up so his back was to the headboard. He pulled in his legs. "Try me."

After a beat, she said, "I haven't been home in about a year."

"Wow. Because of work?"

"Eh." She flipped her phone upside down just so that she didn't have to watch the message try to send itself. "I had time."

He frowned. "Then why didn't you?"

"I've been too busy, I guess."

His eyebrows lifted.

She nodded. Then she shook her head. When she did, it unleashed a wave of jumbled thoughts. "It's complicated."

"Try me." He opened a hand out to her, and she placed hers into his. This would be twice they'd held hands tonight; but this time, she was the recipient of his comfort. It urged her on.

"My parents tried to give me everything I ever needed so I would be successful. We even had a list of things we would do together. But then my dad had his stroke," Geneva said. "And everything changed. No Kilimanjaro for my parents and me. No Machu Picchu. No Grand Canyon. They'd worked so hard with all these plans for retirement, and now that they're retired, they can't do half the things they planned."

His gaze dropped for a beat. "The leather notebook you had with you in Annapolis."

"I still have it." She gestured over her shoulder. "I still add to the bucket list. I like to torture myself with the pressure, I guess."

"I've never known you not to be determined."

"It's to my detriment sometimes. No one holds any of my goals over my head, Bran. But looking at the list and what our family accomplished together, well, it made me want to be more. Over time, I tackled that list. The more I accomplished, the more fun I had, the further away I got from home, and it just got harder to return. For whenever I did, I wasn't sure where I belonged, and how I fit in. By their side to support them? Or out there in the world to make my way? If the notebook is accountability, my parents are reality. And I'm scared—" She swallowed and pushed the rest out. "I'm scared to find out that I haven't done enough, that I've just been meandering, checking off a list that wasn't mine but everyone else's. At the same time, I'm afraid to find out that I've done all that but haven't been a good daughter."

"Did you really want to climb Kilimanjaro?"

"No." She laughed. "I actually don't like camping. Glamping maybe?"

He scoured her face. "It makes sense, now. Your boundaries."

The conversation had happened after the first night they'd made love. They'd been lying side by side, naked, his hand resting on her waist. Vegas lights had streamed through his Airbnb windows. The rest of the family had been out there, partying, celebrating Chris and Eden's nuptials.

I don't want this to be complicated. I can't stay.

"You wanted boundaries, too, for your own reasons. Though it was me who left," Geneva reminded him. "But in this case, with my parents, it's the opposite—"

He frowned. "How do you mean?"

"It's me who has to go home. But it's too late, isn't it? You can't use Filipino time for this."

CHAPTER TWENTY-THREE

Filipino time—a cultural concept that things happened when they happened, that it was better late than never. It had been Brandon's father's excuse when their six-pack had rolled into Mass ten minutes late or arrived at Filipino-hosted parties a half hour after their start time and still were among the first celebrants.

When was Filipino time an admissible reason?

Was it acceptable to be tardy, and was it fair to those waiting?

Brandon shrugged. "I hope Filipino time counts, because it took me a long time to come back here, to Heart Resort. While I give my brother a lot of grief, if the tables had been turned, I would be pissed at me too. I took my sweet time."

Brandon slid brief looks at Geneva, careful not to linger too long. As comfortable as this bed was, he couldn't let himself off guard. The last time they'd been on a bed together, they'd been tearing up the sheets. Her reminder that he'd had his own boundaries was a point of accountability. She was right that it was unfair to blame their breakup on her. She'd just been the one to follow through.

She tugged on his arm. "What you and your brother have going on is completely different. Chris is difficult, and though I can't say you're an easier personality, you are oil and vinegar."

"Don't you mean oil and water?"

She smiled. "Nope. Oil and vinegar. A little shake and the both of you can make something good. Hence how we are barreling toward the grand opening."

As if the world contended, thunder crashed around them.

Brandon swallowed down the uptick of his nerves. "Um, Oscar protests."

She laughed, and the sound of it was soothing. Brandon had missed this, her laugh and being this close to her with her hand in his.

"Filipino time still applies to you, Gen. You can still go back. You can just show up. There doesn't need to be any fanfare."

"Like you did?"

He laughed, though inside an alarm blared. In leaving Annapolis, he'd left a whole lot of unresolved issues and arrived with his own challenges. "Yeah, I guess so. Sometimes the lead-up's the worst part." Brandon thought of his own convictions, of the nervousness he'd carried walking up the steps just a week ago. "What matters is that you show up. Your parents love you. They know that you've been trying to come home."

Her eyes fluttered upward to him. In them was a spark of playfulness. "We're so much alike."

"You're right. And sometimes we mess up. Although," he said, then took a breath, "you should be prepared for the unexpected if you just show up."

"Like what?"

"Oh, I dunno. Like having to plan a grand opening. Or dealing with a storm. Perhaps meeting up with someone you had a heck of a crush on, and then having to face the truth."

Their fingers were linked together now in their own method of play, and Brandon sensed a shift between them. Geneva had inched closer.

"The truth," she whispered.

"That I wasn't perfect that last day we were together."

"Bran—"

"Gen, wait, let me say this," he said, grabbing hold of the moment. His memory cycled back. He'd come home from work to find Geneva digging through the bottom kitchen cupboards. She'd been matching Tupperware covers to containers, and behind her had been a garbage bag of unmatched pieces.

He'd gone off on her. He hadn't been ready for this change, for her to make this change.

He'd told her to go. And when she had, he'd waited to reach out. By the time he had, it had been like coming upon a cold case—past its statute of limitations.

"That night," he continued, "I was scared. I was scared of letting go of anything."

"It wasn't my place to go through their things."

"It was wrong for me to yell. I shouldn't have told you to leave." He shook his head, wishing that he'd done the work back then to let go. He was working on it this very minute, by being there at the resort and gearing himself up to tell his siblings about Mulberry Road's sale. "It was hard for me. Still hard for me."

"I know." She scooted closer. "Filipino time, right?" She offered a pensive smile.

"Filipino time. Better late than never."

He gazed up at her; half of her face was in shadow. He knew that if he came upon her in the dark, he'd know her by touch, by voice, by spirit. That even if years passed and they found themselves on opposite sides of the world, somehow their paths would cross again.

The thought of this bathed Brandon with relief. Much like the small reminders throughout his day that perhaps his parents were milling just beyond reach, Geneva would be too.

He dared to inch closer.

"Bran." Geneva's voice had taken on the quality of warm sugar. At the same time, he said, "Gen."

"Yes," they said simultaneously, and laughed.

"You first," he said.

"I was going to say, if we're so alike, I wonder if you're thinking the same thing I am."

A curl of need started in his belly. "Is this a trick? If I tell you what I'm thinking and it's not what you're thinking, it's going to be mighty awkward because there's a storm outside and this place is as tiny as a matchbox."

Her body seemed to relax; her hand left his palm and crawled up his wrist. It beckoned him to keep going.

"I'm thinking that I want to kiss you again. Is that what you're thinking?" he asked.

Geneva took her bottom lip into her teeth, and Brandon's eyes locked onto her mouth, onto the small peek of her tongue. She nodded.

But he no longer wanted to play this game. Their kisses at the warehouse, in her kitchen, and at the restaurant had been something they'd fallen into. They were instinctive. This kiss would need to be different; it would be decisive and meaningful.

"That's not enough, Geneva. I want to hear you say it." He leaned in closer. "Because I not only want to kiss you, but I want to touch you and take you into my mouth. I want to feel you under me and over me."

Her lips parted minutely, and Brandon heard her exhale. Then she took his hand and placed it at the nape of her neck, his thumb on her carotid.

Her pulse was strong and slow, and when she swallowed, he felt the intimate movement of her throat. "I want you to kiss me." Her voice reverberated so its echo reached him, to his core. "I want all of it."

It was she who leaned forward, and the bravery took Brandon off guard. A part of him still couldn't believe that she was here, and with him. That this moment wasn't just another one of his dreams.

There had been so many dreams. So many questions. So many doubts.

But he pushed all that down and away.

They didn't take their eyes off one another as they kissed. His brain needed to catalog every moment, every breath, every move of her body. How she towered over him briefly, hair falling over his face as she straddled him.

"Gen, you feel so good." He breathed out, resting his hands on her hips, squeezing gently. Her warmth bypassed their clothing. He pushed against her, an instinct, enticing a sweet groan from her lips.

"Bran," she whispered into his ear. "I want it all off."

"Yes, ma'am." He reached behind him and peeled off his shirt with her assistance. She started on her buttons, and he joined her in the endeavor.

The sight of her skin was like coming home. As he splayed his hand on her abdomen and then up to her breasts, all the years melted away. As if they hadn't ended, as if what they were doing was wonderfully old hat, as if every day in the last four years had been spent together.

With a thumb he undid the front clasp of her bra.

She threw her head back in pleasure.

The sight of her neck, the small sign of submission, was Geneva's tell.

So he rose higher on the bed, and supported her back with a hand. He took her into his mouth; he tended to her, noting the little things that made her gasp. He wanted nothing more than to give her everything she sought at that moment, to ease all her thoughts.

Gently, he laid her on her back and, leaning on one elbow, made his way back to her mouth. She ran her fingers up his back, a movement that elicited a lustful shiver, and he had to take a breath.

"Is this okay?" he asked to confirm. He wanted to do this right so that there would be no reason for regret.

She answered by lowering her hand to the zipper of his jeans. With the same deft movement of her fingers, she popped his jeans button open and dragged the zipper down, causing him to shut his eyes.

If this was the consequence for the second time around, for Filipino time, it was all worth it.

CHAPTER
TWENTY-FOUR

They tumbled through the sheets, lost in each other's breaths and heart-beats. Slow and seductively, he peeled off her clothes until they were skin to skin. They moved, creating heat, creating fire, creating noise, until they were much louder than the storm outside. Nothing else mattered but what was happening indoors, between her and Brandon.

Geneva found comfort in Brandon. This, being intimate, was never difficult with him. He read her cues—he clamored for them. His eyes never left her face.

"You're beautiful, Geneva." He looked down from above, with an expression that exceeded sincerity, with such care.

She cupped his cheek. "Don't stop kissing me."

His lips trailed her chin and down her neck to her shoulder, fingers deftly preparing her so her body hummed with pleasure. Inside, she was a coil tightening, to the lust, to the anticipation. He was seemingly taking his time, and she wasn't sure if she would make it.

"Please, Bran . . ."

"Do you have condoms?"

She nodded. Her whole life was with her in this house. "In my bag, at the foot of the bed."

He left her for the moment and returned, though now his expression was determined and serious. He crawled onto the bed, a prowler to his prey. Lust filled, Geneva opened herself to him, beckoning for this moment that she'd been pining for since she'd seen him that first day.

"Gen," he said. "This changes things."

"Yes, I know." She guided him toward her. "It changed from the first kiss."

He entered her, gentle at first, then filling her. She rocked with him; she couldn't get enough. They kissed and nipped, bodies coming together in coordinated movements. Slow at first, and then quickly and swiftly, until the coil unwound and she let go at the same time he did.

Of course he waited for her. Brandon was willing to wait. While Geneva was raring to go, he was patient. He was truly like the foundation of the home, unmoved and solid. While Geneva was trying to renovate and fix, reinvent herself, Brandon remained true, for better or for worse, through all life's storms.

With the release came the rush of emotions. Of regret, of satisfaction, of a wish she could never say. Because there was so much left unsaid, so much in the years that had passed. Like how much he'd meant to her, how she'd measured every man against him since their affair, and how she knew that no one could be like him.

The reality that she'd left him four years ago crashed down around her with the crack of thunder.

Tears sprang into her eyes.

He fingered her hair out of her face. "Hey, Gen. What's wrong. Was that—"

"It was perfect. It was exactly what I needed. What I wanted."

"Me too. But . . . you're crying."

"I'm just overwhelmed with everything I said, with everything we just did." She looked into his eyes, at the trust in them. It gave her the bravery to say more. "I missed you, so much. Back then, I shouldn't have assumed that you were ready to let go like I was. I shouldn't have gone through those cupboards. And I shouldn't have left when you told me to. I loved . . . I love you, Brandon."

"Oh Jesus, Geneva. I love you. I always have. I never should have told you to go." He pressed his lips into a thin line. "I was wrong—you were only trying to help. And we're here, and that's what matters."

"You're right." She was overthinking things again. It was her superpower, this internalization that would drive her out the door and off the resort. She pushed down her lingering thoughts and focused on enjoying the way he held her. "What do we do now?"

"Do you mean like after we have more sex?" His devilish grin appeared.

She nudged him. "Yes, after that. After tonight. Tomorrow when this all passes. What do we say to your sister?"

He placed a finger on her lips. "Please don't ever mention any of my family members when we're naked."

"My bad," she said against his touch.

"I don't want to think about anything or anyone else but you and me. So I guess that means I have to keep you distracted." He leaned down and kissed her bottom lip.

She would allow it to happen.

♡

Geneva rowed the kayak in the still water of the sound. Everywhere was calm: the light-blue, cloud-free sky above her, the dark-blue waters below. The warm summer wind blew gently against her skin.

Finally. She had been in search of this stillness, where there was no pressure to be anywhere, to be anything. She was, finally, content.

There was only one person missing.

In her periphery, the point of a surfboard appeared. She turned— Brandon was by her side, prone on the board. He wore a wet suit; his hair was tousled. His upper arms flexed as he paddled through the waves. He saluted her as if to say, *I'm here.*

Now she was complete.

But, from afar, a sound of an air horn took Geneva's attention. She shaded her eyes with a hand. Squinting, she recognized someone waving a white flag. As in surrender, as in help.

We need to get her. She signaled Brandon, who reflected back an unreadable expression. She pointed in the woman's direction.

"I'm going," she yelled, and began to paddle. Then a cross wave cut through so she was pushed away from the woman as well as from Brandon.

She was being swept out into the Atlantic.

While Geneva didn't get a good look at the woman, she knew innately that the woman was her. And she had been waiting for herself, not Brandon.

So, she left the safety of the kayak to save the woman. She dived into the tumultuous water to save herself.

Geneva's eyes flew open and she gasped, swiftly taking in her surroundings. The room was lit, but beyond, through the loft window, was darkness, still.

She was in Ligaya; the electricity was back on.

Geneva exhaled a breath, and she turned to her right, to Brandon's bare back. Her panic subsided at the sight of him and the black-eyed Susan tattoo.

Geneva had had a similar dream for a while now, though this was the first time it was in the water. It always started out peaceful, and it'd turn into something panic filled, vivid, in her point of view, of her chasing herself unsuccessfully.

And apparently with this last dream, even Brandon's appearance hadn't helped her.

It was as if her ambition was intent on plaguing her both day and night. Whatever this simultaneous restlessness and exhaustion was couldn't be helped by anyone but herself.

Except this time, she noted, she'd jumped into the water.

Geneva reached for her phone. Eleven p.m. They'd only been asleep a couple of hours.

She inched herself closer to Brandon and wrapped her arm around his waist. His body was warm, comforting, and she rested her cheek against his back.

No one had come close to Brandon the last four years. From the men she'd dated after him, she'd wanted everything: friendship, love, trust. She'd wanted perfection, because Brandon had been the rod to measure them by.

Now here he was.

His heartbeat was slow, a metronome of calm. A stark difference from how he had been in their lovemaking, where he was everything active, strong, firm, and, might she say, commanding.

A rush of excitement invaded her body once more, and Geneva squelched a squeal.

Brandon was snoring in this sweet way, so she slipped out of bed and donned his shirt and dug out underwear from her duffel. She climbed down the ladder, used the bathroom. Luna paced behind her as she should have done before the storm began. Then again, if the cat hadn't purposely hidden, then this—them—would have never happened.

"Did you do that on purpose, Luna?" she whispered.

Luna jumped up on the kitchen table.

"Well, thank you," Geneva said, rubbing her behind the ears. The cat leaned against her touch. "He's not so bad, is he?"

She purred, until she seemingly had enough and made her way back up to the loft.

Geneva followed and after her climb glanced at the calendar on her stool, to her original date of departure, which she'd crossed out with a pencil, to the encircled new date, three days from now. She'd done that preemptively as part of her decision-making process, to evaluate how she'd feel leaving early. Next to it was her leather notebook, open from when she'd haphazardly set it down when the lights had gone out. The family bucket list, to a page. One entry stood out: *Fall in love.* The box was checked.

She'd checked it four years ago, a week into her affair with Brandon. She had completely forgotten about that entry, moving on to check the other boxes, and she never looked back.

It was what she did. Would she do it again?

From behind her, Brandon sighed in his sleep.

No, I'm not ready to decide.

Geneva climbed back into bed and slid back to her spoon position.

"Hey." Brandon's voice vibrated through his body. Gently, he turned, and she nuzzled into his chest. If it was possible, he was even warmer, and she snuggled into him as he wrapped his leg over hers, grounding her. "How are you even awake? I'm usually up before you."

"It's still night. I had a weird dream."

"Mmm . . . so it wasn't because I didn't work you out enough?"

Her body flushed all over again, and she nipped at his skin.

"That feels good. More," he groaned.

"Pilyo."

"That's right, *naughty* is my middle name." His hand slid down and squeezed her behind. "Wanna tell me about your dream?"

"You and I were out in the water. You were on a surfboard. I was kayaking."

"Did we hang ten?"

"No, we were literally just sitting there."

"That sounds peaceful."

"It was . . ." Until a wave had swept her sideways, and she'd been too flustered to use the wave to her advantage, to orient herself to face the wave to overcome it, so she'd leapt into the water.

"You're thinking again." One eye opened. "For someone who's supposed to be more expressive than me, you're not saying much."

"Hmm." Geneva snapped out of her last thought.

"Hey." This time, both of Brandon's eyes were open. "Where'd you go?"

"Nowhere. I'm right here."

And she scoured her brain on how she could always be.

CHAPTER TWENTY-FIVE

Day 8
Weather: clear skies, 70°F
Tropical Depression Oscar off the coast of Virginia Beach

Brandon woke to a brightly lit home and Geneva in the crook of his arm, and he grinned like a man who'd just won the lottery. Geneva's face was calm and had a hint of a smile. Her hair cascaded around her face and onto her bare chest.

If this was a dream, he never wanted to wake up.

The clock on the wall told him that it was just shy of six in the morning, which meant coffee time, and he patted the side table for his phone. He remembered that it was downstairs, where he'd ventured for a midnight water-and-bathroom break. There had been a couple of these breaks overnight; he and Geneva had kept each other up, either talking or making love, as well as other wonderful, sinful things that he'd hold in his memory bank forever.

He sat up and took in the remnants of their night—the comforter askew, their clothing spread out around the bed—and his heart leapt. What a difference one night made.

He dressed. All the while, Luna eyed him from the edge of the loft, so he turned while zipping up his jeans. As if the cat didn't know what had gone on last night, but the light of day chased away the denial that the cat was a third-party observer. "Put in a good word for me, okay?" he asked Luna now, knowing how much she meant to Geneva. Today was another beginning in their story, and he wanted all the good vibes, including the cat's blessing.

Luna meowed.

That was a good sign, right?

Brandon picked up around the bed and made a little pile of Geneva's discarded clothing. One thing he'd learned from her from the three weeks they'd been together: she had a thing about things out of place. He plucked her phone off the floor and placed it next to her open calendar and the leather notebook cover, next to the shell he'd given her a few days ago.

His heart warmed. That was, until his gaze wandered to the date, two days from now, encircled.

Brandon backed away from the calendar like it had burned him. It was a reminder of reality. That there were time limits. That there would be decisions, not only for Geneva but for him too.

He wasn't ready just yet.

Behind him, Geneva stirred under the sheets, and his thoughts returned to the present. It was 6:00 a.m. after another storm that he'd been able to endure, helped by the company of the woman he loved, and the first thing he needed so he could process all this was coffee.

After climbing down, he started the kettle for french press coffee, and he opened the door to the cool morning. The waves were lively. Remnants of leaves and tree branches littered the sand. Otherwise, it was as if the peninsula was bathed and refreshed, renewed. Hope was in the air; he felt it in the breeze.

While sipping his first cup, he tidied up the first floor to distract himself, and he grabbed his phone, which was hanging on to its final drop of juice. Notifications littered the screen; he plugged in his phone using Geneva's charger and stood next to the outlet and tended to messages.

"Is that coffee I smell down there?" Geneva's voice was hoarse, tearing his attention away. He backed up to view the loft, to see her sitting up on the bed, a sheet wrapped around her body.

"Yes, and I saved you a cup. Come on down."

"That's so sweet. You and Nita are the only ones who remember to save me a cup of coffee."

"Nita?"

"A good friend of mine, and my assistant."

It dawned on Brandon that there was a whole section of Geneva's life that he didn't know about, and she with his. "Ah. We have a lot to catch up on," he said.

The thought of her calendar popped up in his head.

Stop.

"I'll get some clothes on," she said.

As she got ready, Brandon returned to his phone. His eyebrows rose as he caught up with his family's group chat. He took a sip of coffee and absentmindedly said, "This coffee is so good."

"Isn't it, though?" In the loft, the blanket fluffed upward with a snap. "I was on the road and had very little equipment, so french press was the way to go, and I can't quit it. Beatrice made sure that I had one here when I arrived."

At the mention of his sister's name, the mood plummeted.

"Ugh. I shouldn't have said her name," Geneva said.

"My siblings are like earworms but for the memory. Especially because my phone is blowing up." He scrolled the messages upward, still combing through the one-line responses each of them had answered with. It was common to wake up to the entire family having several conversations, leading to hundreds of messages.

Geneva climbed down. "We'd better call them to let them know we're okay."

He helped her down the final rung, drawn to her. Her hair was up in a bun, exposing the black-eyed Susan at the hairline. He'd been enamored by it all night; he kissed it again. Then, with a hand on her hip, he spun her around gently. She slung her arm across her mouth. "I have morning breath."

He looked into her eyes, then pulled her arm down. Then he kissed her on the lips.

Her eyes fluttered open after the kiss, and he was met with a serious expression. "How do we do this, Bran?"

"What do you mean?" He cupped his hands on her behind and pushed her against him. "I thought I showed you how we do it."

She lightly slapped him on the shoulder. "Be serious."

He kissed her on the neck, hoping to distract her from this avenue of conversation. "I love you."

"I love you too. Bran—"

"And I'm very serious. I'm serious about these buttons totally in the way." He messed with the first button on her pajama top. He wanted to hang on to this moment.

But Geneva wasn't having it. Her face had skewed into an honest-to-goodness frown. So he linked his arms around her back. "Fine. Okay, how do *you* think we should do this?"

"I want to tell Beatrice first, and alone."

"Shouldn't I tell her?"

She shook her head. "No. She's my best friend." She placed a hand against her chest. "I'm having palpitations just thinking of it. Feel."

She took his hand and placed it on her heart. It beat at a runner's pace.

"It's going to be okay," he reassured. And yet, the thumping against his palm had a similar effect on his heart. Any reveal, good or bad, would elicit a major reaction. And would they limit their reveal to the present? Would they have to admit to their affair from four years ago?

The phone beeped with another text. And another. And another. Their eyes locked.

"Go catch up. I'll brush my teeth," she said.

As she scuttled to the bathroom, Brandon scrolled through the texts, finally arriving at the most recent ones, from this morning. "I . . . oh . . . Gen!"

"What's up?" she mumbled, a toothbrush sticking out of her mouth.

"I'm caught up with the texts. My fam's already out and about checking around for the damage. So far, so good on that end. No major damage to the houses, and none behind the gate."

"Well, good. Business as usual," she said, smiling, resuming her toothbrushing.

Then, after a final swipe up of the texts, Brandon moved to perch on the end of his chair.

Beatrice:

We're on our way to you.

Beatrice:

We even have coffee.

The next text was sent to Brandon only.

Gil:

You've got about two minutes before we roll up.

From his night and the lack of caffeine in his system, Brandon stuttered, "G . . . Gen . . . they're on their way to us."

From outside came the thumping music of a radio's bass.

"Is that them?" she asked from the bathroom doorway, glancing down at herself, disheveled in her pajamas.

Voices, several of them, were heard right outside, answering her question.

Geneva scrambled to fix herself, while Brandon stood to . . . he didn't know . . . act normal. He leaned against the fridge, then decided to look into it. He breathed in the cold air, for strength and stealth.

"Here they come," she whispered, just as the screen door screeched open.

"The rescue team is here!" Beatrice announced as she stepped in, and without knocking. She was wearing another one of her colorful dresses, and she peeled off her sunglasses. Behind her were Chris and Gil, holding two large to-go cups of coffee.

"Wow, you guys. Come on in!" Geneva squealed, not convincingly.

Brandon took a carton from the fridge and faced his sister's inquisitive expression. "Hey! What took you guys so long? Anyone want eggs?"

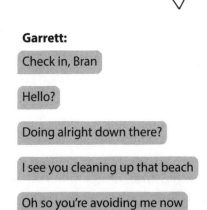

Garrett:

Check in, Bran

Hello?

Doing alright down there?

I see you cleaning up that beach

Oh so you're avoiding me now

If Brandon had not been watching his phone for Geneva's texts, he would have thrown his phone into the water. Garrett was relentless.

Normally, he liked this quality in his friend. Garrett was a fierce negotiator, and he was one of the most determined people Brandon knew. But right then, he wished that Garrett would let up a little. He needed a moment's break, a breather after the best night since forever and after a full day of backbreaking work. He didn't have an answer for him about Mulberry Road, nor did he know what to say about his ultimatum. Everything seemed to fall on the next step, which was to tell the family. Though with how busy everyone was, he wasn't sure when Geneva was going to tell Beatrice.

Tropical Depression Oscar had passed through the Outer Banks with very little damage compared to Maximus. The entire team had been scattered on the resort, cleaning up the beach and debris and inspecting all the homes. That morning, after his siblings had arrived at Ligaya, they'd scooped up him and Geneva to start cleanup almost immediately. Beatrice had naturally recruited Geneva to work alongside her, and Brandon hadn't seen Geneva since.

Brandon entered his apartment. It was still a blank slate without an inch of fabric on the windows or on the floor, and with the barest of furniture. But it was his, and this morning, it took on new meaning. For the first time in years, he was together with his family and the woman he loved. The future held so much hope, and this apartment, in this southern colonial named Puso, he actually felt at home.

With one final look at his phone—with no new text from Geneva— he threw it, his keys, and his wallet onto the coffee table.

He dressed out of his clothes for a quick shower—he assumed that he would see Geneva for dinner and later on tonight—and his phone dinged a text message. He ignored it. It was probably still Garrett. So he took his time and showered and dressed, then, finally, after he felt clean enough, walked out into the living room . . .

And properly jumped back at the sight of his brother, feet up on the coffee table, a hand draped across the couch and the other scrolling up on his phone.

"Dang, Kuya Gil. You scared the living daylights out of me."

Gil twisted in his seat to look at him. He had already changed out of his work clothes into one of his button-down shirts. "You drained the whole resort with that shower. That was twenty minutes!"

He rubbed his hair with his towel. "I didn't realize I was being timed. How did you get in?"

"You left the door unlocked, which was good . . ."

"What's up?" Brandon tossed his towel over the shower door and walked up while throwing on a shirt.

Gil's hand was extended, shaking his phone. Brandon swiped it from him.

Loaded onto the browser was Heart Resort's website, and splashed across the top banner were Geneva and Brandon, foreheads touching. It was both stunning and surreal, how good they looked and how evidently into each other they were.

"Speechless, are you?" Gil remarked. "I mean, talk about a wow-factor home page. It almost looks believable."

Brandon willed his face into a neutral expression. He couldn't say a word. "Tammy did a good job."

Geneva could be telling her right now. Maybe that's why she hasn't texted.

"Uh-huh." Gil rolled his eyes. "Where are you headed to?"

"To the restaurant. I'm meeting with Lainey for the final kitchen walk-through. Why?"

"I wanted to get you alone." He patted the sofa cushion.

Oh, here we go. Brandon's neckline itched. He felt his brother's stare deep in his bones. "I don't need to sit. What's up?"

"You're not going to tell me?"

There were two things he couldn't have yet told his brother, so he played clueless. "I don't know what you're talking about."

Gil heaved a breath. "All right, then. I'm just going to come out and say it. Bran, it's written all over your and Geneva's faces this morning. The two of you are a thing. I get why you're keeping it a secret, and you don't need any of our approvals. But it will be better if you told our siblings rather than them finding out themselves. Despite all the secrets we keep, the expectation is that we're honest."

Brandon shook his head. "That is the most hypocritical thing ever."

Gil bit his bottom lip. "Yep. Pusos aren't perfect. Then again, no one is."

CHAPTER
TWENTY-SIX

"Let's make sure those pillows go upstairs, and yes, that afghan goes down here." Geneva was at the door of Tiwala, which she'd designed with textured fabrics and geometric designs. With her iPad, she checked off the items as they were carried into the house. Beatrice, Eden, and Rhiannon were with her for the final decorating, with the rest of the resort crew done for the day with the storm cleanup. To make up for the delay, they would all need to work overtime the next couple of days.

"There should be two pillows and lamps with the wooden base and, if you can handle it, a rattan bowl still left in the van," Geneva instructed as Beatrice and Rhiannon went out for another load.

Eden peeked from the kitchen. "So . . . Bea said that you and Bran were in Ligaya all night long? Was it . . . *joyful?*"

Her cheeks burned. Geneva had been on her toes after this morning's sudden arrival at her beach house. So she focused on the screen to keep herself steady. "I was glad to have the company."

"Where did he sleep? If I remember, that house doesn't have a couch or a love seat."

Stomping from the front stoop brought the room to silence as Beatrice, with her earbuds in, entered with pillows precariously balanced against her chest.

Geneva pointed to the loft; Beatrice sang and climbed the stairs.

Silence continued, though Geneva felt Eden's stare and silent interrogation.

"I'm a romance writer, Geneva." Eden pretend-swept the floor and glanced up toward the loft. "And romance writers can pick up a trope like no one's business."

To add more space between them and reduce the peer pressure that was working on her, Geneva moved to catalog the half-dozen framed prints leaned up against the wall. "I don't know what you're talking about."

"Just one bed? Forced proximity?" Eden's eyes gleamed with both mischief and warmth, and for a beat, Geneva was tempted. How she wanted to talk to someone about this. How she wanted to share this news, especially with friends.

All morning, she had been on cloud nine or, better yet, rocking in a kayak on top of the waves. Thoughts of Brandon and their night had flitted through her head when she'd least expected it, and she'd found herself grinning like a fool.

But she couldn't yet say a word, not until she spoke to Beatrice first. News traveled like wildfire among the Pusos. They had the kind of ESP that Eden, by way of marriage, possessed. Beatrice had to hear it from Geneva first.

Rhiannon walked in with two lamps and settled them in their required areas. "What's just one bed?"

"Nothing," the two women said.

Geneva coughed. "Rhi, can you grab the last of the framed prints from the van? I'm missing a couple."

"Okey doke."

When the young woman left, Geneva side-eyed Eden. "You know what this sounds like? This sounds to me like *someone* is looking for ideas for their book. Is this projection?"

"No, but as someone who's not a Puso by blood, and impartial to the general drama of this family, my antennae are up. Something is afoot, or perhaps aspark, and I think it's because of you."

"Is *aspark* even a word?"

"No, but as the master of my own universes, I can make it up." She winked.

"Gen!" Beatrice called from above; her head peeked out from the railing. She took off one of her earbuds. "I think I'm good up here. Do you want to check?"

Eden pointed at her. "Uh-huh. Distraction saves you another day. But heed my advice. Clear the air before it ends up biting you in the butt. Trust me."

Geneva, face burning, made a *pfft* noise and rolled her eyes to play it off. Then she hopped up the steps to get the heck out of that room; she knew Eden was right.

She would tell Beatrice after finishing up this house.

When the bedroom came into view, white sheets topped with corduroy pillows on a bed pushed up against a textured wall, all Eden's questions fell away. They were replaced with pride. What a difference a week made. "This is perfect."

"I agree. It's exactly what belief feels like. Classic and reliable."

The way Beatrice complimented her work always touched her. Not once had Beatrice doubted Geneva's dreams. Would Beatrice feel different once Geneva told her about her and Brandon? "Eight houses down, two more to go." Her voice cracked.

"And with six more days?"

Geneva stilled.

Beatrice's face crumpled into a frown. "Two?"

"I don't know," she said, in full truth, and a sliver of guilt wrapped around her like a ribbon.

"But if you decide to stay with me, then you can do more of this. Of anything you want . . . and the sky is the limit!"

The pressure built around her heart, and Geneva resisted it with all her might. She hated pressure; she gave herself enough of it as it was. And now with Brandon . . . what had happened last night was beautiful and momentous. It felt like a step forward toward something positive.

But it wasn't just about them but also about their families and herself. It meant rearranging her work life to accommodate her current commitments. She couldn't just bail—

Then again, she would have to leave someone, and something, no matter what. Whether it was Brandon or Beatrice or Foster's Group or her parents. Never settling down had been her MO; she'd just never looked back, until now, when everything was smooshed into this one couples resort project.

God, wasn't this place supposed to heal relationships, not make them more confusing?

Thoughts swirled into one big messy mush. She pleaded, "Bea."

"I'm sorry." Beatrice raised both hands up in the silence. "I get it. No more pressure."

"I need more time to think about it." *Because I still have to tell you about Brandon.* "Speaking of, can we grab coffee, alone, after this?"

Her expression changed. "I'm here now. What's up?"

"Bea! Your phone's ringing," Eden said from downstairs.

"Hold that thought," Bea said, then bounded down the stairs.

Geneva fluffed the pillows and, before heading down, took in the room once more.

Yeah, she knew what she was doing around here. But the question was, What was she going to do next?

"Ladies, food at the restaurant in a few minutes. Kuya Chris picked up dim sum. Let's wrap up here!" Beatrice said as she climbed up the stairs. "Let's get dessert alone after dinner?"

Geneva nodded. Dim sum sounded perfect, and so did buying her a little more time to think.

CHAPTER
TWENTY-SEVEN

Brandon grunted, lowering the stainless steel table. Mike set down his corner, and they both stepped back and surveyed the room, checking the placement of equipment and the new layout.

"That's perfect," Lainey said, coming from the swinging kitchen door. "Wow. This was the fastest installation ever."

"That's the aim." He nodded at Mike. To the rest of the crew, he said, "Thanks, everyone. That's it for now."

As Mike and the crew made their way out of the restaurant, Lainey pressed on the screen of her iPad. "Check, check, and check." She beamed. "You're all set. I think I'm done here."

Brandon offered his hand. "I want to thank you for everything."

"You paid me."

"But you were flexible as we figured out how to work together, and came up after the storm to see it all the way through."

"Eh." She waved it away. "This isn't my first rodeo into family drama, and it was a good excuse for me to head to the beach." She looked around. "I must say, this is a good-looking kitchen. If you need anything else done, please call me. It was a great break from the tiny houses. Don't tell my boss, but I missed large, complicated kitchens."

Brandon walked Lainey out the front door into the bright sun. "I won't say a word."

"I'm a little disappointed that I didn't get to say goodbye to Geneva. Last we emailed she had a nice plan for the dining room decor. Please wish her happy trails from me."

"I will. I know she's disappointed too. She's been so busy."

It wasn't the entire truth. Brandon had no idea what Geneva was up to or thinking. Geneva had yet to text back. His instincts were warning him that she was pulling away.

But he also knew that lunging for her was the absolute wrong move. *It's been less than twenty-four hours since we made love.* He was jumping to conclusions.

"I'll see you, Brandon."

"Thank you for everything."

Then Lainey crossed the street, narrowly missed by a golf cart whizzing by. "Goodness! This is supposed to be a resort. Ten miles an hour!"

Brandon waved a goodbye as she got into a cart and pulled out.

Another cart swerved into the empty spot. The driver, a Black man wearing a fedora, a tank top, and shorts, stepped out.

Brandon rubbed his eyes to focus. "Garrett?"

The guy looked down at himself. "Is that my name? That's impressive, seeing that you haven't been returning my calls. For all I knew, you were swept up into the ocean. Jerk." He jogged across the street.

Brandon opened his mouth to explain, but before he could, Garrett bear-hugged him. "I'm sorry, man. All I thought of was our last phone call when that storm came through . . ."

The tension in his body left him. Brandon hadn't even thought of Garrett worrying. "I'm okay. And I'm sorry too. I know that I owe you a lot, and so much happened since last night, literally. I don't know where to start."

"I'm glad you're okay. That's what matters."

"Look what the storm dragged in! Garrett Carter?" a voice said.

They both turned. Chris and Gil were coming up the street, both holding plastic bags of takeout.

"Damn. Blast from the past." Garrett bounded over to Brandon's brothers, and they all did a version of a hug. "Let me help you guys."

"You here to clean up this mess? Bran, you should have said. We would have made arrangements for you to stay behind the gates."

"We definitely have room," Gil chimed in, handing Garrett a bag. "How long are you staying?"

"Just a couple of days. I had to talk to this guy here." He eyeballed Brandon.

"Whoa! It looks good in here!" Chris said, upon entering the restaurant.

Brandon was relieved for the distraction from his two worlds colliding. Now he had to pick up the debris. "Head into the kitchen. That's where the good stuff is." As he watched the backs of his brothers disappear into the kitchen, he reached out to Garrett's arm, holding him back.

Garrett set down the bag of food on one of the tables. "You told them, right?"

"Told us what?" Chris asked from the kitchen.

Brandon all but rolled his eyes.

Garrett lit up. "He's got the hearing of a bat."

"I do." His brother hovered in the doorway. "What's going on?"

"We have an offer," Garrett said.

"Offer?"

"Yep." Garrett grinned—pride beaming. As far as he knew, he was doing Brandon a big favor. "An unofficial one for the town house, and it's so good. You really shouldn't walk away." He went on to describe who the buyers were and what their plans were to turn the corner property into a school.

"Wait a second. *Our* town house?" Chris asked.

"I mean, yeah." Garrett's smile diminished. "Mulberry Road."

"It has a project name already?" Gil had entered the doorway, and his mouth was agape. "When did this all go down?"

"I've been hounding him about it," Garrett supplied innocently.

"So you've known?" Chris asked, this time to Brandon. "All this time?"

Garrett halted, and his gaze darted from Brandon to his brothers and back.

"Yeah, I haven't told them yet," Brandon said.

"This makes me the messenger, doesn't it?" Garrett crossed his arms.

Brandon pressed his lips together.

"Let's . . . head outside and wait for the rest of the family, Garrett," Gil said, shuffling past and grabbing the food. "Have you met my kids? Eden's coming down with them."

"I haven't!" Garrett said a little too loudly.

The two erupted into a faux conversation, but as they left, the kitchen fell into a cold silence.

"Why didn't you say anything?" Chris entered the dining room, though he halted several feet away. "You've been home over a week."

"I wasn't sure how to bring it up."

"You just bring it up. You just . . . tell it like it is."

Brandon shut his eyes to keep his thoughts from catapulting to Chris and Eden's wedding. "It hasn't been as simple as that."

"I mean, it is. Besides, it's not really your answer but *our* answer the buyer needs. The house belongs to the four of us."

"Technically, yes. But you've made Heart Resort your home. The sign's here, the whole family's here, and I'm the one left behind. I'm the one living with everything they left behind."

"You've always been welcome to live here."

"Really." A snort left him. "I was run out of here years ago."

"I didn't run you out."

"But it was sure uncomfortable enough that I wanted to go."

Chris pressed his fingers against his forehead. "I'm losing my train of thought here, Brandon, because we've discussed the past already. And even then, it doesn't take away the fact that you've had this offer all this time, whether official or unofficial. You didn't tell any one of us. I'm really disappointed. God, I have Willow Tree to contend with. I don't want to think about you too."

Brandon shook his head, though defiantly. "I'm not seven, or even seventeen. Don't talk to me this way."

"I'm telling you how I feel, and as far as I know, that's fair game."

"Look. It wasn't easy to tell you because I knew you'd react like this. Because it unearths a crap load of things. Figuratively and literally. None of you have stepped back into that town house in months, and when I came to you wanting to move, years ago, you said no on the spot. I couldn't just *bring it up* this time around. I wanted to find the perfect time. But now I wonder if there's even such a thing."

"You agreed to communicate."

From his periphery, Brandon caught shadows in the kitchen. Chris turned. Beatrice showed herself, and behind her was Geneva, eyebrows lifted.

"You're going to sell the town house?" Beatrice asked, looking right at Brandon.

"No, God . . . don't know."

"Kuya Chris, he wanted to sell the town house years ago?"

His big brother groaned.

"Should I . . ." Geneva gestured for the back door.

"Don't." Brandon jumped in; Geneva was like a life raft in this whirlpool. "I want you to stay, please." In the silence Brandon gathered up his bravery. "I mean, let's get Garrett and Gil here. Might as well."

"I'll get them," Beatrice said. "No one say a word until I'm back." She eyed all of them pointedly and walked out the door.

Just then, Chris's phone rang. He looked at the screen. "Damn it. Let me . . . let me take this. Give me five minutes."

Chris exited through the back door, leaving the room empty and quiet. That was, except for Geneva, who looked at him through rounded eyes.

303

"So when were you going to tell me about the town house?" Geneva said, skipping all pleasantries.

He rubbed his head. "Let me guess. You have an opinion too. Oh, wait. You did. Four years ago."

"I . . ."

Brandon winced at his words. He knew that he'd gone too far, but there was no escaping the history they had. That somehow, this town house was coming into their conversation once more. And he was upset. He was angry. At his parents for dying, at his siblings for shackling him to a house that they never visited, at Geneva for leaving him, for not clamoring to scream their relationship into the world.

Everyone left him in some form.

"Why does this matter to you?" he said. "You've already checked out."

"That's . . . what?" She lifted a finger. "We're going to put a pin on what you just said, because I want to make something clear once more. Yes, I did leave Annapolis, and yes, it had something to do with your house and letting go, but it was because *you* sent me away. I apologized for it, last night, remember? But checking out? What is that about?"

He dipped his chin into his chest, regret rushing through him. This restaurant was not the place for this conversation. At any moment, someone was going to walk in, but since everything seemed to be on the table, he launched into what had fueled his every worry since their involvement. "All right. Let's talk about it. You run. You ran from me. You keep trying to run from me. Let me guess—you haven't spoken to Beatrice about us. You aren't convinced of staying. I bet your bags are already packed, right? Your mind is already miles away from here at your next job."

"That's not fair, Brandon. You know why I work so hard."

"And you know why I hold on." He shook his head at the pain building up in his body. "You said to me, just before you left the last time, that you thought I was hanging on to the house."

She nodded, and through her eyes, he saw a perfect clip of the memory play back.

"I did say that. It was after that you told me to go. And I regret that, Brandon. I regret the way I do things, how I walk away."

Her apologies slowed his anger, but the pain remained. He shook his head. "But it was the crux. You wanted to go, and I couldn't."

She nodded. "And now? Can you go? Are you ready to move on?"

He knew what she was asking him, but remembering the calendar on her desk, he looked her in the eyes. In her beautiful eyes. "Are *you* ready to stay? Are you ready to unpack your entire life from that duffel bag of yours? Because whether you leave in six days or two days, you're still leaving, aren't you?"

Geneva's gaze faltered a beat. Not even a beat—a microsecond. In that moment, Brandon understood, as she did, that whether or not he or she was ready, they had to be ready together, at the same time. It would be the only way.

"This is a repeat." He half laughed. "We answered our own questions."

A tear dropped and slid down her cheek.

He looked away—he couldn't do tears.

"I love you, Bran," she said. "You're right, and I'm sorry. But I don't know how to explain that I can't stay, not until I can figure things out."

"I'm sorry too. It's just too bad that love isn't enough, because I have so much for the both of us. Maybe my brother's right? That I'm looking for things that aren't there, and I've got crap judgment."

Geneva pressed her hand against her heart.

But it was Brandon's heart that was breaking. It was shattering into pieces.

Movement from the right took Brandon's attention, and he spun. His siblings were at the door, with Beatrice up front, a hand over her mouth.

CHAPTER TWENTY-EIGHT

Day 10
Weather: overcast, 80°F

Sal and Rhiannon looked at Geneva with stunned expressions from across Ligaya's kitchen table.

"Do you have any questions?" Geneva closed the design binder and handed it to Rhiannon. "You're really at the home stretch, and in fact, you can get started on this house after she's all cleaned."

Rhiannon took the binder into her arms and held it against her chest like a precious package. "How about the last house, Sinta? Are you really going to leave it up to me?"

"Yes." She smiled. "You helped me fix up all of these houses, Rhiannon, and you have a touch. I know that you want to do other things in college, but consider Sinta part of your thesis of everything you learned thus far in this faux internship. Just like the house's name—put everything you love into it."

"I still don't understand why you're leaving now, Ms. Geneva."

"The next job calls." She offered a smile, which was the most she could do. "Thank you for meeting me so early, especially so last minute."

"Of course I was going to come. I wouldn't leave without saying goodbye," Rhiannon said with a stricken expression.

It was a stab to Geneva's heart, and she looked away.

Sal clasped his hands. "We're going to be fine, Ms. Geneva, but the question is, will you?"

"Speak for yourself, Mr. Medina. I'm not ready to do this by myself," Rhiannon said, voice rising to a soprano tone.

Geneva took Rhiannon's hand. "You're not by yourself. First of all, you have this book; you have Sal. And, you have me." She pulled her phone out of her back pocket. "Phone call, video chat. There are no office hours for either one of you, and unless I'm in the middle of something, I'll answer."

"Even if it's a phone call about school? What if I still have questions about that?"

Geneva didn't hesitate. "Of course I'll pick up. I want the play-by-play."

Sal nodded solemnly. "I hope you'll forgive me if I overstep my boundaries here, but please don't be too hard on yourself, Ms. Geneva. Whatever happened, it doesn't mean you have to stay away."

"Well . . ." She stood, the stress of pressure on her temples now heavy and persistent. It was from the last day of work, from tossing and turning in bed last night and the night before, from this anticipation of leaving a place that she'd grown to love. "I wish it could be that easy, but at the very end of it, it's not all up to me. That goes for me coming back." She heaved a breath. "Okay, guys, it's time for me to get ready. I want to see Beatrice before I go. It'll only take me a half hour, forty-five minutes at most. Sal, I'll meet you at the reception office for my ride to the airport?"

"Of course."

Sal and Rhiannon stood, and she walked them to the door. After they hugged, the two descended the steps.

As Geneva turned to walk into the house, she heard her name called.

Beatrice was at the bottom step. She wasn't wearing her sunglasses, and the evidence of the last thirty-six hours of disappointment, shock, and tears was on her face. After all the siblings had witnessed Geneva's conversation with Brandon—a conversation that she would never want to repeat or remember, ever—it had been a somber dismissal for everyone. There were no parting words, not even from Chris. They'd all simply retreated to their corners.

She'd texted Beatrice repeatedly and even shown up at her door last night to no answer. Thank God for Nita, who'd anticipated her departure by scheduling her flight the other day. She and Brandon had made a big enough mess as it was.

"Hey," Geneva said. "I'm glad to see you. I came over last night, but . . ."

"I stayed in Nags Head. May I?" Beatrice gestured to the round table at the front stoop. She lifted a clear container that showcased a purple dessert.

"Ube cake. The big guns. I must really be in trouble. Of course you can come up."

"Chef Castillo brought it in today, and I thought of you immediately." Beatrice trudged up the stairs, her skirt flowing around her. She sat and popped open the clear container. Two forks were laid at its side at the ready.

Geneva picked up her fork and stuck it into the ube cake. Her appetite was nonexistent, but the dessert was so special that she felt compelled to eat it. "I should have been honest. I should have told you a long time ago."

Beatrice nibbled on the cake on her fork. "You should have. But I understand why you kept it a secret. We all keep secrets."

"Not like this. Not this big."

"I own a home that none of my siblings know about, and I want to leave the family business. That's pretty big." Beatrice shrugged. "When did it start?" She lifted her eyes briefly to Geneva's face. It was a demand for the full truth.

So, Geneva told her. As Beatrice took bites of the cake, Geneva recalled their affair years ago, and then their story today. She didn't stop there. She filled her in on her parents, on the two jobs still in limbo, and on her persistent nightmare of being swept away from herself.

Beatrice lowered the fork next to her plate, then looked up. Her cheeks were wet with tears. "I had a feeling. I had a feeling, and I pushed it aside. You were both hurting at the same time. He holed himself up in that house, and you were so out of reach. I didn't know how to help either one of you. Or maybe I was scared to." She reached across to Geneva. "But I'm not upset."

"You're not? But you said you didn't want for us to be together."

"I was presumptuous in thinking that you wouldn't stay together. That's my issue, my hang-up, not anyone else's."

"Bran is one hundred percent right, though. The presence of love isn't enough sometimes. We have to want to accept it, and each other, where we are. Maybe you were right to be presumptuous. You always seem to have a feeling about these things." Geneva swallowed the rising tide of simultaneous heartbreak and relief.

"Can I tell you something?"

"Of course you can."

"I don't hate the idea of you and my brother together. This is me being selfish, but if it brings you closer to me, all the better. You are already my sister." Beatrice offered her hand. "My offer still stands in Nags Head, Geneva, for as long as it takes. Before you and my brother, there was always us. You and I can still be partners even if you and my brother are not."

Geneva took her hand, relief running through her. But what the both of them knew was that as much as they would try to make these words true, Geneva could not return to being a partner to just one and not the other.

♡

Gatlinburg, Tennessee
Weather: partly cloudy, 85°F

At nine that evening, Geneva was driving through a sleepy seniors community. The roads were empty; the streetlights were the only signs of life.

Still, she could've driven down this street blindfolded. All the blocks were reliably square, the houses perfectly spaced apart. It was a planned community that would be accessible for most seniors, with wide sidewalks and even wider streets. Along with the occasional car parked in the driveway, there were also golf carts for the short distance to the park, the community center with a pool, the man-made lake, and the neighborhood grocery store.

She passed a golf cart with a flamingo float secured to its roof, presumably from a lake trip. The sight of it made her smile; she'd seen a share of that in the Outer Banks. And of course there were the golf carts at Heart Resort.

She stifled a cry.

This is a repeat.

Geneva pressed on the gas to distract her crumbling spirit. She rounded the turn, to the sixth house on the right. It had gnomes in the front garden and a bird feeder strategically placed so it could be viewed from the kitchen window. Two chairs banked a small round table on the covered front porch. Parked in the drive was a red convertible Beetle with its top up.

She sniffled as she watched shadows play against the windows of the home. All the lights were on. On the passenger seat, Luna purred her support from inside her carrier. She had been an angel the entire flight, crying only once, when they'd driven off the resort.

I can do this.

It had been eleven months and two weeks since Geneva had been home. It had been a brief stay. She'd been restless and excited, ready to take on one more thing. She'd wanted to go. Being home was a reminder of a life of what could have been. What she'd seen in her parents was the lack of time.

But now, as she got out of her car and dragged the duffel out of the trunk of her rental, she realized that the restlessness was a cover-up. It was a cover-up to avoid admitting that she wanted to reevaluate, that she wanted to rest and maybe even change course. It was a cover-up to keep from digging into her emotions. It was a cover-up for her vulnerability.

The door was already open by the time Geneva stepped onto the sidewalk of the house. The outline of two people darkened the threshold.

You can just show up.

Since leaving the resort this afternoon, she'd finally allowed the tears to flow.

"Neva?" Her mother met her on the walkway. "Oh my goodness." Though shorter, Lisa Harris wrapped a strong arm around her and led her forward.

Her father waited at the door. He was tall, though much leaner now. His smile was sincere, eyes bright.

"I'm sorry I didn't—"

He shook his head, cutting her sentence off. "You're here now."

And he wrapped her in his arms.

CHAPTER
TWENTY-NINE

Day 14
Outer Banks, NC
Weather: cloudy with afternoon sun, 85°F

Heart Resort was back to a bustling, pristine resort. Roads were lined with cars from local businesses invited to the grand opening event, families of resort staff, the press, and the seven couples who'd jumped in as its first customers.

Even the road behind the gates teemed with racing golf carts. As Brandon witnessed another cart fly by, he slipped on his short-sleeve resort polo over his pressed chinos. He ran his hand under his chin and against his cheek, newly shaven for the event.

But despite his outwardly groomed appearance, inside he was a mess.

His phone buzzed with his ten-minute warning for when he had to be at the restaurant. After turning it off and ignoring the hundreds of unread text messages in his family group chat, he stuffed the phone into his pocket and walked out the door.

Chris was waiting for him outside, leaning on the hood of his golf cart. "I thought I'd give you a ride to the site."

Brandon avoided his eyes, and he sure as heck was going to keep trying to avoid his presence. "Thanks, but I'm walking."

"Then I'll join you."

"Suit yourself." Brandon strode down the hill with one brief backward glance at him and Puso in the background. The house was really such a sight, exactly the kind of house their mother would have loved for them to grow up in. His parents used to show them pictures of their family homes in the Philippines, cozy and surrounded by trees. They'd talked about the birds and feeling one with nature. One of the reasons why they'd picked their little town house in Annapolis was because there were still the trees and the beautiful views of the water, though it was proximate to DC.

Did Tennessee have similar foliage? Or did the other places where Geneva had her next projects have Heart Resort's vibe?

Where was Geneva?

How was Geneva?

His brother was making small talk, something about the day's schedule. The tone of his voice was so casual, so nonchalant, and it acted like an annoying poke against his back. Brandon had successfully worked around him the last four days. He didn't want to hear about the bad judgment he had falling for Geneva. Nor did he want to argue about the house. The family hadn't come to a decision on the sale, and after this grand opening, he planned to climb back on the Rubicon and head north with Garrett, who had returned for this event. Everything else he'd face later.

"Hey, can you slow down a little?" Chris said. "Hey. Wait."

Brandon now wished he had taken the option of riding with him in the golf cart. At the very least the length of this conversation would have been cut short. So Brandon stepped out toward the sound of music in the air.

The other day, neither Brandon nor Geneva had needed a single beat to dance to the waltz. At the heart of it, with just the two of them, they were perfect. Or so he'd thought.

I can't stay, not until I can figure things out.

Maybe my brother's right? That I'm looking for things that aren't there, and I've got crap judgment.

Had he really said that to her? Had he categorized her under "crap judgment"?

Behind him, Chris kept talking, and against logical thought, Brandon turned and lifted his arms.

The anger burst forth like lava. It came out hot and unrelenting, no longer held up by a proverbial barrier. "You know what? I'm tired of this—I'm tired of you trying to talk away my anger. I'm going to sell Mulberry Road. Kuya Chris, I can't do it anymore. I can't keep it up—I feel beholden to that house and everything in it. God, I feel beholden to everyone. To you. What I need . . . what I need is for you to support me, in doing what I want to do, at times when I want to put myself first. I need for you to tell me that even if I'm selfish, and even if I make mistakes, that it's all right. That you'll still be there."

"God, Bran." Chris wrapped his arms around Brandon for the first time in forever. It was a real hug. The kind their father used to give them, without pretense. Their father had been a stoic man; he hadn't expressed his emotions and love, unlike their friends' fathers. Their father had shown his love in other ways, much like Chris—in the things they did. But every once in a while, he'd take them into his arms and squeeze them until they all giggled and laughed.

But Brandon wasn't laughing now. He was tearing up. He was crying like a baby, with hot tears that he couldn't halt, not since he'd lost his parents.

"I'm sorry," Chris said. "I know I'm tough to deal with. And that's not an excuse, because I know I should listen."

"I try to do the right thing."

"I know you do. This is all on me. I keep thinking, if Mom and Dad were here . . ."

"I miss them. I'm so mad. I'm so mad they're not here."

"Yeah." Chris kept hold of Brandon, and for that, he was grateful; otherwise he would have fallen apart. "Yeah, me too." He stepped back and laid a hand on each of Brandon's shoulders. "I want to make this better. I want to help you. It's been a bear, trying to make this place work, but I am here. I can come up to Annapolis. I can help get it ready for sale. Anything. You are more important than this town house, and I won't let it get in between us."

Brandon sniffed, but he found that while he felt tons lighter, there was more regret that he carried in his chest. "I let Geneva go."

"Oh, Bran, getting involved with—"

"Please, I don't want to hear—"

"Let me finish. I was going to say that getting involved with Geneva was the smartest thing you ever did, because she is a wonderful person. As are you. Let me help you."

"I don't know how . . ."

Chris slung an arm around his shoulders. "Let me give you a couple of lessons only the husband of a writer can. Have you heard about an arc?"

Brandon shook his head. "How does that have anything to do with Geneva?"

The gate opened, revealing Gil in his golf cart. His face was scrunched into a scowl. "Filipino time doesn't work for grand openings. My God, Beatrice is about to lose her mind. Get in."

Brandon and his brother climbed into the cart, with him in the back seat.

"The conversation isn't finished," Chris said, looking back.

"What did I miss?" Gil said. "CliffsNotes before we get to the ceremony."

315

After Chris delved into the rudimentary explanations, Gil said, "Oh yeah. This is going to be a team effort. Even I know about the grand gesture."

♡

Brandon was not emotionally present at the ceremony. Throughout the welcome speeches, the fireworks, and the welcome barbecue, his to-do list occupied most of his mind. That night, he knocked on Puso's guest room door.

Garrett opened it with a flourish. He was still in the Heart Resort polo—because he insisted that he was an honorary staff member—and the bright logo was matched by a megawatt smile.

Tammy Dirks, the resort PR, was sitting on his bed. She had a glass of something bubbly in her hand.

"Whoa." Brandon took a step back, all at once shocked and impressed. "I mean, hey. Sorry, man . . ."

"Aw, don't leave. It's sparkling cider—want some?" He lifted the bottle for show.

"No, I'm good!" He didn't want to be there any longer than needed. Garrett was a goofball, but a shy goofball, and Brandon didn't want to ruin their vibe. "We can talk later."

"Uh-uh, Bran. Just tell me. Did you guys make a decision?"

"Yep. It's a yes. I want to counter, and I have a bigger plan . . ." He gestured to Tammy, who was now scrolling through her phone. "Let's get on this, after."

Garrett leaned down and whispered, "After this, we're going to walk on the beach. Will Chris mind? I know it's an exclusive resort and all."

Brandon shook his head. "No, he won't mind. And anyway, I won't tell."

Garrett leaned in and slung him into a hug. "Thanks, man. We're okay, right? I know I messed up, twice now. But you and I are partners for the long haul. I was just, I don't know—"

"You were trying to do what's best, and you're right. We have business to tend to. You and I are copacetic. I love you, man." He leaned in for a hug. "I'm just . . . trying to make sure this isn't a repeat."

"Whatever that means, I'm here."

"I know." Brandon, again, was on the verge of another round of tears. He didn't have time for that right now. He had plans to make.

CHAPTER THIRTY

Day 21
Gatlinburg, Tennessee
Weather: clear, 88°F

"So, do you love it?" On Geneva's computer screen, Rhiannon panned across the living room of Sinta. All four walls were painted white, with framed black-and-white pictures of Outer Banks foliage on the walls. The windows had been kept bare, but the love seat overflowed with fluffy, welcoming pillows.

"I love it." Geneva's answer encompassed only a smidge of what she really felt. Her heart was too big for her chest, so proud of this young woman, and so enamored by her work. "You're really a talent."

"And the best part? Look at this." Rhiannon directed the phone through those bare front windows to where the sun was setting.

"Wow." Geneva smiled at that, and at the memory that followed it. Of Brandon helping her kayak out of the sand. Of the two of them running toward the little blue house. Of waltzing. All memorialized on a website she had yet to be brave enough to log on to.

At least, this time, she hadn't hurt quite as much. It was helped by her parents, who cooked her favorite foods, who'd allowed her to open up in her own way. It was also helped by Rhiannon and Sal and

Beatrice, who checked in with her often. Finally, she was supported by Nita, who'd waved her magic wand and gotten Geneva to Chicago for her Foster's Group interview, which she'd realized was not for her and ultimately declined.

"Well, I have to go," Rhiannon said. "I've got homework. Talk to you later!"

She laughed. "Sounds good. See you soon!"

After Geneva hung up, she met her parents at the kitchen island. Her dad was sitting on a barstool, flipping through a magazine. Her mother stirred a pot at the stove, her back toward her. Luna was on her own stool—if she was spoiled by Geneva, Lisa was extra accommodating. The mouthwatering smell of sautéing tomatoes and garlic wafted in the air, and the quiet sadness that she had been keeping inside of her lifted a smidge.

Lisa's hair was a mix of ash brown and silver, a clever combination of high- and lowlights and gray coverage. Her apron was tied into a neat bow.

She picked up the bowl she had preset next to the stove and scooped rice from the rice cooker and then a ladleful from the pot.

When she turned, her face lit. "Hungry?"

"I could smell the food all the way from the bedroom," Geneva said.

Her father grinned. "Your mother's cooking is a lover's call."

Lisa playfully slapped her husband's shoulder. "Pilyo. Your daughter is right here."

Geneva coughed.

"Oh, darling. Here's some water." She poured water from a Brita into a glass and set it in front of her.

Geneva's cheeks burned as she gulped the refreshing water. If only her parents knew that it wasn't their show of flirtation that made her choke up; it was because she'd used that term on Brandon too.

Lisa handed her three sets of utensils to set and placed three bowls of food on the plastic place mats at the kitchen island. Then she popped on a stool next to Geneva.

Geneva's tummy growled. Pork mechado, Geneva's favorite dish, over hot white rice that was sure to burn her tongue—the best kind of rice.

Her parents bowed their heads in quiet prayer, though Lisa didn't prompt Geneva as she used to when she'd lived at home; however, Geneva picked up her utensils only when her parents did, out of respect.

"I love meals with our whole family," her mother said, echoing her thoughts.

"I know. It's especially nice when someone else makes the food," Geneva admitted.

"Sometimes I make so much that I have to give the leftovers to the neighbors."

"They don't mind, believe me. They love your food." Her father's speech was delayed due to aphasia from his stroke, but his eyes were alight.

Geneva took a bite. Yep, her tongue burned, but she suffered through it.

"Breathe, baby." Lisa laughed.

"It's so good." She topped it with a gulp of water, and it bought her some time. These dinners had been vehicles for sharing stories, but she hadn't yet properly explained why she was home. While they never forced the conversation, it still hung over her. With only a day left before leaving for Helena's B and B project, she said, "I'm sorry that I haven't been home."

"Mm." Lisa put a hand on her wrist. "Iha, I'm just happy you're here. No need to explain. No need for sorrys. My only hope is that it won't be too long till your next visit."

Geneva shook her head. "You're letting me off the hook way too easily. I was . . . running away. My priorities—somehow I got them screwed up, and I used my ambition to cover up that I was scared."

"Scared of what?"

"Sitting still. Not accomplishing."

"You're the most accomplished person I know," her dad said. "Even if you didn't accomplish one more thing, you are enough. You have always been enough."

Geneva's eyes watered. She thought of how she'd felt as she'd launched from college, with the pride of her parents behind her, and with the Traveler's notebook in her luggage. She'd wanted to show them what she could do, that she could check those boxes.

The truth was, the pressure had always been inside her, and it had been up to her how she would manage it. "Thanks, Dad."

"We missed you a lot, anak," her mother said. "But now that you're here, the missing is gone." She took a bite of food, a cue for Geneva to take another bite. Which was a good thing because she was half a second from full-on tears.

"I won't wait too long this time, I promise."

She nodded. "And iha?"

"Yes, Ma?"

Her mother's gaze darted between her and her father.

Something was amiss. "What is it?"

"How long have you been here now?"

"I dunno. Five, six days? I had that day trip to Chicago, but yeah . . ."

"Actually it's eleven days and twelve hours."

Geneva's spoon was halfway to her mouth. "Okay."

"That's long enough, don't you think?"

"What do you mean?"

"I mean . . . don't you have work? Besides that one trip?"

"I do. But I don't have to be at my next job for another couple of days."

"But after that job? How about your home?"

"I . . ." Geneva shook her head. "You . . . you always said that home was where you and Daddy were."

Her father cleared his throat. "What your mother meant . . . well, we have been empty nesters for a while now. You have made a life, and at some point you have to return to it. *Your* life, and your home. We know you love us, but we also know you love being out there. And it's okay."

"Anak," her mother said. "Your home doesn't have to be for forever, but it should be associated with something solid and true to who you are. When I immigrated and we moved everywhere, your daddy and I always looked for that special something in a place that said, *This is where I belong. This is where my heart is.* For a long time it was Annapolis. Now it's here. Now you have to find yours."

"But in settling down, I might not get to accomplish everything I want to do," Geneva said.

"Darling, why does it have to be either or?"

"Because time runs out." Geneva halted; she'd run upon her unspoken truth, something she had felt to her core. Something that made her exactly what she was.

Understanding flitted across both of her parents' faces. Lisa put down her spoon and turned toward her, fully. "Don't be afraid of this, anak. Of being sick, of getting old. Of dying. We have been privileged to live this long, to watch you grow to be a wonderful woman. Your daddy meant it for the both of us when he said that even if you didn't accomplish one more thing, that we'd love you still. I know now that you're thinking of legacy, and it's noble. But a legacy doesn't need to be big. It simply means leaving a bit of yourself in some way with the world, with someone. It's making an undeniable mark that is yours alone. But you see, you already have done that. With me, with your father. With your friends."

Lisa had laid all Geneva's fears out at this kitchen island. With that, the pressure-release valve jostled free, and tears sprang from Geneva's eyes.

Luna made a sound, a meow mixed with a yowl, snatching all their attention. Geneva barked out a laugh. "Whoa."

Lisa clucked. "You're right, Luna. How can I forget? If there's any being who is a testament of your ability to love, commit, and make a home, Neva, it would be Luna. You shouldn't underestimate that, anak. Animals are much more discriminating than people, and this one loves you all the way through." She turned to the cat and ran a hand down her back. "Right, baby?"

Luna whipped her tail in pride.

Are you ready to stay? And unpack your entire life from that duffel bag of yours?

Geneva wiped her tears. All this time, she'd thought herself someone who didn't bond or connect. She had considered herself transient and condemned herself to be transient, to achieve her goals all on her own, to remain unattached. When actually she was deeply connected to people.

Her mother stood and went to her stationery drawer and brought back a letter. After handing it to Geneva, Lisa stood next to her husband and draped an arm around his shoulders.

"Who's this from?"

"Who else?"

Geneva looked at the Nags Head postmark, then to the left, to the Heart Resort return address. Above it was Brandon's name.

"Neva," Lisa said. "We can tell you time and again that you are enough, but you need to know for yourself. A way to do this is to surround yourself with people who love you just the way you are."

Geneva unfolded the piece of paper. The header: *Proposal for Illinois Way.*

CHAPTER
THIRTY-ONE

Day 40
Outer Banks, North Carolina
Weather: clear skies, 72°F

Eden:

She's on her way

Geneva:

Thank you, Eden

You're a lifesaver for keeping it a secret

And for sneaking me the keys

Eden:

Are you kidding?

I love this so much

I love a good heist

Also the resolution is the best part of Act 3

Geneva:

Resolution?

Act 3 of what?

Eden:

Never mind!

Good luck!

Geneva tucked the phone in her messenger bag and paced Beachy's foyer, and she wrung her hands. She peeked out the front door each time she passed it, anticipating Beatrice's arrival. Her speech was prepared, practiced during her flight, her drive from the airport, and her gathering of all the materials to hopefully aid in this conversation.

Minutes passed but Beatrice had not yet arrived. Geneva opened the front door—where could she be? Geneva had an extensive plan; she'd elicited the help of Eden, a woman who had shown she could keep a secret, to iron out the details. She only had this one day to spare, after Helena's B and B project, before she headed up north.

That future trip depended on this one.

"Geneva?"

Geneva spun around, to Beatrice, who emerged from Beachy's back entrance. She covered her mouth with a hand.

"Argh, I didn't think you would come from the back."

"There was no parking out front," Beatrice said, through the hand still covering her mouth. "What . . . what is this?"

"It's your design consult." Geneva bit the side of her cheek as a wave of nervousness washed over her. She turned to what Beatrice was looking at: windows with several different curtains hanging from their rods, six swatches of paint colors on the white walls, three samples of flooring on the ground, three paper samples for an accent wall. "I figured that we could start with these, narrow down or go a different direction if you wished. I scoured your Pinterest board and—"

Geneva was bowled over by Beatrice's bear hug. She wrapped her arms around Geneva's upper body and squeezed. "I can't believe you're here."

She grunted against her friend's tight hold. "I told you I'd design Beachy, didn't I?"

Beatrice let go; she had tears in her eyes.

Geneva's heart broke. Crying was not what she'd expected. "Oh no. You don't like it. I shouldn't have—"

"No! I love it. I love it all. It's going to be so hard to pick. But . . . seriously, Gen. What does this mean?"

Geneva took Beatrice's hand in hers. "I thought about Beachy, and you, a lot."

"I thought about you too. Every day."

Geneva couldn't smile hard enough. "When I went to Helena's B and B, I realized that life changed for me, tremendously. Personally, professionally. And I want more and different in my career. I want to build something with someone who I respect and look up to and who I consider my sister. I would be honored, if you were still willing, for me to come on board, to take Beachy to the next level."

"Yes, yes, yes." Beatrice hugged her once more. "Absolutely. Yes." Then her expression changed, as if she'd come upon a realization.

They both knew that Beatrice didn't come solo, but with an entire family, including Brandon.

"There's a second part of this, Bea." Geneva took a breath, to brace herself. "I love Brandon, still, and he wrote—"

"I know, and you don't have to say another word," Beatrice interrupted with a smile. "Just go. Go get him, and the both of you come home."

CHAPTER
THIRTY-TWO

Day 42
Annapolis, Maryland
Weather: sunny, 55°F

Brandon paced the front walkway of the Illinois Way flip. He glanced at his watch for the twelfth time in the last twenty minutes, and he peered out onto the circular driveway that led to the house.

No dice.

"Don't worry, man," Garrett bellowed from the second-floor window, or what would be the second-floor window. As of right then, there was no real second floor, because the flip had uncovered some structural issues they couldn't ignore.

"What if she doesn't come?" Brandon spun around and yelled up, "I mean, look at all this." Lifting his arms, he gestured to the would-be house.

"This, you mean, the potential greatness of a vacation home?"

"No—this mess! Who wants a mess? I mean, I'm overwhelmed myself."

"Are you serious right now?" Garrett disappeared from the window, and seconds later, he emerged from the doorway. "This is beautiful. This is a remaking. This is a renewal. There's nothing more pure than that."

Brandon lowered his face. "I can't do this. She must have laughed at that proposal letter. What was I even thinking? She's not coming. Maybe it's too late."

Strong hands landed on his shoulders, grounding him. "Bran. Hush."

"You're right. I need to take a breath." He looked up at his friend, the epitome of optimism. Garrett had been his rock as he'd negotiated Mulberry Road's sale, when he'd reached out to Geneva. He was smiling, and it rounded up the last of Brandon's motivation. "And if she doesn't come, I'm going to try again. Maybe I can go to her, or will that be stalkerish?"

"No, it's not about taking a breath. Just shh," his friend said, then turned him around.

To Geneva.

For a beat, Brandon was stunned. Then he choked out a response. "How did you . . ." He glanced back; Garrett waved a goodbye.

"I walked up. I parked down the road." She gestured down the driveway. "I couldn't . . . I needed to get out some energy before we talked. Because I was shocked at getting your letter." She shifted on her feet.

"How . . . how was your last job?" His mind was reeling, and by making this small talk, he could figure out if he was seeing an apparition.

"I decided to forgo the job at the hotel chain. It was too . . . I dunno . . . basic." She shrugged. "After my last job at this awesome resort, everything pales in comparison. I went on to Helena's B and B, finished that up; then I whipped on to my next project for a check-in, and now, well, I'm here."

"Wow, that's a lot," was all he could say. He dug into his memory for his prepared speech—he'd been planning this moment for weeks—but she gently pressed a finger against his lips.

"Please," she said, eyes glassy. "Me first, Bran. I know I left twice now, and you have every reason to think me flighty and unreliable, but I need to tell you something: You don't have bad judgment. You are kind and forgiving and empathetic. What I had to figure out had less to do with whether or not we would work but more with what I wanted for myself. For me to be the person I aspire to be. So, I went home and spent some time with my parents, and you were right. It was better late than never, because they reminded me that the best thing about their lives was their relationships with good people."

"That's great, Geneva." His voice croaked.

"I'd been so focused on making old new, fixing things to modernize them. Working at Heart Resort taught me that the imperfect can be beautiful, and cherished, and remembered. I want to be around people who feel this same way. I want to be around people who know me and love me for who I am, and I want to spend my life with people I love. With you. Bran, I want to unload this duffel. I might have spent years running toward opportunity, but leaving something—you—has been the worst. I don't want to go anywhere else without you."

Brandon squeezed Geneva against him. Her body was strong against his, a reflection of her will. It dawned all at once how lucky he was, that he was surrounded by the strongest individuals. Being around them, and being around Geneva now, made him a better person because they challenged him as much as they supported him. "You were right. I needed to let go."

"That was wrong for me to say. I had no right."

"No, no, it wasn't wrong. You were spot on. You weren't asking me to let go of my parents. You were just asking me to be with you. You were asking me to open my heart to trust you, and twice I was stubborn and defensive. Twice, I showed you that I wasn't ready to take the risk. But I am now."

Brandon had so much more to say, about everything that had transpired, about dealing with his siblings as they had tackled their parents' things, in the process of selling Mulberry Road. But one piece of news took precedence. "This is my new house."

She looked up at him, then stepped back. "What house?"

"This, um, structure." He hiked a thumb behind him.

Her eyes lit. "Illinois Way is *your* house."

He nodded. "A vacation home, maybe even an investment home. But it needs a lot of help. And, I was hoping that you could be the one to help me. It's got good bones, a really strong foundation. Some structural issues but fixable." Brandon's cheeks warmed. "It has . . . a lot of potential. Lots of room for improvement for someone who's willing to give it a little TLC. And, I thought that with my construction knowledge and your design genius, we could do something special here—"

Geneva stood on her tiptoes and kissed him, halting his words. "You want me to what?"

The kiss reset him. It bolstered him to say the next words with conviction. "I want for us to be together, wherever that may be. Here, or in a tiny house, or anywhere else. I'm free. Garrett and I—we've been talking, about what we both want, about what's best for P&C Homes. You've made a business being a mobile entrepreneur, and I think I can make a go at that too. Will you . . . can I . . . go with you?"

Silence descended around them while Brandon waited for her answer.

Geneva blinked up at him. "Do you mean that?"

"I do."

"With Luna?"

"Is that even a question? Yes." He felt a slice of worry. "Will she have me?"

"Oh, I think so." She grinned. "She lets very few people pet her. My parents, Beatrice, Nita, and you . . . you picked her up. She *let* you pick her up. I think you passed her test."

"Then I'm a very lucky man with more to love."

She reached for her back pocket and produced a card. She pressed it into his hand. "All right, here is my counterproposal. I'm so impressed with the local printers, by the way. They did this for us in a couple of hours."

"Local printer?" Brandon examined the card. It was a business card for Beachy. Geneva's name was under his sister's.

"What do you think of the Outer Banks as home base?" She smiled up. "Because there's no more running for me. I'm at the finish line."

EPILOGUE

Six months later
Heart Resort, North Carolina
Weather: full sun all day and a perfect 70°F

"Did you pack your running shoes?" Geneva whispered to Brandon. She looked over at the line of words in the document he was signing, where it said, under activities, *Couples hike on Pea Island.*

"Of course I did," he said. "I wanted to get a run in before our 5k. What I don't have are hiking boots."

"Me either," she whispered. Now she was worried. Would her running shoes be ruined? They needed to last until their race, which she and Brandon had been training for. "Did you sign us up for hiking?"

"No, I didn't, I swear. My siblings are punking us."

"Actually," said a voice behind them, and Geneva turned as Chet Seiko walked into the Heart Resort office with two resort backpacks in his hand, "we created a custom set of activities that could be beneficial to your relationship goals, all of which are a surprise. Much of the experience is the couple traversing the unknown together. Thank you, by the way, for volunteering as guinea pigs for this new programming."

"Volun*told* is more like it," Brandon said.

"It will be good for us," Geneva noted and bit her cheek, musing, *Your first surprise is literally here, Brandon.*

Brandon grumbled. He was, as expected, exhausted from their red-eye from San Diego. Geneva had pitched Beachy home wares to a chain of high-end boutiques; Brandon had tagged along—he was also in between consulting a major home renovation with Garrett—and they'd made a small vacation of it. Geneva was on a high from the short getaway; she'd landed the account and had even met up with Nita, who now worked with Beachy. It would only get better now that they were back home in the Outer Banks.

Topping her to-do list was, finally, this reveal.

"After you sign the bottom of those forms, I can give you these bags, and we can have Sal drive you to your beach house."

Geneva's heart began to beat in earnest as she scribbled her signature. She nodded at Chet, who handed each of them a backpack—to her, the green backpack, and to Brandon, the blue.

"Thanks," Brandon said.

"We should check what's in the backpacks, shouldn't we?" Geneva's voice croaked. Her heart rate sped up. "What's in your bag, Brandon?"

"We can unpack in the beach house. Which are we staying in, Chet?"

"Sinta."

"Babe, let's see what's in your backpack," Geneva insisted. He already knew that they were staying in Sinta—it was written on the contract.

"Oh, that's the one you didn't get to finish, right, Gen?" Brandon asked. "Or was that Ligaya?"

"It was both." Geneva's nerves frayed. "But anyway, look inside your backpack. In fact, let's look together."

"Goodness, fine." He unzipped the large compartment and peeped inside. "There's nothing in mine."

"What?" She darted her gaze at Chet. "What do you mean?"

"Let me . . . um . . ." Chet left the room hurriedly.

What the heck? "Where are you going, Chet?" She'd coordinated everything down to the second, to make sure the black velvet box was placed in the blue—in Brandon's—backpack.

She set down her green backpack on the table while she searched all the blue backpack's pockets. The speech that she'd rehearsed ran through her mind. This was supposed to be the perfect setup: being in the place where they'd fallen back in love, with Brandon's family—who had given her their blessings over video chat three days prior—waiting outside the door for confirmation that she finally put a ring on it . . .

"Where is it?" she yelped in panic.

"Geneva Roque Harris."

The sound of her complete name snapped her out of her running thoughts. From the green backpack, Brandon pulled out her leather Traveler's notebook.

"How did that get there?" Geneva was confused. She'd left the notebook in her suitcase, currently in one of the white vans, waiting for transport to Sinta. Or she thought so, anyway.

"You're not the only one who can coordinate," Brandon said, handing the notebook to her.

Dangling from the bottom was a bookmark charm. A shell. She opened the book to the first page of a brand-new notebook insert, to a line item next to an unchecked box. Written in Brandon's distinct handwriting, it said: *Marry me.*

She looked up just as Brandon dropped on one knee. He was holding a teal velvet box.

She gasped.

ACKNOWLEDGMENTS

The beginnings of the Puso family came to me while at a romance writers' conference in 2019, but it was only when we (as in our family and most of the world) began sheltering in place for COVID-19 that the full concept materialized. Along with my sourdough bread, I baked up the final image of a private heart-shaped resort where couples could escape and work on their relationships, run by a family that had its own issues of the heart. Literally. *winks* In my own need to escape, I dived into the synopsis and the first chapters with reckless abandon. I threw everything I love into it: the magnificent Outer Banks (my family's most favorite destination, especially south of 12), tiny spaces (we are an RV family), the naming of homes, and my Filipino American culture.

This book would not have come to be without my literary agent, Rachel Brooks, who not only continues to champion my work but champions me. She took this pivot and ran with it with enthusiasm. Enter Lauren Plude and her perfect editorial suggestions that pushed me to dig deep. Writing requires vulnerability; writing and editing during COVID times could be *unprecedentedly* difficult without an editor who believed in the heart of your book. I'm so lucky to have an editor who saw Brandon and Geneva for who they are, and for what they are to one another.

To Anh Schluep, Jillian Cline, Lauren Grange, Susan Stokes, Riam Griswold, and the entire Montlake team for your unyielding support.

Amy Concannon and Christina Carrasco, for our chat on design and business. April Hunt and Jeanette Escudero for reading an early copy and tearing it to pieces. Sanjita E. and Maida Malby, for your intimate insights. All mistakes are mine and mine alone.

To Kristin Dwyer of LeoPR, who is a pillar! Our phone calls during COVID times where we talked more about life than about books have been such bright spots. The complete #girlswritenight ensemble: April and Jeanette, along with Annie Rains and Rachel Lacey, for our everyday check-ins, sprints, gossip, and laughter. #5amwritersclub, for your company in the wee morning hours, especially Annie. Tall Poppy Writers for your support, partnership, and friendship, especially Sonja Yeorg, Amy Impellizzeri, and Amy E. Reichert. #Batsignal: Mia Sosa, Tracey Livesay, Nina Crespo, Priscilla Oliveras, and Michele Arris for your friendship and acceptance. Fellow titas: Mia Hopkins, Sarah Smith, and Maida Malby.

To readers, bloggers, reviewers, booksellers, and librarians: thank you for picking up my books, for sampling that first page, for reading to "The End," for reaching out with your encouragement, and for sharing my books with others! I heart you!

My parents, who have shown such fortitude in their lives; my brothers, JR and Racky, who are the best brothers an ate could have. My sisters, Connie and Aimee and Liz, and mother-in-law, Cheri: I love you! Greg, who endures my collection of journals and planners, who has shown what it is to compromise, to support, to love. My plotting partners, Marshmallow and now Graham, who whisper their suggestions through their kisses. And finally, my Fab Four: Greg, Cooper, Ella, and Anna. Everything you are is everything to me.

ABOUT THE AUTHOR

Photo © 2020 Sarandipity Photography

Tif Marcelo is a veteran US Army nurse who holds a BS in nursing and a master's in public administration. She believes in and writes about the strength of families, the endurance of friendship, and the beauty of heartfelt romance—and she's inspired daily by her own military hero husband and four children. She hosts the *Stories to Love* podcast, and she is also the *USA Today* bestselling author of *In a Book Club Far Away, Once Upon a Sunset, The Key to Happily Ever After,* and the Journey to the Heart series. Sign up for her newsletter at www.TifMarcelo.com.